THE THIRD DRAGON

FRANK SIMON

THE THIRD DRAGON

BROADMAN
& HOLMAN
PUBLISHERS

NASHVILLE, TENNESSEE

F
SIM

0-8054-2444-X

Published by Broadman & Holman Publishers,
Nashville, Tennessee

Dewey Decimal Classification: 813
Subject Heading: FICTION

Scripture citation is from the NKJV, New King James Version,
copyright © 1979, 1980, 1982, Thomas Nelson, Inc., Publishers.

1 2 3 4 5 6 7 8 9 10 06 05 04 03 02

For John W. K. Simon

Table of Contents

Acknowledgments

I want to thank the people who helped make this book possible:

My wife, LaVerne, first editor and my sweet helpmate.

For all those who prayed for this book, but especially Bill Plate, Carl Hammert, and Larry Murphy. Special thanks goes to Commander Hammert for information on Navy P-3 subhunters.

Scott Chapman, for a kid's-eye-view of the sport of rock climbing.

My friend and agent, Les Stobbe.

Leonard Goss, for his help and encouragement.

Prologue

Major Larry Best pushed open the door to Dogpatch Inn, the name for the Army Air Corps mess hall, and stepped out into the warm tropical night. A light breeze swept over Tinian, carrying the rich earthy smells of palm trees overlaid by a faint scent of salt and rot, an ever-present reminder of the South Pacific's embrace. On other occasions, this might have had a tranquilizing effect, but not tonight.

Larry stood motionless on the wooden decking as others hurried past him. He thought about the earlier briefing, how the Old Man had told them the bomb they were carrying to Japan had the power of twenty thousand tons of TNT. Even though the CO never mentioned the source of this unthinkable power, Larry suspected what it was. Several days ago he had said as much to Commander John Morris, their navy weaponeer. There had been no reply, but the look in the older man's eyes told Larry he was right.

So, what was a Christian to make of this? He had felt no qualms about joining ROTC in college or volunteering for the Army Air Corps. He had measured these acts against his faith and decided it was right to defend his country against the brutal aggression of Nazi Germany, Fascist Italy, and Imperial Japan. Did the destructiveness of the weapon make a difference? The air corps' B-29s had already inflicted horrific casualties by fire-bombing Tokyo and other major Japanese cities.

He ran a hand through his thick black hair, which, as usual, was a mess with his cowlick standing up in back. The door at his back banged again.

"Forget your way back to the hut?" a familiar voice said, as Captain Dennis Roundtree joined him.

"No, Captain. Did you sleep through your classes when they covered respect for superiors?"

"No, sir. I'm always respectful." He threw off a casual salute as if to prove his point.

Larry returned it. "I see. You ready to go?"

Dennis took his time answering, toeing the bare wood planks with his shoes. "This is what we signed up for, sir. The Old Man says go—so we go."

"You didn't answer my question."

"Yes, sir. I'm ready."

Larry stepped down onto the hard-packed coral, his copilot at his side. "Good. Then let's get on with it."

They walked in silence through the pools of light near the clustered buildings. They changed into their coverall flight suits at the hut and grabbed their flight gear. What this was varied by crew member. Larry picked up a Zane Grey novel while his copilot grabbed a *Life* and a *Stars and Stripes*. Outside, they jumped into the waiting jeep. After picking up Commander Morris and his assistant, Lieutenant (jg) Sam Owens, the driver roared off for the flight line.

Larry tried to maintain his composure as the jeep's headlights illuminated objects moments before they were left behind in coral dust. He hoped the driver wouldn't end their mission by piling up on the way to the plane. But as the aircraft CO, he felt he couldn't order the man to slow down. Somehow this didn't mesh with his image of a bomber pilot.

He saw the bright glow long before they got there. The jeep made a final skidding turn and roared toward the waiting B-29. Larry gaped at the sight. He should have expected it, he knew, but he still was surprised. A long line of spotlights bathed his bomber like an insect a moment before annihilation in a flame. The name, *Little Brown Jug*, stood out in black block letters against the brilliant silver nose. The large windows above looked black in contrast.

His aircraft hadn't had a name until recently. He had considered and rejected many possibilities. He admired the names some of the other pilots had chosen: *The Great Artiste*, *Top Secret*, and *Bock's Car*, for example. He had considered *Very Best* but had finally decided to borrow the name of the popular Glenn Miller song because of what it meant to his wife, Elizabeth. Well, it appeared the name would go down in history for other than musical reasons, assuming their mission was successful. Army photographers swarmed around the bomber, taking pictures from every conceivable angle. Several motion picture cameras stood off to the side on their heavy tripods as the operators waited for the crew to arrive.

"Would you look at the brass!" Dennis shouted from the back to make himself heard over the roar of the jeep.

"This isn't a milk run, Captain," Larry replied.

"I know, but . . ."

The driver brought the jeep to a sliding stop.

Larry turned his head. "Commander, are you and Sam ready for the beauty pageant?"

"I'd as soon skip it," the navy weaponeer replied. "But, if we must . . ."

"I believe this is a command performance."

The four officers got out and joined the rest of the crew. For the next twenty minutes they formed lines in front of their aircraft, and the flash-bulbs popped. Larry began to wonder if this would force a delay, but finally it was over. The crew boarded the *Little Brown Jug* and began their preflight checks. Before starting his tasks, Larry obliged the photographers by waving to them from the open cockpit window.

He and Dennis made their rounds outside, checking the engines for leaking oil or hydraulic fluid and to make sure all the instrument covers and pins had been removed. Larry hadn't expected to find anything wrong, and he didn't. After all, the 509th had the best maintenance crews in the air corps. They better not find anything wrong.

Larry boarded the aircraft and hurried forward. He paused at Staff Sergeant Herb Wilson's station.

"Think this crate can make it to Japan and back?"

The flight engineer grinned. "Bet my life on it, sir."

"That's what I want to hear. Has the ground crew run the props through?" He knew the answer but had to ask it anyway. The B-29's Wright Cyclone engines sometimes collected oil in the bottom cylinders. Cranking such an engine usually broke it.

The older man didn't seem to mind the question. "Yes, sir. All four were pulled through twelve blades."

Larry nodded. If the ground crew could pull the engines through three revolutions, there was no problem with pooled oil. He continued forward and climbed into the left-hand seat. He was grateful for the crew he had trained with for over a year. They truly were the best in the air corps.

He switched on the intercom and keyed his mike "Let's crank 'em up. Sergeant Wilson—start number three."

"Yes, sir. Starting three."

Dennis turned to look out his window. "Three's turning. Four blades . . . eight . . . twelve . . . ignition!"

The whine of the starter was replaced by the powerful rumble of the 2,200-horsepower engine. Larry watched the oil pressure come up. The fuel pressure was steady. No problems so far.

"Starting four," Herb announced.

After it was running, Larry looked out his window at number one. After three revolutions, fire shot out of the short exhaust stacks on the outboard engine. Soon all four were running as smoothly as high-performance eighteen-cylinder engines can run. Larry checked the luminous dial on his watch. It was now 2:30 A.M. The whole procedure had taken a little over a half hour after beginning the preflight check. *Not bad,* he thought. *Hope the rest of the mission goes this smoothly.*

Larry set the brakes and signaled for the chocks to be removed. Waving to the observers, he released the brakes and began taxiing toward the southwest end of the runway. The heavy Superfortress jounced over the uneven coral taxiway, following the same path three weather planes had taken over an hour ago. Once out of the floodlights' glare, the warm tropical night took over. Except for their landing lights, it was pitch black.

Larry made the final turn and applied the brakes to halt the heavy bomber. He felt his pulse quicken as tension began to take its toll. They were heavy—very heavy. The *Little Brown Jug* was carrying seven thousand gallons of high-octane gasoline and a single nine-thousand-pound bomb. The B-29 shuddered as Larry ran the engines up. All the gauges looked good.

"How's it look, Herb?"

"Smooth as silk, Major. Couldn't be any better."

"Roger." He glanced at his watch. It was 2:50 A.M. Now all he had to do was get his overweight Superfortress airborne. This was no insignificant task, as the blackened hulks on Tinian testified. He switched the radio to the tower frequency.

"Victor Seven Five to North Tinian tower. Ready for takeoff on runway Able."

"Victor Seven Five. Victor Seven Five. Cleared for takeoff."

The air was stifling in the cockpit as the lone bomber stood poised on the longest runway in existence, ten thousand feet of graded coral. Their landing lights carried less than half the length of the strip, runway lights marking the rest. Where these ended, almost two miles away, was the tropical South Pacific, ready to receive them if the B-29 could not carry aloft its enormous overload. Just two miles to get a sixty-five-ton plane airborne, a plane crammed with gasoline and the heaviest bomb ever made. Larry knew they could make it, with some to spare, unless they lost an engine. But that was unpredictable.

"You ready?" Larry asked.

Dennis wiped his hands on his flight suit. His forced grin looked positively sepulchral in the purple-green glow from the instrument panel. "Roger."

Larry locked the brakes and pushed the throttles all the way forward. The *Little Brown Jug* shook as the engines roared.

"You've got max power," Herb announced over the intercom. "Everything looks fine."

Larry ran a hand over his lean face, trying to massage away the accumulation of tension. He looked beyond their landing lights where the runway lights seemed to come together and released the brakes. The overloaded plane started rolling but not as rapidly as on previous missions. It seemed to crawl down the runway instead of surging forward. But all too soon, the snail's pace became the thunderous lurching of a juggernaut. A tight knot formed in Larry's stomach as the runway end markers raced toward them in a mad rush. He resisted the temptation to pull back prematurely on the yoke. He stole a glance at the air speed indicator as the jiggling needle crept molasses-like toward their liftoff speed. The lump in his stomach turned to ice: only five knots to go, but they were nearly out of runway. Then the needle hit the magic number. Larry pulled back smoothly on the yoke. The bomber hesitated for a heart-stopping moment then started its ponderous rotation. The huge wheels left earth, and Tinian surrendered to the Pacific at the same moment.

Larry shifted his full attention to the plane's instruments as the B-29 staggered into the featureless blackness. There were no reliable references except those vital gauges. Dennis reached over and activated the landing gear. The welcome whine of the wheels coming up was barely audible over the thundering of the engines. Larry leveled out and let the struggling plane pick up air speed.

It took several tries before he got his voice to work. "That's about as close as I ever want to come."

Dennis cleared his throat as he squirmed in his seat. "We earned our flight pay on that one," he said with a forced grin. He glanced at his watch. "I make the takeoff time oh-two-fifty-seven," he said as he made an entry in the flight log.

Larry trimmed the aircraft for a slow climb and made a leisurely turn to 338 degrees, their heading for Saipan. Two minutes later he heard the Tinian tower clear two more B-29s for takeoff. One carried scientific instruments to measure the bomb's explosive power while the other would provide photographic coverage, from what everyone hoped would be a safe distance. Both aircraft carried atomic scientists and photographers in addition to the regular crews.

They were approaching forty-five-hundred feet when Larry felt a light tap on the shoulder. He jumped as his concentration broke. He turned and saw John Morris. If the commander had been worried about the takeoff, he didn't show it. But then, Larry had never seen the naval officer perturbed. He was the most professional and single-minded man he had ever met.

Now John's job would start. A tall officer stood behind him, his pinched, narrow face echoing his spare build. Lieutenant (jg) Sam Owens lacked the composure of his boss. The young man was still clearly nervous from his recent scare. Larry smiled in spite of the situation.

"May we start now?" John asked in a quiet voice.

"Anytime you're ready. We'll try and keep her steady for you. Should be fairly smooth until we get near the Empire."

John nodded a silent thanks and walked back to the forward bomb bay, ushering Sam before him.

* * *

Sam flipped on the bomb-bay lights and rigged the portable work-lights while the weaponeer started removing the access covers from the huge casing of the "Little Boy." John's blue eyes crinkled behind his large, horn-rimmed glasses as he prepared the bomb's interior. He winced once and withdrew a bleeding thumb, cut on one of the sharp, smoothly machined parts. He looked at the nick briefly then resumed the dismantling, working by feel most of the time.

He removed a final bolt and slid the part to one side. He looked at Sam's tension-drained face for a moment then got to his feet, ignoring the pain in his joints. He walked to the large bucket lashed to the forward bulkhead of the bomb bay and removed the lid. Inside were the beautifully machined rings of plutonium. He donned his gloves and carefully picked up the rings and struggled with them over to the bomb. He inserted them quickly, but with infinite care, into the receptacle. He returned to the bucket and removed the smaller, but still hefty, slug and hurried to the bomb's tail section. He squinted down the "gun barrel" and slipped the slug inside, following it with the explosive charge. Done, he stood back and looked at the partially armed bomb.

Sam's relief was clearly visible.

John began the reassembly process with care as his assistant set up the test equipment for wiring the device. Finally John stood back and wiped his hands on his clean overalls, smudging them with dark streaks of graphite lubricant.

"Well, Sam," he said. "Ready to hook it up?"

"Yes, sir."

John reached into the casing for the first cable set and started making the connections. He worked slowly, taking care not to short any wires. He reached for the test prods after each connection was made, making sure the wiring was correct before proceeding.

Finally it was done. John stood painfully and looked at the black box perched on the bomb. Every test light was green. The bomb, if it were dropped then, would detonate—according to the instruments.

Sam broke the silence. "Will it work?"

John paused before answering. "That is the question of the day," he said slowly. "The scientists say it will. The black box says it's wired correctly. If each of the arming devices works, if the charge goes off, if the theory is right. . . ."

"The one in New Mexico went off."

John smiled at the young man's obvious uneasiness. "That one was carefully assembled, tested, and set off on top of a tower. They had the finest experts in the world standing by and plenty of room to work in." He swept his hand around the crowded bomb bay. The plane lurched as it hit an air pocket.

The commander glanced at his watch and turned toward the cockpit. "Come on. We're done here."

* * *

Larry scanned the vast panorama ahead of them. The visibility was excellent, the sky a deep blue relieved here and there by fleecy, white clouds. The early morning sun streamed through the right-hand cockpit windows, a minor distraction to him but more of a bother to Dennis.

Larry yawned. It was 7:42, and they were already almost five hours into the mission, steady on a course of 332 degrees. They had rendezvoused with the other two B-29s almost two hours ago over Iwo Jima. For now, everything was routine.

The excitement of the takeoff had long since worn off. This might be a historic mission, but getting to the target was one monotonous ride. And the drone of the engines did bring on drowsiness.

Larry rubbed his eyes and took a sip of his coffee. It was strong and hot, and it provided the jolt it was supposed to. He heard a sound and turned to see the navy weaponeers walking onto the flight deck.

"John. Steady enough for you back there?"

"No complaints. We're all done. The bomb is assembled, wired, and tested. As far as I can tell, we're ready."

Larry looked at the graying commander, wondering if he would continue. The man seemed uneasy.

"I see. Anything else?"

"That's about it. The rest is up to you, Major."

Larry nodded. "Appreciate the work you and Sam did down there. A bomb bay isn't the best workshop in the world."

John snorted. "You can say that again. Still, it was adequate."

"Good. We formed up with the instrument and photo planes over

Iwo, and the weather planes report fair visibility over the primary." He paused. "So, it looks like it's on."

John nodded. "Yes," he said.

"OK. Why don't you and Sam try to find a comfortable spot and get some rest. We're about an hour and a half from the IP Sergeant Wilson has sandwiches and coffee."

"Thanks. Don't feel like eating, but I think I'll try some coffee."

He and Sam sprawled on the flight deck behind the pilots. Sam picked halfheartedly at a sandwich while John sipped at his coffee. The flight deck tilted slightly and the roar of the engines increased as the *Little Brown Jug* began its slow climb to thirty thousand feet. Larry scanned the instrument panel. Everything was as it should be. The B-29 droned into the gathering morning with its cargo of death.

An hour later, Larry looked down on the islands off Honshu. They looked beautiful and peaceful from thirty thousand feet—toylike— unreal. Larry found it hard to believe, truly believe, that this was all real, that there were people down there, people who would shortly witness the harsh dawning of the atomic age.

He felt no compunction about dropping the bomb, however. This war would only end when Japan's leaders decided the price of continuing was too high. Despite the horrific casualties and destruction to date, the Imperial government had not yet come to that conclusion. And Larry had seen the casualty forecasts for operations Olympic and Coronet, the inva- sion of the Japanese home islands: 750 thousand American casualties and 250 thousand American deaths and several times as many for the Japanese. If their mission could prevent that. . . .

He craned his neck forward as the great bomber crawled inexorably toward Honshu. Up ahead it was becoming hazy, and large white clouds were beginning to form.

"That doesn't look so good."

Dennis looked up from the instruments. "No, it doesn't. It's clouded up since the weather ship flew over. Maybe that will help with the flak and fighters."

Larry frowned and looked over at his copilot. "Lot of good that'll do us if we can't see the target."

He turned toward the east then brought the bomber around in a wide, left-hand turn, circling the immense Tokyo Bay. Larry locked out all external thoughts as he responded to the bombardier's directions. Their course settled on 260 degrees—almost due west. Ahead lay the IP, the initial point from which no deviation from the bomb run could be made. They droned on over a patchwork quilt of brown, black, and green, with Tokyo Bay off to their left.

"That's it," said Major Cliff Haynes over the intercom. "I just lost sight of the IP. I have a good radar picture, but we have to bomb visually."

"Yeah, I know," Larry snapped. He frowned and rubbed his bristly chin as he looked down at the obscuring clouds. "What do you recommend?"

"Let's try again. There are plenty of holes in the clouds. Maybe the IP will be clear on the next pass."

"Roger. The brass said Tokyo if at all possible, and we've got enough fuel."

He well remembered that part of the briefing. Kill the fanatics who refused to give up, and the war would be over, or so they hoped. Although Osaka and Nagoya were their alternates, the desired target was Tokyo. Larry had the distinct impression that the visual rule could be bent, if not broken, as long as the bomb hit the designated target. But did he dare do it?

He waited out the next run with growing apprehension. Sam Owens went forward and peered into the bombardier's radar scope. Larry considered ordering him back but decided Cliff could take care of himself. The bombardier's eye was glued to the eyepiece of his Norden bombsight as he made tiny corrections.

"Come on . . . come on," Cliff muttered. Then came a pungent oath. "Lost it again!" He looked around. "I say we try one more time. I had it right until the last moment. There are still holes in the clouds."

"OK. Once more, then we go to Nagoya."

Again he brought the B-29 around for another run. So far there had been no flak and no fighters. Apparently the Japanese didn't consider a single bomber much of a threat. Well, that was about to change. Soon they were again on a course of 260 degrees.

Cliff turned around. "I can see the IP."

Larry peered through the cockpit greenhouse windows. "Are you sure? There's a thin cloud layer up ahead."

"I know, but I can see through it. See? There's the river, and that's the bridge."

Larry turned to Dennis. "You see it?"

The copilot leaned forward as if this would improve his vision. "Roger. I see it." He pointed.

Larry checked again. It was like looking through a sheer curtain. The IP wasn't all that easy to identify even in perfect weather because Tokyo had many rivers and even more bridges. But there it was. He was almost positive. "Concur. Can you see the aiming point?" This was three minutes beyond the IP, and Larry couldn't make it out.

"Not yet," Cliff admitted. "But I will before we release."

"Roger. See that you do."

"Yes, sir."

Several minutes later the bombardier assumed his usual hunched-over position, eye buried in his beloved bombsight. "I have the IP."

Larry breathed a sigh of relief. The seconds ticked off slowly as they flew over the city. With ninety seconds to go, he took his hands away from the controls. "It's all yours."

Cliff made no reply, but from that point the corrections he entered into the bombsight directed the bomber's autopilot. Sixty seconds before bomb release, he flicked a toggle switch that activated a high-pitched radio tone.

"How does it look?" Larry asked. It was difficult to positively identify objects on the ground, but he knew that Cliff had a better picture in the bombsight.

There was a slight pause. "We're on target."

Well, it's on automatic now, Larry thought, as he waited to regain control of the plane.

At the end of the sixty seconds, the radio tone ceased, the pneumatic bomb-bay doors whooshed open and the "Little Boy" tumbled out.

"Bomb's away!" Cliff shouted.

The B-29's nose leaped up sharply in response to the loss of nine thousand pounds of dead weight. Larry pushed forward on the yoke. "Goggles, everyone!"

He slipped his on and found he couldn't see the instrument panel. Near panic gripped him until he realized they would be heading away when the bomb went off. He pushed the goggles up and found that Dennis had his up as well.

Larry cranked the bomber into a diving 155-degree right turn designed to carry them away from the bomb's blast at full throttle. He half-heard the coded radio message in his earphones indicating that the three instrument packages had been dropped and the parachutes had deployed. The air pockets pounded them painfully as the B-29 strained, carrying them as far from ground zero as possible.

The strident electronic scream ceased abruptly, fifteen seconds after the drop. The bomb's first fuse had armed. The second, a barometric fuse, was to arm when the bomb reached two thousand feet. Then everything would depend on the radar fuse, set to detonate the bomb after the nineteenth reflection from the ground, forty-three seconds after the drop.

Larry rolled the bomber out of the punishing turn. He thought about putting on the goggles again but decided he was safe with the target behind them. The next forty-three seconds seemed like an eternity. The only sound came from the four Wright Cyclones carrying them, hopefully, toward safety. Larry felt as if something unknown, something dangerous was about to spring on them and tear the giant bomber from the sky, scattering them all to their deaths.

He checked his watch. Fifteen seconds to go. He counted to himself, reached fifteen and continued on. His heart was in his throat. He reached twenty and started to worry.

"Major Best?" came a voice over his shoulder.

Larry glanced back. Commander Morris held his goggles in his hand. Larry had to swallow twice before he could answer. "Yes?" he croaked.

"I believe we have a problem."

"What?" Larry asked, knowing the answer but not daring to state it.

"I think it's a dud. Tell the others to keep their goggles on, but the bomb has already reached the ground. Something kept it from going off."

Larry spoke into the intercom. "Listen up. Keep the glasses on until I say otherwise." He flicked off the switch and turned. "What happened, John?"

"How should I know!" snapped Morris in an uncharacteristic fit of pique. "Could be almost anything! All I know is it was working when it left the plane. The timer delay worked, so I guess it was one of the other fuses or a wiring failure—perhaps wind buffeting broke something loose on the way down."

"But that thing's built like a battleship."

The older man bristled. "I know that! I'm the one that put it together!" He paused. "I don't know what happened! Maybe we can recover it after the war and find out. But until then. . . ."

Larry felt sweat break out in his armpits as he thought about the colonel back on Tinian. "The Old Man will have my head for this! And if *he* doesn't, General LeMay will!" He saw John cringe.

The weaponeer uttered a sharp curse. "I know, I know! But we followed the book *all* the way. That bomb was working when we dropped it! The brass can make of that whatever they want." He looked down. "There are two more bombs on Tinian. Maybe the other missions will have better luck."

"I hope so," Larry said, but somehow it wasn't any consolation. "Maybe the Hiroshima flight will go better." Then the utter frustration of it all hit him. "But I wanted this to work! Hitting the Jap high command was our best shot for a quick surrender—I know it!"

John shrugged. "Yeah, I agree."

He keyed the intercom. "OK, everybody, you can remove your goggles now."

Larry could almost feel the cloak of secrecy gathering around them as the *Little Brown Jug* flew through the beautiful morning. Sam Owens stepped away from the radar and joined his boss. Larry couldn't help but notice the mixture of fear and confusion. He could tell something was really bothering Sam. Anger flashed over him. This junior officer wasn't the one that was going to get hit by this mess.

"Do you have something to say?" Larry snapped.

The young man looked at his boss as if for guidance.

"I asked you a question, Lieutenant!"

"Sir, I was watching the scope. We started the run before we reached the IP. The bomb landed short."

Cliff Haynes charged onto the flight deck, fire in his eyes. *"I did no such thing!"* he shouted, the veins in his neck standing out like cords. "We hit the IP right on the money!"

Sam backed away a little, but a look of determination came to his eyes. "No, sir! We hadn't reached it when you announced it."

"What do *you* know about it? I'm the bombardier, not you!"

"Cliff, that's enough," Larry intervened.

"But, sir, this idiot's insulted me!"

"I *said* that's enough! We've got enough to worry about without getting in a fight. Calm down. We've got a long flight back to Tinian."

He sneaked a glance back at Sam. The young lieutenant was looking at the deck. For some strange reason, Larry wondered if the young naval officer might be right. He sighed. It really didn't matter—not now.

1

USS *Tennessee*

Don Stewart frowned and clamped his eyes tighter shut, his bushy, brown eyebrows seeming to guard his fitful sleep. Doris shook him again, this time with more authority. He awoke with a start and looked over at his wife. He sighed and looked at his watch before he realized how futile it was. Not only did he have the wrong time, he had the wrong day, ever since they had crossed the International Date Line earlier in the flight. It was Monday, October the thirteenth—he had lost an entire day, and it felt like it.

Doris smiled at him. She was an attractive brunette and petite, weighing little more than a hundred pounds, in sharp contrast to her husband's hulking two hundred plus.

Now fully awake, Don returned the smile. Doris pointed past him out the window. There, partially obscured by the wing of their United Airlines 747, was the ground, a jumbled, dingy brown, relieved here and there by patches of green. The shadows were long and black, and there was an all-pervading, orange-tinted haze. He quickly scanned the sky, a habit second nature to a career air force pilot.

He saw the glint in her eyes as she took inventory. The love he saw echoed his own, and he liked the way she stuck her arm through his and squeezed. His pulse quickened. She had his undivided attention.

"What are you thinking, Grandma?" Don asked in his friendly gruff voice. The reference to Grandma Moses was because of Doris's interest in painting. She certainly wasn't the grandmotherly type.

She squeezed his arm again. "That blue uniform doesn't do you justice." Her eyes paused at the gold oak leaves that designated him a major. "But I do like those better than the silver bars."

"Yeah, I was glad to see the railroad tracks go," he chuckled. "We could be looking at light colonel pretty soon. We're not brass yet, but we're gaining on it." He took her small, soft hand into his large mitt. Soft and small, he thought, like a little bird.

His smile faded as he remembered something.

"What's the matter?" Doris asked.

"Just thinking about my mother. Saying good-bye was one of the hardest things I've ever done. I'll probably never see her again, at least on this side."

"I know, dear." Doris snuggled closer to him, resting her head on his broad chest. "I'll miss her too." She reached into her purse for a tissue. "After you and I got married, I was surprised to find out she was about my best friend."

He looked down at his wife's tears and didn't know what to do. "I didn't mean to upset you."

"It's all right. It's part of life."

"Yeah. I know she misses Dad." He felt a stinging sensation in his own eyes. "Those two were quite a pair. I really was blessed with my parents."

"Yes, you were. But it's in the Lord's hands now." She looked up at him, smiling now. "He can handle it."

Don sighed. "I know. But I hate cancer. It's such a horrible disease."

"Yes, dear. But we have to let it go."

She was right, he knew. "Yes, Grandma."

She punched him in the ribs.

"Take it easy. I don't want to end up in the hospital."

She ceased hostilities.

Don glanced out the window. "What do you think of our new duty station so far?"

"I think it's a little early to tell."

"Hmm, I guess so. Well, you let me know if you don't like it, and I'll tell the ambassador we can't stay. Once he finds out how henpecked I am, I'm sure he'll understand."

"Oh, sure," she said, trying to look aggrieved but not succeeding.

The two seats directly in front of them popped upright suddenly. "Look at that!" a boy said, taking absolutely no pains to keep his voice down. "Bet that's Tokyo."

There was the sound of jostling. "Hey!" came a girl's voice, definitely indignant. "*Let me see!* Quit hoggin' the window!"

"Bug off! This is *my* seat!"

Don looked at his wife. She looked back at him with an expression that told him this was a job for father. He sighed and undid his seat belt.

He stood, bumping his head painfully on the overhead luggage compartment. He towered over his son and daughter as they continued their fight. The conflict lasted a few more seconds until twelve-year-old Michael looked up. He was a younger edition of his father, down to his unruly brown hair. Nine-year-old Leah scrunched up her face and punched her older brother. Then she as well noticed that the law had arrived. They both adopted their practiced "What did I do?" expressions.

"All right, you two," Don said in an attempt to sound stern. "Knock off the horseplay. I want to hear a little quiet up there."

"Yes, sir," said Michael quietly, as he frowned and cast his eyes downward.

"Yes, sir," echoed Leah.

Don sat back down and massaged the top of his head. Doris smiled at him. It was in his mind to ask why it was the dad's job to settle these wars, but a strident gong preempted him. The seat belt signs had flashed on.

"Ladies and gentlemen," came a weary female voice. "We're beginning our approach to Narita International Airport. Please bring your seats to a full, upright position and fasten your seat belts. We will be landing in approximately fifteen minutes. Thank you."

Don had never cared for long flights with his kids, and one lasting nearly a day was almost too much to bear. But it was almost over. Soon they would be on the ground and headed for the Imperial Hotel in Tokyo.

A frazzled-looking flight attendant walked down the narrow aisle. She looked from side to side, making sure all seat belts were fastened.

* * *

Don held Doris's hand as he paused in the arrival lounge and looked around. Michael stood at his side while Leah stuck close to her mother. Don couldn't say, exactly, what he had expected Japan to be like, but it wasn't as different from America as he thought it would be, at least so far. Although some signs were in Kanji, most were in Roman lettering as well. The bustling terminal was clean and orderly, although quite crowded.

Don spotted an air force second lieutenant holding a sign with STEWART written in large block letters. Don waved.

The young officer hurried over and saluted. He was quite average, with a medium build and brown hair and eyes. But what made him stand out was his smile.

"Major Stewart," he said, shaking hands. "I'm Fred Brown, attached to the embassy. I've got a van and driver to take you and your family to the Imperial Hotel. You'll be staying there temporarily until you're assigned a private residence. If your baggage made it this far, we can pick it up and be on our way."

"Sounds good to me. Fred, this is my wife, Doris."

"Pleased to meet you, Mrs. Stewart."

"Likewise, Fred," Doris replied.

"I don't know who these midgets are," Don continued with a broad grin. "They followed us off the plane."

"Aw, Dad!" Michael complained.

Leah let her displeasure be known with a hot look.

Don adopted a contrite expression. "Oh, my mistake. Fred, these are our kids, Michael and Leah."

"Pleased to meet both of you. Welcome to Japan."

This seemed to mollify them.

"Shall we head for baggage pickup?" Fred asked.

"By all means. I'm looking forward to crashing at the hotel."

"Well, I'm afraid you've got one more ordeal before we get there." He glanced at his watch. "It's just after five, ah, 1700, and Tokyo rush hour traffic is in full swing. It may take us an hour or so to get there. And believe me, you've never seen anything like Tokyo traffic."

They picked up the luggage, which was only slightly more beat up than when it had been surrendered at Los Angeles International. They walked out of the terminal. A maroon van was parked in a loading zone. The driver, dressed in a black uniform and cap, was polishing the paintwork with a cloth. The vehicle was immaculate, both inside and out, without a dent on it. The driver rushed over and helped load the luggage. He put the last piece in and closed the rear door.

"Major, this is Kinji Gusawa, our best embassy driver. He prefers *Gus*. Gus, this is Major Don Stewart, his wife Doris, and Michael and Leah. I think I got that right."

The man gave a quick, shallow bow. "Pleased to meet you, Major Stewart, Mrs. Stewart," he said in fairly good English. He turned and looked seriously at the children, who were regarding him with awe. "And boy-san and girl-san." The driver regarded them and seemed to read their minds. "Would you like to ride up front with me?"

They both beamed and looked around at their father, who nodded. They all piled into the van.

Gus was an excellent driver, Don was relieved to find, after hearing stories about the dreaded kamikaze taxi drivers. He drove the van with extreme caution, his eyes never leaving the crowded street. But their progress was slow, since the traffic was creeping. They were surrounded by more vehicles than Don had ever seen in his life, and the variety was amazing. There were small personal cars interspersed with busses, trucks, and construction equipment. Gus took every safe advantage he could, but their pace was snail-like. The small man took it in stride and even seemed relaxed. Motor scooters and small motorcycles darted in and out of the traffic with what appeared to be reckless abandon. Many were ridden by Japanese executives wearing suits, ties, and crash helmets. Some were delivery vehicles with strange, shock-mounted containers in back.

The buildings seemed to increase in height by steps as the travelers ground their way toward central Tokyo. Gus pulled up on a choked freeway. The traffic was moving at ten miles an hour, scarcely faster than the surface road, but it was steady.

Michael and Leah were all tourist as they looked at the strange sights. The Tokyo Tower stood out in the golden, late afternoon sun. A patch of green appeared in the distance and grew larger and more distinct as they approached. It was a huge, parklike area in the heart of the city, exquisite gardens with manicured lawns and painstakingly placed trees and shrubs, with buildings placed where they appeared to belong. Graceful pathways wound through the vast park and over even more graceful bridges. The whole area was double guarded, once by thick, gray stone walls and again by wide moats.

"The Imperial Palace. Something, isn't it?" Fred asked.

"I'll say," Don agreed, Doris nodding also. The kids were lost in their own world.

Two bellhops in bright uniforms rushed out to the van as Gus drove up in front of the Imperial Hotel. The driver parked and walked around to the passenger doors, holding them open. He spoke rapidly to the bellhops, instructing them concerning the baggage. Don got out and stretched his legs.

"Guess I better go check in," he said.

"Already done," Fred replied. "I've checked you in—rooms 2404 and 2406. Here are your cards. The attaché staff will take care of anything relating to the hotel. You'll be assigned a private residence before too long."

Don took the cards and smiled at the lieutenant. "Thanks, Fred. Seems you've thought of everything. We're kinda bushed, so I appreciate it. Looking forward to doing something about this jet lag."

The young officer hesitated. "Uh, there *is* one more thing I have to tell you. Sorry to be the bearer of bad news, but Colonel Dill asked me to tell you that the ambassador is giving a cocktail party tonight at 8:30. The colonel said 'if you weren't too tired from your trip.'"

"Command performance," Don translated.

Fred shrugged in sympathy. "Yes, sir. Sorry."

Don smiled at him in spite of the situation. "Don't worry about it. We'll be there. Might have to enlist your aid in keeping both of us awake. Should we get a taxi?"

"No, sir. I'll send a car for you around 8:15, if that's OK. The driver will phone your room when he arrives."

"That's fine. And thanks." Don stopped as Doris tugged at his sleeve.

"Honey? What about Michael and Leah?"

"Oh, sorry," Fred interjected, "I forgot that detail. The embassy has child care. They'll have plenty to do, constant supervision, and they'll be close to you."

"You said the magic word as far as Doris is concerned," Don said. "She's a full-time mom. Again, we appreciate your assistance."

"Just doing my job. Oh, one other thing and then I'm gone. It's not customary to tip the hotel personnel. They'll add the gratuity to your bill. Well, guess I'll see you at the party." He turned to Doris and the children. "Mrs. Stewart, pleasure meeting you. Michael and Leah." He turned and hopped into the van, and Gus drove off into the gathering dusk.

"Well, Mrs. Stewart. Shall we see our temporary quarters?"

The bellhops gathered up the luggage and led their guests inside. The Stewarts paused, gawking at the spacious lobby. *Very nice,* Don thought. He knew some of the history. The original Imperial Hotel had been built in 1922 from a Frank Lloyd Wright design. It had stood on pine pilings over a sea of mud and had survived the devastating earthquake of 1923 as well as World War II. But the old hotel was gone now, replaced in the 1970s and 1980s by two medium-rise towers. It was still a favorite of visitors to Tokyo.

"Wow, Dad," Michael yelled, "Look at that!"

He ran through the guests in the lobby and up to a roped-off display, his sister not far behind. Their parents followed more sedately, their eyes drifting upward in awe. It was a pagoda model nearly reaching the lobby's lofty ceiling. Its exquisitely carved white walls stood out against the more subdued backdrop.

"That really *is* something," Don agreed. "But, come on. We have to get ready to go to the embassy."

Michael looked as if he wanted to discuss the matter further, but one look from his father convinced him otherwise.

The bellhops saw them to their rooms on the twenty-fourth floor, bowed, and let themselves out. Don looked through the connecting door, watching as Michael and Leah started exploring their room. Deciding the hotel was not in imminent danger from their mischief, he closed the door and walked to the window where Doris waited. He put his arms around her slim waist. The Imperial Palace grounds, just to the east of the hotel, were a rich, verdant green in the sunset.

"Beautiful, isn't it?" he asked.

"Hmm," she agreed.

A suspicious creaking noise sounded from the adjoining room, only partially muffled by the closed connecting door. Doris looked at her husband with silent communication. He sighed, dropped his arms and walked to the door. He opened it and worked up a stern expression.

"If I have to come in there I know two brats who're going to be awfully sorry!"

The sounds from the sturdy beds ceased immediately.

"You two get cleaned up. We're going down to dinner in a few minutes."

"'K, Dad," Michael said.

Don closed the door and returned to his wife, rolling his eyes as he did so. She laughed. "Our little angels," she said.

"Your idea of divinity's different from mine," he said with feeling.

The unimportant, petty details of human existence suddenly fell away as he saw her standing there before the window. This was the person he had been one with for over fifteen years, the one who truly loved him. And he loved her, and they both knew it. He held his arms apart, and she came to him. Their lips met as he gently pulled her soft body against his. The kiss quickly turned hot and the embrace powerful. He felt her response, and there was no question about his.

"Oh," she gasped, pushing away, catching her breath. "Give a girl a minute, will you?"

"Not a chance," he said, his eyes appreciating her. "C'mere, woman!"

She glanced quickly at her watch, doing a quick calculation. She smiled up at him and walked to the connecting door. She opened it and poked her head through.

"Michael—Leah. I want you ready to go in about a half hour. Be sure to wash up. *Now!*"

"Yes, Mom," came two voices.

Don felt his pulse quicken as she closed the door and locked it. He watched her lithe movements as she returned to the bed and started pulling the spread down. He came up behind her and encircled her waist.

"Need some help?" he asked.

"Tend to your business," she told him.

"Yes, ma'am."

And he did.

* * *

The ride in the embassy van was calm and relaxing compared to the earlier trip to the hotel. Michael and Leah, their restless energy undiminished, were in the front seat thoroughly enjoying the brilliant kaleidoscope of neon lights that was nighttime Tokyo's trademark. The parents watched from the backseat. Don, as a rule, cared little for command performances, where the officer was expected to fill out the guest list of his superior. But this was somehow different. Perhaps it was the newness of the assignment or being in a foreign country. He squeezed Doris's hand, and she returned the pressure.

The van pulled up in front of the embassy and stopped. The driver got out and opened the doors. The Stewarts entered the large, modern building. An employee took the children by their hands and ushered them away to the child-care center.

"Hello, Major Stewart—Mrs. Stewart," said a voice behind them. Don turned and saw Lieutenant Brown approaching, martini glass in hand, a broad smile on his face. This was an aspect of military social life that Don found difficult—how to be in the world but not of it.

Don smiled at the young officer. "Getting started early, I see. Has the parade cranked up yet?"

"No, sir," Fred laughed. "But it's gonna any second now. I could say that we were waiting for you, but that wouldn't be true. However, Colonel Dill is quite anxious to meet you. Actually we're waiting for the navy. They and some Japanese dignitaries are the guests of honor. The captain of the USS *Tennessee* and a few of his senior officers are coming. You may have read about it in the papers. A ballistic missile sub tied up at a Tokyo wharf is a big thing. Supposed to be a goodwill, show-the-flag visit, but certain Japanese groups have been quite vocal in their opposition. The ambassador's anxious that the visit goes well. I believe he would prefer to avoid any nasty incidents."

"Fred, you are a facile young gentleman, and I appreciate the briefing."

"Just doing my job. Can I get you and your wife a drink?"

Don smiled as he took a breath. "Suppose you could fetch us some 7UP?"

The young man blinked. "On the rocks?"

"Yes, please."

He turned and made his way across the crowded floor.

Don looked about the large ballroom, which was all aglitter under enormous crystal chandeliers. Nearly a hundred people were present, gathered into numerous small self-important groups. Each colony tended to be of the same type: four or five air force uniforms here, a group of navy blue coats there, others in ambassadorial cutaways.

A few minutes later Fred returned with three clear tumblers arranged in a precarious triangle.

Don cocked an eyebrow at him as he took two of the glasses, giving one to Doris. "You get a 7UP too?" Then he noticed there weren't any bubbles in Fred's glass.

"No, sir. Couldn't balance a martini glass with the tumblers so I got my refill this way."

As a rule, Don made it his practice to mind his own business. "I see. Well, take it easy there."

"Oh, I always do."

Doris took a prim sip and immediately seemed to forget the glass was there. Don tried his 7UP, resisting the urge to drink all of it. A wry grin came to his face as he remembered an embarrassing incident at a former duty station. It had been another command performance, and he had been very thirsty. He had gotten a tumbler of his usual 7UP with ice and promptly drained it. Two more glasses quickly followed, all under the watchful eye of his then commanding officer—no teetotaler but no friend of lushes either. The following day Don had found himself on the colonel's carpet facing a considerable head wind until he had finally convinced his boss that it had been only soft drinks.

Don turned as the din of surrounding conversations lulled. Out of the corner of his eye he saw a flurry of navy blue and gold. A navy captain entered the ballroom trailed by two commanders. As if on cue, another door opened, and a distinguished-looking gentleman in an evening cutaway walked slowly through the guests, talking earnestly to a Japanese official at his side. The navy types, the civilians, and an anxious-looking air force colonel converged. The other guests broke up their cliques, preparing for the amenities.

"Here we go," Fred whispered in Don's ear. "The uncomfortable looking officer is Colonel Dill, your new boss. He's doing about mach 1.5, aimed right at Ambassador Dewey. The gentleman next to the ambassador is Mr. Fujii, a member of the Diet and responsible for persuading the Japanese government to allow the *Tennessee*'s port call. The new arrivals are Captain Allender, the sub's CO and two senior officers. I forget their names. One's the XO. Perhaps we should get in line. I'll introduce you to Colonel Dill and the ambassador."

Fred led the Stewarts to their proper position in the long line and talked with them as the queue snaked its leisurely way past the distinguished guests.

At last they were before the ambassador. Don's first impression was favorable, he was surprised to find, since his mental image had been more pessimistic. The man appeared pleasant and genuinely interested in his guests. He was beginning to gray at the temples, but he showed no signs of middle-age spread. *He obviously takes physical fitness seriously,* Don thought. The gray eyes were sharp and clear. He was almost as tall as Don but had a lighter build.

"Mr. Ambassador, may I present your newest air attaché, Major Don

Stewart, and his wife Doris," Fred began. "Major and Mrs. Stewart, this is Ambassador Victor Dewey."

Don noted that the ambassador's handshake was firm and sincere. "Mr. Ambassador, I'm very pleased to meet you."

"And I'm pleased to meet you, Major Stewart—Mrs. Stewart. May I present my wife, Ann." Mrs. Dewey turned. She was a large blond and obviously accustomed to her position, but in a way that spoke of duty rather than pride. The two couples said the necessary pleasantries. Then the women entered into earnest conversation while the men felt each other out in the brief moments allowed.

Finally Victor said, "It was so nice of you to come this evening. I regret the inconvenience since you just got here, but I felt it important that you meet these people. The *Tennessee's* visit is high profile, to say the least. I'll be meeting with you and Colonel Dill later on this week. I'm looking forward to getting to know you."

Don mumbled the appropriate words, and collected Doris's arm.

"Hon," she said with a pout, "what's the hurry? We were talking about Ann's shopping trip to Hong Kong. She's going Wednesday. Do you think I could go soon? There's so much we could get."

Don had to laugh. "The hurry is that we were holding up the line, dear. As to the other, there'll be plenty of time for you to go to Hong Kong. I don't think they'll sell out."

Further down the line Fred introduced them to Colonel Allen Dill, who appeared to have the weight of the embassy squarely on his shoulders. He was turned partly away from the line talking to a navy lieutenant. Allen looked at the other man, his full lips pursed in agitation. His brown eyes peered out from behind massive, horn-rimmed glasses. He had a respectable assortment of medals on his uniform coat. His wife, Helen, seemed a little uncomfortable, but she greeted the newcomers warmly as her husband finished his talk. The lieutenant finally hurried off as if grateful to escape. Allen smiled as he turned and greeted Don and Doris, but it was clear his mind was elsewhere.

Fred led them away with an attention to duty that was beginning to wear on Don, even though he liked the young officer. The Stewarts met Mr. Fujii and the navy officers from the sub. Finally they were done.

"I know this has been torture for you two," Fred said as they cleared the reception line. "I tried to make it as painless as I could. That's it for the official requirements." His infectious grin returned. "I'm sure no one'll notice if you slip out, as long as you don't trip over something."

Don had to laugh. "Thanks, Fred. You did a great job, and we appreciate it. And you're right—we're pooped. Think we'll head back to the hotel. What time should I make my appearance tomorrow?"

"I'd recommend around 0830, sir." Fred hesitated a moment. "I think you'll find Colonel Dill a fine officer when you get to know him. He was kind of pressed when I introduced you this evening. Pressure gets to him. But he's one of the most considerate bosses I've worked for. For what it's worth."

Don smiled as he remembered the rather brusque introduction. "I think I catch your drift. Thanks for filling me in. See you in the morning."

After collecting their children, the Stewarts made a quick trip to the Imperial Hotel in an embassy van. Finally in their room and under the covers, the last thing Don remembered was leaving a wake-up call with the hotel switchboard.

* * *

The man cursed as the dew-laden bush loomed out of the darkness. The branches scratched his face while the leaves showered him with water droplets. He touched his cheek and felt blood oozing from the cuts. He continued forward again, straining to see the dial on the metal detector he was carrying. The saucerlike coil scraped the ground, making a slithering noise as it bumped along the wet grass. The earphones were completely silent.

He continued on through the park, trying to watch for the half-seen obstructions. He moved the detector in wide sweeping arcs, growing dizzy as he concentrated on the silent earphones. He willed them to make a noise, but they would not. He stopped and poked a test button on the handle. A loud buzzing noise told him the instrument was working.

Another man caught up with the detector operator and gestured impatiently for him to continue. They started forward again and had not gone five feet when the earphones emitted a shrill electronic scream. The operator shouted in pain before he could catch himself. He fumbled with one hand to turn the volume down, almost dropping the detector in the process. Finally he got the level adjusted and started moving the coil from side to side, forward and back, getting an idea of the buried object's size and depth. He made his inspection swiftly but with the care of a professional who knew exactly what he was doing.

Finally he took off the earphones and laid the detector on the ground. He spoke rapidly to his companion. The other raced away over the dew-covered grass.

For nearly five minutes the detector operator waited. The only sounds were from the late-night traffic on the nearby streets, but not a sound came from the park itself. Not a bush stirred in the dead calm. He shivered in the chill night air. The humidity was palpable.

The man turned and looked through the gloom. He heard muffled footsteps approaching, punctuated by an occasional sharp crunch of a dead branch being stepped on. Many were coming. He was almost sure who they were, but fear of the unknown still gripped him. He longed to click on his light but knew what would happen if he did. He waited.

Then he saw dim amorphous shapes materializing out of the murk like ghosts. These ill-defined blobs resolved themselves into black silhouettes. The leader walked over to the detector operator. Another man joined them. He had a thin shadow, and he was not very tall. His nervousness was obvious even in the darkness. The thin man listened as the operator and leader discussed the finding.

Finally the leader ordered the workers to begin digging. They worked frantically, tearing brutally into the earth. Picks made short work of the first few feet, then they switched to shovels. They toiled without break as the mound of dirt grew. Finally the depth of the hole forced all the diggers out but one.

A sharp metallic "clang" sounded. The thin man uttered an anguished shout. He shook visibly as he clambered down into the hole. He clicked on a hooded flashlight and began scraping dirt away from the exposed metal with a spade, treating the object as if it would shatter if he touched it the wrong way. It was a large cylinder, rust encrusted and pitted with age. He scraped some more until he could get an idea of the circumference.

He uttered a single curse, all the more striking because of the quietness of the night.

The light clicked off, and it and the spade came hurtling out of the pit. One of the workers cursed as the shovel struck him. The leader silenced him with a slap across the face.

A light from outside the group snapped on, bathing the scene with a blinding glare. Police whistles shrieked, and for a moment the tableau remained static. Then the men ran pell-mell across the park away from the light.

The thin man scrambled out of the hole and shielded his eyes, trying to see. He ran a few steps but stopped as the whistles sounded again. An order rang out in Japanese. Again he turned and faced the light. He reached into his jacket pocket and pulled out a gun. He fired three wild shots. The thin man fell backward to the ground as a single shot was returned.

* * *

A very annoying sound managed to push through into Don Stewart's dreamland. Then something poked him in the back. He pried his eyes open and heard a sleepy voice in his ear.

"Phone's ringing, dear," Doris said.

Don reached for it and somehow fumbled it into his hand without dropping it.

"Good morning, sir," said a cheerful voice with a slight Japanese accent. "It's seven o'clock."

"Oh. Thank you," he said.

"You are most welcome, sir," she replied.

He replaced the receiver, smiling at the operator's polite efficiency.

"Mm, time to get up already?" said a voice on the other side of the bed.

Don groaned as he sat upright on the huge king-size bed. He rubbed his eyes vigorously and frowned. No doubt about it. Jet lag was still with him.

"Have to. But no need for you to get up. I'll call from the embassy when I know how my day's going."

"'K."

She rolled over and pulled the covers up.

Don got up and stumbled toward the bathroom.

2

Sam Grayson Owens

It was 8:30 when Don Stewart walked through the heavy embassy doors. He was still marveling over the breakfast at the Imperial Hotel. He had debated whether to try a Japanese breakfast or stick with the American menu. He had decided on the latter, and the ranch-style breakfast had been excellent. He resolved to try the other tomorrow.

He looked around the spacious lobby and flagged down a passing airman who directed him to Colonel Dill's office on the second floor. He took his time on the ornate stairway, admiring the tasteful decorations. *Well, this is my office for the next few years,* he thought. He paused at the heavy wooden door with Dill's engraved nameplate on it and knocked. A muted "come in" sounded from inside.

Don opened the door and looked in. Allen Dill was sitting at a magnificent hardwood desk. He looked up and stared at Don through horn-rimmed glasses, his face blank for a moment. Then a ready smile appeared.

"Come in, Don," he said, standing and shaking his new assistant's hand.

"Welcome to the organization." He paused. "I apologize for dragging you and your wife to that reception last night, but I wanted you to meet those people. Having our navy boomer tied up at a Tokyo wharf is important to the State Department." He frowned. "Naturally there are some who would like to see us rip our knickers over it."

"I understand, Colonel. It gave Doris and me a head start in getting acquainted."

Allen nodded and sat back down, motioning Don to an overstuffed chair beside the desk.

"Good, good. Oh, please call me Allen. I'll feel more comfortable."

"Allen," Don said, a little self-consciously.

A look of puzzlement replaced Don's smile. "I feel sort of like I missed the punch line. I gather that the *Tennessee's* visit is important, but are the Japanese really all that sensitive about it? After all, they're into nuclear projects themselves now."

Allen sighed as if the entire problem rested on his shoulders. "Unfortunately, they are. They're into nukies of course, but some Japanese groups get pretty rowdy, especially the left-wingers. And the *Tennessee* being a fleet ballistic missile sub makes it worse than if it was an attack boat. And it's not anchored out in Tokyo Bay. The *Tennessee's* tied up at Harumi Wharf, a little over three kilometers from here."

"What are the reactions so far?"

Allen snorted. "Just look at these English language newspapers."

He waved at a stack of papers on the corner of his desk. Don turned his head to the side so he could read a headline. The type was large, black and to the point: "U.S. ATOM SUB ENDANGERS TOKYO."

"Are they all that bad?" Don asked.

"That's the worst one. But they're *all* talking about it, even the moderate press. And there's precedence for this sort of trouble, which is why we're being careful. Back in 1968 a nuclear attack boat visited Sasebo, Japan." He paused. "They happened to be in port over May first."

Don rolled his eyes. "May day."

"You bet your little red book. As you might guess, we were set up. The local communists planted a report that the sub had discharged radioactive waste into the harbor. They said we were killing fish and poisoning the people and that the U.S. and the Japanese governments didn't care. It wasn't true, of course. Our navy and the Japanese officials conducted a thorough inspection that proved it, but the damage already had been done. Naturally I want to avoid that."

"I see." Don nodded as he reviewed the problem. The fall of the Berlin Wall had taken some of the stridency away from the Cold War's East-West conflict, but leftists of various flavors still made their presence known.

Allen frowned. "And, if our plate wasn't full enough, a tropical storm is brewing some fifteen hundred miles off the coast. The weather gurus predict it'll turn into a typhoon and start heading toward Japan in the next day or so. The *Tennessee*'s captain isn't happy about it, but Tokyo Bay is well sheltered."

"Will it hit Tokyo?"

"Too soon to tell, but it looks likely."

"That sounds nice."

Allen looked over at a thick manila file folder on the corner of his desk. The frown eased and the smile returned.

"Enough of that. I've seen your file. You have a nice record. I'm proud to have an officer of your caliber in my organization."

"Thank you, Allen."

"We can use a man like you, and I think you'll find this tour reflects favorably on your career." He flipped a page. "I noticed that this is your first tour in the Far East."

Don nodded. "It's my first duty station outside the U.S. Don't know why. I sure haven't avoided it."

"You'd be amazed at how many do. The air force has changed a lot since I was a first lieutenant."

Don scanned his boss's medals with respect. Allen had been where the action was, that was for sure.

"Doris and I were delighted when we found out about our posting," he said.

"I think you'll find it interesting." He glanced at his watch. "Well, I'm sure you'll want to get settled into your office. As you know, you're the assistant air attaché under me, but you'll find your duties broad and varied. We assist the ambassador and provide intelligence for the air force and DOD. This makes our work patterns quite flexible."

Don got up. "I'm a quick study. Which way is my office?"

"To the left, two doors down."

* * *

Don spent the next hour and a half sitting at his desk, reading general information publications. A brief foray outside his office had yielded the location of the break room. He sipped on a cup of coffee as he finished scanning yet another report. He eyed the cover. *They sure look nice,* he thought, *but where do they get these writers? Probably makes the Congressional Budget look like a thriller.* He jumped as his telephone gave an imperative ring. *Who would be calling me?* he wondered as he picked up the receiver.

"Major Stewart," he said.

"Don, this is Allen." His boss sounded a little stressed. "I need you in the ambassador's office on the double."

"Yes, sir. I'll be right there."

"Fine. You know where it is?"

"Yes, sir. I saw it this morning."

The phone clicked dead. Don slowly replaced the receiver, wondering what could be so urgent on his first day. He got up and put on his blue coat.

He went down the stairs and across the entrance hallway, stopping outside the ambassador's door. He knocked on the heavy wooden door. A marine orderly opened it and stood to the side as Don entered the luxurious office. Ambassador Dewey was seated behind his desk, Allen standing at the side. They both looked toward him. They were not smiling.

"Come in, Major Stewart. Colonel Dill has just brought me some rather disturbing news." The ambassador paused for a moment and looked past Don to the marine. "That will be all. Please tell my secretary we aren't to be disturbed."

The corporal clicked his heels. "Yes, sir," he said as he turned and left the room. The door shut with a solid thump.

"Now, gentlemen," Victor said. "My secretary handed me this when I came in this morning." He picked up a single sheet of paper, then tossed it aside. "It's a memo from the Tokyo Metropolitan Police Department. Seems an American was killed last night in Hibiya Park, near the Imperial Palace." He glanced at Don. "That's right across the street from the Imperial Hotel. It happened around two this morning. But what's *really* strange is that this memo is from the Internal Security Division. Not many people know about them. They keep tabs on Japanese subversives and terrorists.

"Anyhow, I'm sure you catch the drift. They think this American was involved in some way with a terrorist group. I needn't tell you how sensitive this is, especially right now."

Victor paused. "The police are asking for our help. I've talked it over with Colonel Dill, and we agree it would be a good idea to have one of our people work with the Internal Security Division. Major Stewart, we think you're the one for the job."

"Anything else we need to go over?" Victor asked Allen.

"No, sir. I think that covers it. I'll keep you posted on what we learn. If there's nothing else, Major Stewart and I will go back to my office and go over the details."

"Yes, well, thank you, gentlemen."

Don could sense his boss's tension as they walked back to his office. Allen opened the door, went in, and sat behind his desk, avoiding eye contact. Don entered and closed the door. Allen waved absently at a chair beside the desk, and Don took it. Allen remained silent for almost a minute.

Finally he looked up, a frown on his face. "Man's name was Sam Grayson Owens. Strange background. Take a look." He pushed a thick folder across his desk.

Don picked it up and began scanning the thick sheaf of papers. Owens had been *one* unhappy man. He had a long list of convictions, crimes ranging from shoplifting to disorderly conduct to two instances of armed robbery. In recent years he had joined a series of survivalist organizations, most of which Don had never heard. He had married twice, but neither marriage had lasted long. His father and mother were dead, and he had no siblings. Then, approximately a year ago, Sam Owens had dropped out of sight after a run-in with a sheriff near Cut Bank, Montana.

Don flipped nearer the back and stopped. His eyebrows went up when he realized how thorough the man's dossier was. Here was his father's service record. Sam Byron Owens had been in the navy, serving as an ord-nance officer, and his last duty station had been on Tinian, where he had worked for a Commander Morris, both assigned to the 509th Composite Group.

The name "Sam Owens" had rung a bell the first time he heard it. Now he remembered why. Years ago, Don's father, Bill, had been on the staff of the base commander at Lowry Air Force Base in Denver. Don remembered overhearing a conversation between Colonel Larry Best and his father.

Bill knew that Larry had been in the 509th Composite Group on Tinian and had remarked on the two naval officers standing with the crew in front of a B-29. He asked Larry if they had been involved in either of the atomic bomb missions. Don still remembered the stricken look on Larry's face. The older officer explained that everyone in the 509th had been involved in one way or another. He had worked with Commander Morris and Lieutenant (jg) Sam Owens, both navy weaponeers, but pointed out that those men hadn't been involved with either Hiroshima or Nagasaki.

Don looked again at the father's record. This Sam Owens had to be the same one. Then he silently chided himself—*Stick to the facts, Stewart! What difference could it make?*

Don looked up and replaced the folder on Allen's desk. "You're right," he said. "Not a pretty picture."

"That's putting it mildly," Allen agreed with a sour expression. "Some-times I think the life-goal of some people is to cause as much trouble as possible.

"That's from our sources. I don't know what the Japanese have, but you can bet there's more. Probably just as nasty too."

"Guess I'll find out pretty soon."

"I'm sure you realize how sensitive this is. Keep me posted. Let me know the minute *anything* new turns up."

"Yes, sir. Who is my contact at the Internal Security Division, and when do I go?"

Allen referred to a scrawled note in front of him. "Man's name is Toshiro Okawa," he said. "Mr. Okawa wanted to meet with someone this morning. After checking with the ambassador, I told him we'd have someone over there at 1300. That OK?"

"Yes, sir. I'd like to look this over." Don picked up the folder again. "You said *Mr.* Okawa? He's not a police officer?"

"He's attached to the Metropolitan Police Department, but technically he's a civilian. Odd, but that's the way the department is set up.

"By all means, take the folder along. If you need anything else, let me know. Okawa-san's office is in the Tokyo Metropolitan Government Office Building. I know time's short, but get as familiar with Owens's background as you can. We don't want to look unprepared."

"I'll do the best I can, sir."

Don returned to his office and closed the door. He sat down at his desk and went over the dossier again, this time more carefully. His frown grew steadily worse. *This is like examining the contents of a sewer,* he thought. Sam the younger had even been accused of a failed plot to blow up the Capitol in Helena, but he dropped out of sight before he could be apprehended.

After reviewing the father's record again, Don was even more convinced that this Sam Owens was the same one Larry Best had known. But so what?

Don had an impulse to call Larry but wondered if he should. How likely was it Larry knew anything about the son? But Colonel Dill had ordered him to be prepared.

Don glanced at his watch, noting it was just after eleven. Quick arithmetic told him it was after 7:00 P.M. in Denver. Of course, it was Monday there instead of Tuesday, courtesy of the international date line.

Don got Larry's number from information in Denver and punched it in. He sat back in his swivel chair and stared at the file folder in front of him. The phone rang three times.

"Hello?" a man's voice answered.

"Larry, this is Don Stewart."

"Don! How are you?"

Don smiled at the friendly voice from half-a-world away. "I know I'm supposed to say 'fine,' but right now I'm up to my hip pockets in alligators."

"You got orders as air attaché to Tokyo, right?"

"That's a roger. This is my first day, and already something juicy has fallen on my plate."

"Well, if the younger Stewart is anything like his dad, that's not a problem." He paused. "Is this a social call?"

Don took a breath. "About half-and-half. I like to keep in touch with old air force friends—mine *and* my dad's."

"I understand. I thought the world of your old man. I miss him. Listen, I'm so sorry about your mother."

Don felt his throat tighten. "Me too. It's especially hard for us being so far away. But, we had some good visits before we left. She belongs to the Lord, so I know I'll see her again."

"Amen to that. She's a wonderful lady. I'm also mighty impressed with her son, and being brothers in the Lord makes it even nicer."

Don smiled. "Thank you. The feeling's mutual."

"So, how can an old broken-down retiree help you?"

"Larry, something's come up that I'd like to run by you, if you've got the time."

"Sure. You don't have to ask. What is it?"

"An American was killed in a police raid at a Tokyo park last night—something to do with a Japanese terrorist group. The ambassador has assigned me as liaison to a Japanese security group, and I'm trying to get up to speed before I go over there."

"OK, but I don't see what this has to do with me."

"The American's name was Sam Owens."

The line went silent.

"I remember you talking to Dad about a Sam Owens you knew on Tinian—a navy weaponeer assigned to the 509th. The dead man's father was Sam Byron Owens. I have a copy of his service record, and it says he was assigned to the 509th. I think I know, but is this the same guy?"

"Sounds like it," Larry said in a subdued voice.

"Did you know the son?"

"No. I never ran into Sam after the war—the father, I mean."

"I know I'm grasping at straws, but is there anything about him that might explain why his son would get mixed up in a Japanese terrorist group?"

"No!"

The abruptness of Larry's answer gave Don pause. "Larry, exactly what did Sam Owens do on Tinian? I know he wasn't on either of the atom bomb flights."

"I can't tell you that."

"What? Everything about the Manhattan Project has been declassified for years. What's the problem?"

"Didn't you hear what I said?"

Don's eyes grew wide at his friend's obvious anger. "Yes, Larry. I heard you. I'm sorry if I said something I shouldn't have."

"Forgive me. Guess I'm getting crotchety in my old age. But there really are some things I can't talk about—even now."

"Related to the 509th?"

"That's correct, and that's all I can say."

"OK, I understand. I'll let you go. Got to finish getting ready for my meeting."

The voice on the other end of the line seemed to brighten, but Don knew it was forced. "Nice to hear from you. Defense attaché duty is nice, from what I've heard. Probably spoil you rotten for regular military duty. Tell Doris and the kids hi, and I expect to see you next time you're in the States. Hear?"

Don said what was expected and slowly hung up the phone, feeling depressed and uneasy. He didn't know what he had expected but certainly not the reaction he had received. Larry had obviously known the elder Owens, and something about their past was still classified. *Why in the world would* that *be?* he wondered.

Don returned to the folder and went over it one last time. He was about midway through it when a knock sounded at his door.

"Come in," he said.

The door opened just enough for Fred Brown to stick his head in. "Some of the guys are going over to the Tokyo Prince Hotel for lunch. Wanna go along?"

Fred's cheerfulness was refreshing after his own dour thoughts. He glanced at his watch.

"Don't think I better. I'm due at the Tokyo Police Department after lunch, and I still have work to do. Can I get a rain check?"

"Sure. See you later."

The door closed. Then the phone rang. Don struggled with his irritation at the interruption as he grabbed the receiver. "Major Stewart."

"Major, this is Ambassador Dewey. Could you come by my office?"

"Of course, Mr. Ambassador. I'll be right there."

He put on his coat and hurried downstairs. The marine orderly let him in, then left and closed the door. Victor seemed quite uncomfortable, which puzzled Don.

"Please sit down, Major."

Don took the indicated side chair.

"I noticed from our file that you have two young children." He glanced at a folder on his desk. "Michael and Leah."

"Yes, sir." *What is this about?* Don wondered.

"My grandson, Matt, is coming to visit us, arriving tomorrow." He cleared his throat. "He and his mother have been here several times, but this time Fran—my daughter—isn't coming. She's—she's having a lot of problems right now. I won't bore you with the details. But, I was wondering if you could include Matt in some of your kids' activities?"

Don's mind shifted into turbo. He knew the right answer, and only part of it had to do with this being the *big* boss. Victor hadn't said much, but there was no doubt that his grandson needed help. "Yes, sir. Doris and I would be glad to help."

"Fine, fine. I appreciate it." He glanced at his watch. "I know I'm taking away from your preparations. We can discuss the details later."

Don got up. "Any time, Mr. Ambassador."

"Thank you."

Don left and hurried back to his office. He had less than a half hour to get ready. *That's a laugh,* he thought. *How in the world can I get ready for this? What I know is flying fighter aircraft. This is politics. What do I know about that—or want to?*

3

Toshiro Okawa

Toshiro Okawa sat at his small desk, his face impassive as he meditated. The American military officer would arrive soon, he knew. But right now Okawa's thoughts were many miles and more than half a century away. To be precise, they were on the island of Okinawa and with a man he had never met: Yoshio Okawa, a young Japanese lieutenant in the Imperial Army.

His grandfather's life had ended on that island, since it had been the emperor's will that Okinawa be defended to the last man. Yoshio had carried out his duties faithfully, with honor to the emperor, his homeland, and his family—a family consisting of a wife and a young son, Shintaro—Toshiro's father. But Yoshio died on Okinawa, as had almost all the Japanese who fought there, and his body had never been found.

Okawa's memories shifted slightly in location but not in time, to the stories his father had told him, stories that had terrified him as a young boy, how his grandmother and her son had fought for survival in the bombed-out ruins of Tokyo.

Toshiro could still remember his father's tears as he told of the fire-bombing raid that had killed his mother. The younger Okawa had sat spellbound as he saw the horror in his father's eyes.

There had been no getting away from the all-consuming firestorm that had enveloped much of Tokyo. They had run and run until young Shintaro could run no more. With the unbearable heat at his back, he knew he was dead. His mother screamed. Shintaro turned to see a burning wall fall, crushing her. The last thing the boy remembered was staggering away in an attempt to escape the inferno. Then he tripped and tumbled forward and everything went black.

Shintaro had been very surprised to wake up the next morning. He had fallen into the muddy banks of a rubble-choked river, the only way he could have survived. The smoke was still very thick, and it had a horrible stench to it. Shintaro crawled out of the river and wandered for days in the ruins that had been Tokyo, eating and drinking things he couldn't remember. Finally a stranger had taken him to a police sub-station. The horror had finally ended when his aunt and uncle had taken him into their home and raised him as their own.

Toshiro's father was dead now, but he had carefully explained how things had been. The American assault on Okinawa had killed Toshiro's grandfather, and their B-29s had killed his grandmother and almost killed his father. Those fire-bombing raids had killed more Japanese than the atomic bombing of Hiroshima and Nagasaki. And, remembering the pictures of charred bodies stacked six and eight feet deep, Toshio couldn't really say that their deaths had been any less horrible.

Toshiro's father had told him how, after the war, the Japanese had viewed the American giants with respect and awe. The emperor had told them they would follow the American general's orders, and they had. But this respect had diminished over the years. Regardless of their basic goodwill, individual Americans had done bad things, things that Okawa had seen many times. These giants were not all kind, and they certainly were not all-knowing. Many had little appreciation for Japanese culture, coupled with the worst that an unprincipled, ignorant soldier can do in a country he sees as filled with inferiors.

Okawa swallowed down his distaste. Soon he would be meeting this American, Major Stewart. He sighed. This was business, and he would do his duty.

* * *

It was twenty minutes to one when Don walked out of the embassy. Gus was waiting beside his sparkling van, smiling as broadly as ever. They made the short trip quickly.

The Tokyo Metropolitan Government Office was a large, imposing building across the street from Mitsubishi Bank and just down the street from the Imperial Palace. The guard inside directed Don to an office on the second floor. Don stood for a moment outside the plain door, then entered. The secretary in the cramped reception area looked up.

"Major Stewart?" she asked in a soft, lilting voice.

"Yes. I'm here to see Mr. Okawa."

"Yes, sir. He is expecting you."

She got up and led him down the narrow hallway to a door at the far end. She opened the door and bowed as Don walked past her.

A short, middle-aged Japanese stood. He was thin and wiry looking, and his civilian clothes were loose and baggy. He hesitated a moment then extended his hand. Don took it and was surprised at the strength of the grip.

"Major Stewart, so good of you to come and help us in this matter," Okawa said. His accent was heavy, but his diction was precise. There seemed to be a faint hint of reproof in the greeting, Don thought, a hint that was reinforced by something in Okawa's expression.

Don forced a smile. "I'll be glad to help, any way I can."

Okawa waved toward a utilitarian chair as he sat down behind his small desk. His eyes never left the American, seeming to analyze him down to the smallest detail. Don grew uncomfortable under this open appraisal.

"Now," Okawa said, "shall we look at this situation?" He smiled at Don, a smile devoid of warmth.

Okawa gave Don a brief review of the incident in the park, concluding with what he knew about Sam Owens, which was considerably more detailed than the American's information.

"What is the name of this group?" Don asked when Okawa had finished.

"*Pikadon-ha.*"

Don grinned. "You'll have to explain that, Mr. Okawa."

Okawa's expression changed not at all. "Literally it means something like 'lightning-boom group.' Actually, *pikadon* has come to mean 'atomic bomb blast' since the Pacific War. Owens was with them for almost a year. He left your country in late 1999 as an employee of the W. W. Matthews Company, an importer of eastern goods. He worked in their Tokyo office and was officially their employee up until yesterday. It was a good cover, and although we had him under observation, he had not done anything we could arrest or deport him for."

"Is there more?"

"Yes. We have had the Pikadon-ha under observation for many years. They want a radical change in our government, by any means possible, including terrorism. At first they limited their activities to the political: rallies, demonstrations, attempting to elect members to the Diet. But lately they have become restless because they have had little success. Most

Japanese are conservative and seem likely to stay that way. This finally caused the Pikadon-ha to turn to terrorism."

"Sounds like the *Aum Shinrikyo.*"

Okawa shook his head. "No, the *Aum Shinrikyo* are obsessed with spiritual corruption, as they define it."

"Obsessed enough to turn sarin gas loose in the Tokyo subway system," Don observed.

"That is correct. In 1995 they killed eleven and injured thousands. The two groups *do* agree on terrorism, but the Pikadon-ha are interested in one thing only—political power."

"So, what do they want?"

Okawa looked at the American a few moments before answering. "Naturally, the first thing is political power. That and state ownership of the large companies, the expulsion of foreign companies, a ban on foreign investment." He paused. "And above all they want the expulsion of American military bases and an abrogation of treaties—all treaties. As you probably know, they tried to assassinate Prime Minister Chodo recently. The attempt failed, but they killed one bodyguard."

Don struggled to maintain what he hoped was a friendly smile. "I see. What were they doing in the park?"

"That we are not sure. We found an unexploded American bomb at the bottom of the hole, and they left an American mine detector behind—the latest army model I am told. They also abandoned a high capacity hydraulic lift. Apparently whatever they are looking for is quite heavy. The bomb was not their goal, I would think."

"Not unless they're crazy. Those old bombs are quite sensitive. A sneeze could set them off."

"Yes, Major, I am quite aware of that. Your army graciously supplied explosives disposal personnel to take care of the bomb."

"I'm glad they could be of assistance," Don said, thankful for at least one kudo for team USA.

"So, do you have anything to add that might shed light on this mystery?"

Don felt like shrugging, but he didn't. "Not a lot. Your intelligence is quite good. All I can add is that the dead man's father was Sam Byron Owens."

Okawa nodded. "Yes, a member of the illustrious 509th Composite. That seemed irrelevant to our investigation. Also, I was sure you were aware of the younger Mr. Owens's problems with the law, and so did not mention that either."

Don's smile finally disappeared. "I stand corrected. Your intelligence is *excellent.*"

"Thank you, Major. You are very kind to say so."

"Mr. Okawa, I'm here to help in any way I can. The ambassador is as concerned about this as you are. What can we do to help?"

A wry smile came to Okawa's lips. "That is a good question, Major. It would help if we knew what the Pikadon-ha are planning. Reports from our contacts suggest an action soon, something extreme I have no doubt. The Pikadon-ha have stated openly that they will stop at nothing—terrorism, assassinations. But so far we have not been able to penetrate their innermost circles, and we have lost several men trying. I am at a loss. However, I have an operation planned for tonight. You may join me if you wish, and your duties do not interfere."

Don sensed again a faint note of criticism making it hard to keep smiling. "I'll be glad to. What did you have in mind?"

"A sumo wrestling match in north Tokyo."

Don blinked in surprise.

"Strictly business," Okawa continued. "Although I suppose it would not hurt to mix a little pleasure in."

"Whatever you say."

"Good, good. I hope you enjoy it. We are going to see a sumo wrestler named Akira Moriya. He is not a champion but still quite good. He weighs 305 pounds, so he would be a match for either of us, I am sure. He is also in the Pikadon-ha, which is why I want to talk to him. We do not know his exact position but suspect he is quite high. I plan to take him into our headquarters for questioning."

"Isn't it a little unusual for a sumo wrestler to be a subversive? I mean, sumo is related to the Shinto religion, isn't it?"

Don watched Okawa's reaction. He seemed a little surprised at what Don had said. Was there a hint of grudging respect?

"You are right, Major Stewart. It *is* unusual. That is something I would not expect an American to know. You must have studied Japanese history. The Shinto religion is what Westerners would call reactionary. They believe in the ancient traditions, respect for the emperor, for ancestors, things like that. What you would call a referee is modeled after a Shinto priest. The wrestlers pray before their bouts, and they use elaborate rituals before bodily contact is made. The arena is covered by a roof similar to the ones covering Shinto shrines. But strange or not, Moriya *is* a member of the Pikadon-ha."

Okawa gave Don his business card. "Here is my card in case you need to reach me before this evening."

Don took the card, noting Okawa's hesitancy.

"Tell me, Stewart-san," Okawa said finally. "How do you like our country?"

Don tried not to show his surprise. "I like it very much. I'm looking forward to my tour of duty here, and that goes for my family as well. My wife can't wait to start on her shopping list, and the kids are excited about exploring Tokyo. Doris is looking forward to getting back to her painting because there are so many subjects here."

"Your wife is an artist?"

"Yes, and quite good, I might add. She especially likes landscapes and still lifes."

Okawa nodded. "That is good. I would think she would appreciate our art."

"I'm sure she will."

Okawa stood. "Until this evening then."

Don returned to the embassy and spent the rest of the afternoon reading about Japanese subversive groups in general and the Pikadon-ha in particular. Around four he called Allen's office and found out Owens's body had not been claimed. Somehow this did not surprise him.

* * *

Don unlocked the hotel door and walked in. Doris stood by the window contemplating a canvas sitting on an easel. She turned and smiled. She put down the palette and brush and hurried over.

"Hi, dear," she said.

He kissed her, feeling his tension and concern ease a little.

"How was your day?" Doris asked.

"Strange." He encircled her waist as he guided her back to the painting. "I see Grandma didn't take long getting back into the art business. Couldn't wait for our household effects?"

"Did you know there are more than two hundred art galleries on the Ginza?"

"No, I didn't. Did you know you answered my question with a question?"

She poked him in the ribs.

"Ow." Don rubbed his side then picked up a paint tube. "Where'd you get this stuff?"

"There're also a lot of department stores around here. We may miss being near the Ginza district when we get permanent housing."

"Maybe." He turned the tube sideways. "The writing is in Japanese. What color is this?"

"Sap green."

"How can you tell?"

"The color band on the tube. See?"

"OK." He looked over the incomplete painting. "Imperial Palace Grounds. Unusual perspective."

"True. Not your usual landscape. But then, I can't get up close and personal, so it's either paint from our window or use a postcard."

He nodded. "I like it. You show promise as an artist."

"What do *you* know about it?"

"I know what I like." He pulled her close and kissed her again, this time with more attention to detail.

"Hmm," she said when they parted. "I think we agree on that."

"It's a little warm in here, don't you think?"

Before she could answer, the door to the adjoining room banged open, and Leah rushed in, her expression one of complete outrage.

"Michael's hogging the TV remote!"

Don struggled to maintain a smile. "My day was fine, Leah. Thank you for asking."

Her pout, grand before, became magnificent. "Daddy, make him share!"

Doris inclined her head and whispered in his ear. "So, how will the Supreme Court rule?"

"Michael!" Don said, raising his voice.

"Yes, sir?" came the reply from the other room. However, the boy did not appear.

"In here, please!"

Michael trudged in moments later, his eyes laden with dread. Leah's pout segued into a look of triumph.

"Did you kids have fun today?"

Michael and Leah looked at each other, obviously confused.

"Yeah," Michael answered finally. "We saw some parks and went in some stores." His face lit up. "Then we rode around on the subways—they're everywhere! It was cool! Mom said there's even a Disneyland here." He looked up at his mother. "When can we go?"

"We'll see," Doris replied. "We're not settled in yet."

"But Mom . . ."

"Later, Michael."

Don looked at his daughter. "Did you have a good time today, Leah?"

Her excited expression changed to a look of distress. "Daddy, Michael was—"

"How was your day?" Don interrupted firmly. "I really want to know."

She looked down. "It was OK, I guess."

"Only OK? Riding on the subways. Shopping. Bet you saw a lot you've never seen before."

Her eyes lit up. "Yeah! Daddy, they have these large dolls dressed in fancy Japanese dresses. And later we were going by this place that had lots of flashing lights and all this noise. People were playing these games with small marbles. The marbles fall down, bounce off pins and fall in holes. Then more marbles pour out. It was cool!"

Don looked at his wife for guidance.

"It was a *pachinko* parlor. They're like vertical pinball machines that you put ball bearings in. The place was jammed with them, and I think all of them were in use. Sounded like a army on roller skates, and the lights. . . ." She rolled her eyes. "Naturally the kids were fascinated."

Don turned back to Michael and Leah. "So, you two had fun today?" He saw their suspicious expressions.

"Yes, sir," Michael said in a subdued voice.

"Yes, sir," Leah echoed.

"And we're supposed to be kind to each other, and that includes sharing. Michael, were you hogging the remote control?"

"Dad." He drew the word out into at least two syllables. "Leah was being *such* a pest."

"You didn't answer my question. Well, were you?"

Michael looked down. "Yes, sir."

"See!" Leah said.

Don turned to his daughter. "This isn't about getting even, young lady. Have you ever been selfish?" She turned away. "Look me in the eye," he added.

She did so. "Well . . . maybe a time or two."

"A time or two!" Michael exploded.

"I'm talking to your sister," Don said before returning his attention to Leah. "So, you've been selfish too. Listen, both of you. You're brother and sister. Michael, you're supposed to look after Leah, and I want *both* of you to be nice to each other and that includes sharing. Understand?"

They both said yes, not liking it but understanding that it was the right thing to do.

"Good," Don concluded. "I love you, and I want what's best for you both. You can go now, but remember what I said."

They disappeared quickly, obviously glad to get away.

"Not bad," Doris observed when the connecting door finally closed.

Don grinned. "Sure makes you believe in original sin, doesn't it?"

Doris laughed. "Yes." Then the smile faded. "You had a strange day? Can you talk about it?"

"Yes. Nothing classified, at least not yet. Strange isn't exactly accurate; weird is more like it. An American by the name of Sam Owens got himself killed in Hibiya Park last night—right across the street. He was associated with a Japanese terrorist group called Pikadon-ha. The ambassador has assigned me as liaison to a Japanese security group. I'm working with Mr. Toshiro Okawa."

"Sounds like you had to hit the ground running."

"It was rather brisk," Don said with a wry grin. "But the weird part is that Owens's father, also named Sam, was part of the 509th Composite Group on Tinian. Larry Best knew him."

"That is odd."

"Oh, it gets better. I called Larry today, and he clearly didn't want to talk about it. He even snapped at me when I pressed him. Apparently I really hit a nerve."

"That doesn't sound like Larry."

"No, it doesn't." He paused. "And there's more. I have to meet Mr. Okawa tonight at 7:30. We're going to a sumo wrestling match."

"What?"

"One of the suspects is a wrestler named Akira Moriya."

"What will you be doing?"

Don grinned. "Watching men the size of buses trying to make grease spots out of one another."

Doris laughed. "Besides that."

"Don't know. That's up to Mr. Okawa. But I presume he wants to talk to Moriya. And I'm instructed by the ambassador to help in any way I can." He snapped his fingers. "Which reminds me. We have something else to do for the ambassador."

"Oh, what's that?"

"His grandson, Matt, is coming for a visit—by himself. Seems Fran, the ambassador's daughter, is having problems. Ambassador Dewey asked if we could include Matt in the activities we're planning for our kids. I said yes. Hope that's OK." He saw the concern in her eyes.

"Well, of *course* it is. Poor little guy. How old is Matt?"

"Er, that didn't come up," Don said, aware that he had fallen short of the information women considered vital. "I'm guessing he must be around Michael's age, or the ambassador wouldn't have asked."

"You will find out?" Doris asked.

"Yes, dear." He glanced at his watch. "Quick dinner in the hotel restaurant?"

"Sure. I better get ready. Mind checking on the kids?"

"Yeah, guess I should. It's pretty quiet in there."

He opened the connecting door and looked in. The TV was on, and Michael and Leah were seated before it on the floor, legs crossed underneath them. Two pairs of eyes were riveted to the glowing screen.

A sharp-looking woman in a white dress danced onto an all-white set holding a plastic squeeze bottle of blue liquid. If her beatific expression was any indication, this elixir had magic powers and life without it was not worth living. Two children joined in the dance, with an accompaniment that sounded like a pack of cats fighting to the death. Then the lady in white showed what her squeeze bottle would do, which was quite amazing. Finally the commercial ended.

There was a slow dissolve to the program. Don noted with surprise that it was a Bonanza rerun. The camera panned slowly around the Ponderosa, taking in the snow-capped mountains, the deep blue sky, and the tall fir trees. A cut to a close-up of Hoss Cartwright showed him big and determined. Apparently someone had done something he didn't like. Hoss opened his mouth and a high, squeaky Japanese voice came out.

Don's mouth fell open, and he looked at the screen not believing what he was hearing. Then he howled, tears rolling down his face.

Michael and Leah frowned at him in annoyance.

"Dad," Leah whined. "We're trying to watch the show."

Don wiped his eyes with the back of his hand. "Sorry. I just never thought of Hoss Cartwright that way. You two understand what they're saying?"

"Not really," Michael admitted. "But it's easy enough to figure out what's going on."

"That's good. But time to get ready for dinner. Old Dad has to work tonight. I'm going to see a sumo wrestling match with a Japanese policeman."

"Oh, wow!" exclaimed Michael. "Can we go?"

Don grinned. "Not this time. This is business, so I doubt Mr. Okawa is expecting any munchkins. But we'll see a match sometime. Now get ready for chow."

Don saw a bright flash in his son's eyes and knew the young mind had jumped track.

"Oh! Dad!" Michael said. "Will I be able to do my rock climbing in Japan?"

Don thought about it. "Well, I'm not sure, but I guess so. I think rock climbing is a worldwide sport. Tell you what. I'll find out at the embassy. How's that?"

"Great!"

Michael turned and dashed into the bathroom.

Don wasn't sure how he felt about his son continuing his rock climbing. He liked the confidence-building aspect of the sport, and it was relatively safe on prepared sites and in rock-climbing gyms. However accidents still happened occasionally. Don realized he couldn't protect his kids from everything. It wasn't possible. He returned through the connecting door and closed it.

* * *

The waiter took the parents' orders, then turned to the children. Don watched Michael and Leah as they ordered from the menu. With great dignity, they laced a few Japanese words with a liberal assortment of English modifiers. The waiter said *"hai!"* after each item, giving the impression he understood them perfectly. He got a clarification on a few entries from Doris then left the table.

"Well," Don said, "you two are wasting no time learning Japanese."

"Sure, Dad," Michael replied, kicking absently at a table leg. "The people at the hotel and in the shops help us."

"That's good. You're not being pests, are you?"

"No, sir," Michael replied with a frown. "We wouldn't do anything like that."

Don looked around at Doris, barely able to suppress a grin. She smiled back at him.

The meal arrived before Don had an opportunity to worry about the time. He and Doris had tempura with all the trimmings, while Michael and Leah had, much to Don's surprise, hamburgers. After their valient efforts to order in Japanese, Don had expected nothing less than sukiyaki, or some such.

By Stewart household standards, the dinner was uneventful. Leah managed to tip over her glass of water (which she called *mizu*), spilling it on her mother. Then Michael doctored his hamburger with mustard and catsup and picked it up. But before he could take a bite, the bottom fell out, dumping the patty, relish, and bun into his lap with a loud plop. He looked at the mess for several seconds, as if wondering where it had come from, then nonchalantly picked up the pieces, assembled them, and resumed eating as if nothing had happened. Leah, her earlier accident forgotten, looked mortified. Don seemed oblivious as he and Doris enjoyed their tempura.

Only when the dinner was over did Don turn his thoughts to what he would be doing that evening. Again he wondered, could a sumo wrestler *really* be involved with a Japanese terrorist group?

4

Akira Moriya

The crowd outside the arena was larger than anything Don had ever seen. Japanese were packed so tightly about the doors, it was hard to see how anyone could get inside. In contrast to the polite social interactions Don had observed so far, he was surprised to see men barge through the crowd, callously jarring others as they shoved their way toward the doors. It was evident that this was not accidental, and women were not immune from the treatment. Those who were shoved did no more than shrug and quickly look away, apparently without anger. It looked as if all the spectators were intent on maintaining isolation, at least on the nonphysical level. Don saw Okawa looking at him.

"Most Americans find this hard to understand," his host said. "We Japanese have a reputation for courtesy. This is true on a personal level between friends and in social contacts with individuals, but it does not extend to groups of strangers. We live in a crowded land, Major. We cannot afford to become involved in the lives of all those around us. So we look after ourselves and ignore the jostling others give us."

Okawa shrugged his shoulders. Don couldn't tell if this was an explanation or an apology.

"However," Okawa continued with a wry smile, "*we* do not have to shove our way through this crowd, in case you were worried about that."

He brought out a badge in a plastic wallet and led Don around to a side door. He flipped the badge at a determined-looking man in a black robe and exchanged a few sentences in staccato Japanese. The guard bowed and held the door open for them. He bowed to Don as he went by, and the American smiled back. It was not returned.

The arena was jammed with people, men mostly, seated in boxes near the ring or in western-style seats in the balcony area farther away. All the boxes had rice mats and cushions to sit on. Most had four occupants, although a few had less. Don found it hard to believe that the throng outside would find places. It seemed as if everyone was smoking, causing the far reaches of the arena to be hazy and indistinct. The ceiling-mounted lights lanced down in bold shafts that seemed almost solid.

Okawa led Don through the crowd. He showed an attendant his badge. The man admitted them to a roped-off section of boxes that was nearly deserted. He pulled out two cushions, placed them on the mat, and motioned Don to one. The American sat down awkwardly and crossed his legs Indian-style, trying to ignore the popping noises in his knees. Okawa smiled and descended in one graceful movement. Don frowned and looked down at the tiny circular ring, determined not to admit his discomfort.

They didn't have long to wait. The referee came out and started chanting in a piercing, singsong voice, punctuating his speech with sharp movements of a square fan. The billowing sleeves of his purple robe flapped like some huge bird. He wore a high black cap.

"See that structure above the ring?" Okawa asked.

"Yes."

"It is like the roof of a Shinto shrine. And the official in black is similar to a priest."

Don studied his host, wondering where this was going. He hoped he wasn't violating Japanese etiquette. "Mr. Okawa, may I ask you a personal question?"

"I guess you may," Okawa replied with obvious reluctance.

"This makes twice we've discussed the Shinto aspects of sumo wrestling. Spiritual things interest me. Are you a follower of the Shinto religion?"

Okawa's eyes were even more guarded now. "No. That means nothing to me."

Don felt a tightness in his throat as he wondered how to proceed. "I see." He waved a hand toward the ring. "All cultures show an interest in powers beyond what we can see, but there's only one way that answers all questions."

"You are a Christian," Okawa said. It was not a question.

"Yes, I am. Are you interested in Christianity?"

"Forgive me, Major, but no. I am comfortable with my own beliefs."

"As you wish. If you change your mind . . ."

"The matches are about to begin."

The referee concluded his preliminaries. The ponderous sumo wrestlers paraded onto the platform, led by a current champion. Each wore an ornately designed apron.

Okawa leaned toward Don and nudged him. "Those aprons are given to the sumos. They are very expensive, costing many thousands of your dollars."

Don looked at the policeman in surprise, then back at the ring.

Each of the sumos had his raven hair done up in a tight topknot and wore a scanty black loincloth under his apron. The crowd thundered its approval as each was introduced. The sumos were the largest men Don had ever seen—not one was under two hundred pounds, and one weighed in at over four hundred.

Soon the introductions were over, and the giants returned to the dressing area. The referee called for the first match.

Two sumos entered and strode slowly down an aisle, seemingly oblivious to the wild cheering all around them. Their immense bellies quivered with each step as they entered the ring and went to their respective corners.

Don expected things to start right away, but they didn't. The referee said a few more words, obviously a prayer of some sort, but then seemed to lose interest as he stood silent and immobile in the center of the ring. The sumos appeared unaware of each other and in no hurry to begin. The one nearest Don stooped nonchalantly and scooped up a fistful of salt with a hand the size of a baseball glove. He scattered the salt over the mat, chanting and bowing as he did so. He repeated this several times, with minor variations as his opponent did likewise.

Finally they turned simultaneously, faced each other, and hunkered down, bearlike arms held at the ready. Then they froze, regarding each other like immense people-shredders. One made a move, unmatched by the other. Both turned away and returned to their corners as if they had decided to call the whole thing off. They ignored each other again as they repeated the purification process of salt throwing and praying. Apparently shortcuts were not allowed, as this ritual took as long as the first time. Again they broke off just when mayhem seemed imminent.

The wrestlers faced each other for the third time. Okawa touched Don on the arm and nodded toward the ring. The American peered through the miasma of smoke but could see nothing different about the two sumos. A fraction of a second later the two sprang at each other with a vicious speed Don wouldn't have believed possible. The mountains of flesh slammed into each other with a "smack" that sounded like a thunderclap in the now-silent arena. The sumos strained against each other, their huge thighs knotted with effort and their ample middles shaking as each tried to throw the other off balance.

Don anticipated a long, drawn-out match, but seconds later one of the wrestlers lost his footing. The other charged forward like an enraged buffalo, pushing for all he was worth. The off-balance sumo reached the ropes, tried to regain his balance, then toppled over the edge like a human avalanche, falling into the spectators below. Most scrambled to safety. However, two frail-looking men were not so fortunate and were trapped beneath the flailing sumo. The crowd roared its approval.

The fallen sumo got ponderously to his feet, apparently unaffected by his fall. He graciously helped the two unfortunates to their feet. They beamed at the wrestler as if this were an unexpected bonus. The sumo climbed back into the ring, and both wrestlers bowed as the referee intoned a short prayer punctuated by the flapping of his fan. Finally it was over, and the hulking contestants left the ring.

Four more matches came and went with much the same results, with minor variations that seemed significant to the spectators. Then Okawa nudged Don as the sixth pair entered the ring.

"The one on the right is Moriya."

Moriya looked to Don much like the others, ponderous and powerful. But there seemed to be something different about this man. The other sumos, for all their ferocious attacks, had a serenity about the eyes that spoke of a gentle nature. But there was none of this in Moriya. His eyes were cold, black, and hard.

The match preparations seemed much the same, but Don thought Moriya seemed more intent on getting to the physical contact. Moriya won his match handily, and both sumos retired from the arena amid a general uproar. *This was the man Okawa wanted to question?* Don wondered. He looked toward Okawa.

"We must wait," said the Japanese. "Moriya will be praying after his match, and then he will dress. We will leave shortly."

A few minutes later, Okawa led the way down to the dressing rooms, his badge opening the doors. They walked through the dark, musty corridors. A door opened and a sumo came out, surprisingly graceful for all his bulk. He seemed not to notice the two intruders as he walked past. Another sumo followed the first. Don was dimly aware of a muted roar as the two wrestlers made their way into the arena.

Okawa stopped a black-robed man and asked him a question. The man pointed to a door a few feet farther down the corridor. Okawa gave a brief bow and walked over to the door. Don listened as Okawa gave the door a tentative knock that sounded thunderous in the empty corridor. Although Don could hear faint sounds elsewhere, none came from this room. Okawa tried again. Again silence.

The policeman grasped the knob and turned, slowly pushing the door open. Don looked in as the crack widened, revealing more and more of the cramped dressing room. It was dark inside. The dim light from the corridor threw a wedge of light into the room, but it didn't reach the far wall. Okawa started in, reaching for the light switch as he did. Don followed.

A bulky shadow in the corner exploded into movement. The huge shape rushed toward them. In what seemed like slow motion, Don saw Moriya plow into Okawa, lifting him off the ground, hurling him back through the door and against the corridor wall. Don tumbled backward as he received glancing blows from both Okawa and Moriya.

Okawa shook his head and cried out as he scrambled to his feet. He grasped his left shoulder, his breath hissing from the obvious pain.

The policeman staggered off down the corridor behind Moriya. Don stumbled as he got up and had to hurry to catch Okawa. Past him, the huge robed figure neared an exit. Moriya hit the door without trying to open it. The lock and jamb splintered as the door crashed open.

Don caught up with Okawa at the exit and slid to a stop. A rather short man in a dark suit stood in their way. He held a .44 Magnum that dwarfed his gun hand. Black unblinking eyes watched them with no emotion at all.

Okawa stepped back from the man, taking care to avoid any sudden movements. The man remained there, still as a statue and just as silent. Don could hear people moving about in the corridor behind them, but no one approached. Finally the man turned, vanishing as quickly as he had appeared. Don followed Okawa out onto the street. The man was gone.

"What was that all about?" he demanded.

"We are close, Major Stewart. Closer than I thought. Moriya must be near the top."

He gasped as he moved his shoulder.

"You're hurt," Don said.

"I am OK!" Okawa snapped. Then he seemed to regret it. "Thank you for your concern, but the pain is going away."

Don debated with himself. It really wasn't his business. "Don't you think you should have it looked at?"

Okawa sighed. "Yes, I suppose that would be wise. There is a hospital near here."

They made the trip to the hospital in dismal silence, Okawa insisting that he could drive. They pulled up at a rather dreary looking brick building. The emergency room doctor examined Okawa and ordered an X ray. After reviewing the film, the doctor told Okawa he had a deep bruise, but nothing was broken or sprained. He handed the policeman a packet of pain pills as he finished filling in the hospital report.

Okawa didn't say a word as he drove Don back to the Imperial Hotel. Don was concerned about Okawa's condition, but the man seemed unwilling to talk about it, or the run-in with Moriya.

"Will you be all right?" Don asked when they pulled up in front of the hotel.

"Do not be concerned!" Okawa snapped.

"OK," Don replied. Although he was concerned for Okawa, the officer's abrasive temperament was beginning to wear Don's diplomatic skills a little thin. "What do I tell my boss? Are you closing the Owens case?"

Okawa sighed. "No, Major. We cannot afford to do that. The government is anxious to put an end to the Pikadon-ha. What happened tonight shows we are getting close." He paused in obvious distaste. "It appears that Mr. Owens was deeply involved with whatever they are planning. And I need not remind you that your government is vitally interested in this, especially at this time."

Don frowned and checked what he wanted to say. Diplomacy came hard for him, because he was used to saying what he thought. "As you wish. So, when do you want to see me?"

Okawa shifted. "The doctor said I should take a few days off. I told him I could not, and he—the doctor suggested I was not being wise."

"I think he was giving you good advice. That was some hit Moriya gave you."

"We finally compromised on one day."

"So, day after tomorrow."

Okawa nodded.

"What time?"

"Would ten o'clock be convenient?"

"Fine. I'll see you then."

* * *

Moriya watched the American get out of the car. *So, this is where he is staying,* he thought to himself. Even though he had only seen the man for a moment, every detail was etched into his memory. A big man, even for an American, but no match for a sumo. And, like all Americans, a meddler in affairs that did not concern him. But who did he work for—surely not the police. The U.S. Embassy was a possibility, but it could just as easily be a nearby military base. Whoever the man was, Moriya knew he would have to watch him—and take him out if necessary.

* * *

Don was more tired than he realized. He unlocked and pushed open the hotel room door. Doris looked up from the novel she had been reading, lowering it to the bed. She smiled, got up, and went to him. She gave him a long, lingering kiss, which he returned with feeling as she got his attention. His former concerns receded a little as he rearranged his priorities.

"Hi, dear," he said. "It's been a long day." He watched her eyes as they took a quick inventory.

"I can see that," she said. "What happened?"

Don sat in an easy chair, and Doris took the one beside it.

He closed his eyes. "Okawa was right. That sumo wrestler—Akira Moriya—*is* in with the Pikadon-ha. Either that, or he *really* has a thing about privacy! Okawa and I went to talk to him after the match. Moriya blew past us like we weren't even there. Bruised Okawa's shoulder and knocked me down!"

Doris put her hand to her mouth. "Oh, no! Don, this isn't part of your job! You're not a policeman!"

"You're right about that." He took a deep breath. "But unfortunately there's more. We chased Moriya outside and ran into a gunman who held us while his friend made his getaway."

"Don! You *have* to talk to Colonel Dill!"

"Oh, I will—in the morning." He paused, knowing she wouldn't like what he had to say next. "But Okawa wants me back in his office day after tomorrow."

"Why? Owens is dead. His connection with this terrorist group is over. Why do the Japanese need your help?"

"I wish it were that simple. Look. I don't know what Allen will say, but I can guess. The visit of the *Tennessee* is critical to the United States, and an embarrassment to the Japanese, especially with the noise the Pikadon-ha are making about it. Owens's involvement makes it *our* problem, like it or not."

Doris frowned. "I *don't* like it."

"Neither do I, but my opinion doesn't count for much."

He saw her jaws tighten, a sure sign she was mad. But then her eyes lost their flash of anger, changing instead to concern and love. In the twelve years he had been in the air force, she had finally come to peace with the sometimes extreme demands of service life. But they didn't have to like it, and Doris certainly didn't.

"I know, dear," she said finally. Her smile was genuine and full of love.

He sighed, suddenly very tired. "We better hit the hay. I need my sleep."

He saw an impish glint come to her eyes. "Too tired for close formation flying?" she asked.

He grinned. The euphemism dated back to their honeymoon when he used it to describe an activity high on their list of priorities.

"When I get too tired for that, give me my lily and put me in the box."

She sprang to her feet and started toward the bathroom. "Now don't fall asleep while I'm gone."

"Don't worry about that."

5

Plans for the Unknown

Don finished shaving and returned to the bedroom. He and Doris had decided on an early breakfast to give Don more time to plan his day and what he would say to Colonel Dill about last night's incident. By mutual consent, they decided to let the kids sleep in.

Don smiled in appreciation as Doris finished brushing out her hair. He kissed her gently.

"You look great," he said, really meaning it.

"I didn't have time to do it right," she began.

"Hush. You're talking about the woman I love."

She finally returned his smile. "Well, thanks."

"Ready for breakfast?"

She glanced toward the kids' room. It was peaceful. "I guess so."

They ate a quiet breakfast in the hotel coffee shop and afterward walked hand in hand to the lobby. They didn't say much, but Don knew Doris was thinking about what had happened last night, and what could have happened. He didn't blame her. He had been thinking about it too.

Don promised to call around noon, if he could. It was with a heavy heart that he kissed his wife good-bye.

* * *

Don waited until 9:30 to stop by Colonel Dill's office, giving his boss enough time to get his day started. Allen was surprised when he heard about the assault but saw no reason to call off the project. Don returned to his office and continued his research. He found no shortage of material, provided by the Japanese government as well as U.S. intelligence sources.

Near noon Don remembered a task that had been pushed to the back of his mind. He looked up Fred Brown's extension and punched in the number.

"Lieutenant Brown."

"Fred, this is Don. How are you?"

"Fine, Major." There was a pause. "How's your project going?"

Don felt a jolt of undefined dread. "That's hard to say. You heard about the American that got killed—Sam Owens?"

"Yes, I did. I also heard the ambassador assigned you to help the Japanese police. Making any progress?"

"Not a lot. Mr. Okawa—my Japanese contact—says the Pikadon-ha are involved, but we don't know what Owens was doing with them."

"Pikadon-ha! Whoa! They are some nasty dudes, from what I've heard. Hope you're being careful."

"I'm trying to. But that's not why I called. My son, Michael, is into rock climbing. Are there any rock-climbing sites or gyms in the Tokyo area?"

"I'm sure there are. Let me check on it and get back with you."

"I appreciate it—no hurry."

"Glad to help."

"Thanks. Talk to you later."

* * *

After taking time out for a quick lunch, Don continued his research well into the afternoon. Around two, he heard a knock on his door. It opened, revealing Victor Dewey with a rather sheepish grin on his face.

Don jumped to his feet. "Mr. Ambassador, please come in."

"Are you busy?"

"No, sir. What can I do for you?" Don came around and offered the ambassador one of the side chairs while he took the other.

"My grandson is coming in around four."

"Oh, yes—Matt. I remember you telling me. I told Doris, and she's looking forward to having him meet Michael and Leah."

"I appreciate your kindness. I'm at a complete loss when it comes to entertaining kids—and with Ann being in Hong Kong. . . . I'll do the best I can for Matt while he's here, but he needs to be with kids his own age."

"I understand. I'm sure Matt will have a good time. Doris enjoys out-ings with our kids as much as they do. I'll check with her tonight and see what she has planned. When do you think Matt would like to join us?"

"Tomorrow, if that's convenient. I could call your hotel tonight to firm up the details."

"That will be fine." Then Don remembered something. "Oh, how old is Matt?"

The ambassador looked up for a moment. "Uh, let's see—I think he's . . . yes, he's twelve now."

"Same age as Michael. They should get along great."

"Yes, well I must be off."

They stood up.

The ambassador's discomfort was evident. "Major Stewart, you're helping me with a difficult family situation. I appreciate it."

"You're welcome." He paused. "Sir, Doris and I care. We're praying for Matt."

Victor looked shocked and uneasy. "You are? Well—thank you."

He hurried out and gently closed the door.

* * *

"That is the man!" Moriya said pointing.

Takafumi Hasagawa nodded and got out of the car. He was wearing an expensive gray suit and blended in well with the Japanese businessmen walking past the entrance to the Imperial Hotel.

The American disappeared through the doors. Hasagawa increased his pace while maintaining his composure. He entered the lobby and looked toward the elevators. There he was, and the elevator doors were opening. Hasagawa rushed over and stepped through as the doors were closing. The elevator started up. It made several stops before reaching the twenty-fourth floor.

Out of the corner of his eye, he saw the American start to move and followed him out, keeping a comfortable distance. The man up ahead stopped, pulled out his card key, and plunged it into the lock. Hasagawa walked past as if going to a room farther down the corridor. Now he had the number.

* * *

Don considered the evening meal in the hotel restaurant a success, as the only casualty had been a tipped-over glass of water. Leah, the usual culprit, had been innocent this time, much to Michael's chagrin. The

Stewart's young son practically had ensured his own downfall after bragging that he never spilled anything.

After dinner, the Stewarts had returned to their rooms. Around eight, the phone rang. Don picked it up.

"Major Stewart," he said.

"Good evening, Major. Ambassador Dewey here. Can we talk?"

"Yes, sir. We've been expecting your call."

"Good. Well—Matt is here. Even with the long trip, he's pretty wired, but I think he's about to crash." Victor paused. "I told him a family on the embassy staff had kids his own age, and that he would have someone to play with. Major, I think it only fair to warn you that Matt can be difficult. He has trouble relating to people he doesn't know, and this doesn't bring out the best in him. But I think I convinced him he'll have fun, at least I hope so."

"Don't worry, Mr. Ambassador. Doris and I are used to what kids can get into. Matt will fit right in."

"Thank you, Major. What time should I send Matt over?"

"How about nine? Doris is taking them to the Tokyo Tower first and then over to Disneyland around lunch time."

"That sounds great!" Victor said, his voice picking up. "Matt will love that. The embassy limo will have him there at nine."

"Very good, Mr. Ambassador."

"Thank you, Major. Well, good-bye."

"Good-bye, sir."

Don replaced the telephone receiver and turned to Doris. "That was the ambassador. An embassy limo is bringing Matt over at nine." He paused. "Reading between the lines, sounds like Matt is a little wild. Are you sure you're up to it?"

She took his hand and squeezed it. "In my own strength, no. But we'll pray about it."

"Yes, we will," Don agreed. He kissed her gently, grateful once again for the one God had given him to live his life with.

* * *

The next day, Don hurried into the embassy to prepare for his mid-morning meeting with Okawa. On top of his in basket was a bright yellow folder with a red sticky note that said "FYI," signed by Fred Brown. Don opened the folder and found the results of a rather thorough Internet search. One web page listed the rock-climbing gyms in Tokyo. Another described the Okutama Climbing Area west of Tokyo, including maps on how to get there, what the weather was like, accommodations and camping, and climbing shops.

"Well," Don said to himself. "This should make master Michael happy."

He set the folder aside and reviewed his official correspondence. There was nothing new on the Pikadon-ha—at least from U.S. sources. Don began to brood over his encounter with Moriya.

* * *

Don left the embassy around 9:30. The veil of depression hanging over him lifted a little during the taxi ride to the government office building. It was a beautiful day. A light breeze had blown the dreary smog away, removing its acrid sting. The air was clear under the blue sky. The early morning sun bathed the city with warm red tones, giving everything a soft, roselike glow. On arrival, Don paid the driver and got out.

He was ushered into Okawa's office a little before ten. Then his earlier glow drained away like a deflated balloon. Okawa winced as he got up. The events at the sumo arena came flooding back.

"Good morning, Major Stewart. We have additional news on the Pikadon-ha, I am afraid. Please sit down, and I will bring you up-to-date."

Don took the indicated chair, and Okawa sat down behind his desk.

"How is your shoulder?" Don asked.

"It hurts some, but the pain medication helps. I have full use of the arm."

"I'm glad to hear that."

"There were three more diggings last night," Okawa said, "all within a mile of each other."

"Have they found—whatever they're looking for?"

"I would say no. One hole contained a section of cast iron sewer pipe, probably leftover from a construction project. Another had a large machine, so rusted we couldn't tell what it was. The terrorists even excavated inside a shop near the Imperial Palace, digging right through the floor. That turned out to be an unexploded bomb. Your U.S. Army took it away. But whatever they're looking for, they seem to be in a hurry."

"So it would seem," Don replied. "But why?"

"I wish I knew. But we do know that the Pikadon-ha are becoming restless. They have made no progress in changing Japanese policy, and I am sure this is bothering them. They are getting desperate, I think."

He paused and started doodling on the front page of a newspaper on his desk. He darkened the lines around the picture of a submarine.

"Stewart-san," Okawa continued, "the Pikadon-ha have been particularly vocal about the *Tennessee*. These mysterious diggings—and Mr. Owens's death—started after this visit was announced. There have been several so-called communiqués threatening mass killings unless we cancel *Tennessee*'s port call. We are not positive the warnings are serious, but we think they are. Our government feels this pressure, I assure you. Your ambassador feels it as well, which is why he assigned you to me."

Don felt his irritation rising, which he knew from experience was not good. He tried to remember the diplomatic part of his job as he struggled to remain calm. *Why is Okawa prodding me?* he wondered. Why not say what he thought and get it over with, rather than engaging in verbal thrusts?

"Yes, I *know* the ambassador is concerned!" Stewart said with more force than he intended. "Owens's death and his apparent association with the Pikadon-ha caused Ambassador Dewey to assign me to you, and I promise I'll do *everything* I can to help. I understand the *Tennessee's* visit is sensitive, but that's a side issue. Now! *What* can we do about your terrorists?"

Don saw Okawa's eyes widen at this directness. "Thank you, Major Stewart—I knew I could count on you. What I want to know is: *what* are the Pikadon-ha planning, and *what* was the late Mr. Owens doing with them?"

"That should keep us busy for a few minutes," Don grumbled, not yet over his irritation.

Okawa actually smiled. "Why, Stewart-san, I think I can allow you a little longer than that." Then the smile disappeared. "But not much, I fear."

Don took a deep breath. "I understand."

"So, your thoughts, please."

"From what you've told me, we better find out what the Pikadon-ha are up to and quick. Owens's connection worries me. His dad was an explosives expert, but all we know about the son is that he was a malcontent, and malcontents often have nasty habits. Maybe they're planning a bombing—a government building maybe, or a public gathering—I don't know. But if that's it, why all the digging near the Imperial Palace? They're obviously looking for something, but what? It just doesn't make sense."

"There I have to agree with you," Okawa said, casting his eyes downward.

"Have you scheduled any special patrols at night?" Don asked.

"Nothing out of the ordinary. We are on high alert, of course, but Tokyo is a very large city."

"I understand. But all these diggings are within a mile of each other. Why not concentrate your patrols there for a while and see if we can catch them?"

Okawa rocked back in his chair. "And what happens if I do that, and they strike somewhere else? Or another terrorist group, for that matter. There are others, unfortunately."

"The final decision is yours, Mr. Okawa. The Pikadon-ha seems to be the most dangerous group, and we know where they're operating right now. However, they, or some other group, could hit somewhere else—I know that. You would be taking a chance."

Okawa's smile was faint. "You realize who gets the blame if things go wrong."

Stewart nodded. "Yes, I do."

Okawa played with his pen as he thought it over. "Major Stewart, I like your suggestion. It could be dangerous, but I think it is worth the risk. Would you care to join me? Could be a boring night, but perhaps we will be lucky."

Don didn't see any way to refuse. "Wouldn't miss it for the world. Where do you want to meet?"

"I will call your office after we have planned the operation."

"Very good," Don said as he stood up. "I guess I'll see you tonight."

6

Matt Porter

Doris shaded her eyes as she scanned the traffic rushing past the entrance to the Imperial Hotel. She had no trouble identifying what she was looking for once the long black limo turned the corner. The luxurious car made a leisurely turn into the drive and pulled to an elegant stop. The doorman descended like a falcon on the rear door. The man opened the door, and out stepped a slightly overweight twelve-year-old boy. The doorman looked shocked, as if his pockets had been picked. Young Matt Porter ignored the man and walked to where Doris, Michael, and Leah waited.

"Mrs. Stewart?" the boy asked.

"Yes. And you must be Matt Porter. Pleased to meet you." She shook his hand, which seemed to surprise him. "Matt, I want you to meet Michael and Leah." She turned and stepped back a little.

"Hi, Matt," Michael said.

"Hi," Matt responded, shaking Michael's hand.

Leah hung back.

"That's my sister, Leah," Michael explained. "She's shy around strangers."

"I am not!" Leah said in a sudden huff.

Michael arched an eyebrow as only a twelve-year-old can. "Then what are you standing back there for?"

Leah finally moved. "Hello, Matt," she said, standing still as a statue.

"Shake hands," Michael hissed at her.

She shot her brother a hot look, then shook hands with Matt.

Doris struggled to maintain a straight face. She found the social fumbling of young people amusing, but she also enjoyed being with them. She liked doing the things they found interesting and didn't consider that undignified at all.

"What are we doing today?" Matt demanded, looking Michael in the eye. Then he glanced at Doris.

"First we're going to the Tokyo Tower," Doris answered. "Then we'll spend the rest of the day at Disneyland."

"Disneyland!" Matt whooped. "Way cool!" Then he stopped. "Did you say 'Tokyo Tower'?"

"Yes. It offers a breathtaking view of Tokyo. The brochure says you can even seen Mount Fuji on a clear day."

"I've been there already!" Matt snapped. "Let's go straight to Disneyland."

"But there are lots of things to do at the Tower. They have a wax museum, a trick art museum, and an aquarium."

Matt rolled his eyes. "Yeah, but that's nothing compared to Disneyland. I say we ditch the Tower."

Doris glanced at Michael and Leah. Their astonished expressions said it all. Doris offered a silent prayer for wisdom. "We're *going* to the Tokyo

Tower," she said. She made eye contact with Matt to make sure he understood she meant business.

"Um, well, OK." He turned toward the waiting limo. "Climb in. I'll tell the driver where we're going."

Doris set her jaw. She walked to the passenger side front door, opened it and looked in. She smiled as she saw Kinji Gusawa. "Hello, Gus. How are you today?"

"Fine, Mrs. Stewart. Are you and the major well?"

"We are."

Gus glanced toward Michael and Leah. "And Michael and Leah. Are they enjoying Tokyo?"

"They're having the time of their young lives. We're going to the Tokyo Tower this morning and Disneyland in the afternoon."

He nodded and smiled. "Ah, an excellent plan." He got out of the car. "Let me get the door for you."

"Oh, don't bother. We're taking the subway."

Gus's eyes grew round with shock. "You are?"

"Wait a minute!" Matt interrupted. "I'm not riding on no subway!"

"You shouldn't use a double negative," Leah piped up.

Matt turned on her in confusion. "What?"

"You used a double negative," Leah informed him. "That's not good English. A double negative makes a positive. It means you *are* riding the subway."

"And we are," Doris interjected.

"I didn't say any such a thing!" Matt said, raising his voice to almost a shout.

"Calm down," Doris said.

"I'm not . . ."

She caught his eye again. He stopped in mid-sentence. Doris fixed him with her "take no prisoners" expression and watched as the hostility melted away into doubt.

"OK," he said finally. He turned to Gus. *"Sayonara."*

Gus nodded. "Good-bye. Call the embassy if you need me."

"Wakarimasu."

Gus got back in the limo and drove off.

"You know Japanese?" Michael asked.

"Of course. I've been here lots of times."

"Sayonara I understood, but what does *wak* . . . whatever you said, mean?"

A gloating smile came to Matt's pudgy face. *"Wakarimasu* means 'I understand.'" He cast a wary eye at Doris. "And if I need to, I *will* call him."

Doris smiled. "So nice to have an expert with us. Now, shall we go?"

She consulted a map, oriented herself, then pointed. "That way."

* * *

The thin man in a conservative gray suit looked like he belonged in the hotel, but he didn't. The large rectangular case slung over his shoulder bounced against his hip as he walked along.

The man walked up to room 2404. He unzipped a compartment in his carrying case and pulled out a small box with a keypad. The box trailed a wire cable with a plastic card on the other end. The man inserted the card and waited. The LCD screen displayed a string of numbers. The man punched these into the keypad and then hit the pound key. The lock's green light came on. The man entered and quietly closed the door.

He saw what he wanted immediately. He walked to a picture on the far wall and took it down. *Perfect,* he thought. He pulled out a wireless transmitter and attached it to the back of the picture. After replacing the picture, he hurried to the telephone and examined it. He took it apart and inserted another transmitter, connecting it to the phone's tiny wires. He put the phone back together and made sure it was as he found it. One quick look around and he left the room.

* * *

Doris and the kids walked to the entrance of the Hibiya Line and descended the stairs. Doris bought them tickets. A southbound train roared into the station a few minutes later. They boarded, the doors whooshed shut, and the train accelerated toward the next station. Soon they pulled into Onarimon. Doris led the way up into the sunlight. She looked around, thankful for the clear day.

"Viewing should be excellent," she said.

The Tokyo Tower looked like the Paris one designed by Eiffel, except it was painted red and white. Michael and Leah gawked at the lofty structure while Matt pouted. Doris held the door for them, then purchased tickets for the wax museum and both observatories—the main one and the one near the top of the tower. She considered buying admission to the aquarium but decided not to press her luck.

"Let's see the wax museum first," she said, handing out the tickets. "Then we'll go up to the observatories."

"I've already seen it," Matt grumbled. "It's not that great."

"Maybe there's something new," Doris suggested.

"I doubt it."

"Shall we?" she ordered, pointing toward the entrance.

Inside, they passed statues of Jody Foster and Julia Roberts. Michael pronounced them "cool" without dissent from Leah or Matt. Up ahead Doris saw a figure and pose that looked vaguely familiar. As she got closer, she saw it was Marilyn Monroe standing on a grate holding her skirt down. The sign informed her the scene was from *The Seven Year Itch*.

"What's that?" Matt demanded.

Michael peered at the sign. "It's from a movie. Wow! Look at that! It was made in 1955!"

"Ew! Prehistoric!"

"Boys, 1955 isn't *exactly* the dawn of civilization," Doris said.

"Near enough," Matt said.

Doris shrugged. She was used to Michael and Leah commenting about how things had been in the olden days, back when she was a girl. However, this movie *had* been filmed a long time ago, quite a few years before even she was born.

Michael and Leah were enthralled with the lifelike statues of famous politicians and stars. Although Matt tried to look blasé, Doris noted his interest as well. They passed through the rock-and-roll section. A large portion was devoted to Frank Zappa. Doris read the enthusiastic blurb about him and decided the Japanese were enamored with strangeness. Next came Jimi Hendrix, Jimmy Page, and Peter Gabriel. Matt complained because none of the recent MTV stars were there.

Doris saw something she recognized and ushered the kids along as fast as she could. "Look! It's Snow White and the seven dwarfs."

A photographer stood beside his camera and tripod. He approached Doris and bowed. "Would you like a picture of your children with Snow White?"

This sounded good to her. She turned. "How about it?" she asked. Leah nodded her head vigorously. Doris saw Michael was interested as well.

"Naw, that's kid stuff!" Matt grumbled.

Doris saw Michael jump and his smile turn to a look of apprehension. "I don't guess so," he said.

Doris gritted her teeth and turned to Leah. "OK. Leah, go stand by Snow White, and the man will take your picture."

Leah looked over at Michael then back at her mother. "Are you sure it's OK?"

Doris laughed. "Of course it is. Go ahead."

"But what about Michael?"

Doris paused and eyed her son. "Michael's made his decision. Now, do as the man says."

The photographer coached Leah, positioning her between Snow White and one of the dwarfs. When he was satisfied, he took the picture. Moments later he handed it to Leah. She beamed as she ran her fingers over the print's glossy surface. Doris paid the man.

After leaving the exhibit, Doris felt an undefined dread and wondered what it was. Muted screams came from speakers up ahead. Finally Doris saw a sign announcing the torture room.

"Finally something interesting," Matt said as he took the lead.

Leah hung back with Doris, and Michael looked like he didn't know what to do.

Matt turned back. "Come on! This is cool!"

Doris made her decision. "Come on. Let's go to the main observatory. We need to move along if we're going to get to Disneyland by this afternoon."

"But I want to see this!" Matt insisted.

Doris approached and looked him in the eye. "I'm all for having fun, Matt," she said. "But let me explain something. While you're with me, I'm responsible to your grandfather for you. That means if I say we're not going to do something, then we're not going to do it. Do you understand?"

"But . . ."

"I said, 'Do you understand?'"

His scowl looked capable of souring milk. "Yes."

"Good. Now, follow me."

They took the elevator to the first level of the two-story main observatory, a little less than halfway to the top of the tower. Tearooms and shops were clustered in the center section while floor-to-ceiling windows provided a panoramic view of the sprawling city of Tokyo. Windows in the floor offered a rather disconcerting view of the ground, a hundred-and-fifty feet below. Michael and Leah ran to the windows and looked all around. Matt joined them while trying to conceal his interest. Doris followed them as they made a slow turn about the four points of the compass. After this they went up to the second level. The view was the same, but there were more shops.

"Look! A toy store!" Matt shouted.

He charged inside without a backward glance. Michael and Leah followed while Doris brought up the rear. As she passed through the entrance, a fluffy white robot sprang to life.

"Konnichiwa," it said, blinking its bright eyes at her.

Doris stopped abruptly and laughed. "I don't speak Japanese," she said and continued on into the store.

"I said, 'Good afternoon,'" the robot said. "I speak English also. What is your name?"

Doris stopped and turned around, not believing what she was hearing. She turned in a slow circle, looking for someone feeding the toy lines through a microphone.

A clerk approached and bowed. "That is RobiFriend. It has a powerful computer chip and understands many Japanese and English phrases. It appears intelligent, but it is only responding to words programmed into its memory."

Doris laughed. "I see. Well, it certainly surprised me."

"Why don't you answer RobiFriend's question," the man suggested.

"Me? Talk to a toy?"

"What could it hurt?"

Not a thing, Doris thought, *unless you happen to be on the stuffy side.* And she certainly didn't see herself as that. She approached the toy.

"My name is Doris." She saw her kids and Matt approaching.

"Most pleased to have the acquaintance of Doris," RobiFriend said.

Doris turned to the clerk. "His English needs a tune-up," she whispered, to keep the toy from hearing.

The clerk nodded gravely. "Yes, I am afraid that is true. The toy salesman told me they are still working on the export model. This is the Japanese model, however it has a test version of the English program."

"I do not understand," RobiFriend replied.

"How are you?" Doris asked the machine.

RobiFriend turned his head and blinked his eyes. "I am most OK, if you are pleased."

Doris suppressed a giggle.

"O-namae wa, nan desu ka?" Matt said.

"What did you say?" Michael whispered.

"I asked him his name," Matt whispered back.

The electric eyes turned on Matt. "RobiFriend *to mo shimasu.*"

Matt bowed. *"Domo arigatoo."* He then turned to Michael and Leah. "He says his name is 'RobiFriend.' I thanked him."

Michael shook his head. "That's pretty good."

"Not bad," Matt allowed.

"Would you like to buy for children?" the clerk asked.

Doris felt the fascination fade. "No, thank you."

The man bowed and returned to the back of the store.

They returned to the broad walkway around the observatory windows. The space next to the toy shop was boarded up. She could hear hammering sounds coming from inside.

"Wonder what that's going to be?" Doris asked, scanning the Japanese sign.

"It's going to be a tearoom," Matt replied.

"There's sure enough of those," Doris said. "You guys ready to go to the special observatory?"

"Yeah!" Michael said. Then his excitement faded as he saw Matt's jaded expression. "I guess so."

Doris found the elevator lobby. She handed the attendant the tickets as they entered. Moments later the doors closed, and the glass-sided elevator began its ascent to the top. More and more of the sprawling city came into view the higher they went. Finally the elevator's whine stopped, and the doors opened.

Doris led the way around the circle of windows.

"Look," she said, pointing to the southwest. "There's Mount Fuji."

They continued around in a clockwise circuit. To the north they saw the Imperial Palace.

"That's the embassy," Matt said.

"Where?" Michael asked.

"That glass building about halfway to the palace."

"Oh, yeah."

Soon they were around to the Tokyo Bay side.

"Hey!" Matt said. "There's the sub!"

Doris looked down on the wharf so far below. The sinister black shape was sharp and unmistakable in the clear air. Doris felt a shiver run down her spine as she thought about what the boat contained.

After completing their circuit about the observatory, Doris ushered the kids back into the elevator. They descended to the lower observatory and got out.

"Come on!" Matt ordered as he headed toward the other elevator lobby. "We've seen all this! I wanna go to Disneyland."

Doris glanced at her watch. It was almost noon. She looked around and saw a tearoom with a good view. "Let's have lunch here. Then we can take the subway to Disneyland."

Matt whirled around, his eyes blazing. "I've had enough! We can eat at Disneyland! Now, *come on!*"

For a few moments Doris was speechless as she struggled with her surprise and growing anger. She closed her eyes a moment and prayed a silent prayer for wisdom. When she opened her eyes, Matt still faced her, openly defiant.

Doris took a deep breath. "Matt, I am responsible for you until Gus picks you up, and while you're with me, you *will* do as I say. Is that clear? Do you understand?"

Matt's eyes flicked over Michael and Leah, then zeroed in on Doris. "*They* may have to do what you say, but *I* don't." He pulled a mobile phone out of his pocket, flipped it open, and punched in a number.

"What . . ." Doris began.

Matt took a cautious step back as he waited. "Gus!" he said into the phone. "Come get me!"

Doris debated on what to do and finally decided to wait. She watched Matt, wishing she could hear what was being said.

"No, I'm all right. Just come and get me." Matt paused and glared at Doris. "I'll be waiting in front of the Tokyo Tower." He listened for a few moments. "*No,* you can't speak to her! Now do what I say, and come get me!" He punched the "end" button and shoved the phone back into his pocket.

Doris saw the look of utter disbelief in her children's eyes. To Matt she said, "Come on."

"Where?" he demanded suspiciously.

"Down to the street so we can wait for Gus."

"Don't bother! I know my way around."

"You don't listen very well. I'm responsible for you until Gus gets here. Now come with me!" Her voice rose at the end.

They rode the elevator down in an uneasy silence. Doris took Matt's hand at the bottom and led the way toward the entrance. Matt tried to get loose, but Doris only clamped down harder. She held his hand until they arrived at the entrance drive beside the parking lot.

They didn't have long to wait. Several minutes later a familiar black limo pulled into the drive and stopped. Matt started for the back door without a backward glance but halted when it opened. Doris watched as Ambassador Dewey emerged and closed the door.

"Uh, hi, Granpa," Matt said.

Victor glared at him. "Don't 'hi Granpa' me! Get in the car!"

"But . . ." Matt began.

"Get in the car! Now!"

Matt hurried over, opened the door, climbed in, and shut it. Victor followed with his eyes then turned back to Doris. She saw the anger in his eyes turn to embarrassment.

"I'm sorry, Mrs. Stewart. I apologize for Matt's behavior."

"That's all right, Mr. Ambassador."

He shook his head. "No, it's not. You were very kind to take Matt under your wing. I know I shouldn't make excuses, but maybe if my daughter wasn't having . . ." He waved his hand. ". . . all her troubles, things would be different." He shrugged. "But I'm boring you with my problems."

Her heart went out to him. "It's obvious Matt is troubled. Don and I have prayed for him—and his situation. We really hoped this outing would be good for him."

He lowered his head. "Thank you for your concern. I hoped it would be also."

"And we'll include your daughter in our prayers as well."

Victor's expression was a combination of gratitude and embarrassment. "Hmm, well, I thank you. That's very kind."

"If things change, we'd be glad to have Matt with us again."

Victor's eyes widened. "You can't mean that, not after what he just did."

Doris took a breath. "Yes, I do." She lowered her voice. "He needs help, Mr. Ambassador. I won't deny he was trouble—he was. But if Don and I can help, we'd like to. I can't think of anything more worthwhile than guiding a youngster."

He nodded. "Thank you. I'll keep that in mind." He sighed. "But for right now, I need to get him out of your hair." He glanced toward Michael and Leah and lowered his voice again. "I can see you have two fine kids. I hope Matt didn't spoil their day."

Doris smiled. "Oh, they're quite durable at that age."

Victor nodded. "Well, good. I guess we'll be off. Good-bye."

"Good-bye."

Victor went around to the other side. Gus got out and opened the door for the ambassador. Moments later the black limo purred off in the direction of the embassy.

Doris turned back to Michael and Leah. Both of them stared at her as if they didn't know what to say. Doris ransacked her mind searching for something to bring this horrible event to a close, something to return things to normal. But it wasn't that easy, she knew. Actions have consequences. Finally she pointed to a bench.

"Let's go sit down."

She sat with the Tokyo Tower at her back, Michael on one side and Leah on the other.

"Why did he do that?" Michael asked finally.

"He's hurting inside," Doris said. She wrapped her arms around both her children and hugged them. "I love both of you. You're very precious to me and your father."

"I love you, Mom," Michael replied.

"Me too, Mom," Leah echoed.

Doris hugged them again. She felt a stinging sensation in her eyes. People walked past, both tourists and Japanese. The sounds of traffic seemed to heighten her feeling of sadness. *Snap out of it,* she thought to herself. *You have your children to look after.*

"I have a suggestion," Doris said finally. "Let's not go to Disneyland today. Let's go tomorrow and spend the whole day. That will give us more time to enjoy it." She glanced at her watch. "It would be around two by the time we got there. What do you say?"

Michael shrugged. "OK." He looked into her face. "But tomorrow we stay the *whole* day, right?"

Doris nodded. "The *whole* day." She turned to Leah. "How 'bout you?"

"Yes, Mom."

Doris hauled a Tokyo tourist book out of her purse. "What about going to the zoo? I don't think it's far." She turned to a dog-eared page. "Yes. Here it is. Ueno Zoo is a few miles north of here. We can take the Hibiya Line right to it."

"Is that the one we came down here on?" Michael asked.

"Yes. The guide says it's a small zoo, but it has two giant pandas from China, along with all the regular critters."

A tentative smile played about Michael's lips. "Critters?"

Doris feigned innocence. "All right—what then?"

"Animals?"

Doris glanced at Leah. "Critters or animals?"

"Animals, Mom."

"Guess I'm outvoted. OK, animals. There's also an excellent restaurant in Ueno Park." She glanced at the guide. "Ueno Seiyoken Grill. Let's see. Oh, look. Their specialties are fried grasshoppers and pickled frog tongues. Doesn't that sound delicious?"

Michael eyed his mother suspiciously. "Is that *really* what it says?" he asked.

Doris struggled to maintain a straight face. "Would your mother kid you?"

He nodded. "Yes."

Doris turned to Leah. "What about you, munchkin?"

"I'm not a munchkin."

"Oh, I don't know about that. You look an awful lot like a munchkin to me. But forget that. Wouldn't you like to eat some pickled frog tongues? Sounds finger-lickin'-good to me."

"It doesn't say that." She hesitated a moment. "Does it?"

Doris pretended to look at the guide book again. She rolled her eyes. "Oh, goodness. My mistake. *Wrong* restaurant. The Ueno Seiyoken Grill serves western food. And I had my mouth *set* for grasshoppers." She hugged them. "What about it? Want to see the pandas?"

"Yeah, Mom," Michael said.

Doris got up. They started walking toward the Hibiya Line subway station. Doris was grateful for the resiliency of young minds. She would do her best to make sure Michael and Leah enjoyed the rest of the day. Later she would go over the incident with Don. Then they would pray.

7

Pikadon~ha

Don yawned as he got out of the cab and paid the driver. He glanced at his watch. In fifteen minutes it would be midnight. He knew he should be thinking about the operation with Okawa, but his mind kept turning back to Matt Porter and what had happened earlier in the day. Don had prayed with his wife about the situation—and about the stakeout with Okawa. Now it was time to leave it with the Lord.

Tokyo nightlife was in full swing as people thronged the brightly lit street under garish neon signs. Don looked around, feeling completely out of place in his ill-fitting worker's twills. That they were new and stiff only added to his discomfort. He had gotten the outfit at Okawa's suggestion, who had assured him that a U.S. Air Force uniform would definitely be out of place.

Don was on time, but where was Okawa? A dilapidated delivery van screeched to a stop at the curb and sat there rumbling. Pungent blue smoke drifted out from underneath. Don peered into the dim interior.

The man behind the wheel, seated on the far side, waved at him. Don hesitated, then stepped closer and stuck his head in the window. It took a moment, but he finally recognized Okawa.

Don's concern about his disguise dissipated when he saw how Okawa was dressed. They were, apparently, going to be workmen that evening. Don couldn't read the sign on the side of the truck but assumed it said something like "Okawa & Sons Plumbing—24 Hour Service." He pulled on the door handle but found it jammed. Don tried again, but still it refused to budge. Finally he yanked with all his strength and heard something inside break. The handle flopped down like something dead. The door sagged as Don pulled it open. He winced at the hideous screech of tortured metal.

Don smiled with the satisfaction that the inanimate object had not won. He slid into the frayed and torn seat and pulled the door shut. It made a clumping noise but refused to latch. Don slammed it, but it only rebounded. He jerked it as hard as he could with no more success.

"Where did you get this piece of junk?" he demanded, looking around at Okawa.

"Why, Major Stewart. An undercover vehicle should look the part, should it not?" He shook his head. "And now you have damaged it. You will have to hold the door while I drive."

Don couldn't help smiling. "OK. Ready when you are—I guess."

Okawa roared off down the narrow street. Don struggled to remain upright as he held on to the sprung door. *We must look like a pair,* he thought as they sped along.

Okawa turned with reckless abandon onto Uchibori-dori, which bordered the Imperial Palace grounds. The wide street curved around to the left. The city lights reflected brightly off the wide moat running parallel to the street. Okawa finally pulled into a large park, found a parking place and stopped.

"This is, as you would say, our stakeout," he announced.

Don grinned in spite of his nervousness. "The air force doesn't do stakeouts."

"I stand corrected, Stewart-san. But since you are temporarily assigned to the police, perhaps I am not too far off."

"I concede your point."

"This is Kita-no-maru Park," Okawa continued. "Nearby is the Modern Art Museum and the Science and Technology Hall. After plotting the other diggings, I decided this park would be a likely target. I have men here and in other sites nearby. Ready for a long night?"

Don felt an icy chill. "As ready as I'll ever be."

He put a hand on the door and pushed. After trying to swing open during the entire trip, it was stuck fast. Okawa walked around to the passenger side and watched. Don shoved and pounded, but it did no good.

"Major, perhaps you had better go out the driver's side," Okawa suggested.

Don frowned. "I'll get it open!" he snapped.

Okawa backed away.

Don lay down on the seat and pulled both feet back as far as he could. Then, with all his strength, he uncoiled, striking the door as hard as he could. It broke free and flew open, the edge whistling through the air. It reached the limit of the hinges and continued on around, slamming against the side of the truck. The top hinge broke with a sharp snap, causing the door to droop at a drunken angle. Don lowered his legs, wincing at the pain in his shins. He smiled as he stepped down, as if he always got out of vehicles that way. He tried to close the door, but the remaining hinge broke. The door clattered to the pavement and wobbled for a moment. Don tried for an apologetic expression but failed. That door, he thought, had got what it deserved.

Okawa peered into the truck through the gaping hole. "Stewart-san. I am afraid I shall have to send this vehicle to the garage. You really must be more careful."

Don wondered if he was serious. Then he saw Okawa's faint smile.

"It's easier to get into now," Don observed.

"Yes, but perhaps there is a problem with safety." Okawa led the American into the park. "I will have to think about it."

Don felt a sense of eager expectation as they walked along. It gradually grew darker as they left the street lights behind. Up ahead they met three men. Each bowed to Okawa and looked at Don with obvious surprise. A heavy plastic ground cloth was spread beside some dense bushes. Don noted the commanding view of the park between the Science and Technology Hall and the moat.

He heard footsteps behind him and turned. A large man approached from the direction of the parking lot. There was nothing soft about this man, Don noted.

"Ah," Okawa said, turning. "Stewart-san. This is my assistant, Michihiko Sawara. Sawara-san, this is Major Don Stewart from the American Embassy."

Sawara bowed slightly. "Major," he said, his English as good as Okawa's, "I am pleased to meet you. You are helping us tonight?"

"That's the idea," Don said. "How much help remains to be seen."

"We will all do our duty," Okawa said.

He and Sawara spoke in rapid Japanese for several minutes. Then Sawara turned and disappeared into the park.

"Sawara-san will be at another location," Okawa explained. "But now, let me see about something to drink."

He said something to one of his men, and a large thermos was brought out along with five cups. The man with the thermos poured the steaming black coffee.

"I am afraid there is no sugar or cream," Okawa said. "All we have is the coffee."

"That's fine with me. I prefer it black anyway."

It was hot and bitter, Don noted. He was sure it would keep them awake.

"Ah, that's good," he said, grateful for the caffeine. The evaluation was more diplomatic than truthful.

Okawa cocked an eyebrow at him as he sipped his coffee in silence.

The initial exhilaration, thinking of what might happen, soon dimmed into boredom. Don and Okawa squatted on the tarpaulin while the three officers fanned out, joining the others waiting in the park. Okawa checked with them periodically on his handheld radio.

The night traffic sounds drifted into the park, muted and strange. The lights from distant streets gradually became hazy as a light fog began to settle, spreading a clammy cloak over everything. Don shivered and gratefully accepted another cup of coffee when Okawa offered, but it was lukewarm now and delivered none of the earlier satisfaction.

Don glanced at Okawa and wondered about the wisdom of his suggestion for increased surveillance. Unpleasant thoughts ran through his mind, propelled by the inactivity. Would the Pikadon-ha return, as he expected, or would they wait? Maybe they had already found what they wanted—whatever *that* was. Perhaps they knew the police were looking for them. Don shook his head. Thoughts like these were not helping any.

Several more radio checks came in with nothing new. Don looked at Okawa each time to gauge his reaction. The policeman seemed calm and unaffected.

Don shifted again, trying to get comfortable but finding it impossible. Okawa's radio crackled and a voice rattled something off. Okawa acknowledged, turned off the radio, and shoved it into a pocket. He pulled out his automatic and picked up a flashlight.

"Time to go," he whispered to Don. "One of my officers spotted some men entering the park. They have a sticklike object with them; he could not see what, but it must be a metal detector. They are headed this way." He grabbed the edge of the tarpaulin. "Help me roll this up."

They hid the cloth under a bush. The policeman pointed toward the moat, and they started walking in that direction, keeping among the shrubs as much as they could. Okawa stopped periodically to listen, but there was nothing to hear except the distant sounds of traffic. The fog grew heavier, making it harder to see.

Don strained his eyes to make out the indistinct bushes and trees, expecting gunfire to explode out of the dripping darkness at any moment. Somehow he couldn't forget the terrorist at the arena, and his .44 Magnum and his obvious willingness to use it. Don felt a chill run down his spine as he realized these people didn't care what they did to those in their way.

Okawa motioned toward a particularly large bush that loomed suddenly out of the mist. Don followed, trying to walk silently over the dew-laden grass. The wet slithering sounds seemed unnaturally loud in his ears. He shivered as chill droplets of water fell onto him from overhanging branches. Okawa blended with the towering bush until Don could barely see him. Don hoped he was equally inconspicuous.

Don tried to forget the chill and wetness as they waited. His heart raced as he imagined the terrorists approaching, expecting dark shapes to come drifting out of the mist at any moment. But the long minutes dragged by without sight or sound, other than the incessant dripping.

He had to force himself to be patient. The others would be coming slowly, he knew. Searching for a metallic object in a fog-shrouded park would take a long time, and they had to avoid detection while they were doing it.

Don flexed his shoulders, trying to ease the tension. But the nagging pain would not go away. He was reaching back to massage an aching muscle when he heard it. The unmistakable sound of a cracking twig came out of the fog. Don turned his head as he tried to isolate where the sound had come from. But it seemed to come from everywhere and nowhere, the tendrils of mist seeming to distort sound as it did the light. Whoever it was had to be close for the sound to be so loud.

Stewart saw the detector first. The saucerlike shape came drifting out of the fog like a miniature spacecraft. Then he saw the pole attached to it and finally the inky blob of the operator. Other shapes materialized, looking like a ghostly convoy working its way through a dark and lonely channel.

Although Don knew he couldn't be seen, he backed farther into the bush. The way the man with the detector was shuffling along, he obviously couldn't see where he was going.

The black shapes crept forward. There were six of them. The man with the detector stopped and swept the instrument in a loose circle. He moved about slowly, describing a large area on the ground. One of the other men stepped up and whispered to the operator. Finally the operator pulled the earphones off and set the detector down.

Don tapped Okawa on the shoulder but was answered by a restraining hand. Four of the men took up shovels and started digging. Two watched from the side as dirt flew out of the hole.

Okawa drew his gun and tapped Don on the arm. He then pulled a slim object from his pocket and held it to his lips. A shrill whistle pierced the silence. Okawa tore out from under the bush and started running toward the terrorists. Caught by surprise, Don had to struggle to catch up.

The group froze for a moment, reminding Don of grave diggers. Then they started to run back the way they came, but their hasty retreat was cut off by more whistles up ahead, and then from the sides. They stopped. One of the terrorists pulled something from his jacket and fell to the ground. Flame spat from the gun. Don heard a thin whine close to his left ear. Okawa hit the ground with a grunt. Don fell down beside him. Okawa fired once, and the man in the grass screamed and tried to stand. He staggered a few steps then fell forward on his face. The others remained where they were.

Again the whistles sounded, but much closer now. The sound of pounding feet came through the darkness. Black shapes materialized out of the mist as the policemen surrounded the diggers. Okawa got up, brushed himself off, and joined his men.

Don rose, not quite as easily as Okawa, and turned to face the direction the terrorists had come from. He felt his spine tingle as he thought he saw movement. He squinted, trying to make out what it was. There seemed to be something near a bush about twenty feet away, a shape slightly darker than its surroundings. But he wasn't sure.

"Major, please come here," Okawa said behind him.

Don glanced at Okawa, then turned back to the bush. The shape was gone now, but he thought he saw a branch moving in the still night air.

Don walked back to where Okawa was. "I think one of the terrorists was hanging back—over there." He pointed. "But he's gone now."

"Quite possible. But I think these will lead us to the others. I want to get them to the station at once so we can begin the interrogation."

Okawa's officers handcuffed the intruders and administered thorough pat-downs. In less than a minute they were walking back toward the Science and Technology Hall.

Don felt his dread ease as the group walked out onto the deserted parking lot behind the building. Then he stopped as he heard the sound of a roaring engine coming from somewhere up ahead. A nondescript van swerved around the corner, tires howling on the wet pavement.

Okawa was quick. If he hadn't been, Don knew they would have died on the spot. Okawa screamed at his men and pointed back toward the interior of the park. He then grabbed Stewart with a grip that felt like a vise and pulled him along. Don stumbled back into the park in confusion. His heart pounded as adrenaline coursed through his veins. Don heard at least two more vehicles follow the first.

A light clicked on near the city entrance to the park, casting a bright glare through the trees and bushes. Seconds later Don heard a loud whoomp. He glanced back, but all he saw was flickering red reflections. Whatever it was, it burned furiously.

"Major, you must run faster," Okawa gasped. "If they catch up with us, we die."

Don heard pounding feet behind them, and knew they were close— very close. A gun roared. Don ducked involuntarily. He saw a muzzle flash off to the side and felt something snatch at his coat.

"Down!" Okawa hissed as he shoved Stewart under a soggy bush. Don wriggled around until he was facing back the way they had come. Okawa trained his gun toward the unseen attackers. Off to the side, Okawa's men hit the ground, trying to force the prisoners down as well. The terrorists bolted for freedom, all but one disappearing into the mist. An officer grabbed the handcuffs of the unlucky one and jerked him to the ground.

Don estimated ten or so men were firing on them but with more show than accuracy. Okawa raised his gun and squeezed off a careful shot. The leading man tumbled forward and lay still. The other gunmen fell to the ground and continued blazing away. Most of the shots were wide, but some were uncomfortably close. Okawa took four more deliberate shots, but the return fire seemed undiminished.

"I am out," Okawa whispered. He pulled out a box of shells and started reloading.

Don heard more men approaching. The gunfire, which had tapered off, returned with an even greater vengeance. Don wanted to merge with the ground as heavy slugs thudded all around him.

Okawa shouted something in Japanese, then turned to Don. "On your feet! Run! It is our only chance!"

Don's heart pounded as he staggered to his feet. He stumbled into the bush behind him and almost fell. He stood there. Any moment he expected to feel a bullet rip through his body, ending it all. Something tugged at his arm. The mad scene swirled around him like a dingy kaleidoscope, everything happening in slow motion.

Three of Okawa's men, the ones in the open with the prisoner, jumped up and started running deeper into the park. The one holding the prisoner took a bullet in the back and fell, dragging the man down with him. The terrorist wrenched the chain out of the dying hand and raced away.

Again Don felt the insistent tug at his arm. He whirled around and started running, almost throwing Okawa off balance. He glanced off an unseen bush but somehow managed to keep from falling as he raced to keep up with Okawa.

A scream of agony sounded somewhere behind them. Don felt a jolt of pure terror as he struggled to hear over his own labored breathing. The sound of pounding feet, faint at first, grew louder. Don could barely see where he was going, but it seemed the pursuers had no such problem. The squelching thudding came ever closer. Don expected shots to ring out at any moment.

Then he heard another sound. It was a police siren, but it was far away. Don's lungs burned as he gasped for air. He silently prayed the police would hurry, but how would they find them in the darkened park?

Misty points of light danced in the distance as he and Okawa neared the far side of the park. Then they disappeared. Don had only a moment to wonder about this before he plowed into a large bush. He rebounded from the clinging thing, spitting out bits of twigs and leaves. He lurched off again, trying to ignore the lancing pain in his side. Up ahead, Okawa was barely in sight.

Don glanced over his shoulder. His heart froze as he saw a half dozen men charging after him, obviously gaining. He forgot his pain as fresh adrenaline coursed through his veins. His feet seemed detached from his mind as he raced ahead without conscious thought.

A moment later a gun roared behind him, and then another. He started weaving but knew this was futile. Sooner or later they would hit him. Don was on the very edge of panic. He glanced around, but Okawa was nowhere in sight. Another shot. This time he heard the whine of the bullet as it whizzed past his right ear.

"God, help me!" Don shouted.

Without warning he found himself in midair wondering where the ground had gone. As his momentum carried him forward he saw reflections off water. A fraction of a second later he hit. He plunged beneath the chilly waters, his body screaming with shock. He lost all orientation tumbling through the murky depths.

Don's lungs burned like they were on fire. He thrashed toward the surface, fighting the urge to breathe. Finally his head pierced the murky -

surface. He drew in a great draft of air, choking as water splashed into his mouth.

A shot rang out above him. Don heard it hit behind him, but it wasn't very close. Two more followed, equally inaccurate. Don saw dim figures standing above him, but for the time being, the towering stone wall hid him in its shadow. Finally he realized he was in one of the moats that surrounded the Imperial Palace grounds.

Don tested with his feet and found that the water was over his head. He knew it was only a matter of time before they spotted him. Either they would use a flashlight, or one of them would finally spot him against the slightly darker background.

Don swam silently to the wall, keeping his eyes on the terrorists above him. He felt with his feet. Finding a rough crevice, he steadied himself and tried to catch his breath. One of the men shouted and pointed. Another terrorist raised a hand to shield his eyes from the street lights across the moat.

Guns roared overhead, the muzzle flashes lighting up the immediate area. Deadly splashes appeared all around Don. He ducked below the surface and pushed off from the moat wall with all his might. He felt the black water rushing past him, but he couldn't see a thing. He swam in what he hoped was the general direction of the street on the far side of the moat. Occasionally he heard the muted plop of a bullet, but nothing close.

His starving lungs burned. He felt ahead as he swam, hoping to feel the stone wall of the far side, but there was nothing but water. He longed to swim to the surface but knew he was a dead man if he did. He continued on. Finally he knew if he stayed under a moment longer, he would breathe water.

Don thrust upwards, piercing the surface as quietly as he could. He sucked air into his tortured lungs in great whooping gasps, the rank air smelling pure and sweet. He whipped his head around, trying to take in the whole scene in an instant. He found he was near the center of the moat, swimming parallel to it. He trod water and scanned the bank. A shout went up. A muzzle flashed, then another. Soon they were all firing. Water geysered all around him. Then Don heard a siren, but it seemed far away. What he needed was help *now.*

He dove again and swam for the street side of the moat. An icy chill ran down his spine as he realized he was trapped like a fish in a barrel. Even if he made the far side, there was the slimy moat wall to climb. And even if he could climb it, he knew the terrorists would nail him before he got halfway up. But he couldn't think of any alternative.

Don breached the surface again, next to the moat wall. He turned toward the park and waited in agony for the expected bullets to slam into his exposed body. But it didn't happen. The terrorists were still there, but they were firing wildly toward the street at something Don couldn't see. He knew it had to be the police, but the terrorists kept blazing away as if they didn't care. He decided they were either very sure of themselves, or they didn't care. But one thing was obvious: the gunfire from the park was much heavier than what came from the street.

Gunfire erupted from the park, farther down the moat. Muzzle flashes lit up the darkness as the terrorists found themselves in a lethal crossfire. Instead of running, the terrorists turned and faced both threats, blazing away with increased determination. Don marveled at their guts but wondered at their wisdom. Finally they saw it was hopeless. A crisp command rang out, and the black shapes vanished back into the park. Soon all Don could hear was the sound of running feet.

Don turned around and looked up at the top of the moat. He hesitated to shout for help. He knew it had to be the police above him, but who would they take him for?

"Help!" he finally shouted.

He heard the crunch of boots on pavement. A black shape loomed high overhead. A brilliant white beam lanced out, bathing Don in a pool of light. He raised his arm to shield his eyes. Then a disturbing thought came to mind—what if the man didn't speak English?

The man said something in Japanese.

Great, Don thought. "I'm with Toshiro Okawa!" he shouted. "Help me out of here!"

The man with the light turned and spoke to someone Don couldn't see. A few moments later another man appeared with a coil of rope over his shoulder. The man with the light moved his right hand into the beam, revealing a gun. The meaning of the loud click was only too evident. The other man threw the end of the rope down into the water. Don took it and started scrambling up the slick stones, slipping once and cracking his left knee painfully.

Finally he reached the top. He stood dripping as the night chill drove deep into his bones. He swayed with fatigue. The nearest policeman wasted no time in patting him down for weapons.

Don felt a deeper chill unrelated to his soaking. Why hadn't the Pikadon-ha run when the police arrived? Did they really think they could win, or were they fearless? Either possibility was scary.

Don looked at the traffic on Uchibori-dori. The garish artificiality of the mercury vapor lights together with the ignorant bliss of the drivers underscored Don's increasing uneasiness. The contrast with his recent brush with almost certain death made him stop and think. *What have I gotten myself into?* he wondered.

A message came over the police truck radio. One of the officers hurried over and answered it. A few moments later he motioned for Don to join him, pointing to the passenger side door. Don and the policeman climbed in, and they roared off toward the park entrance.

As they approached the turn, Don saw another truck coming from the opposite direction, weaving in and out of the traffic. It beat the police van to the entrance and made a skidding turn up ahead.

The police driver flipped on the siren and jammed the accelerator to the floor. Slowing at the last second, he swerved into the park in hot pursuit. Don watched the red taillights up ahead wink out as the other vehicle made a turn, deep inside the park.

The police van roared over the narrow road. The driver handled it with precision, his eyes never leaving the road. The headlights danced over the roadway as if creating it as they went. Don saw a black shape approaching. He spun his head around as they roared past and got a quick look. It was the blackened remains of a police van, still smoldering. The sight of the charred bodies inside lodged in Don's mind like a spike. He fought his rising nausea as he smelled the pungent stench of burning rubber, overlaid by the sickly sweet scent of burned flesh.

The police van careened into the park entrance. The driver slammed on the brakes as the headlights revealed the other truck parked facing them, its lights off. The police van fishtailed to a stop, less than fifty feet from the other truck.

Don could see the other driver hunched over the wheel, his head turned away from the approaching glare. Dim shapes flitted out of the dark shadows. Suddenly, a man ran out into the police van's headlights. He held a hand in front of his eyes to ward off the glare as he tugged at something in the satchel he was holding. Then he hurled the bag. The satchel arced through the air, hit the pavement and slid underneath the truck.

"Get out!" Don shouted, as he threw open the door.

He and the policeman jumped out at the same time.

Don pointed back the way they had come. "That way! Hurry!"

The two men pounded down the narrow road. Don half-expected a hail of bullets to mow them down at any moment. But then he realized the terrorists would be running away from the bomb also.

The explosion's shock wave threw them to the ground. Don wheezed as the air pounded out of his lungs. His chin hit the rough asphalt, and his mouth snapped shut, catching the tip of his tongue in his teeth. The night erupted in blood-red flames.

Don rolled onto his side. All the sounds seemed hollow and distant, with a ringing noise overlaying everything. He shook his head, but the ringing continued. He turned to the policeman at his side. Don shouted, but he could barely hear himself. The man appeared dazed. Don staggered to his feet, knowing they had to run if they wanted to live. He grabbed the man's arm and pointed.

Don cocked his head to one side as he ran. A disagreeable whining noise insinuated itself through the ringing in his ears. It seemed urgent, somehow, but he couldn't place what it was.

The policeman staggered and fell. Don returned and hauled him to his feet. Don pointed toward the park exit, and the man seemed to understand. The path grew dark as they put distance between themselves and the burning truck.

The policeman stopped and turned back. Don pulled up as well. He looked back and saw the flickering glow through the trees and bushes. The night erupted once more in a brilliant orange flash. The shock wave hit a moment later. The truck's gas tank had finally exploded.

Again Don heard the whining sound. It was louder now, and something seemed to be happening off to the side. He turned. Flashing blue lights. He shook his head, but the grogginess would not go away. Don frowned. What did it all mean? The whining grew louder. Finally he realized it was sirens. The police were close. He saw the kaleidoscope of lights approaching, but they seemed very far away. Would the police cars ever get here? He wondered.

Then they all seemed to arrive at once. Don staggered out of the way, dragging the dazed policeman with him. Three squad cars roared past and squalled to a stop halfway to the burning truck, apparently not wanting to perish the same way. Muzzle flashes erupted again from inside the park. Dark shapes milled around the terrorists' truck as the men clambered inside. The engine roared to life. The truck lurched forward, engine screaming. It sideswiped one of the police cars on the way out.

Don fell to the ground, and the policeman joined him. They watched as the truck roared past and out of the park. The sound gradually grew faint and then disappeared.

Don and the policeman started for the parking lot as others came drifting out of the park. Some gathered around the squad cars while others watched the still-burning van.

A familiar shape came out of the dark and approached the truck. The policeman at his side pointed and said something Don couldn't hear. But the meaning was clear enough.

Don started toward the truck, but his legs were so shaky he didn't know if he could make it. As he approached, he saw the man was Okawa, as he suspected. The men around the officer parted reluctantly to allow Don to pass. Okawa looked at him in obvious surprise. The policeman smiled in obvious relief, but then a look of sadness came over him. He turned back to the man he was talking to. A few moments later they both bowed, and the man hurried away. Okawa led Don away.

"Stewart-san," Okawa began. "I . . . I did not know if I would see you again."

Don shuddered and cleared his throat. "I'm surprised myself. I didn't think I'd make it."

"I must get you back to your hotel."

"What about all this?" Don pointed to the organized confusion all around them.

"Sawara-san can handle it now," he said as he escorted Don to the parking lot.

"How bad was it?"

"I am not sure, but we have lost three men that I know of, and five more wounded." Okawa paused. "We picked up four terrorists—so far—but we will not get much that's useful. Only the leaders know the plans."

They walked on in silence. Okawa picked one of the squad cars and motioned to Don. "Get in."

Okawa helped him into the car and stood there a moment, looking at him. He frowned, walked around to the driver's side, and got in. Okawa started the car and drove out of the park.

Don slumped back against the seat. He was bone tired. But more than that, he was scared. Now that the emergency was over, he began to realize how close it had been. He started shaking and couldn't stop.

"I cannot tell you, Stewart-san, how relieved I was to see you," Okawa said finally. "I feared the worst when we became separated. Had I known this would happen . . ."

Don heard the emotion in the policeman's voice, and it surprised him. He tried to formulate a reply, but he couldn't make his brain work. Despite the car's motion, he felt himself drifting into a sleep of sheer exhaustion. He tried to stay awake but couldn't.

* * *

Don awoke with a start. For a few moments he couldn't place where he was. He only knew he was tired, and he hurt all over.

"Stewart-san," a familiar voice said.

He turned to see the policeman standing by the door. Everything came back in a rush. Don shuddered. They were parked outside the Imperial Hotel. The doorman hung back, looking like he wanted to intervene but not knowing if he should. Okawa helped Don out and inside.

The lobby was deserted. The desk personnel stared in shock at these obvious derelicts trudging in off the street. The doorman finally rushed inside and intercepted them. Okawa flashed his badge, and the man backed off. Don looked down at the muddy water dripping off him onto the carpet as they waited for an elevator.

Arriving at Stewart's floor, Okawa helped him to the door. Don watched the odd play of emotions on the man's face.

"Major Stewart. This is difficult—I want you to know I had no idea this would happen. If I had, I would never have asked for your help."

"I know," Don said. But he was so weary, he said it mainly to be agreeable.

"Please let me finish," Okawa continued, obviously very distraught. "What happened tonight is unprecedented. Terrorists groups are nothing new, and sometimes they do horrible things. But I have *never* seen anything like what happened tonight. The Pikadon-ha are better prepared and more ruthless than I expected. Please forgive me."

Don looked at the policeman in surprise. "There is nothing to forgive." He paused as anger sprang up inside him. "But the Pikadon-ha are another matter! You need to nail those guys, and if it were me, I wouldn't be too particular about bringing 'em in alive!"

Okawa nodded. "I understand how you feel, Stewart-san. But we have established procedures for these things."

Don felt an inner urging. "Sorry—you're right," he admitted. "A Christian isn't supposed to think that way. Please forgive me."

"Of course."

"But, what are you going to do about this?"

Okawa sagged visibly. "The report will go up to police headquarters. From there it will be summarized for the prime minister. Obviously there are many political ramifications, and that greatly complicates things."

"I understand that," Don said. "One other thing . . ."

"What is that?"

"I'm on your side. What happened tonight scared the daylights out of me, but it needed to be done. I respect what you're trying to do."

This obviously touched the policeman. "You are most kind, Stewart-san." He looked right into Don's eyes. "I am in your obligation." He paused as if unsure how to continue. "I have a confession to make. I judged you unfairly when we first met, for which I am truly sorry. You are a man of integrity and courage. I am honored to know you."

"Just doing my job," Don said.

He shivered as he thought that over. The way things had worked out, it really *was* his job. However, he doubted if the ambassador and Colonel Dill would have approved the project if they had known this would happen. But what now? He knew it was far from over.

"A little more than that, perhaps," Okawa said.

"I'll call you in the morning," Don said, knowing this was his assignment until he was relieved. "Do you want to continue looking into the Owens connection?"

Okawa's eyes grew very round. "Surely you do not intend to continue. Colonel Dill will not allow it."

Don shook his head. "I don't know what my boss will do. But until I hear otherwise, I assume I'm still on the job."

"I hope that is the case, Stewart-san. I have come to value your help—

very much. Until tomorrow, then. Good night." He bowed, and it seemed to Don that it was the deeper bow of respect.

"Good night," Don repeated.

Okawa turned and left.

Don fished around in his pocket, wondering if the hotel card key had survived the evening's events. It had. Now, would it work? He inserted it, and the green light came on. *Will wonders never cease,* he thought as he opened the door.

He hoped that Doris would be asleep and he could shower and sneak into bed without waking her. But the bedside light was on. She looked around and dropped her book. From her worried expression, he knew she had not really been reading. She jumped out of bed and ran toward him.

He held out his arms, conscious of how smelly and wet he was. But suddenly that didn't matter. He took her in his arms and pulled her close. He kissed her and felt his fatigue drop back a notch.

"What happened, dear?" she demanded, as she leaned back and started taking inventory. "You're wet. And that smell!"

"It's a long story," he said with a sigh. "Basically, we found out the Pikadon-ha are much more determined and violent than Mr. Okawa expected. We came on a group of them tonight, and they overran the police. It wasn't until reinforcements were called in that we could drive them away."

She looked shocked. "You keep saying 'we.' I don't like this Don. Surely Colonel Dill will pull you off this project when he hears."

Don wasn't sure how he felt about that. He certainly didn't want a repeat of *this* particular disaster. But on the other hand, *someone* had to do something about these people. Terrorists *had* to be dealt with. If he could help, shouldn't he?

"I don't know what Allen will do." He glanced at his watch and was a little surprised it was still working. It was almost four. "I'll find out when I call. But don't get your hopes up. Unfortunately, the late Mr. Owens brings the United States into this."

"But . . ."

"Please, I have to call in."

Don punched in the number for the embassy switchboard and waited. On the third ring the line clicked.

"United States Embassy," the operator said.

"This is Major Don Stewart. I need to speak to Colonel Allen Dill."

"Sir, the embassy is closed, and I can't give out home numbers."

Don struggled to maintain his composure. "Ma'am, I'm the assistant air attaché, and I'm well aware the embassy isn't open at four in the morning. Now patch me through to Colonel Dill's residence—pronto!"

"Sir, I can't do that without authorization."

"Listen carefully! This is official embassy business! If you *don't* patch me through, you'll find yourself on the ambassador's carpet in the morning! Do I make myself clear?"

The line was silent for a few heartbeats. "Yes, sir. One moment please."

The line clicked. Don waited impatiently as the seconds ticked away. The line clicked again.

"This is Colonel Dill."

Don could hear his apprehension. "Colonel, this is Major Stewart. Sorry to call you at this hour, but I have bad news. Okawa's men found a group of the terrorists, and they almost overpowered us."

"What do you mean?"

"I mean that the Pikadon-ha are better prepared than we thought, and they're armed to the teeth." He paused. "Colonel, Okawa and I almost bought it. He lost three men—maybe more."

"This is bad—very bad. I had no idea."

"I know, sir. It surprised Okawa also. They arrested four terrorists, but Okawa doesn't think he got any leaders."

"Are you all right?"

Don sighed. "I'm sore all over but other than that, OK. I'll make a full report in the morning."

"Yes. I hate to ask it, but can you make it in by—say, oh, 0730? The ambassador will want a brief on this ASAP."

"I'll be there, sir. Good night."

"Good night."

The line clicked dead.

"What did he say?" Doris asked. "Are you still on the operation?"

"Please, let's talk about it tomorrow. Right now, all I want to do is take a shower and go to bed."

"OK," she said quietly.

He saw the concern in her eyes but right now couldn't do anything about it. He retreated into the bathroom. He stripped quickly and stepped into the shower, turning the spray on as hard as it would go. He sighed in relief as he felt his sore muscles relax. All he could think about was the cool crisp sheets.

* * *

Takafumi Hasagawa clicked off the recorder. Akira Moriya mulled over what he had heard. He felt his rage building, and was tempted to lash out at Hasagawa. But what he really wanted was to get his hands around the throat of this arrogant American—this meddling *gaijin*. He smiled as he thought about how much he would enjoy that.

"So," Moriya said. "We have his name—Major Don Stewart, a military attaché with the American embassy, working for a Colonel Dill."

Hasagawa nodded cautiously. "Yes, and it seems they know a lot about us."

Moriya glared at him. "They do not know what we are looking for! Or what we will do once we find it!" He paused. "However, we must stop this interference."

"How?"

"I will think about it. There must be a way."

8

Encounter at Disneyland

Don swam toward consciousness from a drugged sleep. He felt something nudging him and wished it would go away, but it didn't. Instead he heard a voice, indistinct and far away. Then he was awake, and the horror of the previous night came flooding back. He shivered.

"Darling, it's time to get up," Doris said.

Don turned over. Doris was standing by the bed, fully dressed. "I wish I could let you sleep, but you told me you had to get up." She reached down and pushed an unruly tuft of hair out of his face. He saw the tension behind her smile.

Don massaged his face. "That's OK. I've got to be at the embassy by 0730."

He groaned as he got up, feeling the muscles that had stiffened during his brief sleep. He noted her look of concern. "Boy, am I sore," he continued, trying to lead away from the subject of the argument they had had only a few hours earlier.

She was silent, in the way he hated. He hobbled into the bathroom and turned on the water. He shaved and dressed quickly.

"Join me for breakfast?" he asked as he finished.

"Mm," she answered, casting her eyes downward.

He forced a smile. "OK, we better go down now."

"Yes, dear. I'll look in on the kids and be right with you."

The dining room was bright and cheerful, but it did nothing to diminish Don's depression. The waiter seated them and stood by for their order. Don gave up on his earlier resolution and ordered an American-style breakfast. Doris ordered the same without looking at the menu.

"I want to talk about this," she said quietly, in that voice that Don had never been able to ignore.

He frowned. "I figured as much." He knew from experience that Doris could be persistent when she felt strongly about something. She understood military duty, and that being an air force pilot wasn't the safest of professions. But he certainly hadn't been flying an airplane last night. He knew she was close to tears.

She leaned forward. "I'm worried, Don. This thing is dangerous. I know the ambassador doesn't want you involved in—in what happened last night."

"No, I suppose he doesn't. But we had no idea anything like this would happen. Listen, I'm not going to get involved in any more police operations. But, there's still the problem of Owens's involvement with the Pikadon-ha."

"Don, it's too dangerous! Tell them you won't do it!"

"Hon, I can't do that. I have my orders."

"But . . ."

"The diplomatic situation with Japan is sensitive, especially with the

Tennessee's visit. Look, I promise I'll be careful. Okawa's concerned about this too. He won't underestimate the terrorists again. OK?"

She nodded. Don suspected this was only a temporary cease-fire, but he was willing to take what he could get.

The waiter brought their breakfast out, set the tray down, and served them. Don tried a piece of buttered toast, but it seemed dry and tasteless. His stomach churned and started making noise. He clamped down with his arm, but it did no good. He looked over at Doris. She was picking at her food. Don forced himself to eat, knowing he needed the energy. He finally called it quits after finishing his eggs and bacon.

"I have to go, dear," he said. "Say hi to the kids."

"I will," she said. She leaned forward and kissed him.

Don got up. Their eyes locked for a moment, and he felt his heart going out to her. Then he turned and walked out.

* * *

Don read over his report, still warm from the laser printer. It was rough but complete, he decided. A knock sounded on his door. It opened, revealing his boss. Don got up.

"Good morning, Allen. I was about to come down to your office with my report." He held up the sheets of paper. "It's not pretty, but it covers the facts."

Allen took the pages and sat down. "Good." His serious expression became more strained as he scanned the report. "I called the ambassador at his residence and gave him a heads-up." He glanced at his watch. "He should be in his office any time now. This will help me with my briefing." He got up, shaking his head. "This is incredible." He looked up at Don. "Nice job. I'll be in my office. I want to read this over again before my meeting."

"Allen?" Don asked.

"Yes?"

"Do you think the ambassador will want me to keep working with Mr. Okawa—after what's happened?"

"I don't know. But considering the political situation, I think it's likely." He paused. "But I can tell you one thing." He flicked the pages with his hand. "*This* isn't going to happen again. Their internal security people know how to deal with terrorists. And I'm sure Ambassador Dewey will make our concerns known to Mr. Okawa. I'll let you know what he says. Now, if you will excuse me." He rushed out.

Don sat back down. Despite the reassurance, he had a bad feeling about the whole situation.

* * *

Doris walked across the broad plaza before the Disneyland entrance and selected a line for one of the ticket booths. It was a perfect day. A light breeze swept the blue skies, moving white clouds along like stately ships. There was still no sign of the typhoon that was wandering around in the Pacific, although the morning newscast said it was expected to turn toward Honshu.

The grounds outside the park were immaculate, and the cheery entrance seemed to beckon. Michael and Leah looked around, obviously excited, as the line inched forward. Doris tried to push her concern for Don to the side, at least for today.

Upon reaching the attendant, Doris stared at the multilingual sign with a combination of sticker shock and information overload. The Tokyo version of the Magic Kingdom offered Disneyland one-day passports; two-, three-, and four-day passports; senior passports; starlight passports; after-six passports; and annual passports.

Doris selected one-day passports, good for general admissions and all attractions, except the Westernland Shootin' Gallery. She gulped as she did a mental conversion from yen into U.S. dollars and forked over her MasterCard. The attendant smiled, punched her magic buttons, and pushed the passports through the ticket slot.

"Thank you," she said. "Enjoy your stay in the Magic Kingdom."

Doris tried to smile, but she couldn't dismiss what this was costing. "We'll try. Thank you."

She led her kids toward the entrance. "Don't lose this," she said as she handed Michael his ticket.

"I won't," he said. He gripped it with determination.

Doris looked at Leah. "Do you want me to hold yours?"

Leah glanced at Michael then stuck out her hand. "No, Mom. I want mine too."

"OK, but be careful. It's very expensive."

"I will." Leah beamed as she took her ticket.

They passed through the main entrance and entered the World Bazaar. Doris was glad she had taken the time to study the Disneyland brochure that morning, as she looked around at the 1900s shops and attractions sheltered under the overhead glass canopy. Although much was different, there were a lot of similarities with Main Street at the original Disneyland in Anaheim. The Tokyo version had a Main Street Cinema, a penny arcade, and even an omnibus ride at the far end of the street at the Plaza. But the World Bazaar had more shops, selling everything from Disney memorabilia to wonderful things to eat.

"Look at all these shops," Doris said, a twinkle coming to her eyes. "I bet we could spend the whole day in here and not see it all."

"No, Mom!" Leah said in shock. "I want to go on the Peter Pan ride."

"Peter Pan?" Michael said with disgust. "That's kid stuff. I wanna go to Space Mountain."

Leah faced her brother, put her hands on her hips and pouted. "Mom! That's not fair! Michael *always* gets to do what *he* wants!"

"Stop it, both of you," Doris said. "We're here to enjoy Disneyland as a family. That means we take turns doing what *each* of you wants."

"Fine," Michael said. "Let's go to Space Mountain."

"Hold on," Doris said. "Don't you think it would be nice if you let your sister go first?" She saw from his eyes that he was not of that opinion. Then something changed and she saw a softening.

"I guess so," he said finally. But he looked like terminal boredom was about to get him.

"That's very kind," Doris said. "We'll do the Peter Pan ride, then we'll go to Space Mountain. OK?"

She heard the echoing OKs, noting that one was more enthusiastic than the other. *I'll take what I can get,* Doris thought to herself. She led the way down Main Street toward the plaza at the far end. A man playing a bicycle piano nodded as he pedaled past going in the opposite direction. The strains of a Scott Joplin rag competed briefly with the surrounding sounds, then lost the battle.

Doris waited for the omnibus to chuff past, then crossed the plaza and walked over the drawbridge and through the portal under Cinderella's Castle. They got in line for Peter Pan's Flight as it snaked toward the entrance. Leah moved forward with every opportunity, barely containing her excitement. Michael looked completely bored, but Doris could tell this wasn't entirely true.

Finally they were inside. Several attendants managed the two-person galleons. One let off those finishing their ride while the other helped those waiting to climb aboard.

Doris tapped Michael on the shoulder. "You and Leah take the first one. I'll be in the one right behind."

"OK, Mom."

The Japanese attendant helped the kids into the galleon and closed the door. He pulled a lever and the ride lurched forward. Doris got in the next boat. Soon she was following her children into the pitch-black night sky of Peter Pan's London. The bright lights of Big Ben and the Tower Bridge loomed ahead. Doris had to admit it was an excellent attraction. She knew Leah was enjoying it, and suspected Michael was, too, although he probably wouldn't admit it.

Soon the ride was over. Doris followed her children back out into the bright sunlight.

"How was it?" she asked.

"Cool, Mom!" Leah said, jumping up and down.

"It was OK, I guess," Michael said. Then he brightened up, "Now, let's go to Space Mountain!"

The line for this ride was longer Doris found as they arrived in Tomorrowland. Michael looked eagerly toward the entrance as if this would speed their progress. After a long wait, they made it.

"All right!" Michael whooped when he saw that he and Leah would have the first seats in the car. Doris got into the seat behind. The attendants locked the bars down and released the car. It rolled forward into Space Mountain and up a steep incline. A loud clicking sound marked their progress toward the top. The car reached it and started down. They roared down a steep hill and screeched around a tight turn. Doris held on to the bar as the car slammed from side to side. She wondered if she would end up bruised.

Finally the ride ended. The car clattered around the final curve and swept back into the open. They were back at the entrance. Doris followed her children out through the exit. Over to the right was the entrance to the Grand Circuit Raceway.

"Mom!" Michael shouted. "Can we go on that!" He looked back, his face a mask of eager yearning.

"What did we decide?" Doris said. She suspected he had not forgotten and that she was seeing convenient amnesia.

"We share," he said. He brightened suddenly. "But Leah got to go first!"

"It's Leah's turn now, then you go again. It'll come out even." Doris turned to her daughter. "What do you want to do now?"

"The Roger Rabbit ride!"

"Oh, gag me!" Michael grumbled.

"You don't have to go on it," Doris said.

"But I won't have anything to do."

Doris struggled to maintain her composure. "Your choice. Now listen to me—both of you. We're here to have fun. We're going to be here all day, so there's plenty of time to do everything. Now, I want this bickering to stop right now, or we'll be doing what *I* want to do."

"What's that?" Michael asked suspiciously.

Doris thought a moment. "Let's see, I think there were several clothing stores on Main Street." She saw he was not convinced.

"I don't think so," he said finally. "You like doing the same stuff we do."

Doris smiled and poked him in the ribs. "You're on to me."

He giggled and jumped away.

"But I *am* serious about sharing. Now come on." She oriented herself. "Toontown is that way." She loved the joy she saw in Leah's eyes.

* * *

The tally was exactly even when lunchtime arrived. Since the kids got to pick the rides, Doris decided it was only fair that she choose where to eat. That, she found, was not easy since the park had no shortage of restaurants. Finally she settled on the Sweetheart Café in the corner of the World Bazaar. This pleased Leah, but Doris could tell the name didn't set well with her son. However, he kept his opinion to himself.

A young woman escorted them to a small table outside, beside the colorful colonnade. They took their seats and looked at the menus.

"Oh, boy!" Michael said. "Pizza!"

"What do you want?" Doris asked Leah.

"Pizza!"

Doris ordered for the kids and selected the ravioli dish for herself. Michael and Leah talked about their favorite rides and what they wanted to do after lunch. Doris looked around, thinking about the strange contrasts all around her. Here they were, on the north end of Tokyo Bay, in a clone of a theme park invented by Walt Disney. The attractions were a combination of familiar Americana spiced with a Far Eastern accent. The faux 1900s café they were in specialized in Italian dishes, but their host was the Meiji Milk Products Company. *Weird,* Doris thought to herself. *But wonderful.*

* * *

There he is, Takafumi Hasagawa thought. The overweight kid matched the pictures exactly. *And there is the embassy driver. Perfect. All I have to do is act quickly.* He knew something could go wrong; there was always that possibility. But he counted on the element of surprise. He shrugged. If that failed, he would use brute force. That was dangerous, but he felt confident he and his partner could handle it. Hasagawa looked down at his "borrowed" Disneyland uniform and decided he was ready. He waited until the kid reached the exit to the ride, then approached the waiting driver.

"Are you Kinji Gusawa?" Hasagawa asked, bowing respectfully. He saw the quick look of apprehension in the man's eyes.

"Yes," Gus replied cautiously.

"Please forgive me. I am Hiroshi Asakura with the Disneyland park police." He flashed a badge, then stuffed the wallet back in his pocket, hoping the driver would not ask for a photo ID. He had one, but the photo didn't match. "I am afraid I have very bad news," Hasagawa hurried on. "The embassy phoned the park a few minutes ago, asking that we locate you." He looked at Matt for the first time and switched to English. "Matt, I'm afraid your grandfather has suffered a massive heart attack."

"What?" the boy stammered.

"Are you sure?" Gus asked.

"The ambassador's secretary was most explicit."

"What hospital!" Gus demanded.

"The U.S. Naval Hospital at Yokosuka."

Gus turned to Matt. "I will take you there at once!"

"Please," Hasagawa interrupted. "The navy has dispatched a helicopter to pick up both of you. It will be arriving at our heliport at any moment. Follow me."

* * *

Michael stood outside the Grand Circuit Raceway entrance as he waited impatiently for Doris and Leah to return. He looked toward the Space Mountain ride and thought he saw Matt. But the boy was far away, and Michael couldn't be sure. A Japanese man approached. Michael guessed it was Gus, but the man had his back to him. Another man walked up. Then he lost sight of them as a large group of teenagers walked past.

* * *

Hasagawa swept his arm toward the Visionarium show and waited. He was prepared to grab the kid if the driver balked, but he hoped it wouldn't come to that. He knew that would be very risky.

"Come," Gus said to Matt. "We must go with him."

Gus started toward the walkway between the show and the Micro Adventure attraction. Their guide led the way about a step ahead. The man watched for the narrow side path and gauged his timing.

"This way," he said, pointing to the narrow alcove with the door that said "Employees Only" in Japanese and English. "I have to check in with our Security Center."

Gus hesitated only a moment, then turned to follow their guide. Hasagawa unhooked the chain barring the path to park guests and dropped it on the concrete walk. In moments they were in a narrow space between two buildings, shielded from the noisy crowd behind them. Hasagawa continued on to the heavy metal door which was slightly ajar. A red light winked on the keypad mounted on the wall.

Gus stopped. "Where are you taking us?" he asked.

"As I said, I have to call our Security Center."

"Where is your radio?"

"I left it at Security. Now, please. I have to phone for a shuttle to take you to the heliport."

Hasagawa started moving slowly to get behind them.

Gus turned to Matt. "Come with me."

The imposter pulled a gun out of his pocket. "Go through the door," he ordered.

"What is the meaning of this?" Gus demanded.

"Do as I say or I will kill you both," the man hissed in Japanese.

He motioned with the gun. For long seconds he wasn't sure what would happen. Finally Gus turned toward the door and ushered Matt before him. Hasagawa followed them in and closed the door.

It was a storage room. Steel shelves lined the walls, loaded with cardboard boxes and cleaning supplies. Several large wheeled trash containers stood in a corner. A man in his underwear sat beside them, his back against the wall. Itcho Unten, wearing a park maintenance uniform, stood over him holding a gun.

"Why are you doing this?" Gus asked.

Hasagawa ignored him. "Tie this one up also," he ordered his accomplice.

Unten stuffed his gun in a pocket, then turned Gus around. Pulling a nylon tie strip out of his pocket, he pulled Gus's hands behind his back and cinched the thin strap tight about his wrists.

Matt started to cry in a long, drawn-out whimper.

"Stop that!" Hasagawa ordered.

Matt hiccuped and wiped his eyes with the back of his hand.

"What about the boy?" Unten asked after he forced Gus to sit down beside the park employee.

"Tie him up and stuff this in his mouth." He held out a cleaning rag. "Make sure he cannot spit it out."

Hasagawa pulled one of the wheeled trash containers away from the wall and opened the hinged plastic lid. He grabbed several bails of cleaning rags and threw them into the bottom.

"Hurry!"

"He will not open his mouth."

Hasagawa grabbed a handful of Matt's hair and pulled. "Open!" he growled in English.

Matt did so, blinking back tears. Soon he was gagged and had a nylon loop tied tight about his wrists. Unten lifted him into the container and closed the lid.

Hasagawa went to the door, opened it, and looked out. "Go," he said.

Unten pushed the trash container through the door.

Hasagawa closed the door and walked back to Gus. He saw the mixture of fear and hate in the driver's eyes, but that didn't matter. The terrorist pulled a silencer out of his pocket and screwed it onto the barrel of his automatic. When he was done, he took deliberate aim and pulled the trigger. The report was barely audible. The park employee fell forward, blood quickly spreading over his white undershirt.

Hasagawa stood before Gus as he calmly unscrewed the silencer. He put it in one pocket and the automatic in the other. Then he looked Gus in the eye. "We mean business, Mr. Gusawa. If you call the police, we will kill the boy. Tell the ambassador we will contact him."

With that he pulled out a knife, unfolded a long blade, and cut the strap tying Gus's hands.

* * *

"Mom," Michael said as Doris and Leah walked up. "I think I saw Matt just now."

"Are you sure?" Doris asked.

"Not really. He was far away—whoever it was—and then I lost sight of him."

Doris shrugged. "Well, I guess it could have been him. It's no secret he wanted to come here, but I'm a little surprised the ambassador let him, after what he pulled yesterday." She paused. "If it *was* Matt."

9

At the Tearoom

Takafumi Hasagawa fought his way through the heavy Tokyo traffic. Up ahead he could see the Tokyo Tower. *Grabbing the kid should please Moriya,* he thought. The Pikadon-ha's leader sometimes did things Hasagawa didn't understand, but he knew Moriya was right about this. The Americans were a real threat to their plans, plans they had perfected through the years. Finally they stood on the threshold of success. The final victory would probably require sacrifice, but Hasagawa knew it was worth it.

He took the exit ramp from the crowded expressway and made his way along the gridlocked surface streets. Finally he pulled into the drive leading up to the tower. He drove around to the loading dock and breathed a sigh of relief. There was the van.

He got out and helped Unten push the trash container up the ramp and into the building. They made their way to the elevator lobby where the attendant commandeered one of the cars for them, ordering the tourists to wait.

Hasagawa took over the trash container while Unten returned to his van. The doors closed. The elevator whined to life lifting him high above the city. The harbor came into view. Hasagawa's eyes drifted over to the hated black shape docked at the wharf. He was glad they were doing something about that. The elevator stopped at the main observatory's lower level, and the doors opened.

Hasagawa took the freight elevator to the upper level and pushed the container over to the construction wall that announced the coming tearoom. He punched in the code on the keypad. The electronic bolt snapped open with a heavy thump. Hasagawa pushed open the construction door and went inside. After securing the bolt, he pushed the container through a door into a back room. He closed the door and bowed. Akira Moriya was waiting for him.

"Did you get him?" he asked.

"Yes. Everything went well."

He threw open the container's lid, and Moriya peered inside. Matt blinked in the bright work lights and squirmed around. Hasagawa kicked the side of the container. "Stop that!" he said in English.

"You released the driver?" Moriya asked.

"Yes. He should be back at the embassy by now."

"Do you think he will call the police?"

Hasagawa shook his head. "No."

"Good." Moriya looked down at Matt. "I believe it is time for me to pay my respects to Ambassador Victor Dewey." He nodded toward the trash container. "Get him out of there and watch him!"

* * *

Moriya took Hasagawa's car and drove north toward the district near the Imperial Palace where most foreign embassies were. He waited until he was near the U.S. Embassy then punched in the main switchboard number on his mobile phone.

"United States Embassy," the operator said.

"Ambassador Dewey, please," Moriya said.

"I'm sorry sir, the ambassador is unavailable. Could someone else help you."

"Tell the ambassador I am calling about his grandson, Matt. I am sure he will talk to me."

"One moment, sir." The line clicked.

A few moments later a man's voice came on the line. "Who is this?"

"Ah, Ambassador Dewey. You *are* available after all. I trust Mr. Kinji Gusawa arrived at the embassy safely?"

"Yes! Now, what have you done with Matt?"

Moriya turned right. "I hope you are not trying to trace this call. If anything happens to me—well, I am afraid you will never see Matt again."

"I'm not."

"Good." Moriya suspected the ambassador was lying but knew they wouldn't have much luck tracing a mobile phone in the city. "Now listen. We do not like you working with the Tokyo Police."

"I don't know what you're talking about."

"Oh, yes you do! Do not try my patience! You are to recall Major Don Stewart at once. If you do not, we will kill your grandson. Do you understand?"

Moriya listened but heard only static.

"Do you understand?" he repeated.

"Yes," came the defeated reply. "But what about Matt?"

Moriya punched the "end" button and turned the phone off.

He smiled to himself as he began a circuit of the Imperial Palace grounds. His eyes scanned the moats, walls, and bridges as he wondered where the bomb might be. He knew they were close—he could feel it. And once they had it, the Pikadon-ha would have the power to force the *gaijin,* the foreign devils, out of Japan forever.

Moriya turned to the southeast and drove toward the harbor. Soon the Tokyo skyscrapers were behind him as he entered the warehousing and manufacturing district near Tokyo Bay. He turned between two long buildings and drove along an empty railroad siding. The left-hand structure had been a foundry at one time, but it had been abandoned several years ago. Moriya parked next to the large doors. A rusty chain and padlock secured those. He parked. The van swayed as Moriya heaved his bulk out. He walked up the steps to the side door, knocked, and waited, aware of the hidden security camera focused on him.

The door opened. Hong Woo-sik bowed and stepped aside. Moriya entered and looked around the cavernous building. He sniffed the air. A pungent metallic smell told him the smelter had been in operation. Heavy metal-working machines stood on their isolated concrete foundations, gleaming under powerful work lights. Machinists operated the computer-controlled milling machines and lathes while other men stood by the electric furnace, located in a corner under a massive hood and chimney. Everything seemed to be waiting.

Moriya had mixed feelings about the North Korean expert. On the one hand, the Pikadon-ha needed expert help to build the bombs, someone who didn't care about what was being smelted and machined. And Hong also had access to tritium through his North Korean contacts. This would boost the yield of the rather primitive plutonium implosion bombs to nearly five hundred kilotons—not superweapons, but enough to vaporize a large portion of central Tokyo. Enough to force the Japanese people to demand vital changes and to eject the hated *gaijin*. But Hong was also a *gaijin*.

"Is there any news?" Hong asked.

Moriya nodded. "We have the American ambassador's grandson. That will remove Major Stewart from the picture."

"Good. But what about the weapon? Have you located the third dragon? Without the plutonium I cannot proceed."

Moriya struggled to maintain his composure. The North Korean's name for the American atomic bomb grated him, although he appreciated the obvious reference to power and authority. And the ultimate goal of all dragons to push aside the clouds and ascend to heaven resonated with Moriya's plans. But the man overstepped, something he seemed completely unaware of. "No, we have not!" Moriya said, sharper than he intended. He tried to relax. "But we are very close—I can feel it. Are *you* ready?"

"Yes. I have trained your men. They are highly skilled, so this was not difficult." Hong swept his arm about the machine-tool floor. "And I must say, I am impressed with the tools. I could not ask for better."

Moriya smiled. "We Japanese excel in these things."

"That is true."

"How long will it take once I have the bomb?"

"No more than a day, perhaps less. All the components are ready: the explosive lenses, the kryton switches, the tritium, the cases—everything. The machinists have even turned out blanks of the implosion cylinders. All we have to do is smelt and cast the plutonium, machine it, and assemble the bombs."

"Good," Moriya said. "You will soon have your plutonium."

* * *

Matt sat on a folded-up cloth with his back against a wall. Construction tools lay everywhere. Sawhorses supported plywood panels.

Exposed ductwork and wiring were visible where some of the ceiling panels had been removed. Long, heavy-duty extension cords lay along one wall. Whatever this place was, it wasn't finished.

Although he didn't know where he was, something about the place was familiar. The fake Disneyland employee sat on a chair watching him and had left him gagged despite Matt's protest. Matt's face still tingled from *that* mistake. The man had jerked him to his feet and slapped him so hard Matt thought his neck would snap.

A few minutes ago Matt had finally worked up the courage to communicate another problem. He had been reluctant to do so until his distress had finally become an emergency. His captor understood his squirming and had cut the nylon strips and led him to a rest room in the back. Matt was surprised to see that the facility was large and modern but rather dirty. He noticed on leaving that there seemed to be another rest room on the other side, the women's room he guessed.

The man strapped Matt's hands and legs again. Matt pushed himself back with his feet, trying to get comfortable. He could hear muted sounds beyond the door to his right, where he guessed they had brought him in. He leaned his head back against the wall and closed his eyes. Occasionally he heard voices behind him, faint, but sometimes clearly enough to pick out a few words. Most of these phrases were in Japanese, but sometimes they were in English.

"*Konnichiwa.*"

Matt's eyes popped open. The greeting had been so soft he almost had missed it. It also had been artificial. He had heard that voice before. *It's that stupid robot!* He thought. Matt knew where he was. *This is where that tearoom is going to be. I'm in the Tokyo Tower.*

10

Operation Canceled

Don tossed the thick report onto his desk. He decided that "Japanese Subversive Organizations in the New Millennium" would have been better titled "More Than You Wanted to Know About Japanese Whackos." The number and diversity of the groups was surprising, and the report agreed with Okawa on one thing: the Pikadon-ha were far and away the most dangerous.

Don jumped as the phone rang.

"Major Stewart," he answered.

"Don, this is Allen! I need to see you at once!"

"Yes, sir. I'll be right there."

Don frowned as he got up and hurried out of his office. Apparently Colonel Dill was in one of his excitable moods. He ransacked his memory trying to come up with what could be upsetting his boss but came up empty. Don's talk with Allen that morning had been pleasant enough.

He knocked on the door and walked in. Dill looked up. There seemed to be a vague sense of defensiveness in his expression.

"Morning, Colonel," Don said as he sat down.

Allen's expression took on a hard edge. "Change of plans, Don. The Owens operation is off."

"What?"

"If you will let me finish!" Allen said, biting off each word.

"Sorry, sir."

"The ambassador called me into his office a few minutes ago. He's decided we have nothing more to gain by continuing. Owens was just a radical creep who got mixed up with some bad people. He's dead now, and we have no business helping the Tokyo police take care of *their* terrorists."

"But, Colonel, this morning you said the operation was still on. I don't understand. What happened?"

"See here, Major Stewart!" Allen roared, so violently a fleck of saliva hit Don. "Let's get one thing straight right now! When I give you an order, I expect you to carry it out—no questions asked! Is that clear?"

For a few moments Don could say nothing. Finally, he said, "Yes, sir."

Don saw the anger in Allen's eyes fade and the hunted look return. He could tell his boss was having second thoughts about his outburst.

"Yes, well. Sorry, Don. Didn't mean to snap your head off, but the operation with Okawa is definitely off. The ambassador was *most* clear on that."

"Yes, sir. I understand." He paused. He most certainly did *not* understand but knew he could not pursue the subject further. "I'll be in my office if you need me." He got up quickly.

"Fine," Allen said with a strained smile.

Don hesitated. "Colonel? Has Mr. Okawa been notified?"

"Not yet. I'll be sending him a memo since it's air attaché business."

"I see. Can I call and let him know this is coming? Last night I said I would call today."

Allen hesitated, then shrugged. "I don't see why not. Go ahead."

Don returned to his office and sat down behind his desk. It felt funny. He had spent a lot of time out of the embassy in the past few days, working on something that scared him. But he realized the importance of what Okawa's organization was trying to do. Now the ambassador had terminated the operation, but the reason Allen had given didn't make sense. That Owens was dead did not take the United States off the hook, the way Don saw it. He shrugged. His duty was to obey Colonel Dill's orders, just as Allen was following the ambassador's.

He eyed the telephone, not looking forward to what he had to do but knowing he had to do it. He pulled out his wallet and extracted Okawa's card. He punched in the number and waited.

"Moshi moshi."

Don smiled at the Japanese version of hello. "Mr. Okawa, this is Major Stewart."

"Major Stewart, I was hoping you would call. I trust you are somewhat recovered from last night's unfortunate incident."

"All things considered, I'm fine," said Don slowly.

"Good, I am glad to hear that. The object at the bottom of that hole was not what they were looking for, I suspect. It was a large cast-iron kettle, buried for quite some time by its appearance."

"I see."

"I am continuing our patrols of the districts near the Imperial Palace. I thank you for suggesting that."

"You're welcome."

"Could you come over to my office this afternoon? I would like your opinion on my revised plans—and I wish to investigate the possibility of involving units of your military special forces. I understand the prime minister's office is also pursuing this with your State Department, but I would appreciate informal talks through the embassy." He laughed. "I suspect that might be faster."

Don dreaded what he had to say. "Mr. Okawa, I'm afraid something has come up. The ambassador has terminated my operation with your office." Don felt Okawa deserved a better explanation, but there was nothing he could add since *he* didn't know what had happened.

"Oh," Okawa replied. Gone was the earlier tone of trust and appreciation. "This is most unexpected, Major. However, after what happened last night, I certainly understand."

Don sighed. "It doesn't have anything to do with that, as far as I know. But as to the reason—I can't say."

Okawa didn't reply immediately. When he did, his voice was low and formal. "Ah, so. Then I must let you go. I know you have important things to do. I thank you for your help."

"You're welcome."

"I appreciate what you did for us and regret what happened more than I can say."

"I understand that."

"One more thing, Major. Despite the ambassador's decision, this matter of Owens and the Pikadon-ha is important. I believe whatever they are planning is dangerous and affects us all. The ambassador needs to be aware of this and realize the consequences."

"I'll do what I can."

Okawa gave a brief laugh and, for a moment, lost his grave tone. "I know you will, Stewart-san. I hope we meet again. *Sayonara*."

"*Sayonara*," Don repeated, aware that his pronunciation was off. The phone clicked dead. Don sighed and replaced the receiver.

A few minutes later his door opened, and Fred Brown's smiling face appeared around the corner. In spite of his concern, Don couldn't help smiling.

"You busy?" Fred asked.

"Come in."

Fred came in and closed the door. He sat in a side chair. "Did the colonel give you a personal tour of the rack?"

"What would you know about that, Lieutenant?"

"Been there myself—more than once." He became serious. "It's no secret when he's upset about something."

"Yes, that's true."

"Please don't misunderstand. Colonel Dill is basically a fine officer, but he *does* let pressure get to him. When his boss leans on him, or he's unsure about something, things can get a little rough. When I see the signs, I make like a shadow."

"I remember you warning me when I first got here."

Fred nodded. "I know. But the surprising thing is that the colonel is also a decent guy, strange as that may seem. If you have a personal problem or need some time off, I've never known him to say no. He really likes people."

"I'll take it on advisement." Don watched Fred. It was obvious he wanted to ask something.

"Something on your mind?" Don asked finally.

"Yes. I was in Colonel Dill's office this morning, and he told me a little bit about what happened to you last night. Is it something you can talk about?"

Don thought a moment. "Don't see why not. Did Allen give you any background info—about Sam Owens and the Pikadon-ha?"

"Yes. In fact he seemed quite pleased with your performance, although he said there would be no repeat of last night. But no details."

"Well, settle back. It's a strange story."

Don was grateful to have someone he could share the whole thing with. He saw Fred's expression change as he filled in the details. There was no question he understood how serious the situation was.

"That's pretty strong," Fred said when Don had finished. "The operation was still a 'go' this morning?"

"That's a roger. Then the ambassador shut it down."

"Why?"

Don frowned. "I wish I knew."

"Think the colonel knows?"

"I'm not sure, but I suspect not. I think he would have told me if he did."

"Maybe the ambassador said not to."

"That's possible, I guess. But Allen seemed very defensive. I think he's as much in the dark as I am. "Anything you can add?"

"Not much, I'm afraid. Japanese radical groups have been getting more violent for some time now. The *Aum Shinrikyo* come to mind. But I've *never* heard of a group with as much firepower and determination as the Pikadon-ha."

"We're agreed on that!" Don said with a snort. "But here's what I don't understand—what was Owens doing with them?"

Fred shrugged. "Good question. Maybe he was their demolitions expert. If he was involved in that bomb plot in Montana, he'd know how."

"OK, but what are they looking for? It can't be those old bombs they've been finding."

"That's for sure. But it's got to be something metallic. Suppose it could be something valuable buried near the palace—maybe something they could finance their activities with?"

"I guess that's possible, but where would Owens fit into that?"

"Don't know, unless he helped them get the metal detector the Japanese recovered—you know, that special army model."

"I suppose. But those guys don't seem to have any problems getting equipment." Don sighed. "I've been wrestling with this for several days, and it makes about as much sense now as it did when I started. And since the ambassador has shut the operation down, I need to get back to learning the routine around here—assuming, of course, that Colonel Dill lets me stay on."

Fred laughed. "I wouldn't worry about that. If *I* can keep from getting fired, you, sir, ought to be golden." He got up. "I believe that was my cue to get lost. No need to hit Brownie over the head to get his attention."

"So, you have a nickname. I'll remember that."

"Might as well, that's what everyone calls me. If you need someone to bounce ideas off, let me know."

"I appreciate it," Don replied, meaning it.

"Right. See you later."

The door closed, releasing Don's mind to roam. He wanted to forget the Pikadon-ha and Owens, but he couldn't. He reviewed the whole sordid mess again, examining every detail. What did it all mean, and what *was* Owens doing with the terrorists? Okawa's last words kept coming back. The Pikadon-ha were dangerous—very dangerous. And despite the ambassador's decision, whatever they were planning affected the United States.

He tried to push these dark thoughts out of his mind. He picked up one of the thick manuals and opened it with a thorough lack of interest. He read the introduction and overview but found it impossible to concentrate. Finally he gave up and slammed the manual shut. He leaned back in his swivel chair and closed his eyes.

Don couldn't shake the feeling that something was horribly wrong, and doing nothing would be the grossest dereliction of duty. Lives could be at stake. He suspected the operation's termination had been forced, but could the Pikadon-ha have that kind of leverage with the State Department? Or was it possible the terrorists had forced the Japanese government to act?

Don went down to the break room, filled his coffee mug, and returned to his office. He sat down behind his desk and sipped the strong brew. He thought of his friend back in Denver. Larry Best knew something about Owens's father, something he couldn't talk about. Don suspected it was in some way related to what the son had been doing with the terrorists. But *whatever* it was, he was sure Larry wouldn't talk about it over the phone.

An idea sparked in the back of his mind. At first he dismissed it as impractical, but it wouldn't go away. If he could visit Larry, perhaps Don could get him to talk. But to take the time off, not to mention the expense—majors didn't roll in wealth, even including flight pay. Then he started reviewing the recent acts of terrorism throughout the world. What if he was the only one who could stop this—whatever it was the Pikadon-ha were planning?

He made his decision. Then something else occurred to him. If he went to Denver, he also could visit his mother. When he and the family had left for Japan, Don believed the next time he saw his mother would be at the throne of God. Perhaps God was giving him one more visit this side of eternity. He felt a stinging sensation in his eyes and felt a powerful inner urging. He picked up the phone and punched Allen's extension.

"This is Colonel Dill."

"Allen, this is Don. I need to see you about a personal matter. Is now a good time?"

There was a slight pause. "Of course, Don. Come on over."

"Thanks. I'll be right there."

Don put down the phone and said a quick prayer. He hurried over to Allen's office, entered, and sat down. Don looked into his boss's eyes and saw true concern there. This surprised him, despite what Fred had told him. After an inner debate, he decided to lead with the secondary reason.

"Allen," Don started uneasily. "I know I just got here, but I'd like to take some leave for a trip back to Denver. My mother lives there, and she's dying of cancer."

"Oh, I'm sorry to hear that," Allen said. "I didn't know. Is your father living?"

Don shook his head. "No, Dad died several years ago, and Mom misses him terribly."

Allen nodded. "I'm sure she does."

"I'd like to see her one more time—and visit with an old air force friend. There's some personal business I need to take care of." Don paused. "I really don't have anything on my plate right now, other than learning how to be an air attaché."

"Of course," Allen said. "I'll have your leave papers cut at once. Will a week be long enough?"

"I'm sure it will."

"When do you want to leave?"

Don thought about that. This was going to be a surprise to Doris and the kids. "I guess as soon as possible."

"OK, and if you need more time, give me a call, and I'll have your leave extended."

"Thank you, Allen. I appreciate it."

"Don't mention it. I'm just sorry about your mother. If there's anything else I can do, please let me know."

Don got up. "I will."

"Oh, one other thing before you go. Hold up on making your flight arrangements. I think I can get you space on military transportation."

"That would be great."

"Let me see what I can do."

"Thank you, sir."

Don went back to his office and thought about what he had committed himself to. He went over in his mind how he would break the news to Doris. Leaving her and the kids in Japan while he returned to Denver might not set well, especially on top of what had happened last night.

About a half-hour later a knock sounded on his door.

"Come in," Don said.

Allen entered, holding an envelope.

Don got up. "I would have come by for that," he said.

"I know," Allen said.

Don took the envelope and a handwritten note.

"Got you an unusual ride home," Allen added as Don glanced over the note. "I checked with Captain Young, the naval attaché. The navy is delivering a P-3 to Greenville, Texas for an electronics upgrade. It's leaving from Yokota Air Base tomorrow at 1430 hours, and Captain Young says they can drop you off at Denver. Should beat commercial air by a wide margin. Oh, and Gus will take you to Yokota."

"Wonderful. Thanks, Colonel."

"You're welcome. Hope your visit goes well."

Don looked at the note again. "Guess I better get a move on."

Allen turned to go. "See you when you get back."

Don watched the door close. Fred had been right. Colonel Dill really did care about people.

* * *

"Don," Doris said in a peevish tone that was unusual for her. "I don't understand this. OK, Colonel Dill pulling you off the terrorist operation is strange, but *why* do you have to go Denver? We don't even have permanent housing, and you're going to leave me and the kids alone to go see Larry Best."

He stopped his pacing and sat on the bed beside her. She turned aside, a clear indication she wasn't ready to be talked out of her irritation.

"I don't blame you," he said heavily. "But I can't let go—it's too dangerous. Larry knows something, but he's not going to talk about it over the phone. He knew the father during World War II, and somehow that's related to what Owens was up to—I know it!"

"He might not tell you in person. What then?"

"That's possible, but I've got to try. Doris—the Pikadon-ha have to be stopped. Okawa says they'll stop at nothing to get what they want. I just can't stand by and watch that happen."

"I still don't see how Larry can help. He knew Owens's father; he didn't know the son—and that was over fifty years ago. Is it really worth it?"

He lowered his head and sighed. "I won't know that until I see Larry."

"There's no other way?"

"Seeing him in person is the only chance I've got." He grinned. "I'm much harder to avoid in person."

He saw her expression soften a little, although the worry was still there. The argument was over. He knew she wasn't happy, but she wasn't one to hold a grudge.

"How long will you be gone?" she asked.

"Allen gave me a week's leave, but I don't plan on being gone that long."

"How long do you think?"

"A couple of days." He thought of his mother. "I'd like to stay longer, but I can't. I've *got* to find out what Larry knows and get back here."

She got up. "I'll help you pack."

"Don't think I can do it myself?"

She poked him in the ribs. "Men don't know how to do it right. If *you* do it, your clothes will be all in a wad when you get there. Besides, you're sure to forget something."

"Oh. Now you've hurt my feelings."

Her laugh was a little strained. "Only telling it like it is."

Don ransacked his mind for a peace offering. "What are you and the kids doing tomorrow?"

"Well, we *were* going to the National Children's Castle before *this* came up."

"Don't let this stop you. Tell you what. Gus is taking me to Yokota around noon. I can spend the morning with you and the kids. What do you think?"

She smiled. "I think I'd like that."

"Good."

Don stood, took her hand, and pulled her up. He drew her close and kissed her. He felt his pulse quicken as he realized the home fires were not out.

11

The Lord's Provision

Don pushed through the doors, oblivious of the beautiful Saturday morning. He handed the attendant the tickets as Doris and the kids preceded him through the entrance of the National Children's Castle. Michael pointed to a sign.

"Look, Dad. The climbing gym is on the third floor."

Don grinned. "What do you know. The tour book was right." He turned to Doris. "I know what Michael wants to do. What about you and Leah?"

Doris looked at her daughter. "Want to try the art?"

Leah nodded vigorously. "Yeah."

Don saw the tension in his wife's eyes. "We'll come find you before I leave."

She forced a smile.

Don took Michael up to the third floor and got him checked in with the attendant who showed him what the gym had to offer. Don sat on a bench and tried not to be nervous as his son used the handholds to climb up and down the walls. Michael was certainly good at it and seemed fearless, although Don knew he was being careful. Still, letting go was hard.

Don reviewed their morning. He and Doris had decided to tell the kids about the trip over breakfast, mentioning his visit to their grandmother but nothing more. They had taken it in stride. Long-distance travel was no novelty for the Stewart family.

Around 11:30, Don coaxed Michael down. Together they located the art room and went in. Don spotted Doris off in a corner, standing behind Leah. As they got closer, he saw they were working on a watercolor of a Japanese castle.

"Very good," he said.

Leah looked around, beaming. "You like it?"

"Yes, I do. Looks like we've got two artists in this family."

This obviously pleased her.

"Time to go?" Doris asked.

Don felt a pang of anxiety. "Yeah. Gus is picking me up around noon."

"You'll be careful?"

"Of course." He kissed her. "I'll call."

"Bye, Dad," Michael said.

"Bye." He hugged his son, then Leah. "You two be good, and mind your mom."

"We will," Michael said.

Don turned and walked out.

* * *

Moriya's hard black eyes watched the maroon van as it entered the hotel drive and stopped. The driver jumped out and started for the door. Before he got there, Major Stewart came out toting two bags. He was dressed in a dark green flight suit. The driver took the bags and put them in the back of the van. The air force pilot got in the passenger side, and the van pulled out into the traffic.

"We must stop him," Moriya said.

"We have the ambassador's grandson," Hasagawa said. "Surely that is enough."

Moriya shook his head. "No. Major Stewart continues to act on his own. We *must* stop his interference!"

Hasagawa nodded. "What do you wish to do?"

"Take his family."

* * *

Don tried to relax on the trip to Yokota Air Base, but he couldn't. His mind kept turning over pieces of the puzzle but to no avail. He had no idea what the Pikadon-ha were planning. What were they looking for? Why had Ambassador Dewey ended the operation with Okawa? It made no sense. Don closed his eyes and tried to relax as Gus drove them through central Tokyo.

Approaching Yokota, Don spotted Mount Fuji towering in the distance, its cinder cone dazzlingly white. On reaching the base, Gus entered the main gate and drove directly to the flight line. There in the afternoon sun sat a Navy P-3C Orion. Gus parked the van next to an air force pickup. Don saw they were none too soon. The crew was already pre-flighting the aircraft.

"I appreciate the ride, Gus," Don said as he got out.

"My pleasure, Major Stewart."

Gus hurried around and opened the van's back doors. Don reached in and pulled his bags out.

"Guess I'll see you when I get back," Don said.

"I will be here."

Don headed for the men walking around under the four-engine sub-hunter. One of the officers saw him coming and turned. He was tall and thin and had a trim mustache. His smile hinted of a sense of humor. Don saw the officer's name on his flight suit patch: "CDR Edward Carpenter, USN." Don popped a salute that was promptly returned.

"Good morning, Commander," he said.

The aviator's eyes darted to the patch on Don's flight suit as they shook hands. "Major Stewart, you're right on time. Welcome aboard."

"Appreciate the ride, sir."

"Please call me Ed. No one around but us aviators."

Don grinned. "Thanks, Ed. My name's Don."

Ed started toward the aircraft. "What do you fly, Don?"

"F-16Cs, at my last duty station."

"The Fighting Falcon. I suspected you were a throttle jockey."

Don laughed. "However, over here it will be anything with wings so I can maintain my flight pay."

"I hear that." The naval aviator stopped before the large, gray transport and looked up. "Hope flying in my trash hauler doesn't contaminate you."

"Ed, I'm not saying *anything* bad about a bird that's taking me to the States." He paused. "Besides, some of my best friends fly trash haulers."

"Well, we'll try to make your flight pleasant. However, the in-flight service leaves a lot to be desired—stale box lunches."

"Same thing in the air force."

Ed motioned toward the ladder. "Follow me, and I'll show you where to stow your gear."

Don boarded the aircraft and placed his bags with those of the flight crew. Ed led the way forward past the electronics stations and up to the cockpit.

He sat down in the left-hand seat. "The jump seat is all I can offer," he said, pointing. "We've got two flight crews for this hop plus the normal operational personnel, so it'll be kinda snug."

Don took the seat behind the pilot. "This will be fine. At least I'll be up where the action is."

Don heard the clumping of boots behind him. Another aviator hurried past and sat in the right-hand seat.

"Don, this is George Zuck, my copilot," Ed said.

"Pleased to meet you," George said, shaking hands.

"Major Stewart is an air attaché with the American embassy in Tokyo," Ed explained. "Captain Young arranged for him to hitch a ride with us to the States."

"Glad to have you aboard, Don," George said. "Did Fast Eddie brief you on our mission?"

Don cocked an eye at the pilot, who seemed absorbed in the preflight checklist. "Ah, no, he didn't. This trip was arranged in a hurry."

"OK. The mission is to drop this bird off at Majors Field in Greenville, Texas, for an electronics upgrade. Our modified flight plan calls for a nonstop great circle flight to DIA to drop you off, then on to Texas."

Don's eyes narrowed. "That's quite a hop for a P-3, isn't it?"

"Roger that. But the jet stream happens to be in just the right place. We'll be cruising at thirty thousand feet with a true airspeed of around 360 knots. But inside the jet stream our speed over the ground will be more like 470—not bad for a turboprop."

"I'll say. Are you detouring the typhoon?"

"A little, but it won't affect us much. The eye is off our flight path. We'll deviate a few degrees until we get past."

"Let's get a move on, George," Ed said as he scanned the instruments.

"Aye, aye, skipper."

The pilots began their checklist. Partway through, George started the engines one by one while the flight engineer monitored his instruments. Ed radioed ground control and received permission to taxi. The ground crew pulled the chocks. One of the airmen saluted. Ed returned it and advanced the power levers. Moments later the lumbering P-3 turned left onto the taxiway that ran parallel to the active runway. Up ahead a heavy transport trundled along, so low it seemed to touch the concrete. The jet blast rocked the navy plane.

"Air force trash hauler, dead ahead," George announced.

Don saw the wide grins on both pilots.

"One of your boys," Ed said.

"Well, this *is* an air force base."

"Roger that. We appreciate your hospitality."

Ed made a quick check on the intercom. All stations were ready for takeoff.

The C-141B turned onto the active runway and started accelerating. It roared past the P-3 with turbines screaming. Ed switched to the tower frequency and reported. Moments later the controller cleared them for takeoff.

Since they had plenty of runway, Ed began the takeoff roll without stopping. He advanced the power levers smoothly as he guided the heavy transport down the runway. The aircraft shuddered and bounced as it picked up speed. Moments later Ed pulled back on the yoke, and they were airborne. Don looked out to the left as they turned toward their initial heading. Mount Fuji's gray-black slopes and snowy crown stood out against the cobalt blue sky.

An hour later Ed looked back. "Wanna fly this bird?"

Don looked through the windshield at the clouds in the distance and felt the familiar urge. "Sure you trust an air force pilot?"

"You bet."

George unbuckled and stepped out of his seat. Don sat down and strapped in. The copilot left the cockpit.

"You've got it," Ed said, taking his hands away. "Go ahead and see how it handles."

"Roger."

Don smiled as he checked the controls for response. The P-3 handled well, despite its size and the heavy fuel load. He began a series of gentle turns, always returning to their base course. "Not bad. Nice, solid feel."

Ed grinned as he shook his head. "I expected more from a fighter pilot. I've got it."

Don took his hands away.

Ed cranked the P-3 over into a steep left-hand turn. Don looked out through the low side windows at the sea so far below. The pilot rolled the aircraft level then executed a right-hand turn that was just as steep.

"Impressive," Don said.

"You should see some of our patrol maneuvers."

A heavyset man appeared in the cockpit holding two mugs of coffee. "Mornin', skipper. Are we dodging icebergs?"

"Good morning, Chief. Didn't mean to wake you up."

"I wasn't sleepin', sir. I was pouring your coffee."

"Hope I didn't make you spill any."

"No, sir. Just wasn't expecting it." He gave the pilot one of the mugs, then turned to Don. "This one's for you, Major. Need any sugar or cream?"

Don smiled as he took the mug. "No, Chief. I like it black."

The older man grinned. "Only way to drink it, sir. Black with a touch of salt."

Don took a sip. It was good, but it did have a slight salt tang. He glanced at Ed.

"Navy tradition," the pilot said. "Right, Chief?"

"Yes, sir."

"What's your estimated time of arrival?" Don asked.

"Ten-thirty hours Saturday, local time. It's almost an eleven-hour flight so you might want to catch a few winks. There are two bunks back aft."

"Thanks. I probably will."

The flight soon became a boring routine of smooth cruising at thirty thousand feet, with periodic course changes to stay on their great circle route. Don soon relinquished the right-hand seat to George Zuck and reclaimed the jump seat behind the command pilot.

Flying to the east put daylight in fast-forward, as each fifteen degrees of longitude advanced the local time one hour. Even though Saturday would become Friday at meridian 180, it would soon become Saturday again as the P-3 raced away from the setting sun. It didn't seem quite right, but they would arrive in Denver at midmorning on Saturday, after a nearly eleven-hour flight. Don shook his head. Several hours later, Don stretched out on a narrow bunk back in the cabin and went sound asleep. But it was not dreamless. His mind churned as he pursued Larry Best all over Colorado, demanding to know who Sam Owens was. Larry never answered. Finally Don felt someone shaking him. He opened his eyes and saw George looking down at him.

"Skipper sent me back. We're approaching Denver."

Don glanced at his watch, then realized it was still on Tokyo time. "What time is it?"

"Ten-hundred hours. Should be on the ground in a half hour."

"Right. Thanks."

Don groaned as he sat up and massaged his face. He got up and followed George forward. The cockpit windows framed deep blue chunks of sky. Brilliant sunlight streamed in. Don sat down in the jump seat and looked down. Fluffy white clouds sailed along over the rugged Rockies.

"Beautiful, isn't it?" Ed said.

"It sure is."

The reason for this trip churned through Don's mind again, zeroing in on the Pikadon-ha and the World War II secret that Larry Best couldn't talk about. The nearness of his destination made his anticipation acute.

Ed pulled back on the power levers. The aircraft tilted down as the turboprop whine decreased.

"We're beginning our approach to DIA," Ed said over his shoulder.

"Good," Don said.

"Don't know what your plans are, but we're coming back this way tomorrow afternoon with a refurbished P-3. We can give you a ride back if you like."

"About what time?"

"Around 1600, local time."

Don thought about all he had to do and his dead certainty that time was running out. "Thanks. Let's plan on it. I appreciate it."

"Glad to help out." Ed took out a card and scribbled down a number. "Here's a number where you can reach me if you need to. But unless I hear from you, we'll pick you up here."

Ed took his place in the landing pattern among the commercial airliners. Soon they were on the ground and taxiing toward the Aerolink freight terminal. The pilot shut down the engines as a man rolled some mobile stairs up to the plane. A navy crewman opened the door. Don walked down the stairs with his bags, followed by the navy crew.

Ed came alongside. "Got your customs form?"

"Yes."

"Good. The inspector will meet us inside the terminal."

They entered the building, and a bored-looking man in a uniform waved a clipboard at them. Don lined up with the P-3 crew, and in his turn, handed over his form. Once the inspector had them all, he put them in an envelope.

"Everything seems to be in order," he said. "Welcome back."

He turned and walked to a small office.

"That's it?" Don asked.

"Usually. Sometimes they want to see more but not often." Ed shook Don's hand. "We'll be heading on. See you tomorrow."

"Right. Thanks."

The crew picked up their bags and left the terminal.

Don stopped a man and asked to use a phone to call the Avis office. The friendly middle-aged man was the shift supervisor. He offered to take Don there, explaining that he was in the army reserve. Don gladly accepted.

The man dropped him off at the rental office. Don thanked him and hurried inside. After waiving the insurance and signing the indecipherable contract, Don was on his way out of the airport.

It was after eleven when he entered westbound I-70. A few miles later he then turned south on I-225. Up ahead were the exits for Aurora, an eastern suburb of Denver. Don's mind spun back into gear as he mentally plotted his course to Larry Best's house. He reviewed in his mind what he would say to his friend, how he would overcome any objections that might arise. Don *had* to find out what Larry knew.

Then he felt an inner urging and recognized it at once. He remembered telling Allen he wanted leave to go see his mother, then mentioned he also had personal business to take care of. That, of course, had been fudging. Don wondered if the Lord's opinion might be a little more pungent than that.

Don found himself thinking about the one who had borne him into the world, and felt a stinging sensation in his eyes. Although Japanese terrorists loose in Tokyo might seem more important, perhaps Don's stated reason for coming was more important in God's eyes. He felt an inner confirmation. But at the same time, he believed the visit to Larry Best was part of the plan as well. It was a matter of having your priorities right.

Don took the Mississippi exit and turned right. The Denver foothills stood out clearly in the distance, the majestic Rockies forming a continuous north-south ridge as far as the eye could see. A gentle breeze blew from the west, cleansing Denver of its frequent brown haze. He turned left at Peoria, then drove to Florida where he turned left again.

A few blocks later he pulled up at his mother's house, a comfortable two-story with a small yard. A familiar Chrysler Town & Country sat in the driveway. Although his mother had decided on hospice care, volunteers from the church provided most of the day-to-day care and companionship. Paul and Karen Easterling headed up this ministry, and the dark blue van meant that Karen was inside ministering to his mother. None better, he thought as he opened the door and got out.

He walked up the sidewalk, climbed the steps, and stood before the door. He felt a momentary sense of helplessness, then rapped softly on the door. He heard quiet footsteps on the tile entryway. The door opened, but it was Paul's blue eyes that looked up at him rather than his wife's.

"Don, come in," Paul said. "What a surprise. Thank God you're here." He took Don by the arm and guided him toward the stairs to the second floor. "Karen's with your mother. The hospice nurse just left—she's doing all she can, but the pain is very bad." He stopped at the stairs and looked into Don's eyes. "I was going to call you around six Tokyo time. Your mother doesn't have much time left." He had to swallow before he could continue. "She's going to be in the arms of the Lord soon. Don, I don't know *how* you got here, but I'm sure glad you did."

"It's a long story," was all Don could say.

They tiptoed back to the master bedroom. Karen looked up, obviously surprised. Don's eyes drifted down to his mother. She was gaunt, even more emaciated than when he had left. Although it was quite warm, a heavy quilt was pulled up snugly under her chin. She turned her head to the side and saw him.

"Don," she whispered. Her scarecrowlike hand struggled out from under the quilt. "He brought you."

Karen and Paul left the room.

It took several tries before Don could say anything. "Who, Mother?" He knew the answer, but somehow he had to ask it.

"I prayed I would see you again." Something glistened in her eyes. Two shining tracks appeared on her drawn face. "I shouldn't have done that." She smiled at him. "We said our good-byes—I have no regrets. I thank God we're all Christians. Next time we meet, it will be in a far better place."

"Yes, Mother."

"I miss your father." She looked toward the dresser. Don followed her eyes, knowing what he would see. There was the wedding picture of Second Lieutenant and Mrs. Bill Stewart, taken in the chapel at the Air Force Academy just after the young officer's commissioning—the beginning of their air force life together. They had seen some interesting duty stations, enduring living conditions most Americans wouldn't put up with. "Till death do us part" had come to them over fifteen years ago. His mother had been alone for a long time.

"I know, Mom."

"It won't be long now."

"Yes," he said simply.

He sat down in the chair beside her bed and took her hand. It was cold, and seemed to be nothing but bones with the thinnest covering of translucent skin. Don didn't see how she could still be living. He felt a brief flash of hate directed toward the cancer that had done this. Then he thought of the Lord, whom he knew cared intensely about what she was going through. And very soon the Lord would do something about it—the final mercy.

He looked down and saw her eyes were closed. He wondered if she was asleep or . . .

"Don," she whispered, not opening her eyes.

"Yes?"

"For some time I've felt another presence in this room. But then I open my eyes, and no one's there. Do you think that's silly?"

Don looked about the room. "No, Mom. I imagine it's an angel here . . ." He swallowed, ". . . to take you home."

She seemed to relax. "That's what I thought. I like that." She paused, then whispered, "I'm tired. Think I'll sleep a while. Don?"

"Yes, Mom?"

"I love you, Son."

"I love you too, Mom."

"I know." She slipped her hand out of his and slid it slowly under the covers. "We'll meet again."

He watched her for several minutes, but she said nothing more. Concerned, he looked at her closely, wondering. Then he saw the gentle rise and fall of her chest. She was in the merciful arms of sleep. Don got up and tiptoed out. Paul and Karen were waiting in the den downstairs. They got up as he came down the stairs.

"She's sleeping," Don said.

"Thank God for that," Karen said. "Best thing for her."

Don rubbed his eyes as he thought about what these two had been doing for his mother—and the others in the church who were critically ill. "I can't tell you how much I appreciate this. Thank you."

"It's the Lord's provision," Paul said. "Thank him. I'm glad he brought you home. I think it meant a lot to your mother."

"It meant a lot to me as well. I didn't think I'd ever see her again."

"Will you be here long?" Karen asked.

Don's other task hit him like a bucket of ice water. "No. In fact, I'm going to have to leave tomorrow afternoon." He paused. "I'm glad I got to see Mom again, but there's another reason I came back—something I can't talk about."

"Something with the air force?" Paul asked.

"Related to it. That's all I can say."

Paul nodded. "Fine. Well, don't let us hold you up. Someone is with your mother twenty-four hours a day."

"Please thank them for me."

"We will."

Don picked up the phone and dialed Larry Best's number.

12

The Answer

Don parked his rental car and looked across the street at the familiar two-story house. Larry Best also lived in Aurora, several miles from Don's mother. Two generations of Stewarts had spent many happy hours in that house, the blessing of a deep friendship born out of military service and commitment to the Lord.

Lowry Air Force Base had been Larry's last duty station, and the Bests had decided they wanted to live their retirement years under Denver's Rocky Mountain grandeur. Elizabeth, Larry's wife, had died years ago, leaving behind an old World War II warrior and a dwindling number of friends. Don swallowed hard as he remembered that the number was about to drop again.

He got out of the car and closed the door. He began to doubt the wisdom of his trip as he crossed the street and walked up to the front door. He reached out and pressed the lighted button, hearing the rich chimes sound inside. For a while the only sounds were the restless breeze and the dying reverberations of the chimes. Then he heard footsteps approaching. The door opened.

Larry stood there for a moment then stuck out his hand. "Don—I'm surprised to see you."

Don shook his hand and stepped inside. "I know. I'm on leave to see my mom." He felt an inward pang of conscience at not stating the other reason. He saw the wary look in his friend's eyes. Larry turned and led the way to the den.

"I'm so sorry about Eileen," he said. "She's a wonderful woman—and an inspiration to us all. I don't think I know a finer Christian."

"Thank you. I was blessed with my parents."

Larry smiled. "Yes, you were. Please sit down."

Don sat on the couch under the picture window.

"Can I get you something to eat?" Larry asked. "I was getting ready to fix lunch when you called."

"Yes, I'd appreciate that."

"I'm having sliced beef on sourdough. That OK?"

"Sounds great." Don followed him into the kitchen.

Larry pulled out the bread and sliced the beef from a roast. He got lettuce out of the crisper and cut up a tomato.

"Want anything else on it?"

"No, thanks."

"Me either. Never could stand mayonnaise or mustard, but Elizabeth loved 'em." He stacked up the thick sandwiches. "What do you want to drink? Iced tea, soft drink?" Larry's smile widened. "Your usual?"

In spite of everything, Don laughed. "I'll *never* live that down." He shook his head. "I wish Doris wouldn't tell that one on me."

"The base CO thought he had a real lush on his hands, as I recall."

"Yeah, well, 7UP *does* look like something a little more potent."

"Which is part of the idea, right?"

"Yeah, I guess."

"Seriously, what do you want?"

"Now that you mention it, a 7UP *would* be nice."

Larry put ice in two glasses, popped the top on a 7UP can and poured. He fixed a Coke for himself and led the way into the breakfast area off the kitchen. They sat, and Larry offered thanks for their food. They talked about Don's impressions of Tokyo, and whether Larry was still hitting the slopes in the winter. He was. But by tacit agreement, they stayed away from the reason Don had come.

When they finished their lunch, Don went back to the den while Larry cleaned up the table. Don looked around, admiring the collection of large color prints of Colorado landscapes. Larry had taken up photography after retirement, and like everything he did, he took it seriously.

"Nice work," Don said as Larry came in.

"Thanks. I really enjoy traveling around shooting those."

"I bet you do," Don said as he sat down on the couch.

Larry sat in his swivel recliner.

"So, how was your trip?" he asked.

Don saw the wariness return. "Tiring, even though I got some sleep. Suffering from jet lag, I guess—propjet lag to be exact."

"Oh?"

Don grinned, but it was weak. "The naval attaché arranged a ride for me on a Navy P-3. It was interesting, and it beat the commercial schedules by a long margin."

"I see," he said.

Don felt the tension growing. He wondered again why his friend didn't want to talk about the Pacific war. The silence grew as Don searched for a way to broach the subject. Larry saved him the trouble.

"Let's get down to it," he said wearily. "I know what you're here for, but for the life of me I don't understand why. So I guess you better tell me."

Don cleared his throat. "It's about the Owens thing, as I'm sure you've guessed. Sam Grayson Owens, son of a 509th navy weaponeer, got himself killed working with a Japanese terrorist group call Pikadon-ha."

"Must be pretty serious for you to come all the way to Denver to ask me about it."

Don shrugged. "I knew you wouldn't talk to me over the phone."

"You're not going to get much further in person, old friend."

"Look, Larry. This is vitally important, or I wouldn't be here. You know I don't go off on wild tangents."

Larry nodded, and the anger drained from his face. "Yeah, I know you don't. But believe it or not, what you're asking about is still classified, and I can't tell you why."

"I guess I'll have to accept that, but I sure don't understand."

"I'm not going to discuss the logic of national security with you," he said with a sour frown. "OK. Why don't you tell me about these terrorists. No promises, but I'll think about it."

Don reviewed the entire situation, describing the mysterious diggings and what he had learned about the Pikadon-ha. Larry listened carefully. Don saw the color drain from his friend's face when he described the brutal firefight in Hibiya Park.

"Wow," Larry said. He rocked back in his chair and looked at the textured ceiling.

"Mean anything?" Don asked.

"I'm afraid it does. Let me think."

Larry stood up and walked over to the fireplace. He looked up at a framed document hanging over the mantle. The title said "The President of the United States of America" in bold, black letters. Underneath was the president's seal of office. It was the commission of Second Lieutenant Larry Best, United States Army Air Corps.

Finally he turned around. "Don, if it was anyone else, I wouldn't tell you. But you need to understand one thing: what I'm going to tell you was, at one time, the most highly classified secret this country ever had. I doubt anyone currently in the Department of Defense is aware of it, but you know that makes no difference. I could get in deep trouble if this leaked out and someone started digging."

"I understand."

He seemed to relax a little. "I hope you do." He came back to his chair and sat down. "I'm not sure how much you know about what I did in the war, but let me tell you about one of my missions. I've never talked about it to anyone, for reasons you're about to find out.

"You know I was in the 509th Composite on Tinian near the end of World War II. Did I ever tell you about any of the missions leading up to the two atomic bomb drops?"

"Not that I recall. I knew you were in the 509th, and of course I know the history of Hiroshima and Nagasaki."

Larry's expression turned sour. "Well, stand by, because there's more to the story. You've seen pictures of my plane—the *Little Brown Jug*?"

"Yes. I remember the picture of your crew standing in front of it."

"Then you probably remember the two naval officers. One was Lieutenant (jg) Sam Owens—father of *your* Sam Owens. The other was his boss, Commander Morris, who was my weaponeer."

"I figured that."

"OK. But did you know that the *Little Brown Jug* was the first aircraft to drop an atomic bomb?"

Don stared at his friend as he struggled to understand. "What?"

"It *wasn't* the *Enola Gay*, and Hiroshima wasn't the first target. We dropped a gun-type plutonium weapon on Tokyo on 20 July 1945."

"How can that be?" Don asked, struggling to catch up.

"Easy," Larry snorted. "It didn't go off. We looked for it after the war but never found it."

Don closed his eyes as some of the pieces started sliding together. Now he understood Larry's earlier reaction. Don opened his eyes again and saw a wry grin on his friend's face.

"Going too fast for you?" Larry asked.

"No. Press on."

"OK. Not much more to tell. We dropped the bomb on Tokyo to eliminate the Japanese high command, only the bomb turned out to be a dud. Sheds light on some strange things in the historical record."

"Such as?"

"Our failure caused little notice, but Tokyo Rose reported that a single bomber passed over Tokyo that morning, taking the inhabitants unaware—look it up." He laughed. "She said that these sneak tactics were aimed at confusing the minds of the people. Well, that particular mission was designed to do a lot more than that!"

"OK, I understand so far. But why couldn't we find the bomb after the war? You must've known where it landed."

Larry shrugged. "That's the sad part. We *thought* we knew where it landed. We looked all around ground zero for months but didn't find a thing. We finally decided we must have missed the drop point. Don, that bomb could be anywhere."

"Which explains the secrecy."

"You better believe it. We couldn't admit to the world that we'd lost the blasted thing."

"How could you miss the drop point? Weren't you bombing visually?"

Larry hesitated. "Supposed to be. But it was hazy, and clouds messed up our first two approaches. On the third try, Cliff Haynes, our bombardier, said he had the IP—the initial point. Once I accepted that, the rest was up to him."

"Where was the target?"

"Near Shibuya-Ku, north and west of Tokyo Bay."

"That name sounds familiar. Is it close to the Imperial Palace?"

"Yes. It's a few miles west of the palace grounds."

"So, what do you think happened?"

"I'm not sure. I've thought about this for years. Cliff said he had the IP, so I went with him. He was the expert. But it was awfully hazy that day, and there are lots of rivers and bridges in Tokyo."

Don nodded. "That's true enough."

"After the drop, Lieutenant Owens claimed that Cliff made a mistake—that the IP he supposedly identified was several miles east of the real one."

"How could Owens possibly know that?"

"He was looking through the bombardier's radar scope."

"I see. And Haynes was using the bombsight?"

"Right. He was looking through all that haze trying to identify one particular bridge on one particular river. Still, he was the expert with all the training. Cliff was livid when Owens piped up saying he had missed the IP. After that, Owens kept his mouth shut. We all believed Cliff, so that's what the army based the subsequent search on."

"What do you think about it now?" Don asked.

"Through the years I've wondered. And from what you've told me about this terrorist group, it sounds like they're looking for the bomb. It also sounds like Owens told his son where he thought it landed. And since we didn't find it, I'd say there's a good chance Owens was right. Those radar pictures were quite good, if you knew how to read them."

"And apparently he did."

"Yes. He saw the detail map at the briefing, same as we did." He paused. "Do you think the terrorists have found the bomb?"

"I don't know, but that brings something else up. The ambassador shut down my operation."

"What did he do that for?"

Don shrugged. "I don't know, and I don't think my boss does either. But the last time I talked to Mr. Okawa, the Pikadon-ha were still digging around. So, no, I don't think they've found it."

"I hope they don't."

"Where do you think it landed?"

"At this point, I'm inclined to believe Owens. I think we dropped early, which would put the bomb somewhere around the Imperial Palace grounds."

Don felt frustrated, with nowhere to turn. He now knew what the Pikadon-ha were looking for, but he couldn't do anything about it since the ambassador had removed him from the operation. To make matters worse, what Larry had reluctantly shared with him was for his ears alone—he couldn't tell Okawa. The ticking of the grandfather clock in the hall grew loud, filling the void of the lengthening silence. One further question came to mind.

"I've never been in any of our nuclear programs. Will the terrorists be able to set that bomb off if they find it?"

"They won't set *that* one off," Larry said with a snort. "It's the *pluto-nium* they're after. There's enough in that bomb to build several devices. Unfortunately, bomb plans are easy to come by. All they have to do is cast the implosion cylinder and machine it. No problem getting machine tools in Japan. All the other parts—shaped charges, kryton switches, etcetera—are either readily available or easy to make. Mount the thing in a box, hook up a triggering device, and you're in business."

"How big would it be?"

"Oh, around footlocker size, maybe a little larger. Remember the suitcase bombs the Ruskies misplaced after the U.S.S.R. disintegrated?"

"Yeah. This is much worse than I thought." He looked into Larry's eyes. "Thank you for talking to me. I'll keep it to myself."

Larry shook his head. "Do whatever you have to. If those terrorists get that bomb, you've got to stop them. If you need to bring me into it, that's OK. If I had understood what you were working on, I wouldn't have given you such a hard time. Sorry."

"I understand." Don thought a moment. "I have one more question. Would you describe the bomb?"

"I'll do better than that." He got a pad and pencil and drew a quick sketch. "I'm no artist, but this is sort of what it looked like. I've jotted down the vital stats—weight, diameter, length, and so on. And, if memory serves me, this is where the inspection hatches are." He tapped the drawing.

"Thanks," Don said, as he folded the drawing and put it in a pocket.

"What will you do now?"

Don took in a deep breath and let it out slowly. "I wish I knew. I'm hitching a ride back to Japan with the navy crew that brought me here."

"When?"

"Tomorrow afternoon."

"Join us at church tomorrow?"

For the first time that evening Don's burden seemed to lift. "Yes. I'd like that."

"Good. I'll come by for you. Are you staying at your mother's house?"

"Yes."

"I usually go to the 9:30 service. That OK with you?"

"Fine."

* * *

The Easterlings were still there when Don got back to the house. Around three the hospice nurse came by and verified what he suspected. His mother was in a coma. The nurse said it was not likely she would come out of it. She couldn't give an estimate of how long Eileen had, but the end was clearly in sight—a few days at the most.

Don urged Paul and Karen to go home, that he would watch his mother until Sunday morning. They gratefully agreed.

He waited until four o'clock to place his call to Tokyo. Doris picked up on the second ring.

"Hello," she said.

"Hi, hon. I'm in Denver."

"Don! I'm glad you called. How are things?"

"About as expected. I had a nice visit with Mom—we talked some. That was a blessing. Right after that she went into a coma. Looks like this is it, although she may hang on for a few days. She's not in pain."

"Thank God for that. I'm glad you were able to talk."

Don felt a tightness in his chest. "Me too."

There was a pause. "What about the other?" Doris finally asked.

"Let's just say that Larry opened my eyes. I'll tell you about it later."

"OK. When are you coming back?"

"Good news there. I'm hitching a ride with the same crew I flew over with. They're coming through Denver tomorrow with a refurbished P-3. We leave here at four in the afternoon. Don't know exactly when we'll arrive in Japan, but it will probably be early morning Tuesday, your time."

"I can't wait. I miss you."

"I miss you too. How are the munchkins?"

She laughed. "They're full of energy, but they miss their dad."

"Tell Michael and Leah I love them."

"I will."

"I love you."

"Love you too."

Don hung up the phone after their good-byes.

13

Added Insurance

Don spent a surprisingly restful night at his mother's house. He checked in on her several times before going to bed. She had a peaceful expression and was obviously in no pain. Don turned in early in hopes of synchronizing his biological clock with Denver time.

Sunday morning he woke up at seven and checked on his mother but found there was no change. The hospice nurse came in at eight and adjusted the pain medication pump. Don fixed breakfast, then dressed for church. By the time he was ready to leave, the doorbell rang.

"Good morning," Don said as Paul Easterling came in.

"Morning. How's your mom?"

"About the same. She doesn't seem to be in any pain."

"Good. Are you going to church?"

"Yes. Larry Best is coming by for me."

Paul nodded. "He drove up right behind me. You go ahead. We'll take care of your mom."

Don felt a tightness in his chest. "Thanks. I appreciate it."

Paul gripped his arm. "You're welcome. See you after church."

The weather was still clear, with a light breeze that kept the brown haze away. Larry waved from inside his Chevy Suburban. Don hurried over and got in.

"Good morning," Larry said. "How's your mom?"

Don sighed. "Still in a coma. Hospice doesn't think she will last long, which is a blessing. Paul is watching her."

"Yeah, I saw him go in."

Larry put the heavy car in gear. Don watched the familiar neighborhood sweep past, reflecting on the fact that his home-away-from-home would soon be no more, and both his parents would be waiting for him in heaven. His mind rebelled against his imminent loss, but then he realized it was for the best. And the Lord had given him one more visit with his mother, one that he hadn't expected.

Larry turned into the church lot and parked. Don greeted the members he knew, mostly older folks. They all asked about his mother. He felt his answers were inadequate but appreciated the genuine outpouring of concern.

Don sat with Larry about halfway down and near the aisle. He followed on the overhead screen as the opening hymns swept past, but he really wasn't engaged. After the announcements, the pastor approached the pulpit and gave the opening prayer. Afterward he arranged his Bible and looked up at the congregation.

"This morning I want to talk about living in the Spirit in an uncertain world. The world is full of evil. Sin abounds, and no one seems to be able to do anything about it. What should our response to this be? I'm going to suggest that 1 John 4:4 is a good place to start. 'You are of God, little children, and have overcome them, because He who is in you is greater than he who is in the world.'

"The apostle John also lived in a wicked age, and he's saying that Christians *have* overcome—past tense—it's a done deal. The Holy Spirit of God has already done it."

He paused for a moment and shuffled his notes. "I didn't plan on saying this, but I know of an excellent example of living in the Spirit. Many of you are praying for Eileen Stewart, a longtime member of our church. She's been a widow for many years and has seen her share of grief. Very soon now, she will be with the Lord. *There* is a woman who lives by faith, not by sight." He paused. "I visited with her a few days ago, and I can tell you this: she's ready to go, and she *knows* who's going to receive her. As I was leaving, she told me she was praying for me and our church. I can't tell you how much that meant to me."

Don looked at him. He wondered if the pastor had seen him, but he didn't think so. Don considered his mother's life and had to agree. As a service wife, she *had* lived through a lot: worry over her husband's safety, Don's own scrapes while growing up, the difficult living conditions military dependents had to endure sometimes. But she had come through it all with a peace that surprised Don, now that he thought about it. And she was handling her final illness the same way.

The rest of the service passed in a blur, but Don had heard the message, and felt encouraged by it. Afterward he saw the pastor's obvious surprise at seeing him. Don shook his hand and thanked him, then made his way into the fellowship hall. Others came by to talk with him and say how much they appreciated his mother. Don realized that what he had heard was important, but how to apply it was the problem. He knew that putting the Bible into practice was not always easy. And sometimes God allowed bad things to happen.

* * *

Don checked his watch as he waited in the Aerolink freight terminal at DIA. The Navy P-3 was due any time. The shift supervisor had come by a few minutes ago with word that the pilot had reported beginning his approach.

After church, Don and Larry had gone out for lunch. Upon returning to his mother's house, Paul told Don that her condition was unchanged. Don went in and saw his mother, seemingly in a serene sleep. He bent over and kissed her, but there was no indication she knew he was there. Finally he decided to return to the airport and await his ride and the long trip back to Tokyo—and whatever awaited him there.

Don heard a faint whine approaching. He picked up his bags, went to the door, and looked out. A gray Navy P-3 was taxiing toward the terminal. As he watched, the two left-hand propellers began to slow as the aircraft rolled to a stop. Don opened the door and started walking. An Aerolink employee rolled the stairs into place as a navy crewman opened the door.

Don hurried up the stairs and into the aircraft.

"Good afternoon, sir," the young enlisted man said. "Want me to take your bags?"

"No, thank you," Don said. "I know where they go."

"Commander Carpenter said he'd like to see you in the cockpit ASAP."

"Thanks. I'll be right up."

Don stowed his bags and hurried forward.

"Afternoon, Ed," he said as he sat in the jump seat.

The pilot looked around. "Hi. How are you doing?"

That, Don thought, *is a good question.* "Fine," he replied.

Engines one and two were turning again. Ed advanced the power levers and started taxiing. "Next stop is Hickam Air Force Base. With the jet stream against us, we don't have enough range for a nonstop."

"I understand. What's your estimated time of arrival in Hawaii?"

"Twenty-one-thirty hours local time. We'll be on the ground about an hour. Touchdown in Yokota should be around 0230 hours on Tuesday." He grinned. "Gonna lose that day you got back yesterday, or whenever it was."

The P-3 trundled along, sandwiched between a Delta 767 and a United 777. After a short wait, the Delta flight roared off down the runway. Another Delta flight landed, then the tower cleared the P-3 for takeoff. Ed pushed the power levers forward, and the subhunter accelerated. Soon the runway markers were flashing past. The pilot pulled back on the control yoke, and they were airborne. The P-3 climbed into the bright blue sky and turned to the west.

* * *

Toshiro Okawa sat back in his chair. A combination of frustration and apprehension played over his face as he weighed his options. The Pikadon-ha had been busy the previous night—another deep hole and another piece of forgotten junk. Okawa genuinely missed Don's help and advice and the resources available through the American Embassy. Although he suspected it was futile, he had decided to call Don, to see if there was any way to reestablish his cooperation. He waited until 8:30, time enough for Don to get into his morning routine. Okawa punched in the direct number. The number rang once, then a recording came on.

"This is Major Don Stewart. I'm on leave until 31 August. If you need immediate assistance, press zero. Otherwise leave me a message. Thank you."

Okawa hung up the phone. He wondered why Don would take time off so soon after beginning his new job. He wondered if his absence was related to the terrorist threat, despite Don telling him he was off the operation. Then another thought: had the air force officer really gone anywhere, or was he staying at the hotel? He finally decided a trip to the Imperial Hotel couldn't hurt.

* * *

Doris smiled as Michael and Leah tore about their room getting ready. As soon as she had suggested going to the Hibiya City Ice Skating Rink, the morning doldrums had disappeared. Both kids were afraid they would miss something unless they left immediately. Doris suspected she would not see such performance once school started.

"Mom!" Michael shouted. "I can't find my jacket!"

"Did you check the closet?" Doris asked.

She heard him run across the carpet and the door open.

"Oh, *here* it is."

Leah came through the connecting door wearing blue pants and a matching pullover. "Is this OK, Mom?"

"That's fine."

"Do I need a coat?"

"That pullover looks heavy enough, but why don't you take a jacket just in case."

"OK." She disappeared into the next room.

Finally they were ready. Doris herded them down the elevator and through the lobby. She hadn't heard from Don since he called the previous day. She hesitated, then made a detour to the front desk. A clerk approached.

"Yes, may I help you?" the young man asked.

"I'm Doris Stewart, room 2404." She began writing. "If my husband calls, this is where we'll be." She gave him the note.

"I will take care of it."

"Thank you."

Outside, Doris looked around.

"Are we taking the subway?" Leah asked.

"No, it's close enough to walk. Let's go."

A truck roared up the curb and screeched to a stop. The back doors banged open, and three men jumped out. Two grabbed Michael and Leah and jerked them off their feet. Both children started kicking.

"Mom!" Michael shouted.

"Stop!" Doris screamed.

The other man grabbed her, covering her mouth with one hand. She bit down hard. The man yelped in pain but did not let go. He dragged her backward over the sidewalk to the back of the truck. Doris saw Michael and Leah inside the dim interior, both held securely. She stumbled, then felt herself being lifted. Her captor threw her inside. She landed on her side. Bright flashes clouded her vision as pain shot straight to her brain. The door slammed shut, plunging the back of the truck into blackness. A dim light clicked on. The truck lurched into motion, tires squealing.

"Oh, God," Doris moaned. "Help us!"

* * *

Okawa knocked on the door to room 2404 and waited. He had considered calling before coming to the hotel but decided it would be harder for Don to avoid him this way. After trying several more times, Okawa returned to the lobby. He went to the desk and caught the clerk's eye.

"May I help you, sir?" the young man asked.

Okawa held out his badge. "Have you seen Major Stewart—room 2404?"

"No, but Mrs. Stewart left him a message on her way out. She said that if he called, this is where she would be."

"I see. When did she leave?"

"Less than a half hour ago."

Okawa hesitated briefly. He did not like prying. "Please bring me the message."

The clerk bowed, went to the boxes, and returned with a slip of paper.

"Thank you." Okawa read the note then returned it.

He left the hotel, drove to the ice rink and parked. He hurried inside and found the manager. Moments later the music stopped as the speakers fell silent.

"Will Mrs. Don Stewart please come to the office for important information."

People turned around and looked toward the entrance, but no one came forward. Okawa had the manager repeat the message two more times, but there was no response.

Okawa tried to avoid the obvious, hoping there could be some other explanation. But the fact was, Mrs. Stewart and her children were not where she said they would be, and she had left the message in case her husband called. That meant he was away somewhere. *Could this be connected with the terrorists?* Okawa wondered. He got in his car and put in a call to his office, ordering a surveillance expert to meet him at the Imperial Hotel.

A half hour later, Okawa stood outside room 2404 armed with a passkey. The man with him scanned the door with a bug detector. Then he knelt and stuck a fiber optic probe under the door. He flipped open an LCD screen and watched as the miniature TV camera panned the room. The man stood and nodded. Okawa opened the door and stepped back.

The man picked up a detector and slipped the earphones on. He went in alone. After checking that room he repeated the procedure in the kids' room. When he was done he came out into the hall and gently closed the door.

"Well?" Okawa whispered.

The man removed his earphones. "There are two bugs in the first room, none in the second. One is behind a picture, the other is in the telephone."

"Show me."

Okawa opened the door to 2404 again. The expert walked to the wall and pointed to the picture. He also indicated the phone that held the bug. They returned to the corridor and closed the door.

"Each bug has a mike and transmitter," the expert said. "Both are active."

"Any chance they know we found them?"

The man shook his head. "No. I was very careful."

Okawa nodded. "Thank you." He glanced at the large aluminum case sitting in the hall. "You have surveillance devices?"

The man looked offended. "Of course," he said.

"Install one in each room, but leave the phones alone."

The man bowed and went about his work. In a few minutes he was finished. Okawa returned to the front desk and reserved the rooms on either side of those rented by the Stewarts. Then he placed a call to his office and asked Sawara to come to the hotel.

Okawa went up to room 2402 and waited. Fifteen minutes later he heard a soft rap at the door. He got up and let Sawara in.

"Bad news," Okawa said. "Mrs. Stewart and her children are missing, and someone has bugged their rooms."

"When did this happen?" Sawara asked.

"A short time ago. I just returned from the Hibiya Ice Rink where she said they would be. She left a note at the hotel in case Stewart-san called—he is on military leave, I found out this morning."

"Where did he go?"

Okawa shrugged. "I wish I knew. I came over here looking for him."

Sawara's frown grew deeper. "This is very bad. What are you going to do?"

"What I must. Please file the missing person reports for me and direct all communications concerning this to my office alone. Also, draft a memo for my signature notifying the U.S. Embassy of the incident and bring it back here. I will take it to the ambassador personally."

"Yes. Anything else?"

"No. Please hurry."

Okawa let him out, then resumed his pacing as he thought of all he had to do. Most of his men were assigned to nightly patrols around the Imperial Palace grounds. But it was a vast area, extending over many city blocks, and Okawa's resources were stretched to the limit. Although he knew the Pikadon-ha were still digging, his men had not been able to catch them at it—not since the incident in Hibiya Park. He shuddered. He didn't want to go through *that* again.

Okawa wondered again where Don Stewart had gone, but even more troublesome was the whereabouts of his wife and children. To all these worries he added one more. He really needed more help.

*   *   *

Doris waited alone in horror, unable to see anything. Immediately after their abduction, the men had gagged them and put heavy bags over their heads. Doris remembered cringing as one of the men pulled her hands behind her back and tied them with something thin and smooth.

Several times in the short trip she thought she heard muffled groans, but she wasn't sure.

Finally the truck stopped and the doors banged open. Although she heard shuffling and dragging sounds, she couldn't tell what was happening. Then someone came and jerked her to her feet. She almost fell as she was forced to step up into something that had rough sides. Impatient hands forced her to lie down. Something closed with a loud thump. Then she felt a lurch as whatever she was in started rolling.

A few minutes later she felt the unmistakable sensation of an elevator ride, followed by another one. Shortly after that, someone pulled her to her feet and jerked the bag off her head. Doris blinked in the sudden light. She looked around. It looked like they were in a room under construction. Her knees grew weak in relief. There were Michael and Leah sitting against the wall, apparently all right. And beside them sat Matt.

* * *

"The ambassador cannot see you," the secretary told Okawa. "He is in meetings all day."

"I am afraid I must insist," Okawa said. "I am here on official police business concerning American citizens." He held up a folder.

"I'll take it for him."

"This is quite sensitive. I must give it to Ambassador Dewey personally."

"I'm sorry, Mr. Okawa, but I have my orders."

"May I suggest you check with the ambassador? Please inform him that if he does not see me, I will inform the prime minister's office."

The secretary frowned but placed the call. After a short conversation, she got up and escorted Okawa to the ambassador's office, then left without a word. The marine sentry opened the door, and Okawa went in. The marine closed the door.

Ambassador Dewey was seated behind his desk. He looked up at the policeman, obviously worried. Apparently remembering protocol, Victor stood up and came around his desk.

"I understand you need to see me," he said, shaking Okawa's hand.

"Yes, Mr. Ambassador. It is most important."

"Shall we sit at my conference table?"

They sat down, and Okawa placed the folder on the glass surface.

"What is this about?" Victor asked.

Okawa flipped the folder open and gave Victor the memo. "I have filed missing person reports on three American citizens: Doris Stewart, Michael Stewart, and Leah Stewart."

Victor closed his eyes and rocked back in his swivel chair. It was several moments before he opened his eyes. "What happened?" he asked finally. His voice was low and devoid of emotion. He seemed preoccupied to Okawa.

"I fear they were abducted somewhere between the hotel and the Hibiya City Ice Skating Rink." Okawa gave Victor the details. He concluded by saying, "Since Major Stewart is attached to the embassy, I felt you would want to know personally."

Victor nodded. "Yes, of course." He paused. "You are quite right, Mr. Okawa. I have a request."

"Yes, Mr. Ambassador?"

"Because this involves embassy personnel, please direct all communications concerning this to my attention only. I want to handle this myself."

"Of course, Mr. Ambassador. I will see to it." This surprised Okawa, but he knew it was the man's prerogative. He thought of a ploy that might shed light on this growing puzzle. "I would like to ask a question, if I may—a request actually." He saw the man's frown deepen.

"What is it?"

"Would you reassign Major Stewart to help me in the Pikadon-ha case?"

"Absolutely not!" Victor snapped. Then his angry scowl softened. "Sorry. No, Mr. Okawa. That has already been decided, and I am *not* going to reconsider it. I cannot justify embassy involvement in a Tokyo police problem."

"I see. Then I will trouble you no further. I will keep you informed on the Stewart case." He paused. "And I will direct all reports to you personally." He stood up.

Victor got up. "Thank you, Mr. Okawa."

They shook hands, and Okawa left.

* * *

Victor returned to his desk chair and sat heavily. He put his elbows on the desk and his head in his hands. *Now* the Pikadon-ha have the Stewarts also, he thought. He shuddered. He didn't doubt the warning—if he interfered, they would kill Matt. And there wasn't a thing in the world he could do about it.

14

Return to Tokyo

Don made a quick trip inside Base Operations as the P-3 was being refueled at Hickam Air Force Base. It was fully dark now. Rich tropical smells swept over him from surrounding Honolulu. He did a quick calculation and realized it was early afternoon in Tokyo.

He borrowed a phone and punched in the number. He counted the rings, hoping he could catch Doris in. After eight rings, though, he knew she wasn't and hung up. Much as he wanted to talk to his wife, he knew that finding her, and two restless kids, in on a Monday afternoon had been a long shot.

Don walked out into the night and back to the flight line. After boarding the P-3, he decided to try and get some sleep. It would be a long flight into Yokota Air Base.

* * *

The man waited at the pedestrian entrance to the parking garage as he made sure he was alone. It was nearly 11:00 P.M., but the Tokyo traffic was still quite heavy. The Pikadon-ha had changed tactics since the encounter at Hibiya Park. The search teams were smaller, often just one person, and they were more careful. The police were doing everything they could to stop what *they* considered to be a terrorist threat. The man snorted at the thought. It was worth any cost to rid Japan of the hated *gaijin*.

The man held up his low-light binoculars and scanned the buildings across the street. He took his time as he studied the green image, looking for anything out of place. When he finally decided it was safe, he stuffed the binoculars into a nylon bag and picked up the metal detector. He hurried across the street and into the narrow pathway between two buildings. The sidewalk dropped down into a sunken garden, completely surrounded by low office buildings all around.

The garden was deserted, the man was glad to see, but the ornamental lighting worried him. Not knowing where to shut it off, he dug around one of the lights until he found its cable. He slipped on gloves, cut the insulation off the wires with his knife, then shorted them with the blade. There was a bright flash, and the lights winked out.

The man waited for his eyes to adjust, then started forward with the metal detector. He was prepared for a boring night, since he had yet to find anything, so he was quite unprepared when his earphones shrieked as he moved the detector next to a towering shrub. He pulled the earphones off and looked down at the lighted meter. The needle was pegged. The buried object had a lot of metal, whatever it was.

The man felt a brief jolt of excitement, until he remembered all the other chunks of metal they had uncovered recently. He knew it was unlikely that this was what Moriya was looking for. But they had to check. He hurried off to find a public phone.

* * *

Hong Woo-sik yawned as he stumbled through the darkened garden. He tried to hide his irritation at being called out every time a team found something. But since the American's death, he was the only one who could identify what they were looking for. He had lost a lot of sleep during the last week, and in each instance, it had been a false alarm. He was sure this time would be no different.

Hong stepped cautiously toward the dark shapes that loomed suddenly in front of him. He had no desire to tumble down a hole. A man clicked on a hooded light and directed the beam down the earthen shaft. Hong reached the hole and looked down. His heart skipped a beat.

"Give me that!" he snapped.

The man handed him the flashlight. Hong played the narrow beam over the large rusted object. It was obviously a bomb and a huge one—much larger than any conventional bomb. The tail fins were still attached although bent. He eyed the diameter as his hope became certainty. The bomb was *exactly* the right size. He swallowed nervously. After all this time, they had finally found the third dragon—it couldn't be anything else. He was a little surprised that such a heavy weapon wasn't buried deeper, until he remembered how deeply the sunken garden was depressed. He was standing well below what had been grade level in 1945. He handed the flashlight back. At last it was time to get to work.

Hong ordered the digging crew back into the hole, with instructions on how much farther down they had to go. Behind him stood his head machinist, waiting beside his elaborate toolbox. Hong whispered a few instructions in the man's ear, then hurried out of the garden. It was time to call Moriya.

* * *

A little over an hour later, Hong and Moriya were standing at the edge of the pit. "There is your dragon," the North Korean said.

"Is that all you need?" Moriya asked.

"Yes. We have removed the plutonium—the rings and the slug in the tail. Nothing else is of any use."

Moriya looked at his men. "Bury it. I want this garden looking exactly as you found it."

He and Hong began walking away.

"How long?" Moriya asked.

"Within twenty-four hours."

"For both devices?"

"Yes."

* * *

Don yawned as he walked away from the Yokota Air Base flight line. The night was pleasant and calm, despite the fact that the typhoon was now less than eight hundred miles away and approaching. Don's mind had been racing ever since George Zuck had awakened him. But Don was also weary and looking forward to getting back to the hotel. He was grateful to see the familiar van in the parking lot. Gus helped him load his bags. Don climbed into the front seat and settled back for the long trip.

He had been thinking about what he should do. He had tried and rejected a dozen plans involving the embassy and the State Department. Even though Don knew what Larry had told him was true, he also realized it would be hard to prove. He pondered again the ambassador's abrupt decision, but he still couldn't make sense of it. Don tried to relax but couldn't.

* * *

Okawa sat in an easy chair in room 2402 of the Imperial Hotel. Across from him, Michihiko Sawara sat at a small table monitoring the bugs in the Stewarts' rooms. That Mrs. Stewart and her children had been kidnapped by the Pikadon-ha Okawa felt was almost a certainty. He thought again about the ambassador's reaction on hearing about it. *What did it all mean?*

He had sworn the hotel manager to secrecy and instructed him to keep hotel employees away from the Stewarts' rooms and the ones assigned to the police.

Now all Okawa could do was wait and hope.

* * *

Don got off the elevator and trudged up to his room. He set the bags down, opened the door, and went inside. He saw the lights were on, and wondered if Doris was already up.

"Honey, it's me!" he raised his voice.

He entered the bedroom and stopped cold. An icy chill shot through his veins as he saw the bed was made up. He ran to the connecting door and opened it. Michael and Leah's room was deserted as well.

Behind him the phone rang. Don returned to his room and hesitated. On the third ring he picked up the receiver and lifted it to his ear.

He swallowed hard. "Hello?" he croaked.

"Major Stewart, how was your trip to Denver?" a man asked. His English was good but with a pronounced accent.

"Who are you?" Don demanded.

"Let us not play games, Major. As you have just discovered, your wife and children are missing."

"What have you done with them?"

"If you wish to see them again, listen carefully. We know about your trip to see Larry Best. You are to cease interfering at once. And make no mistake—if you contact Mr. Okawa, we will know it. Disregard this warning, and we will kill your wife and children. Do you understand?"

"Yes," Don said in a low voice.

"Good. I am sure you know we mean what we say. Be assured we are watching every move you make. Oh, and one other thing. We know you are on leave for a week. Do not leave the hotel. If you do, we will know. Disobey in any way, and you will regret it."

"But . . ."

"Good-bye, Major Stewart."

The line went dead.

* * *

"Did you get a trace?" Okawa asked.

"Yes," Sawara replied. "A pay phone in Koto-ku near the harbor. I dispatched a unit to check it out, but . . ."

"Yes, I know!" Okawa snapped. "They will be gone."

He grabbed a pad and printed something in large letters. He got up and walked to the connecting door and stood there for a moment.

* * *

Don sat down beside the phone and closed his eyes. He felt dead inside. Fear welled up and threatened to overwhelm him. Don struggled to fight it down. There was no way out. If he did nothing, millions might die. He was convinced the Pikadon-ha would eventually find the bomb since they knew approximately where it had landed. But if Don acted, the terrorists would kill his family.

Even if he *did* decide to do something, *what?* No one knew where the terrorists were. And once they found the bomb, it would be all over. Don wondered if they would use nuclear blackmail or simply build their bomb and set it off. Thinking it through, he doubted the Pikadon-ha would give any warning.

A click sounded from across the room. Don looked up, and to his horror he saw the door to the corridor opening. Okawa stood there motioning for him to be silent. The policeman came in and held up a sheet of paper. Don read the scrawled words:

YOUR ROOM IS BUGGED
COME WITH ME

Don felt his fear return, but what could he do? He got up and followed Okawa outside. The policeman quietly closed the door and took him next door. Don saw Sawara, recognizing him from the fiasco in Hibiya Park.

"They cannot hear us now," Okawa said, "We must talk."

"I can't. The Pikadon-ha . . ."

". . . have your family," Okawa finished for him. "Yes, I know. I am truly sorry, Stewart-san."

"You knew about this?" Don asked, his anger rising.

"Please keep your voice down. I found out after I came here to see you. Your wife left you a message at the front desk saying she was taking the children to the Hibiya City Ice Skating Rink. She apparently never made it."

"What happened?"

"That is all I know."

Okawa paused. "I called your office earlier. Your recording said you were on leave for a week. Where have you been?"

Don shook his head. "I can't discuss that."

The policeman's voice took on a hard edge. "You *must* cooperate, Stewart-san. Forgive me, but the only hope your family has is if you help me. We are all in grave danger until we catch these terrorists."

Don thought it over. Colonel Dill, on the ambassador's orders, had terminated his operation with Okawa. But circumstances had changed, and there was no way he could safely contact his boss. Besides, something about the ambassador's sudden decision just didn't ring true. And on a personal level, doing nothing would doom his family as surely as defying the Pikadon-ha. All things considered, he had no other option. Only one thought lingered.

"What if the terrorists find out?" he asked.

"They will not. I want you to come to my office. I cannot deactivate the bugs, of course, so I will detail a man to stay in your room to make them think you are still here."

"What about food?"

"Since they said not to leave the hotel, you will order from room service. One of my men will deliver it."

"How can I do that if I'm in your office?"

"I have had an extension installed there."

Don nodded. "I see."

"I have tried to think of everything, Stewart-san. Will you help me?"

Don looked at his pleading eyes. He knew he had to do it. "Yes."

Okawa bowed. "Thank you. Now, where did you go?"

In that moment, Don thought of his mother, knowing she would soon be with the Lord. He swallowed the lump in his throat. "I went to Denver—to see some friends. One of them knew Sam Owens's father, and he told me what the Pikadon-ha are after. They're looking for an atomic bomb."

Okawa's eyes grew very wide. "What?"

"It's a long story. The short version is we dropped it on Tokyo during World War II—before the Hiroshima mission—and it didn't go off. It's still out there somewhere, and the plutonium in it is what they're after."

"I see."

"As you probably know, making a nuclear device is straightforward, once you have the fissionable material. The tools are readily available in industrialized countries, and plans are available everywhere."

"How long does it take to make one?"

"I don't know. But from what my friend said, the process isn't complicated, given the materials and the right tools. A short time, I would guess."

"Does your friend know where the bomb fell?"

"Not exactly. If Owens's father was right, it should be in the vicinity of the Imperial Palace grounds—right where the terrorists have been digging."

"Do you know what it looks like?"

Don nodded. "I have a drawing."

"Good. I think I will split my teams. One group will look for the bomb, while the others search for the terrorists."

"Sounds like a good idea. What do we do first?"

"Wait while I arrange your transportation." He glanced toward his assistant. "Sawara-san will make you a little less conspicuous."

As Okawa let himself out, Sawara picked up a small case. "Please, Major Stewart. If you will come with me." He went into the bathroom. Don heard water running in the sink.

"What are you going to do?"

"Dye your hair black. Please, we must hurry."

Don sighed but did as he was told. He took off his shirt and stood there as Sawara applied the smelly dye and combed it in. A few minutes later he was looking at himself in the mirror. His hair was, indeed, raven black.

"Now, back in here, please," Sawara said.

Don took the indicated chair while the policeman sat beside him and opened the makeup case again.

"Now, look straight ahead. Pay no attention to what I am doing."

Don looked up from the neat assortment of jars, brushes, pencils, and rags. He locked eyes with Sawara.

"You are not listening, Major."

"I'm listening. Just what are you doing?"

The policeman smiled. "Changing your appearance. I believe you call it a disguise. Now, please. Look straight ahead."

Sawara opened a jar and dabbed a cotton pad in it. Then he methodically applied the coloring to Don's face, neck and upper chest. After that came his hands, up to mid forearm. Just when Don thought the worst was over, Sawara started thinning his eyebrows with some small scissors. The final step involved careful work with several black pencils.

"There," Sawara said. He held up a hand mirror. "How does it look?"

Don's first impression was that he was looking at a stranger. He had to admire Sawara's skill. The policeman had given Don a reasonable resemblance to a Japanese.

"Not bad," Don said. "Sure doesn't look like me."

"I think that is the idea."

A few minutes later Okawa returned and looked Don over. "Excellent. Now, put these on, please." He pointed to a pair of charcoal slacks and a dark blue sport shirt hanging in the closet.

Don dressed quickly. When he was done, Okawa checked the corridor, then stuck his head back in. "Please follow me. We will go down the stairs."

Okawa led the way to the stairwell, opened the door and went through. Don followed. The door closed after him. He walked to the edge of the landing and looked down the stairwell shaft. He sighed as he realized how far down he had to go.

Okawa stopped and looked back. "Please, Stewart-san. We must hurry."

Don caught up and stayed with him. Around and around they went as they passed floor after floor. Finally they stopped and Okawa escorted him through double doors out onto a loading dock. Several men were examining a shipment of produce. One looked up for a moment then returned to his work.

Okawa stopped at one of the garage doors and started pulling on the chain hoist. The roll door clattered up revealing a van, backed so close to the dock that it touched the hotel's exterior. Stewart jumped down into the truck, almost falling as he slid across the slick metal floor. Okawa joined him. As the driver pulled away, Okawa slammed the rear doors, plunging the interior into darkness. A few moments later an overhead light came on, providing dim but adequate illumination.

After a short ride, the truck came to a stop and started backing up. The horn sounded once. Don heard the sound of a door opening. The truck backed in and stopped.

Don followed Okawa through the back way and into his office. The room was cool and dark as the policeman neglected to turn on the light.

"Please sit down," Okawa said. "Can I get you anything to drink? Are you hungry?"

Don sat in an easy chair beside the desk. "No, not right now."

"Do you want to rest? I can have a cot set up for you."

Don shook his head. Even though he was tired, he knew he couldn't sleep. "No, I got some sleep during the flight back. What are your plans?"

"Start looking for the bomb, now that we know what we are looking for."

15

The Countdown Begins

Doris scanned the cluttered room with growing anxiety. She didn't know where they were, but she had figured out they had been there around twenty-four hours, since the muted sounds outside had ceased for a long time, then recently started up again. She also had decided their captors had to be members of the Pikadon-ha—nothing else made sense.

Most of the time they had two captors, although at times one would leave. The men stayed in the front room except for periodic checks on their prisoners. She and the children were on a routine now. The guards allowed them to visit the rest rooms, always cutting their nylon ties, then applying new ones when they returned.

They were released one at a time for meals. Doris still remembered the first time. One of the guards had warned them against crying out. He had told them it wouldn't do any good and would only result in them being gagged all the time. That had been enough for her. She looked forward to these brief periods of relief, freed from her bonds and having the sodden rag out of her mouth. But after each meal, back in it went.

Doris knew her kids were scared, but they were bearing up bravely. Matt, on the other hand, was not faring as well. Although he didn't cry out, he was obviously terrified, and frequently broke down in tears. Her heart went out to him as she wondered about the trials he must have seen in his short life.

Doris squirmed around, trying to find a comfortable position, but it was impossible. The nylon straps held her wrists and legs securely, limiting her ability to move about. She closed her eyes and prayed for their safe release.

* * *

Moriya rushed through the door of the former foundry. He struggled to maintain his composure, relying on his years of training as a sumo wrestler. Their goals were nearly in his grasp, the result of careful planning and hard work. Turning back the vile Western tide that fouled Japan's shore had to be done, despite the traitors in the current government. Moriya saw Hong consulting with one of his machinists. The North Korean saw Moriya and came over.

"What progress have you made?" Moriya asked.

"We are on schedule. I have smelted and cast the plutonium cylinders, and they are being machined at this moment. Once that is done, it is a matter of assembly." He motioned toward the large workbenches. "Every part is checked and ready."

"When can I have the bombs?"

"Around six or seven tomorrow morning."

"Is it possible to have them sooner?"

Hong shook his head. "No. The work must be done carefully to assure success."

Moriya held his impatience in check. "I see. Then I will expect them at that time. See that you do not disappoint me."

Hong bowed. "You will have them."

Moriya hurried out and got in his car. He looked up at the sky as he drove toward the harbor. Light clouds were blowing in from the east, and the wind was picking up. The typhoon was drawing near, another reason for concern. It was going to be close.

Moriya drove to the secluded wharf well off the interconnected waterways that radiated off Tokyo Harbor like spiderwebs. He drove onto the dock, parked, and got out. He walked to the edge and looked down. A fishing trawler rode the light chop, tugging gently at its lines. Its deck was deserted. Moriya walked down the steep gangplank and boarded the boat. Hearing a noise forward, he followed it through a propped-open door down into the engineering spaces. Kiyoshi Katsube looked around. He wiped the wrench he had been using and set it down.

"Are you prepared?" Moriya asked.

"Yes. I was replacing a fuel line filter. The boat is ready."

"What about your first mate?"

"Isomura-san will be coming on board this evening. When do I pick up the bomb?"

"Hong says he will be ready between six and seven tomorrow morning." Moriya paused. "Wait here for me. I need your help in an important matter. After that, you will pick up the device at the foundry. There must be no delay once we start. We will coordinate the exact detonation time then."

Katsube bowed. "I will await you here."

Moriya returned to the deck and looked toward the west. There, amid the tall office buildings of the central city, stood the red and white needle of the Tokyo Tower.

* * *

Don looked up as Okawa returned to his office. Although his disguise was excellent, they had agreed it would be better that the American remain inside while Okawa organized the search teams.

"That took longer than I thought," Okawa said as he sat behind his desk. "My men are spread very thin, but we have four new teams searching for the bomb."

"Were the Pikadon-ha active last night?"

"Yes, they were. We found one hole, but they didn't finish it."

Don arched his eyebrows. "Oh? Did one of your patrols scare them off?"

"I do not think so. The site is quite secluded, and I have no report of any of my men going near there."

"Maybe they found out it wasn't the bomb?"

Okawa shook his head. "No. We checked with one of our metal detectors. It was the right size and mass. We dug it out and found an abandoned storage tank."

"Why did they stop digging?"

Okawa frowned. "I do not know."

"No other sites?"

"Not that we have found so far."

"What are your plans for this afternoon?"

"I will be visiting the search teams."

"Do you think it would be safe for me to go with you? Sitting here doing nothing is driving me nuts."

Okawa looked him over. "Sawara-san did a good job. From a distance I would take you for Japanese. Yes, I think it would be safe. However, before we go, I think you should order lunch from room service." He tapped his watch.

It took Don a few moments to understand. "Oh, right."

He still wasn't used to ordering meals he would never eat. He decided on a hamburger, fries, and a large Coke. Using the hotel room extension on Okawa's desk, he placed the order.

"Shall we go?" Okawa asked.

They went out the back way. Okawa got in the police car. Don stood by the passenger side door and looked up. The wind was still light, but the cloud cover was increasing. He opened the door and got in.

"What's the latest on the typhoon?" he asked.

Okawa started the car and backed out. "It is supposed to come through sometime late tomorrow."

"How bad do you think it will be?"

"That is hard to say. At least it is not yet a super typhoon. There will probably be utility outages and damage, of course. But villages on the coast and in rural areas will be hit harder."

"How will it affect your operation?"

"We will continue. We have no choice."

Don thought of the difficult search they had to do. He felt a stinging sensation in his eyes as he looked out at the vast city. Doris, Michael, and Leah were out there somewhere. But where?

* * *

Moriya waited impatiently as the crowded elevator made its quick trip to the Tokyo Tower main observatory. The doors glided open, and the tourists scattered like so many ducks. Moriya frowned in contempt as he went up to the second level. He approached the door into the tearoom and waited for the pedestrian traffic to thin. He then punched in the access code, stepped through the door, and shut it.

Hasagawa was sitting in a folding chair. Unten looked through the door then returned to guarding the hostages.

"Your bomb will be ready early tomorrow." Moriya smiled as he thought of Hasagawa's dedication to their cause. "I will bring it over myself and help you set it up. It is an honorable thing we do, Hasagawa-san."

Hasagawa bowed. "It is my duty."

"Yes. And mine."

"What about the Americans?"

Moriya thought a moment. "I think it just that they perish in the atomic explosion. After all, their country supplied the plutonium. And after tomorrow, Japan will be rid of the *gaijin* forever."

That he would be safely outside the city he didn't mention. Someone had to be available to lead Japan through the chaos that was coming. The people would demand answers and a way out. Moriya had those answers.

* * *

Don and Okawa spent the rest of the day checking on the search teams as they prowled around the business district between the Imperial Palace grounds and the main Tokyo train station. By late afternoon Okawa's men had found two contacts, both of which turned out to be false alarms.

Don looked up at the sky as Okawa drove north along Hibiya-Dori beside the Babasaki Moat. The overcast was complete but still light. The typhoon had slowed but was still expected to come on shore tomorrow. It was warm and muggy.

The radio crackled to life. Okawa grabbed the mike and answered. After a terse conversation in Japanese, he turned to Don.

"Another contact a few blocks from here," he said. He turned on his emergency lights, pulled into the intersection and turned around. He sped south down Hibiya-Dori, stopping behind a truck blocking the left-hand lane.

Don got out and followed Okawa as he hurried down the walk between two buildings. Sawara waited for them in the sunken garden, standing beside a tall bush. Workers were already digging.

"We may have something," Sawara said.

"How did you find it?" Okawa asked.

Sawara pointed to the decorative lighting. "Building management reported vandalism to the outdoor lights—someone dug up a power cable and shorted it. The officer taking the report forwarded a copy to our department, since the location is near the palace. I ordered one of the search teams to meet me here."

"Good. Any progress?"

"Yes. There is something down there, and it is the right size. But someone has been digging here recently. The ground is quite soft."

"Gardening, perhaps."

Sawara shook his head. "I think not. It goes deeper than that."

Don stepped forward until he could look down into the hole. The diggers were down a little over three feet, it looked like, and digging frantically. One of the shovels rang like a bell as it struck something. The workers slowed and concentrated on clearing the dirt away from the rusty object. Don watched as bent tail fins were slowly revealed.

"It's a bomb all right," he said.

"Is it the one we are looking for?" Okawa asked.

"Too soon to say."

But even as he said it, Don had the feeling it was. He watched as the diggers revealed more and more. Once he saw the bomb's diameter he was sure.

"That's it," Don said. "I have a bad feeling about this."

The dirt level dropped lower and lower as more of the bomb was exposed. Finally Don could see the first inspection hatch. The cover was missing. He waited until it was clear.

"I need to go down and look," he said.

Okawa gave the order, and the men came out of the pit.

"Does anyone have a flashlight?" Don asked as he jumped down in the hole.

Sawara got one and handed it to him.

Don knelt down and peered into the black hole, fearing what he would see. He clicked on the light and pointed the beam inside the heavy casing. It was empty. The cavity that should have held the rings of plutonium was completely bare. Don stood up and checked the tail assembly. The slug was gone as well. An icy jolt shot straight to the pit of his stomach.

Don looked up at Okawa. "The plutonium is gone. The Pikadon-ha have their bomb."

16

Defying Dill

Don followed Okawa into his office and sat down. Up until an hour ago, he had hoped that Okawa's men would win the race to find the plutonium. But they hadn't. Don thought of the sheer size of Tokyo. How would they ever find the terrorists in time? Don recalled vividly what Larry had told him. Building a fission bomb was not all that difficult, provided you had the plutonium. And thanks to a blunder in 1945, the Pikadon-ha had what they needed. Now millions would probably die because he and Okawa had failed; among them were Doris, Michael, and Leah.

"What will you do now?" Don asked. His heart wasn't in it, but he had to ask.

"Search for their bomb factory," Okawa said.

Don struggled with his fear. "OK, but where?"

"Run-down warehouse and manufacturing districts, to begin with. Sawara-san is coordinating the search teams now." He paused. "I understand the odds are against us, but we *must* continue. It is not over."

Don felt his roiling thoughts swirl to a stop. It really wasn't over yet, but that missed a most important point. Whatever happened fell within the sovereignty of God. Whether God allowed the terrorists to succeed or not, Don knew nothing could remove him or his family from God's love. But ultimately, the good he planned for them would be fulfilled in eternity. And, if he allowed, that might be very soon. Don felt an inner peace and knew its source.

"You're right," Don said finally. "It's not over yet."

"So, what are *your* plans?"

That caught Don by surprise. He hadn't thought about how this affected his duty as an air force officer and an air attaché. But had conditions really changed?

"I'm not sure. Technically I should report this to Colonel Dill, except I'm not supposed to be working with you. If I report in, he'll likely can me."

"And you are still on leave, I believe?" Okawa observed.

"Yes, I am."

"I need your help, Stewart-san. I would hate to lose you through a technical misunderstanding with your boss. I cannot decide for you, but . . ."

Don nodded. "I see your point. OK. I'll stay with you as long as I'm on leave."

"Very good."

Something nibbled around the edges of Don's mind, a thought that wouldn't go away. At first he rejected it, but the more he considered the idea, the more sense it seemed to make. "What if I could get another officer to help?" he asked.

Okawa seemed surprised. "What do you suggest?"

"Lieutenant Fred Brown. He's on the air attaché staff with me."

"What about your boss?"

"That part I don't know. But Fred knows what I'm working on—up to when I left for Denver. He's a resourceful guy. I think he might agree to help us."

"I will accept whatever help I can get. Use my phone."

He turned his elaborate phone around and pushed it toward Don.

Don punched in Fred's direct number, hoping he hadn't left for the day. After the third ring, the line clicked.

"Lieutenant Brown speaking. Can I help you?"

"Fred, this is Don."

"Hi! You back from leave?"

Don took a breath. "I'm back in Tokyo but decided to stay on leave. I'll be back in the office next week." He paused. "Listen. Could you come by after work? There's something I'd like to discuss with you."

"Sure," Fred replied after a brief pause. "Are you at the hotel?"

Don put his hand over the mouthpiece and looked at Okawa. "Can you send a car for him?"

Okawa nodded.

"No, I'm not. I'll have a friend send a car for you."

"What's going on?"

"I'll explain when you get here. Trust me. It's important."

"OK."

"When will you be leaving?"

"I was getting ready to go when you called. I can leave any time."

"Good. You'll be picked up outside the embassy. See you in a little bit."

"OK. Bye."

Okawa took the phone back. "I will send a car."

* * *

Hong examined the implosion cylinder with care, turning it in his gloved hands. He wore a protective suit and breathed through a filtered mask. He admired the mirrorlike finish on the plutonium as he looked for imperfections. He didn't find any, not that he expected to. This cylinder was exactly like its twin. Hong returned the device to the metal work surface under the vented hood.

The most important job was done—also the most dangerous, since tiny particles of plutonium were deadly if ingested. But Hong knew the precautions to take, since he had had much experience in handling radioactive elements.

He turned toward the waiting workers. Everything was ready. It would be a long night, but by morning the bombs would be ready. Then Hong's job would be done, and he could leave the people of Tokyo to their fate.

* * *

Don got up as Fred entered Okawa's office. The driver who brought him turned and left.

"Don?" Fred asked. "What's with the getup?"

"It's a long story," Don replied, shaking his hand. "I'll explain in a bit. Thanks for coming." He turned to Okawa. "This is Toshiro Okawa."

Okawa stood up and held out his hand. "Lieutenant Brown, Stewart-san has told me a lot about you. I am pleased to meet you."

Fred smiled as he shook Okawa's hand. "Pleased to meet you, Mr. Okawa." He cocked an eyebrow at Don. "I'm not sure what Don told you about me. Maybe you should hear my side of it."

"Entirely complimentary, I assure you," Okawa said. "Please sit down."

Fred's smile faded as he took the chair across from Don's. "Mind telling me what this is about?"

"Remember our talk about the Pikadon-ha before I went on leave?" Don asked.

"How could I forget?"

"Well, I visited an old air force friend in Denver—he was in the 509th Composite during World War II." Don took a deep breath. "The terrorists were looking for an atomic bomb we dropped on Tokyo—a bomb that failed to go off."

"What?"

"Let me bring you up to speed. But before I do, the most important point is this. Okawa and I found that bomb a little while ago, and the plutonium is missing. The Pikadon-ha have everything they need to build a nuclear device."

Don filled him in on what Larry Best had revealed and the recent operations with Okawa. He made the briefing terse, but complete—Fred needed to know everything. He saved the devastating news about Doris and the kids until last.

All the color left Fred's face. "That's horrible! I'm so sorry. I had no idea. Have you heard anything?"

"Not since they called and threatened me. That's all I have. Any questions?"

Fred shook his head. "No. I see how all this fits together now. What do you plan on doing—and how can I help?"

"Okawa has officers out looking for the bomb factory. I'm helping him, and I'd like you to join us. Can you do it?"

"I can, but what about Colonel Dill? Shouldn't we go to him with what we know? Your family's been kidnapped; you've actually found the missing bomb. Don't you think he'll act?"

Don shook his head. "No, unfortunately I don't. I've thought about it, but there isn't enough time. Tokyo would be in ashes before we cut through the red tape." He pondered the ambassador's inexplicable decision. "Besides, I'm convinced the ambassador would can the operation if we asked."

Fred nodded. "Yeah, from what you told me, I bet he would too."

"What do you say?"

"I'll do it."

"Any trouble getting the time off?"

"No. My current project is doing research on U.S. military bases in Japan. I was planning to go to Yokota tomorrow, but I can postpone it."

"Thanks." Don turned to Okawa. "What do you want to do?"

"I would appreciate your assistance in planning. In an emergency, perhaps you could help me contact your military bases."

"We can sure try," Don agreed.

"Good. First I suggest Brown-san change out of his uniform into something less conspicuous."

Fred shrugged. "OK. But I didn't bring any civvies with me."

"That is not a problem. I can provide what you need."

Fred glanced at Don. "This won't require any, uh, makeover, will it?"

"No, Lieutenant. I doubt the Pikadon-ha know about you." Okawa stood up. "Please come with me. First your clothes, and then I will show you and Stewart-san my operations room."

* * *

Doris struggled against despair as the second day of their captivity came to a close. The muffled sounds of activity outside their prison had ceased quite some time ago. She still didn't know where they were, except it seemed to be a public place. That was frustrating, being so near help but not being able to do anything about it. So far their captors had been very careful. Her earlier hopes of escape had faded long ago.

Doris looked around at the kids. Michael seemed to be bearing up, and Leah as well. Doris was proud of them. But Matt she wasn't as sure about, although he had stopped crying. Now he seemed resigned to his fate.

Doris closed her eyes and leaned back against the wall. She felt the sharp jabs of fear and doubt begin again. What the terrorists planned she didn't know, only that it was extremely evil. As black thoughts circled around her, Doris was surprised when the words of a hymn sprang unbidden to her mind:

> This is my Father's world, O let me ne'er forget that
> though the wrong seems oft so strong, God is the ruler yet.

The mad echoes ceased. Doris shivered in appreciation of the truth as she began to pray.

* * *

Don sat at the long conference table in Okawa's operations room. People came and went. Some held whispered conversations with Okawa while others updated the large status board and map at the front of the room.

Fred sat by Don's side. It was late. After the initial adrenaline rush, Don had hoped that the massive search would turn up something quickly. But hour after hour, all the reports had been negative, as the police continued searching industrial sites. The large clock seemed to be ticking away the last minutes for the people of Tokyo. And somewhere in that vast city were Doris and the kids.

Don closed his eyes and offered up a silent prayer.

17

Rewarding Hong

Moriya watched the work with growing impatience, but he knew better than to interfere with Hong. The old steel building creaked and groaned as the wind started gusting. A light rain pelted against the roof, a peaceful preview of what was to come that day.

Both bombs were ensconced in sturdy metal boxes mounted on heavy castors. Hong tested the circuitry of one of the bombs, step-by-step. He watched a testing meter as he applied probes to all the internal connections. Apparently satisfied, Hong flipped a switch. A row of green lights winked on. Large red numbers began counting up, stopping at 3:00.

Hong then went through the same exasperating routine with the other bomb. Finally he looked up.

"They are ready," he announced. "All that remains is attaching the radio links." He pointed out three boxes sitting on the workbench. "One for each bomb, plus a spare. And here are your keys."

Moriya accepted the heavy brass keys, each suspended from a beaded chain. He smiled as he realized the power he held in his hands, then slipped them into a pocket.

"Do you have any questions about the radios or keys?" Hong asked.

Moriya forced a smile. The North Korean's patronizing tone infuriated him. "You have explained them well. Connect the radio link to the cable, then arm the device by turning the key to 'ready.' Pressing the 'count-down' button on either bomb triggers both of them, three minutes later."

"Very good," Kong said. "And the emergency override?"

Moriya gritted his teeth. "Turning the key to 'manual' and pressing the 'start' button begins the countdown."

"On that device only," Hong said. "The other bomb is unaffected."

"Yes, I know that."

"Excellent. Then I turn the dragon's twins over to you."

Moriya bowed. "Thank you. You have done well. I will not forget your service to us."

"You are welcome. Since my work is done, I must leave now. I hope my transportation has not been affected by the typhoon."

"Do not worry. The bullet trains are still running. I will take you to Tokyo Station myself."

"You are most kind."

They put on raincoats at the door. Moriya motioned for Hong to go first. The North Korean opened the door, revealing the early morning blackness. A sudden gust of wind jerked it out of his hand and threw it crashing against the side of the building. A fine mist swirled in from the drizzle. Moriya shut the door as he followed Hong out.

He watched as Hong ran for the car, his shoulders hunched against the rain. Moriya went around to the driver's side and opened the door. The car swayed as he got in. He started the car, turned, and accelerated down the road between the two buildings, tires hissing over the wet pavement.

He flipped on his lights as he drove through the gray dawn. The fine rain cut diagonal paths through the white beams.

Moriya turned south toward the harbor. A few minutes later he saw Hong shift in his seat.

"Is this the way to the station?" he asked.

"It is quicker if I take the expressway."

Moriya watched the North Korean out of the corner of his eye. His arm shot out the moment he saw Hong move. Moriya's huge hand closed about the other man's thin wrist and squeezed. Hong screamed as the bones crunched and broke.

"What are you doing?" the man gasped.

"You know too much," Moriya said.

Hong turned and unlocked the door with his left hand. Moriya grabbed him around the neck and pulled him over, twisting suddenly. Hong's neck broke with a loud snap. He slumped over against Moriya, who threw him against the opposite door like a rag doll.

Moriya continued on to the wharf and parked beside Katsube's boat. He walked around to the other side, opened the door, and threw Hong over his shoulder. He stepped nimbly down the slick gangplank. Looking forward, he saw Katsube coming out of the pilothouse.

"Come help me," Moriya ordered.

"What happened?"

"I could not take the chance Hong would betray us. Have you got a place we can hide the body?"

"Yes. Follow me."

Katsube led Moriya below deck and forward, stopping before a large locker. The sailor pulled out a key, unlocked it and pulled the door open. Moriya dropped Hong to the deck and pushed him inside. Katsube locked the door.

"I need you back at the factory," Moriya said. "The bombs are ready."

"Isomura-san is in the engine room. Shall I bring him?" Katsube grabbed his raincoat.

"No, leave him here to watch the boat. He can help you load the bomb when you get back. We must be careful. We are very close now."

Moriya and Katsube returned to the open deck. The small boat danced lightly on the chop, tugging against the lines which held it against the wharf. A steady rain pelted down, raising myriad splashes in the water around them. Both men walked up the gangplank to the wharf above.

* * *

Don entered the operations room after visiting Okawa's office and sat down.

"Did you order your breakfast?" Fred asked.

"Yes. Eggs, bacon, and toast. I can't get used to ordering room service from here. Is Sawara back with our chow?"

The sound of approaching footsteps answered that question. Don turned as Sawara entered carrying a large sack. When Okawa's assistant had suggested McDonald's for their breakfast, he had gotten an enthusiastic response from Fred, and the choice had been OK with Don. Okawa's had been the only dissenting vote, but the policeman had graciously submitted to the majority. Sawara, like many Japanese, seemed to think the golden arches a worthy import, along with the red-and-white motif of KFC.

"What have you got there?" Okawa asked suspiciously.

"An assortment," Sawara replied. "Mostly Egg McMuffins, French fries, and coffee. I also ordered a few Teriyaki McBurgers if anyone is really hungry."

"Such as yourself?" Okawa asked.

"It has been a long night."

"So it has," Okawa said. He turned to Don and Fred. "My apologies for the food, but it is better than visiting the vending machines."

Sawara emptied the bag on the table. Fred grabbed an Egg McMuffin and unwrapped it. He sat down and began eating. Don decided that sounded as good as anything. He picked up an Egg McMuffin and a cup of coffee and sat back. He closed his eyes and gave silent thanks for his food. When he looked up, Okawa was looking at him with a puzzled expression on his face. Then the policeman nodded and resumed eating.

Don pried the lid off his coffee and took a sip. It was warm, rather than hot, and a little bitter. But he felt the caffeine bite almost immediately. He unwrapped the Egg McMuffin and started munching. He had to agree with Okawa. It was better than nothing.

* * *

Doris waited for the morning ritual. She noted the return of the muted sounds beyond their prison, her only clue that another day was beginning. As if on cue, one of their captors came in with sacks of food. Doris knew the drill by now. The man would feed them one at a time, starting with Matt, followed by Leah and Michael. Doris would be last. In the interest of efficiency, Doris suspected, the man allowed each person a trip to the rest room after the meal, before reapplying the ties.

As she expected, the man stooped down and cut the straps binding Matt's legs and arms. The man removed Matt's gag, looked at it in obvious disgust and threw it down. He dropped one of the sacks beside the boy.

Matt pulled the containers out of the bag and began eating ravenously. Doris watched him, again wondering what he had endured in his short life. Personal responsibility was one thing, but being in a loving, nurturing family did make a difference—a big difference. It was obvious that part of Matt's problem was not his fault, and being the grandson of a U.S. ambassador had not made up the difference.

Matt gulped down the last bite and looked in the bag to see if he had missed anything. His captor pointed toward the rest rooms in the back. Matt struggled to his feet and started walking.

* * *

Moriya backed the van into the Tokyo Tower's loading dock. The rain cut off as he came under the overhang. He stopped well clear of the rear platform and parked. He got out, hurried around to the back, and opened the rear doors.

Moriya looked for a ramp but didn't see one. He cursed. In his hurry he had forgotten to bring one. Moriya wrapped his arms about the box, turned, and lifted it up to the platform. He closed and locked the doors, then climbed the steps and pushed the large black device in through the swinging doors and down the corridor to the elevator lobby.

The attendant saw him coming, and after dispatching the current car, held the next one. Moriya hurried aboard without a word. The elevator accelerated upward toward the main observatory. Moriya looked out through the slanting rain at gray, metropolitan Tokyo. In the distance he could barely make out the black shape of the *Tennessee*. He clinched his teeth at this insult to Japan's sovereignty.

The doors opened at the observatory's lower level, and Moriya pushed the bomb out. There weren't many tourists about because of the weather. He looked at those he passed, curious what their reaction would be if they knew what was near them. He rolled the box to the freight elevator and pressed the button. The doors opened, and Moriya rode up to the upper level.

He pushed the bomb over to the tearoom, then waited until he was alone and punched in the security code. The bolt thumped open with an electronic buzz. He pushed the bomb inside and locked the door.

"Is that it?" Hasagawa asked.

"Yes, except for the radio link. I left that down in the truck." Moriya looked around. "Where is Unten-san?"

"Feeding the hostages."

"Send him down for it while we go over the bomb's procedures."

"But what about . . ."

"Send him down now! We still have much to do!"

Hasagawa stepped to the door leading to the back room and looked in. "Unten-san. Come here, please."

The man appeared a moment later.

"Go down to my truck in the loading dock," Moriya said. "There is a small box in the back. Bring it up." He handed the man his keys.

As soon as Unten was gone, Moriya opened the control panel and began explaining the bomb's operation.

* * *

Matt finished and flushed the toilet. He hurried through washing his hands, wiping them on his grimy jeans. He knew from experience that their guard would punish him if he took too long. When he had first been kidnapped, he had assumed it was for ransom. But the appearance of Mrs. Stewart, Michael, and Leah had confused that idea. *Why ransom an ordinary officer's family?* he wondered. It just didn't make sense.

He opened the rest room door and trudged into the back room. He made a face as he dreaded the nasty-tasting gag. He turned the corner and expected to see the guard waiting for him, holding the nylon straps to bind him. But he wasn't there. Matt stopped. He looked at the Stewarts and saw Michael watching him. Matt frowned. *Probably wants me to hurry so he can have* his *breakfast,* Matt thought. *Well that's tough.*

He heard the murmur of voices in the front room but couldn't understand what the men were saying, only that they were speaking Japanese. *Where is our guard?* Matt wondered again. Although he was scared, his curiosity prodded him on. He tiptoed to the door and listened. He found he could pick out a few words, even though the men were talking very fast.

He had to look. With fear approaching panic, he took a quick peek around the doorjamb, then pulled back immediately. He gasped. One of the men was the largest he had ever seen—an absolute mountain. Matt knew he had never seen *him* before. The other was the man who had snatched him at Disneyland. Matt hadn't seen him much since then, since he remained in the front room most of the time. The men had been hovering over a large black box. The huge man had been dangling a key from a silver chain. Clearly, he was explaining something.

Matt concentrated hard, wishing he knew Japanese better. The black box had electronic controls. A radio was to be connected to it by a cable. The key was for turning it on. The big man was warning the other to be careful once the bomb was armed. He heard the word *Shiohama* and recognized it as a district in Tokyo, although he couldn't remember where it was. Then he heard the word *pikadon.* He frowned. He had heard that word before, *now what did it mean?*

A sharp "thwack" sounded up front. Matt felt his insides turn to ice. Terror threatening to overwhelm him, he chanced another look. He saw their regular guard come through the front door, holding a small black case. Matt pulled back immediately. Sweat broke out in his armpits as he realized he didn't have much time. He wasn't supposed to . . .

Matt stopped as he thought of something. The man had apparently forgotten that he was loose. Would he remember? Matt felt his heart beat faster. He hurried back to his place, sat down and wiggled up against the wall. He glanced toward the open door. No sign of the guard. Matt frowned as he stuffed the gag back in his mouth, securing it with the cloth strip. He hoped the knot looked right.

Then he remembered the nylon ties. He jumped to his feet, raced over and grabbed a new one. He returned to the wall and sat down. He placed the tie over his ankles and tucked the loose ends under his legs. Deciding it looked right, Matt put his arms behind his back and tried to relax.

Then he remembered. *Pikadon* meant "atomic bomb."

* * *

Moriya turned as Unten came in. "Bring it here," he ordered.

He took the case and opened it. He lifted a plain aluminum box out and placed it in a depression next to the bomb's control panel. He plugged a cable into the radio relay and watched as the indicator lights flashed. Finally the green light winked on, indicating that the internal diagnostics had been successful. Moriya smiled. There was only one further thing to do. He pressed the red test button on the relay. The green light winked three times then remained on. The radio had successfully communicated to its twin. The red light labeled "link active" remained dark.

"It is ready," Moriya said. He inserted the brass key but did not turn it. "Do you remember the procedure?"

"I wait until I see the 'link active' light come on. Then I turn the key to 'ready.' When Katsube presses the 'countdown' button on the other bomb, my timer will start. Three minutes later, they both go off."

"Correct. This should happen by late afternoon. It depends on how long it takes for Katsube to check the other bomb and get underway for the sub."

"I understand."

"Good. Now what if the light does not come on?"

"At midnight I turn the key to 'manual' and press the 'start' button. I do the same thing if the police discover me."

"Yes. But that will not happen. The operation has gone perfectly. The bombs will go off as planned. Do you have everything you need?"

"Yes."

"Good. Remember. This is the last time we will talk. From here, I go to make sure Katsube is ready. Final victory is within our grasp!"

"It has been a long time."

"It has. Now, I must take Unten-san with me. We need him on the boat."

Hasagawa bowed. "I will not fail you."

Moriya returned the bow. "I leave everything in your hands."

He hurried out, taking Unten with him.

* * *

Matt heard the thump of the lock and knew it was the outside door. He watched the doorway. He was surprised when the other terrorist came in. *Where was their regular guard?* he wondered. Matt watched as the man stalked over and looked down at him. The man's eyes darted to the empty food sack.

Then he turned to Leah. He cut her nylon ties and removed her gag. Matt saw her glance his way. He silently willed her to mind her own business. After a few moments she opened her sack and started eating.

"Hurry!" the man ordered.

18

A Way Out

Moriya drove cautiously toward the harbor through the steady rain. The gusts were beginning to pick up, but nothing like it would be when the typhoon came ashore. The traffic was noticeably lighter now, as those still in the city headed for shelter.

Moriya's mind raced as he reviewed his personal plans. As the Pikadon-ha leader, he would be in a special bunker north of Tokyo when the bombs went off. There he and the other leaders would rally the Japanese people, shaping their inevitable outrage over what they would see as an American atrocity. This would be easy, considering the warnings already given—warnings ignored by the traitorous government.

Moriya could barely contain his elation. It was going to work. After all their efforts, they were going to succeed. Only a few more steps remained.

He turned onto the wharf and parked beside the boat. He and Unten ran through the rain, down the gangplank, and aboard the boat. Forward, the pilothouse door opened and Katsube poked his head out. Moriya led the way inside the cramped space. Water dripped off their raincoats. Isomura stood in a corner. Moriya's eyes went to the large black box lashed into a corner.

"Have you set it up?" he asked.

"Yes, as you instructed," Katsube said. "Everything is complete except testing the radio link."

"That will work. I tested the one on the tower bomb before I left. But just to be sure."

He watched the green light as he pressed the test button. The light winked three times, then remained on.

"It is ready," Moriya said. "Did you go over it with Isomura-san?"

"In complete detail. Either of us can operate it."

"Good. Then we are ready."

"What are your instructions?" Katsube asked.

Moriya paused. "I think we will take advantage of this storm. We will wait for it to intensify. That will make it easier to approach the submarine without detection."

"I understand."

"I will remain for a while. The rest I entrust to you, Katsube-san."

"You can rely on us."

Moriya turned. "I brought Unten-san along to assist Isomura-san."

"Good. We can use the help."

"Now we wait."

*   *   *

The lights went out. A moment later a battery-powered emergency light clicked on, bathing the back room with a dim, yellow light. Metallic creaks and groans, muted earlier, stood out as the ventilation fans whined to a stop. Doris saw movement out of the corner of her eye. To her surprise, she saw Matt getting to his feet.

She heard someone approaching from the front room. Matt threw himself down and thrust his hands behind his back. A powerful beam of light lanced through the doorway. Doris squinted as the blinding glare hit her in the face. The flashlight moved slowly over Michael, then Leah, before coming to rest on Matt. Doris prayed the guard wouldn't see he was free. The beam remained on the boy for a few moments then went off.

After a few minutes, Matt got up again. He glanced toward the door, then ran to a toolbox, returning with a pair of scissors. He knelt beside Doris and snipped the nylon bands off. Doris pulled her gag out. She started to whisper something, but Matt was already working on Michael and Leah. Matt returned to Doris.

"We've got to get out of here," he whispered.

"Wait," Doris said. "We can't get past our guards."

"But we've got to do something," Matt said, his voice rising a little. "There's a bomb in there, and they're going to set it off."

"Sh-h-h. They'll hear us." She saw the panic in his eyes. "Matt—listen to me. You have to get a grip on yourself."

"You don't understand. It's an *atomic* bomb."

"What? Are you sure?"

"Yes. I heard them say *'pikadon.'* That's what it means."

Doris felt a jolt of icy fear as part of the puzzle slipped into place. *So that's what the* Pikadon-ha *were doing—that's why they were digging around the Imperial Palace. They were looking for an atomic bomb!* Matt was right. They *had* to do something. But what?

Michael and Leah crawled close.

"Maybe there's another way out of here," Michael whispered.

"Wouldn't do us any good," Matt said. "The elevators won't work with the power off."

"Then we'll use the stairs."

"Don't you know where we are?"

"No."

"The Tokyo Tower," Matt said. "There are no stairs. The only way down is the elevators."

"What about the people up here when the power went off?" Michael asked. "Maybe they have emergency power for the elevators."

"That's a point," Doris said. "If there was only some way past the guards."

"Maybe there is," Michael said.

"How?" Matt asked. "Those guys are armed."

Michael looked up. "The false ceiling. We could use one of the work ladders to get up there. I can walk across the ceiling grid until I'm over the outer observatory. Then drop down."

"You can't do that," Matt said.

"Yes I can. I'm a rock climber." He glanced up. "Climbing over that would be easy."

"What if they hear you?"

"I can be quiet. Besides, with all these noises, they won't be able to hear anything."

Doris saw him look to her. "Are you sure you can do it?" she asked.

"I can do it."

She felt a renewed twinge of fear. But what other choice did they have? "OK," she said. "Be careful."

* * *

Don looked at the color printout of the latest weather map. A large white spiral rested on the blue Pacific Ocean, with the edge of the clouds overlapping eastern Honshu. The eye of the typhoon was still out at sea, but it would be coming ashore before long. The gusty winds were still moderate, as was the rain. But that would change soon. The lights had gone out once, but power had been quickly restored.

"That looks serious," Fred said.

Don set it aside. "Yes, it does. And it'll only make our job that much harder."

He got up and approached the large map of metropolitan Tokyo. Okawa and Sawara consulted as they checked the latest reports. Okawa pushed another blue pin in the Shinagawa-ku district.

"More negative reports?" Don asked.

"Yes, I am afraid so."

"I had a thought. The terrorists probably have their bomb by now. If we find the factory, it probably wouldn't do us any good. You might consider looking for the target instead. The Pikadon-ha have been most vocal about the *Tennessee's* visit. What about the area around Harumi Wharf?"

"They also could use a boat," Fred suggested.

Okawa put his finger on Harumi Wharf, then traced the surrounding harbor. "A boat *would* be a good choice, Brown-san." He glanced at Don. "However, it could as easily be a nearby warehouse or factory. We will look for both."

* * *

Moriya looked out at the harbor through the large windows in the darkened pilothouse. He was impatient to be on his way but would not leave until he was sure the mission would succeed. The chop along the sheltered wharf was a little worse but still not bad. The wind moaning through the rigging was still below gale force. But that would change once the typhoon's wall cloud came on shore. Moriya knew that would be hours from now.

But it was time for the next step. Moriya walked to the bomb and looked down at the control console. The green light was still on. Moriya turned the brass key to the ready position. A few seconds later the "link active" red light winked on. Moriya turned back to Katsube.

"It is armed now," he said. "Pressing the 'countdown' button will set both bombs off in three minutes."

* * *

Hasagawa listened to the creaking and groaning coming from all around him. He had heard these sounds before but not this loud. He knew it was because the wind was rising. Soon his long wait would be over, once the boat made its approach to the submarine.

He jumped as the "link active" light on the black box came on, even though he had been expecting it. He turned his brass key to the ready position. He knew it would still be awhile before the countdown started, but this was the next-to-last step. The red "countdown" indicator read exactly 3:00—three minutes to detonation and the beginning of the new Japan.

Hasagawa thought about checking the hostages but decided not to. They had eaten breakfast and been allowed to visit the rest rooms. Although Unten had left sacks of food for lunch, Hasagawa saw no need to feed them or allow them to visit the rest rooms. *What did it matter?* They would all be dead in a few hours.

* * *

Michael looked up at the ceiling. Matt and Leah stood by the ladder to steady it while his mother watched the door into the front room.

"Be careful," Leah whispered.

"I will," Michael replied.

He climbed up the steps until his face was inches from the ceiling panel. He pushed it up and shoved it to the side. He turned and reached down for the flashlight they had found next to the toolbox. Matt handed it to him.

Michael got on the top step and straightened up, bumping his head on a pipe. He ducked and looked around. It wasn't entirely dark up here. Here and there light came through gaps in the panels and the light fixtures. But he was glad for the flashlight.

He looked around the ceiling grid. The steel latticework was suspended from wires. It looked sturdy enough, but he knew he would have to be careful not to stick a foot through one of the panels.

Michael oriented himself, knowing it would be safer to move away from the front room. Then he stopped, deciding he *had* to take a look at the bomb. He turned around and duckwalked over the metal rails, peeking through the cracks as he went. Up ahead he saw a panel with a notch cut out of it. Approaching it, he saw the opening was off to the side, but there was a support wire near it.

Michael grabbed the wire and leaned out, making sure his running shoes were solidly on the steel beam. There it was. He saw a black metal box with lights and a red readout displaying 3:00. That had to be the bomb. The terrorist who had finished giving them breakfast was standing over it, but Michael couldn't see the other man.

He considered lowering himself further so he could see more. He listened to the tower groaning and decided he wasn't in danger of detection. He stretched out almost horizontal, his nose inches from the notch. Michael looked all around but didn't see anyone else. He was sure the man was by himself.

Michael started pulling himself up. Partway there his left foot slipped off the grid with a loud "twang." He held onto the supporting wire with a frantic grip as his body rotated. He knew that if his other foot slipped, he would come crashing through the ceiling. It held. Michael placed his left foot back on the grid. He glanced through the notch. The terrorist hadn't moved.

Michael pulled himself upright and hurried back the way he had come. Once he was over the back room he turned on the flashlight. The metal framework extended before him to a wall about thirty feet away, which he knew had to be the outer wall of the observatory. A large, square duct ran parallel to Michael's path, ending at the wall. He ran the light over the shiny sheet metal. There was an inspection hatch about six feet away. Michael continued on to the wall and stopped. He carefully removed a ceiling panel.

Looking down, Michael saw the slanted windows and the windows in the floor. He stuck his legs through until his shoes touched the glass. Then he lowered himself down until he could grip the window frame. He climbed down the window hand over hand until he could jump to the floor.

Michael looked all around. The power was still off, but the emergency lights provided ample illumination. He couldn't see anyone, and all the stores on this side were locked. He hurried to the stairs, ran down, and circled the lower floor. It was deserted. Michael tried the elevator buttons, but nothing happened. Not a single indicator light was on.

Michael returned upstairs and looked up through the hole. He grabbed the frame and climbed up into the ceiling, lowering the panel back into place.

*　*　*

Don watched as Okawa pushed more pins into the Tokyo map. But he could tell without asking that the reports were all negative. This was discouraging, but it did narrow down the search.

"It would drive me nuts to do this for a living," Brown whispered. "Looking for needles in a haystack."

"Yes," Don said, "but that's the way a lot of police work is. I'm just glad that Okawa is as thorough as he is."

"I know. Still . . ."

Okawa finished reviewing the latest report and came back to the Americans.

"Anything new?" Don asked.

"No. But we now have police boats patrolling the waters near the submarine."

"That sounds like a good idea."

"Yes. I think a boat could be our worst threat. Sawara-san and I are going out on one. Would you and Brown-san like to come with us?"

"What about room service at the hotel?"

"We can tape your orders before we leave."

"But—"

"Trust me. My people know how to handle this. I think you and Brown-san would be more useful with us."

Don looked at his friend. "What do you think?"

"Beats sitting here."

Don turned back. "We'll go. Thanks."

Okawa nodded. "Come with me, and we'll take care of the recording."

* * *

Moriya tried to hide his irritation as he listened to the weather report over the radio. The typhoon was still on the original track but had slowed in the last hour. He was tempted to turn it over to Katsube and start for the bunker, but he couldn't do it. He *had* to know the boat was on its way.

19

Escape from Tokyo Tower

Doris breathed a sigh of relief as she saw Michael coming down from the ceiling. She thanked the Lord with a silent prayer.

Michael descended the ladder and hurried over. Leah and Matt huddled around.

"The bomb's in there, all right," Michael whispered, "but all I could see was one guy."

"What about the observatory?" Doris asked.

"It's deserted, and all the shops are closed. We're up here by ourselves. It's raining outside—looks like the typhoon is coming in."

"Did you check the elevator?" Matt asked.

"Yes. It's not working."

"Then there's no way down."

"What are we going to do?" Leah asked.

"Mom, I think I know a way," Michael said.

"That's impossible," Matt said.

Doris stared at her son. "What do you mean?"

"I can climb down the outside of the tower and go for help."

"You're crazy," Matt hissed.

Michael turned on him. "I am not. I can do it."

"Quiet, both of you," Doris whispered.

She felt panic welling up inside. She thought of the atomic bomb in the next room, and what would happen to everyone in Tokyo if it went off. She ransacked her mind, hoping there might be some other way. She shivered. The idea of her son climbing down Tokyo Tower in the middle of a typhoon was too much. Michael was good at rock climbing—she had watched him practice. *But this?*

"Mom?" Michael said.

Doris knew she had to say something, but what? This seemed to be the only way, and if the bomb went off, they would all die anyway.

"Mom?" Michael repeated.

Doris felt an inner peace come over her. Although she knew what it was, she still had a hard time letting go. "Yes, Michael?"

"Can I go?"

She took a deep breath. "How would you do it?"

Michael pointed toward the toolbox. "That extension cord looks about a hundred feet long, and it's good and heavy. I can use it to rappel down the tower."

"But how would you get outside?"

"There's a duct up in the ceiling. It looks like it goes to the outside. Please, Mom. I can do it."

Doris felt two conflicting emotions. She was afraid but also proud of him. She struggled not to cry.

"OK," she said. "How can we help?"

Michael looked over at the ladder. "Just hand me up the extension cord."

* * *

Don tugged at his raincoat, trying to get comfortable as he and Fred climbed into the backseat. Sawara and Okawa got in the front. Sawara started the car and drove out of the parking garage. He turned on his lights and windshield wipers as the steady rain swept over them.

Although it was midday, the overcast made it seem like dusk. Bright neon lights reflected off the black-mirror pavement as they drove toward the bay. A few blocks later they passed into a blacked-out section. Sawara flipped on his emergency lights as they entered the darkness.

"The power failures are beginning," Okawa said.

"How bad will it get?" Don asked.

"Could be extensive. Depends on how powerful the typhoon is."

After many blocks they entered a lighted area. There was still some traffic, Don was surprised to see, but definitely light for Tokyo. There were also a few pedestrians out, but most were scurrying for shelter. Don saw the wind turn a man's umbrella inside out.

Sawara slowed and took a side street. Two blocks later he turned again. The engine moaned as they started down a street that was both steep and narrow. A block further they entered another blacked-out area. Don looked out through the windshield. Soon he could see the dancing white-caps on Tokyo Bay.

Sawara turned onto the stone embankment and parked. Fred opened his door, admitting a blast of wind and rain. Don struggled out. A powerful gust threw a blend of rain and salt water into his face, forcing him to squint. Water trickled down inside his raincoat, getting past his turned-up collar. Don looked down at the dock below. A boat bobbed and swayed, snubbing up against its mooring lines.

Okawa led the way. Don and Fred followed Sawara as they descended the stone steps. They crossed the slick gangplank and stepped down on deck. A door opened forward, and a man looked out. Soon they were all inside the snug pilothouse. A light vibration came through the deck from the diesel engines. Two men awaited them.

"Stewart-san—Brown-san. This is Captain Saeki." Okawa nodded toward the sailor. "His boat and crew have been temporarily assigned to my department. Captain Saeki probably knows Tokyo Bay better than anyone else alive."

Don decided the man's appearance bore that out. Saeki's face was deeply lined and had the appearance of worn leather. He had a perpetual squint that made it difficult to see his eyes. He wore a yellow slicker that seemed much more practical than Don's flimsy raincoat.

Okawa said something to Saeki in Japanese. The captain issued a terse order, and the deckhand scrambled out and went aft. Up on the dock, a man threw in the stern line. Saeki engaged the starboard propeller and advanced the throttle slightly. The stern moved away from the dock. With quick movements he shifted to reverse on both shafts as the bowline fell into the water. The boat backed smartly into the bay.

Don looked out the pilothouse side window. He could dimly see the lights of the city. He wondered where his family was.

* * *

Michael stood on the top rung of the ladder and looked down. He had the heavy, rubber-covered extension cord over his shoulder. He fingered the tape he had wrapped about it to mark the middle. Matt was about halfway up the ladder holding the flashlight. Michael took it and prepared to step onto the ceiling grid.

"Good luck," Matt whispered.

This surprised Michael. "Uh, thanks."

Matt returned to the floor.

Michael paused as he saw his mother and Leah looking at him. He forced a smile, then crawled up into the ceiling.

He wasted no time as he clicked on the flashlight and walked toward the observatory's outer wall. Michael played the light over the duct until he located the inspection panel. He stopped opposite it and stepped over. He turned the locking handles and pulled the door off. Sticking his head inside, Michael directed the flashlight down the duct. Down at the end was a wire mesh and beyond that darkness.

Michael crawled inside and found there was just enough room to move on his hands and knees. He stopped at the mesh and looked out. A fine mist swirled over him from the downpour that was inches away. The wind howled and moaned as it tore through the tower. He could hear the creaking and groaning of the steel structure even more clearly now. It sounded like it was about to come apart.

Michael squinted his eyes against the spray as he studied the heavy wire mesh grill. It extended over the entire end of the duct, held in place by large wing nuts. He undid them, lifted the grill off and set it behind him. He inched forward, slowly exposing his upper body to the deluge. He was soaked in moments.

He looked down, his eyes following the observatory windows and the spider work of red girders as they descended into the gray torrent below. The hundred-and-fifty-foot drop seemed like a mile. Michael was confident of his climbing skills, but he knew the steel girders would be slick. And then there was the wind and rain from the typhoon. He didn't want to climb out but knew he had no choice. If he couldn't make it down, they would all die.

Water poured down the slanted windows in sheets. Because of the observatory's overhang, Michael couldn't see the tower girders that were directly underneath, but the tower's outward spread revealed them further down. That was his first objective, but was it too far away? Michael estimated that the first girder he could see was about forty or fifty feet down—near the limit of his doubled-up electrical cord.

He looked up, shielding his eyes with a hand. A warning light was right above him, dark because of the power failure. Michael pulled the extension cord forward and started letting one end down. When he felt the tape marking the middle, he reached up and looped the cord over the light. Then he let the other end fall. It clattered and banged against the windows on the way down, but the sounds were quickly lost in the gale. Michael turned and looked down. The doubled-over yellow cable danced and swayed in the wind. He breathed a sigh of relief. The ends reached the steel girders below.

He took a deep breath and pulled in a long loop of cable, passing it between his legs, over his left hip, across his chest, over his right shoulder and down his back where he gripped it with his left hand. Rock climbers called this technique the dulfer, the simplest method of rappelling. Keeping the cable taut, Michael started pushing himself out over the precipice. The driving tempest finished soaking him. The gusting gale tugged and snatched, threatening to throw him down to his death.

Finally he was out, standing at a sixty-degree angle to the top of the observatory, his feet spread on the slick surface. His sodden clothes chafed, and water squelched in his running shoes. Michael steadied the cable with his right hand as he cautiously paid it out with his left. He walked down the plateglass windows as he left the security of the duct behind. He looked inside as he passed the observatory's upper level. He caught brief glimpses of the deserted interior through the sheets of water.

When Michael reached the bottom of the lower level, he stopped with his feet resting on the bottom of a window. He knew he wouldn't be able to reach the tower girders for about twenty feet or so. If he slipped off the window while still in the dulfer rig, the cable would flip him upside down, throwing him to his death.

Michael squeezed the soft rubber insulation with his right hand and tested his grip. As he hoped, the material was not slick even though it was wet.

* * *

Hasagawa looked up from the bomb's control panel and scanned the room. He stretched his legs to get the kinks out. He had considered sitting down to rest but decided not to. The mission was too important. Besides, it wouldn't be that much longer.

But a little exercise wouldn't hurt. He circled the front room, moving his arms about in graceful arcs. He glanced through the doorway into the back room. Hasagawa took a few more steps then stopped and returned to the door. The Stewart boy was missing!

He pulled his gun and stepped cautiously into the back room, looking about for possible ambush. All he could see was the woman, her daughter, and the ambassador's grandson. The other boy *was* gone! His eyes narrowed. And if the boy *was* gone, that meant they were all loose.

"Get up!" he ordered.

They sat there looking at him.

"Get up, or I will shoot her!" Hasagawa pointed his automatic at Leah.

Doris got to her feet and removed her gag. Leah and Matt did the same.

"Where is he?" Hasagawa demanded. He struggled for control as they stood there silent. "Tell me where he is, or I will kill you all! I will find him anyway. He cannot get out of the observatory." He aimed the automatic at Leah again and cocked the hammer.

"He's up in the ceiling," Matt blurted out.

Hasagawa's eyes darted to the stepladder and saw the missing ceiling panel. He released the automatic's hammer and set the safety. "Get down on the floor, all of you!"

He bound their legs and arms with nylon straps. He considered putting their gags back in then realized how ridiculous that was since the observatory was deserted.

Hasagawa got a flashlight from the front room and returned to the ladder. He climbed up until he was on the top step. He clicked on the light and searched the space above the false ceiling. The beam reflected off metal straps, pipes, and ducts. One large duct went all the way to the observatory's outer wall. And there, near the end, was a dark rectangle. Hasagawa tucked the gun into his waistband and stepped up onto the grid.

* * *

Doris watched their captor disappear. She was near panic as she struggled for control. Only minutes ago she had been worrying about where Michael was and if he was all right. Now this. She felt Leah snuggling up next to her.

"Mom, is Michael going to be OK?" Leah asked.

Doris felt the tears coming and had to fight not to break down completely. "That's in God's hands," she said.

Doris expected Leah to say something else, but she didn't.

Doris closed her eyes. What she had told her daughter was all that could be said. How this worked out God alone would determine. She shivered as she closed her eyes and began praying fervently.

* * *

Hasagawa stepped over the ceiling grid toward the open inspection hatch. Just before he reached it he slipped and jammed a foot through a ceiling panel. It fell into the room below as Hasagawa grabbed a pipe to keep from falling through. His balance restored, he pushed the flashlight into the duct and climbed in after it.

He could hear the sounds of the storm more clearly now. He turned the flashlight toward the opening and saw what looked like a solid wall of water. Hasagawa crawled forward until he neared the end, noting the grill as he passed it. Up ahead he could see something hanging down. He approached the edge cautiously. He stuck his head out into the downpour. The roaring wind thundered in his ears. Hasagawa brushed the hair out of his eyes and looked down, following the doubled-up extension cord downward. There, partway down, he could see a dark form clinging to it. It was the crazy American kid! Hasagawa pulled his gun, flipped the safety off, and cocked the hammer.

* * *

Michael went hand over hand down the cable, trusting in his grip to keep him from falling. The screaming gale blew him about, threatening to hurl him to his death. He squinted as the wind-driven spray stung his eyes. The cable swung about like a crazy pendulum. Michael couldn't see the ground, but he knew it was still a long way down.

A beam of light swept over him, illuminating the raindrops like silver bullets. Michael looked up into the glare. An icy jolt of fear shot through him as he realized the terrorist had found him. A yellow flash winked beside the light accompanied by the sharp crack of gunfire. On the second shot, Michael winced. This time he heard the lethal zip of the bullet as it passed.

Michael looked down. He was about ten feet from where the dangling cable banged against the tower girder. Michael loosened his grip and slid downward. The red steel structure rushed up to meet him. Michael knew he had only one chance to grab the girder. If he missed, he would fall all the way to the bottom. He let go and lunged, wrapping his arms about the vertical member. His momentum carried him a few feet farther down and around to the inside of the girder. Michael looked up. He could see a dim glare above him, but he couldn't see the flashlight beam itself. He breathed a sigh of relief. He was out of sight.

* * *

Hasagawa continued to play the flashlight beam over the girders below. After his last shot, he had seen the boy fall. Then a strong gust had whipped spray into his eyes, forcing him to blink. When he opened his eyes, the only thing he saw was the electric cable banging against the tower. He hadn't heard a scream but decided the wind must have carried it away.

Hasagawa breathed a sigh of relief. This threat was now past, not that the boy could have reached the bottom anyway. But now he was sure.

He started to back into the duct when he saw the cable swaying about in the gale. He almost left it alone but finally decided he didn't want this reminder of his failure left hanging there. Hasagawa reached up, lifted the cable off the light support, and let it drop.

* * *

Michael saw the cable start dropping and knew what had happened. He reached out and grabbed it as it flashed past, holding on as the cable flopped about and banged against the girders on its way down. The cable almost tore free of his grip as the slack disappeared. His heart thudded in his chest as he pulled his lifeline back up.

Michael looked down the long, sloping girders that formed the main outer support of one of the tower legs. He followed the curving red metal until it was lost in the driving rain below. The girders were large and

offered ample surface for rappelling. Michael squinted against the slanting rain. Being on the lee side meant that much of the typhoon's force was
broken by the tower structure. Now that he was below the observatory,
this made a lot of difference. Michael shivered as he realized it probably
made the difference between life and death.

He looked up and saw a dark warning light attached to the girder
above him by a round metal post. Michael gathered up the cable until he
found the tape. He looped the cable over the post and pulled it between
his legs, around his seat, and over his shoulder and back. Looking upward
one more time, he came around to the outside of the girder, planted his
feet, and started down.

* * *

Fear stabbed Doris's heart when she heard the gunshots. She fought
against tears as she continued praying for her son. Soon she could hear
the sounds of their captor returning. Moments later he stepped down
onto the ladder and descended.

He was drenched down to the waist. He smoothed back his black hair
as he stood there, the flashlight in one hand and his automatic in the
other. Satisfaction overlaid the look of raw hatred in his eyes. Doris
shivered.

"The boy is dead!" he told her.

Doris broke down completely, tears streaming down her face as she
sobbed. Leah bawled as she squirmed against the nylon straps. Doris
longed for some comfort for herself and her daughter, but there was none.

The terrorist glared at them for a few moments then returned to the
front room.

Doris closed her eyes as she continued to cry. *Why did the terrorist have
to check on us when he did?* she wondered. *Why not later when it would*

have been too late to stop Michael? But, then, is the man really telling the truth? Or could he be mistaken? A fresh wave of tears came. There was no way she could know, and wishful thinking was not the same as cold hard facts.

Another thought came. Doris knew she should pray, but for a time her misery would not let her. Then, as exhaustion came, she gave in.

20

Finding Help

Don watched Saeki as he guided the boat through the busy harbor. Angry waves rose and fell, tossing them about, pushed along by the howling winds. The boat plowed into a wall of water, throwing tons back toward the bridge. Don struggled to maintain his footing. The wave surged past, making the windows go black for a moment. If Saeki was concerned, he didn't show it.

"Wonder how much worse it's going to get?" Fred asked.

"This is only the beginning," Okawa said. "The front edge of the typhoon will be crossing the coast in the next hour or two. Then you will see something."

"I can wait."

Don looked down at the radar screen. There were many bright spots on the display, ships anchored or docked in the bay. One was dead ahead. Don glanced at the scale indicator and estimated the range to be around five hundred meters.

"Is that the *Tennessee?*" he asked.

Okawa asked Saeki something in Japanese and got a reply.

"He says it is," Okawa said. "And so far, we seem to be the only boat out."

Don looked out at the tossing waves, wondering if he was right about the target.

* * *

Michael felt the end of the cable with his left hand and stopped. It was time to retrieve his lifeline and get set for his next rappel. He glanced down but still couldn't see the bottom. The wind roared through the tower and threatened to knock him off the girder. The rain pelting him felt like rocks. His drenched clothes chafed with every move.

Michael looked up and saw a light a few feet above. He pulled himself up to it and stepped onto a horizontal beam. Wrapping his arms around the vertical girder, he pulled one end of the extension cable, watching as the other end snaked up and away. A few moments later it came flying down. Michael held tight to make sure it didn't jerk free. He hauled the cable back up until he found the midpoint. He looped it up over the post holding the warning light and arranged his rappelling rig again.

He swung himself around the vertical leg girder, spread his feet and started down again, paying out the cable with his left hand. The wind tore at him as it blasted through the steel skeleton of the tower.

He had gone about fifteen feet when a powerful gust hit him from the side. Despite a desperate struggle, Michael fell sideways off the girder. His upper body weight immediately flipped him upside down. The cable started slipping through his right hand. He brought his left hand around and grabbed the wire in an attempt to arrest his fall, but he was moving too fast. He gripped the cable harder, hoping he could stop when he reached the plugs on the ends.

He stopped with a jerk when the heavy plugs smacked into his fists. But he was at the very end, and he could feel one of the cable ends working out of his grip. He squeezed harder, but it kept slipping. It popped free suddenly and went rocketing upward. Michael screamed as he fell like a rock.

He looked down through the driving rain. A red horizontal beam raced up at him. Michael twisted in midair and planted his feet squarely on the slick metal. He fell on his face and wrapped his arms around the beam.

In a flash of insight, he realized he still held one end of the cable. The rest of it was rocketing down now and would tear free of his grip unless he acted quickly. He wrapped the end around the beam several times and held on. The loose wire snaked past and fell into the void below, stopping with a snap. Michael clung to the girder for several minutes as his scare wore off.

Finally he hauled the cable up and worked his way across to the leg girder he had fallen from. He found a light and set up his rappelling cable once more. The buffeting from the wind was worse than ever. He started down the girder again. He nearly slipped off again, but he recovered and made it down to the cable's limit. He brought down the line, placed it over a light, and continued what seemed an endless descent.

Sometime later he caught a glimpse of the building nestled under the tower. The leg girder continued to flare outward. Michael looked down but still couldn't see the ground. After several more rappels he finally saw a square concrete post. Relief surged through him as he realized it was the tower leg foundation. He was almost there.

Michael jumped the last few feet onto the large, flat surface. He closed his eyes and said a silent prayer for his deliverance. He walked to the edge and looked down. He saw the sidewalk was about ten or twelve feet below. Michael looped the cable around a girder and lowered himself to the ground.

Michael ran through the downpour to the street and looked around. He couldn't see any traffic, so he started running. The wind was even stronger now, forcing him to lean into it. He reached a major street and looked both ways. He could see the lights of a few vehicles through the sheets of rain, standing out against the surrounding blackout. But none of them were coming his way.

Then he remembered the subway they had taken on their visit to the Tokyo Tower. He turned in the direction he thought it was, but with the blackout and the storm he was far from sure. He had struggled down several blocks before he saw anything familiar. Then, up ahead, he spotted the dark stairway leading down. *Oh, great!* he thought. *The subway won't be running with the power out.*

He approached the steps, then looked down and saw a dim, flickering light. He ran down the steps. At the bottom he paused to look around. The feeble illumination came from emergency lighting mounted on the walls. Hundreds of people stood around in tight groups.

A sudden thought came to Michael. How in the world could he explain the horror of the bomb—who would believe him? But unless he got help, and got it soon, Tokyo would become a cinder.

A man standing a few feet away was looking at him. Michael ran up to him.

"Help! I need the police!" he shouted, out of breath.

"Police?" the man asked, obviously confused.

A woman came over. "Is something wrong?" she asked, her English better than the man's.

"Is there a policeman down here? It's an emergency!"

"Yes. I saw an officer a short while ago." She looked around. "Over that way. Come with me."

She led him deeper into the subway station. Up ahead Michael saw a man in a uniform standing underneath an emergency light. The woman said something in Japanese as they got close.

"You require assistance?" the policeman asked, his English not quite as good as the woman's.

Michael took a deep breath. "Some men have my mom and sister—and Matt Porter."

"Where?"

"Tokyo Tower." Michael paused. "They also have an atomic bomb up there."

"What are you saying?" The man looked at the woman, then back at Michael.

"Please! You've got to do something!"

"Give me the names," the man said, pulling out a small note pad.

"We don't have time for this!" Michael shouted.

"Calm yourself."

Michael's mind raced. "Listen, my dad's name is Don Stewart! He was working with Mr. Okawa in the police department! Call him!"

"Toshiro Okawa?"

"I guess. I don't know his first name."

"Give me your name, and the names of your mother and sister."

Michael did so.

"One moment." The man pressed the transmit button on his radio and reported. After a rapid exchange in Japanese, the officer turned to Michael. "Please to come with me. They are sending a car for you."

Michael followed the man out of the station and back up the steps. They didn't have long to wait. A car rounded a corner, emergency lights flashing. The driver pulled up at the curb and opened the passenger door.

"You are Michael Stewart?" the officer asked.

"Yes."

"Get in."

The policeman pulled away from the curb. He flipped his emergency lights on as he roared through the wind and rain.

* * *

Okawa gave the mike back to Saeki and said something in Japanese. Then he turned to Don. "The police have Michael."

"Where is he? Is he all right? What about Doris and Leah?"

Okawa gripped his arm. "Please. He is OK. He told the policeman that the atomic bomb is in the Tokyo Tower observatory. The terrorists are holding your wife and daughter in a construction site on the second level. They have Matt Porter there as well."

"Take me back!" Don said.

"Calm yourself. That is where we are going now."

"Take me with you!" Don saw compassion in Okawa's dark eyes.

"Yes, of course."

Saeki maneuvered the boat up to the dock. The waves were higher now. The captain spun the wheel and worked the throttles as he made the dangerous approach. The deckhand darted out into the tempest and made his way forward, leaning against the wind. The first attempt to throw the line ashore failed. The man pulled it back in and tried again. This time the man on the dock caught it and tied it up.

Okawa waited until the docking was complete then led the way out on deck. Don ducked his head as the gale hit him full force. Water streamed past the collar of his raincoat and finished soaking his shirt. He squinted against the stinging spray as he fought to maintain his balance on the tilting deck. The deckhand held the gangplank in place. Okawa and Sawara went first, then Don and Fred. They hurried up the stone steps and got in the car.

Sawara drove them through the flooded streets. Okawa picked up the radio mike and spoke in rapid Japanese. When he was done he turned around.

"The policeman who found Michael is returning him to the tower. We will meet them there."

"What about Doris and Leah?" Don felt an inner nudge reminding him of something. "And Matt Porter?"

"Please, I am working on that."

"Sorry."

"The district around the tower is blacked out, so I have called in the maintenance supervisor. He will start the emergency generators so we will have power."

"You're going in to get them?"

"I see no other way."

"But . . ."

"Stewart-san. I will do everything I can to rescue your family. You must trust me."

Don felt the heat rise in his face. He knew Okawa was right, but somehow he couldn't turn loose of his fear.

After what seemed a long trip, but had only been a few minutes, Sawara pulled up behind another police car. A door popped open in the car ahead, and Michael jumped out. Don threw his door open and got out. His son ran into his arms. Don hugged him as he thanked God.

"Are you all right?" Don asked as he released Michael.

"Yes, but Mom and Leah are still up there. And they have an atomic bomb."

"Yes, I know."

"Come with me," Okawa said.

They leaned against the wind as they staggered toward the building underneath the tower. A trash container bounded across in front of them before disappearing into the storm. A policeman stood by the entrance. Don and Michael followed Fred in. Okawa waited for them at the elevators. The indicator lights suddenly winked on. One set of elevator doors opened, and a man stepped in, inserted a key, and turned it.

"I think we are ready," Okawa told Don. "We have restored power to the elevators, but nothing else." He gave a command in Japanese, and two uniformed policemen joined him and Sawara.

"Take me with you!" Don said.

"No, it is too dangerous. You must leave this to us."

"What if you have to disarm that bomb?"

Okawa hesitated. "You know how to do that?"

"Larry Best told me how they're made." Don knew this was a stretch, but he was desperate.

"Very well. But stay back."

"I want to go!" Michael said.

"Stay here," Don said. He saw his son's pleading eyes and understood. A lump developed in his throat. "You did your part, son. You escaped and came and got us." He paused. "I'm proud of you, Michael."

Michael nodded and looked down.

"Come, Stewart-san."

Don glanced at Fred. He wanted his young friend along but knew Okawa would never stand for it. Don turned and entered the elevator. One of the policemen turned the key and pressed the button for the observatory. The elevator started up, shuddering as the typhoon's winds beat against it. Water streamed down the windows, blurring what little they could see of the city through the gloom.

They were about halfway up when Don reflected on what he had said to Okawa. He knew little more about atomic weapons than Okawa did, and he obviously knew nothing at all about what the terrorists had built. But his claim had gotten him included in the assault team. He only hoped he would not be called on to disarm the thing.

The elevator reached the observatory's lower level, and the doors opened. Dim emergency lighting greeted them. Don followed the policemen as they took the stairs to the second floor. They paused at the top, then slowly approached the temporary wall. Okawa and Sawara pulled their automatics. The policemen stood back, cradling submachine guns with long magazines.

Okawa stepped close and examined what he could see of the electrically operated bolt. He turned to one of the policemen and outlined where it was with a finger. The man nodded and approached as Okawa backed away. The officer quietly cocked his gun and flipped the safety off. He took careful aim and held the trigger down, jerking the barrel around in a tight arc. The slugs tore through the wood framing, stitching a semicircle around the bolt.

The moment the firing stopped, the other officer hit the door with his shoulder. It crashed inward and banged against the wall. The other officer rushed in, followed closely by Okawa and Sawara. Don raced through, looking all around. He heard something off to the left and whirled around.

A man was standing behind a large black box. He shouted something in Japanese as he started bringing a gun up. Okawa fired one time. The terrorist staggered backward, dropping his gun. He fell forward and clutched the box. He did something Don couldn't see, then collapsed on the floor. Okawa ran over to the man, covering him with his gun. Then he glanced at the box.

"Stewart-san! Come here!" he ordered.

Don rushed to the box and looked down. Icy fear stabbed him in the gut as he saw the red countdown display. He examined the control panel, noting the brass key and several lights and buttons. All the labels were in Japanese.

"He's obviously armed the bomb!" Don shouted. *"Oh, God! What do I do now?"* he prayed urgently.

"Do something!" Okawa said.

"What does this say?" Don pointed to the key.

Okawa looked. "It is set to 'manual.' The position next to it is 'ready' and the one beyond that is 'off.'"

"What about these?"

"The illuminated button says 'start.' The red light says 'link active.'"

Don turned the key to ready and then to the off position. The countdown continued. The large red display read 2:09. *Two minutes to atomic disintegration.*

"It won't turn off!"

"Stand back!" Okawa ordered.

Okawa said something to one of the officers in Japanese. The man approached and aimed at the box with his submachine gun. Don thought about what was inside, wondering how it was fused and whether this might make it go off. A thought occurred to him. Higher impact seemed safer.

"Hold on!" Don said.

"Move out of the way!"

The flashing red numbers read 1:44.

"Okawa-san!" Don shouted. "Can your men blow out one of the observatory windows?"

"What?"

"Impact with the ground is more likely to stop this thing! Now, can they do it?"

"The glass is very strong, but I think so."

"Do it!"

Okawa gave the order.

Don pushed on the box. It was heavy, and it took effort to get it rolling. He strained as he guided it toward the door. He glanced down as he reached it. The countdown read 1:17. He stopped and watched as the officers aimed at the closest window.

"Hurry up!" he shouted.

Both men pulled their triggers at the same time. The glass exploded into tiny particles. The wind and rain roared in through the jagged hole. Don took a deep breath and started forward with the box, pushing as hard as he could. Faster and faster it rolled across the floor. The window loomed ever larger, like some black hole about to suck him in. Don gave one final shove, then turned aside to avoid going out after it.

The castors banged against the window's lower frame. The box's momentum caused it to pivot forward on the front wheels. Don knew it was close to tipping over but the box stopped just short. It hung there for a moment, then crashed back to the floor.

"Push it out!" Don shouted.

He ran up behind the box as Okawa and Sawara joined him. "Lift!" Don ordered.

He reached under the box, braced himself and pulled with all his strength. It lifted an inch and fell back.

"Again!"

The bomb started up again. Don pulled harder. It rose some more. Finally their burden lessened as the box neared the equilibrium point. It passed that point and tumbled out into the storm. Don staggered forward as he lost his balance. Okawa's arm shot out and grabbed him.

Don stepped away from the window to get out of the wind and rain. He waited to see if they were successful, but then realized he would never know it if they weren't.

The emergency past, he turned and ran back into the room. He stopped and looked around. Seeing the door to the back room, he went on through.

"Don!" Doris sobbed. "Thank God you're here!" Tears streamed down, her face contorted in anguish.

He ran to her, knelt down, and buried his face in her hair. She shook as she cried. Don held her close.

"Daddy!" Leah wailed.

Don put his arms around her also. "It's all right now," he said. "And Michael's OK. He's waiting for us down at the entrance."

Doris looked up at him and broke down again. "The terrorist said he was dead," she said between sobs.

Don stroked her hair. "He's fine. He was the one who brought us here."

He reached into his pocket and gave her his handkerchief. It was drenched, but she took it anyway. "Thank God," she finally managed to say.

Don reached down and felt the nylon straps around her ankles.

Doris sniffed and hiccuped. "Some scissors are in that toolbox over there."

Don got them and freed her, then turned and cut the straps off Leah and Matt.

"You two all right?" he asked.

"Yes, Daddy," Leah replied, wiping her eyes with her hands.

"I'm OK," Matt said.

Don helped them up. He pulled Doris and Leah to him again, then remembered something. He looked toward Matt. The boy hung back.

"We're all in this together," Don told him.

Matt joined the circle and Don hugged him too. "You don't know how I've prayed for you." He saw Matt's wary expression. "Matt, if I had known you were kidnapped, I would have prayed for you too."

"Matt made all this possible," Doris said as she wiped away fresh tears.

"Oh?"

"The man guarding us forgot to tie him up. Matt cut us loose. When Michael decided to go for help, Matt helped him get away."

"Well, then we owe our lives to you," Don said. "Thank you."

"Uh, you're welcome," Matt stammered.

"Come on," Don said.

He held Doris's hand as they returned to the front room. Okawa and Sawara were waiting for them.

"Dear," he said to Doris, "this is Toshiro Okawa."

Okawa bowed in respect. "I am so glad we were in time, Mrs. Stewart. Do you need anything?"

She shook her head and started crying again. "No, we'll be OK." She wiped her eyes with the soggy handkerchief.

Okawa was clearly embarrassed. "Well, good." He turned. "Ah, so. You must be Matt Porter."

"Yes," Matt said.

"I will notify your grandfather of your safety when we get down."

Okawa looked at Doris and waved toward the man standing beside him. "This is my associate, Michihiko Sawara."

Sawara bowed.

"Thank you for saving us," Doris managed to say.

Okawa glanced at Don. "Please. I am in your husband's debt—and your son's. But, may I suggest we go down. We have much to discuss, but other things are pressing as well."

A radio crackled. Sawara held it up and replied. A few moments later he turned to Okawa and Don.

"We just found the bomb. The case is mangled, but the plutonium is still inside. The impact destroyed the triggering device."

Something that had been nibbling at the back of Don's mind finally jumped out. He remembered the "link active" light had been on. "I think we have a problem."

Okawa stopped and turned. "Oh? And what is that?"

"I think there's another bomb."

21

Driving to Shiohama

The boat's rocking motion was definitely worse now. The wind rattled the pilothouse windows as the rain pounded everything exposed. Moriya glanced at the bomb's control panel, then looked again. The "link active" light was out. He cursed.

"What does it mean?" Katsube asked, looking.

"How should I know? It is electronic. It could be anything. The radio probably failed."

"What do we do?"

Moriya was tempted to order Katsube to proceed alone, to set off this bomb manually. It was time for Moriya to be on his way. But the operation had been planned for two bombs. If the failure was in this radio, there was a spare back at the foundry and enough time to get it if he acted now. He grabbed a handheld radio and set it to the same frequency as the stationary unit mounted in the overhead.

"Call Isomura-san," Moriya said.

Katsube pressed a button on the intercom and gave the order. Rain drummed overhead as they waited. Isomura entered the pilothouse and closed the door against the gale.

"Is Unten-san standing watch below?" Katsube asked.

"He is."

"Monitor the radio while we are gone," Moriya ordered. "If there is any problem, notify me at once."

Isomura bowed. "I will."

"Come with me," Moriya told Katsube.

* * *

"Please explain," Okawa said.

Don's earlier relief melted away, replaced by deep dread as he became convinced their ordeal was not over. "Larry Best told me there was enough plutonium for several bombs. That red light said 'link active.' I think they made two bombs and linked them together by radio."

"Why?"

"Probably so they'd go off at the same time."

"Are you sure?"

"I don't see what else it could mean. If so, the Pikadon-ha still have one bomb—probably somewhere close to the *Tennessee*."

Okawa nodded. "I see. What about the destruction of the tower bomb? Do they know about it?"

"I'm sure they do. The 'link active' light was on. The other bomb probably has the same indicator. If it does, it's certainly off now." He paused. "Are your search teams still out?"

Okawa looked grim. "Yes. And, I think it is time to return to the boat."

"Don?" Doris said.

He turned. "Yes?"

"Matt heard the terrorists talking."

Don turned to the boy. "What did they say?"

"Mostly they talked about how to work the bomb. The big guy said they had to connect a radio to it by a cable. Then he explained how the key worked. He said to be careful once the bomb was armed."

"Anything else?"

"Yeah. I heard 'em use the word *pikadon*—that's how I knew it was an atomic bomb. And they said something about Shiohama."

"What is Shiohama?" Don asked.

"I think it's somewhere in Tokyo, but I don't know where," Matt said.

"It is an industrial district close to the harbor," Okawa said. "It is not far from where our boat is."

"Can we go by there on the way?" Don asked.

"Yes. Do you think the bomb is in Shiohama?" Okawa replied.

"I don't know, but it's certainly possible." Don thought a moment. "But I still believe a boat makes more sense."

"I will dispatch some patrols, but we can go by as well." Okawa motioned toward the elevator. "Please. We must be on our way."

The elevator shuddered and groaned as it carried them down to the entrance. Water streamed down the windows blurring the limited view. The elevator reached the first floor, and the doors opened.

"Mom! Leah!" Michael shouted as he came running.

He hugged them both, then turned to Matt. "Thanks for helping. We wouldn't have made it without you."

"Uh, you're welcome."

"Come, Stewart-san, we must go," Okawa said.

"What about my family and Matt?"

Okawa looked at Matt. "Porter-san will be taken to his grandfather, of course." He turned back to Don. "With your permission, I recommend your family go to my office. They will be safe there."

For how long, Don thought, but decided not to say. "I think that would be best."

A lump formed in his throat as he hugged Leah and Michael. "Be good, you two."

"We will, Dad," Michael replied.

"Yes, Dad," Leah said.

Don turned and kissed Doris. "Bye."

"Be careful," she said squeezing his hand.

"I will. Got to go."

She released his hand. Don maintained eye contact for a moment then turned and joined Fred as they followed Okawa and Sawara out of the building.

Okawa stayed busy on the radio as Sawara drove slowly through the flooded streets. The power outages were growing, and the lighted sections became increasingly rare. The car rocked as high winds buffeted them, throwing spray against the windows. Don wondered how Sawara was able to drive at all.

Don didn't know where they were, but every few streets they crossed a bridge. They had to be near the harbor. He looked out through his rain-blurred window. How would they ever find the terrorists in all this?

* * *

Moriya drove the van as fast as he dared, keeping his eyes on the signs and poles along the side of the street. The roadway was completely flooded. The truck made a wake like a boat as it plowed along toward

Shiohama. Its headlights provided what little light there was in the blacked-out section. Katsube sat beside him, not saying a word.

Moriya went over the problem again. Was it really the radio, and if so, was the bad unit at the boat or the tower? He considered the possibility that the police had found the other bomb. Raw hatred seethed inside him as he thought about it. But he finally rejected it as extremely unlikely.

Moriya slowed as he neared the next street, making sure it was the right one. He turned in between the two long buildings, drove to the side entrance and parked.

"Bring the light," he said.

Katsube picked up the flashlight and got out. Moriya heaved himself out and found the water came up over his shoes. He waded to the door and went up the steps. Katsube held the light while Moriya found the right key and opened the door. They stepped inside.

* * *

The policeman pulled up behind the small van and stopped. He had seen the truck go by and had followed with his lights out. He had stopped after the truck had turned between the buildings. After reporting, he had been ordered to approach the occupants and question them. The dispatcher assured him that a backup unit was on the way but would take some time to get there. The man thought it unlikely he had found the terrorists. He had already questioned three motorists.

The officer parked, reached for his flashlight, and got out. He squinted as the gale winds threw spray in his face. Rain forced its way past his raincoat collar, and he hunched his shoulders as he ran for the steps. The water splashed up over the tops of his boots. He paused at the top and checked the door. It was open. He drew his gun and made sure it was ready. He opened the door. Seeing a flickering light, he waited. When nothing happened, he dashed inside.

* * *

Moriya dropped the spare radio when he heard the door bang open. "The light!" he hissed.

Katsube turned off the flashlight, and the foundry was plunged into darkness. Moriya drew his automatic, cocked it, and flipped the safety off.

"Police!" came a shout near the door. "Come out!"

Moriya moved close to Katsube. "Do you know where he is?" he whispered.

"Near the door, I think, but I do not see him."

"When I call, aim your light at the door."

"But . . ."

"Do as I say."

Moriya crept to the side and took a few steps toward the door. When he was sure he was lined up he stopped.

"Come out or I will shoot!" the policeman ordered.

"Now!" Moriya shouted.

Off to his right, Katsube's flashlight clicked on. The policeman brought up a hand to shield his eyes and fired. Moriya took aim and squeezed off five shots. The officer groaned and pitched forward. Katsube's light clattered to the concrete floor and rolled to the side, throwing the room into deep shadow.

Moriya groped through the darkness. He tripped and tried to catch his balance but fell heavily. He crawled to the flashlight and grabbed it. He stood up and approached the downed policeman. He played the flashlight over the man and prodded him with a foot. The man was dead. Moriya turned the beam around. Katsube squinted into the glare, obviously in pain. Moriya felt momentary panic. Without Katsube, there was no one he could trust to carry out the mission.

"Is it bad?" he asked as he hurried over.

"Yes," Katsube wheezed.

He coughed. Blood gushed out of his mouth and pooled on the smooth concrete.

Moriya knew there was nothing he could do. "I am sorry, Katsube-san, but I must leave," he said.

"I know." Katsube coughed again and doubled up in pain. He shook as his lifeblood drained away.

Moriya turned off the flashlight, went to the door, and looked out. All he could see was an occasional dim glimpse of the pouring rain. Everything else was black. That momentarily relieved Moriya, but he knew someone would come looking for the policeman before long. He turned on the flashlight and got the radio.

Moriya returned to the door, tucked the radio under his raincoat, and stepped cautiously down into the flood. The wind shrieked as it blew the rain almost sideways. Moriya reached the van, opened the door, and slid in, setting the radio link on the seat. He wanted to sit and think, but he knew he didn't have time. He started the van and flipped on the windshield wipers. He considered what he had to do. Without Katsube, Isomura would have to replace him, which meant Unten would have to man the engine room. *Could he do it?* Moriya wondered.

He turned around and put the van in drive. Much as he wished to avoid it, Moriya reached down and turned the lights on. The white beams seemed feeble against the downpour, as the sheets of rain limited his vision to no more than twenty feet and often less. But without them, he could see nothing at all.

Moriya pushed the truck as hard as he dared, knowing if it drowned out or he had a wreck, he would have to walk. He reached the street and turned toward the harbor.

* * *

The policeman was getting concerned by the time he arrived at the abandoned foundry. He drove slowly between the two buildings, afraid of running into something submerged or ending up in a hole. Up ahead he could see the police car and something else. The side door to the building was standing open.

The officer parked behind the car and got out. He waded through the water and went up the steps. He pulled his gun and made sure it was ready. Holding his flashlight out to the side, he jumped into the building, almost falling as his boots slipped on the smooth concrete. His heart raced as he steadied himself and panned the light about the cavernous building. His light swept over a crumpled form. It was the other policeman.

The officer continued searching. He noted the other body and continued checking until he was sure there was no one else inside. Then he checked on the fallen policeman and found he was dead. The officer examined the other body and checked for identification. As expected, he didn't find any. He stood up, pressed the transmit button on his radio, and reported what he had found.

* * *

Don watched the two officers in the front seat. Sawara concentrated on his driving while Okawa kept the radio busy. Don tried to get comfortable but finally gave up. He was wet, the raincoat clung to him and the humidity in the car had to be 100 percent. He couldn't see much through the windshield except blurred rain illuminated by the headlights.

Sawara wiped the fog off the glass, but it came right back. The car shook as the winds buffeted it.

"You really think there's another bomb?" Fred asked.

"I'm sure of it," Don replied. "And if we don't find it soon, we're all going up in flames."

"How are we going to find them in all this?"

"I don't know. But we've got to try."

Okawa looked back. "Stewart-san. We just found two men dead in an abandoned foundry in Shiohama, one of my officers and an unidentified man. The officer who reported it says the place is empty now but shows signs it was in use recently."

"You think it's the bomb factory?"

"I think it likely. The foundry has been used recently, and the floor is covered with sophisticated machine tools. I have called in some experts, but I am sure they will confirm my suspicions."

"Is your officer sure the bomb isn't there?"

Okawa shook his head. "There is nothing there. He checked the building thoroughly."

"I guess that points to a boat."

"Could be a building close to the water," Fred suggested.

"That is possible," Okawa agreed. "But I agree with Stewart-san. I think a boat makes more sense."

"What do you plan to do?" Don asked.

"Return to our boat and continue searching. I have already directed our patrols to concentrate in this area."

Don sat back in the seat. He admired Okawa's determination, even though it seemed so hopeless. Don didn't know how this would work out, but resisting evil was the right thing to do. He felt the heavy weight of what they were up against, and it was staggering. But at the same time, he felt some inner reassurance. This he didn't understand, but he knew its source.

* * *

Isomura looked out the pilothouse windows toward the wharf. Most of the time he couldn't see it since the power was off. It was late afternoon now, and the thick clouds and heavy rain made it seem like midnight. All Isomura could see outside was varying shades of shadow. He had the top-side lights extinguished to make it just as hard for anyone approaching to see the boat. The only exception was the console lights on the bomb. He thought about the difficulty of navigating in the storm and was glad that responsibility belonged to Katsube.

He looked toward the north. For a moment he thought he saw something, a glimmer of light. He continued to stare until he was sure. There was a dim glow coming from the direction of the street which led to the wharf. Isomura hoped it was Katsube and Moriya. If it wasn't he knew it could mean trouble.

He looked at the boat's radio and was tempted to use it. But Katsube had said it was only for emergencies. Isomura knew what Moriya would do to him if he disobeyed. It should be the two of them returning, but what if it was the police? Isomura decided to take precautions.

He pressed the intercom button. "Unten-san. Start the engines."

"Tell me how to do it again."

Isomura cursed. "Go to the forward control panel. First turn on the ventilator fan and let it run for fifteen seconds. Then close both master switches and press the port engine starter button. When it catches, release it."

"Which side is port?"

Isomura gritted his teeth. "The left one! And do not start the starboard engine until the port one is running! Touch nothing else."

"One moment."

Isomura looked out at the wharf. The glow was brighter now, and it was approaching. He hoped Unten would remember the ventilation fan since an engine room explosion would be disastrous. He felt a vibration in the deck. *Good.* The port engine RPM gauge was registering a low idle speed. A few moments later the starboard gauge sprang to life as well. Isomura inched both throttles forward a little and saw both meters pick up. They were ready to cast off if they had to, which presented the next problem. It would be difficult to get underway with only two crewmen and no dockhand. Well, no point in worrying about that unless he had to, he decided. But, he had best be prepared.

He keyed the intercom again. "Come up here and bring a fire ax with you."

"Where do I find one?"

Isomura struggled for control. "See the locker that says *Fire*?"

"Yes."

"Look inside. There is an ax hanging from clips. Now get up here!"

A few moments later Unten opened the starboard pilothouse door and came inside. He stood there holding his ax as water streamed off his raincoat. The boat rolled and pitched, rubbing against the heavy rubber fenders.

"Is anything wrong?" Unten asked.

"Someone is approaching." Isomura pointed to the approaching glow. "If it is the police, we must get underway."

"Just the two of us?"

Isomura glared at him. "Do you see anyone else?"

He turned back to the dock. He knew it couldn't be Katsube and Moriya because the vehicle was moving very slowly, obviously searching. It was quite close now, but still difficult to see because of the rain. Then a searchlight came on, pointing a finger of light at the murky harbor waters. In a few more moments it would reveal the boat.

Isomura turned to Unten. "Go aft and cut the stern lines! They are doubled up so be sure you cut them all!"

The man started to move.

"Wait!" Isomura roared. "Listen! You must do exactly as I say or we die! After you cut the stern lines, go forward and stand by the forward lines, but do not cut them until I signal you! Understand?"

"How will I know?"

"I will give one blast on the horn. Have you got that?"

"Yes."

"Do it! Cut the stern lines now!"

Unten hurried out the port door and ran aft. Isomura shifted the starboard transmission into forward and advanced the right-hand throttle a little as he spun the wheel hard to port. He felt rather than saw the slack disappear from the aft lines. He opened the port door and looked aft. He thought he could see a shadow hunched over close to the rail. A few moments later he saw the stern start moving away from the dock. The blurry shadow hurried forward.

Isomura pushed the starboard throttle forward. The deck vibration increased and he heard the engine sounds pick up. The stern was swinging faster now. He gauged the moment, then hit the horn button. A deep bellow sounded overhead. Isomura pulled back on the throttle and turned the wheel back to amidships. He threw both transmissions into reverse. A quick glance at the dock told him the car had stopped. He thought he could see shadowy figures approaching. Isomura ran both throttles forward. The boat started backing into the storm-tossed waters of the harbor.

Isomura turned on the radar and regretted the boat did not have a Global Positioning Service (GPS) receiver. They were entirely dependent on his navigational skills and the radar, which was nearly useless as the typhoon intensified. Well, he would have to do the best he could. The pilothouse door rattled, and Unten came in. Isomura shifted into forward and turned the boat around. Soon they were heading out into Tokyo Bay.

22

Sayonara Shiohama

The radio crackled. "*Sayonara* Shiohama."

Moriya cursed. The coded message meant that Isomura was moving the boat to avoid capture. First the run-in with the police, now this. He felt the noose tightening about his neck, but he was not done yet. As long as Isomura evaded the police, all Moriya had to do was go to their alternate port, a floating dock in Kawasaki. The only problem was the time it took to get there in the middle of a typhoon.

He picked up the radio. "*Konbanwa* Shiohama," he said. Isomura would know that he understood and would meet him at Kawasaki. He smiled ruefully. *Good-bye Shiohama* and *good evening Shiohama* might not be sophisticated, but they did the job and didn't tell listening ears much. He regretted not fitting the boat with encrypted radios, but what was done was done. The important thing now was to finish the mission. And that Moriya was fully committed to doing. With Katsube dead, it was up to him.

Moriya turned to the northwest, deciding he didn't want to chance either the Rainbow Bridge or the Tokyo Port Tunnel. Although either of these would have been faster, assuming they were open, it would also be more dangerous. The last thing he needed was to be trapped by the police on an expressway. Water thundered against the underside of the van as he drove as fast as he dared through the secondary streets north of the harbor.

* * *

Sawara slowed down. Don assumed they were getting near the dock, but he couldn't tell from what little he could see. Howling gusts rocked the car and rain hammered on the roof. Okawa acknowledged a radio report and turned.

"A patrol reports a boat getting underway near Shiohama. They were in such a hurry, they cut the mooring lines."

"Do you think that was them?" Don asked.

"Seems very likely. The location is convenient to the foundry. I have alerted the other patrol boats."

"How many do you have out there?" Fred asked.

"Three, including Captain Saeki's boat."

"That doesn't sound like enough."

"It is a large harbor," Okawa agreed.

"Why did they go back to the foundry?" Don asked.

"Perhaps they forgot something," Okawa suggested. "My men are still investigating. Maybe the reason will turn up. But first we must find that boat."

Okawa parked the car, and Don opened his door. The wind tore it from his hands and whipped it around, breaking the hinges. He stepped into the water and tried to close the door, but it wouldn't budge. He followed

Okawa to the steps where Sawara and Fred waited for them. Down below the boat plunged and bobbed, fighting against the lines that held it to the dock. The deck lights were on, and a spotlight lanced through the rain, illuminating the dock and the steps leading down to it.

Don squinted against the driving rain and leaned into the wind. He followed Okawa down the slick steps. Once he had to reach out and steady the policeman when a savage gust threatened to hurl him off. Finally they reached the dock. Two deckhands motioned for them to come aboard as they struggled to keep the gangplank from being carried away. The deck tilted alarmingly as it rose and fell five or six feet with every wave.

Sawara went first. He timed his dash, and went across as the boat rose on a wave. The deck descended like an elevator just as he reached it. Sawara's feet flew out from under him and he tumbled into a winch. One of the deckhands helped him up. Okawa went next and managed to keep his feet. Don glanced at Fred. The young officer waited until the boat was on the way back up and ran for it. Don came right after him. They both slipped when they hit the slick deck. Okawa steadied Fred, while Don grabbed a cable lifeline.

The deckhands brought the gangplank aboard. Don felt the deck's vibration increase. One of the deckhands raced aft and took in the stern line after a man on the dock untied it. The stern swung outward as the deckhand went forward to receive the bowline.

Don followed Fred and the policemen up and into the pilothouse. Captain Saeki spun the wheel and worked the throttles, backing the boat away from the dock. He flipped off the deck lights. The blurry view of the foredeck winked out. Don held on as the boat took on an alarming rolling motion.

* * *

The van's lights picked out stalled cars up ahead. Moriya cursed. Two cars sat abandoned on the narrow street, blocking it. Both were lying at an angle, indicating an unseen hole in the street. He had no choice but to turn around.

Moriya retraced his path a block and took a side street. He turned northwest again at the next block, hoping to make up for lost time. Water peeled away from the van in waves as Moriya drove through the blacked-out section. He dodged another abandoned car, slowing as he passed.

Moriya saw headlights flick on behind him. He watched his rearview mirror as a murky white glow appeared. Moments later emergency lights started flashing.

Moriya pushed the van even harder. He slowed briefly at the next corner and turned to the right. The van bucked and bounced as it plowed through the hubcap-deep water. The police car made the turn behind him, not gaining but not falling back either.

Moriya knew he had to do something quick. He checked his automatic to make sure it was ready. Moriya saw the next corner approaching. He switched off his lights and turned left, judging it from memory since he couldn't see. A little farther he jammed on the brakes and turned hard to the right. The van slid, ending up pointing in the opposite direction.

Moriya watched the approaching glare. The police car rounded the corner, emergency lights flashing. Moriya rolled down his window, picked up his gun and aimed at a spot on the right-hand side above the headlights. He waited a few moments, then carefully squeezed off four shots. The police car lurched to the left and bounded up onto the unseen curb. It crashed through the plateglass window of a storefront, stopping suddenly.

Moriya flipped on his lights and roared away, spray flying. He turned back to the northwest at the next corner and resumed his course. After crossing the Sumida River he turned back to the south. Now all he had to do was drive through the city center, over the Tama River, and into Kawasaki.

* * *

The policeman groaned as he sat up straight. Windswept rain poured in through the shattered windshield. Pulverized safety glass littered the front seat and floor. Both headlights were out, but the emergency flashers lit the ruined restaurant with a garish light. The policeman snapped them off in irritation. He winced as pain shot through his left shoulder like a hot knife. He felt the area with his right hand. His fingers came away warm and sticky. For the first time he realized he had been shot. Pain washed over him, and he almost fainted.

He looked down at the radio. It seemed to be working. He lifted the mike with his good hand and called in.

* * *

Okawa hung up the mike and braced himself against the violent pitching and rolling of the boat. He turned to Don and Fred.

"One of my men was fired on near Chuo-ku," he said. "He was hit in the shoulder, and it caused him to wreck his car."

"Same people as at the foundry?" Fred asked.

"I am sure that is the case."

"Do you suppose they're trying to get back to the boat?"

"Yes. I believe the boat was waiting for them when we found it."

"So, if we could figure out where the boat is going . . ." Don said.

"That is what I was thinking," Okawa said. "The fugitives are going toward the north and west, which suggests they are heading for the western shore of Tokyo Bay."

"That covers a lot of territory," Fred observed.

"It does. But I think we can assume they would choose a rather run-down section, some distance from Shiohama but close enough to allow them to come back to the submarine."

"Where, do you think?" Don asked.

"Somewhere around Kawasaki."

* * *

Don gripped a bracket to keep from falling as the boat took a violent roll. Okawa was in the middle of a radio transmission in which he was mostly listening. Several times the policeman had looked at Don. He was not smiling.

"My office is holding a call from Ambassador Dewey," Okawa explained. "He insists on speaking to you."

Don took a deep breath. He should have expected this, he knew, but the urgency of finding Moriya and the other bomb had chased it from his mind.

"Is the radio secure?" he asked.

"It is."

"OK. Tell them to patch the call through."

Okawa gave the order and handed Don the mike.

"Mr. Ambassador, this is Major Stewart," Don said.

"Major, I'm calling from my residence, and Colonel Dill is here with me. I'm going to put us on the speakerphone." The radio's speaker made a twanging noise. "There. Can you hear me?"

"I hear you fine, Mr. Ambassador."

"Good. As I'm sure you know, the police were just here returning Matt to me." There was a long pause. "First of all, I want to thank you—and Michael—for all you did in finding and disarming that bomb—*and* for saving Matt's life."

"Only doing my job. However, I'm awfully proud of Michael. Without him, we'd all be dead now."

"I'm proud of him too—and grateful. However, what you did wasn't exactly your job."

Don glanced at Fred, who looked rather concerned.

"Mr. Ambassador, I considered giving Colonel Dill and you some excuse—I'm still on leave and decided to volunteer my time to Mr. Okawa—something like that. But, that wouldn't be honest. I know I was disobeying Colonel Dill's orders—your orders."

For a few seconds the radio remained silent.

"This incident is closed, Major," the ambassador finally said. "If you had *not* gone against orders, Tokyo would be in smoking ruins. But what I really meant was, you went above and beyond your duty. I appreciate it, and I'll make sure it's recognized in your service record."

"Thank you, sir. But, we have another problem."

"What's that, Major?" Allen asked.

"Colonel, we believe the Pikadon-ha have another bomb."

"What? Are you sure?" Even over the radio Don could hear his boss's voice go up several notches.

"Virtually positive. The terrorists had enough plutonium to build several weapons, and the controls on the one we found said it had a radio link."

"That's very bad news."

"There's more. The police have found the bomb factory. An officer apparently surprised at least two terrorists. The officer was killed, along with one of the terrorists. Another patrol discovered the boat we think is carrying the bomb, but it got underway before the police could stop it."

"That boat could be anywhere by now," Allen said.

"That's true, but Mr. Okawa thinks it's heading for Kawasaki. Another patrol was shot-up near Shiohama. If that was the terrorists, they're probably trying to get back to the boat. The direction they're going suggests a rendezvous somewhere on the western side of the bay."

"What are your plans, Major?" the ambassador asked.

"Sir, Mr. Okawa has three boats out looking for the terrorists, as well as shore-based patrols. I'd like to stay with him. We probably don't have much time."

"I agree. Is there anything we can do?"

Don started to say no. Then he thought of something that *might* help, but would the ambassador go for it? "I think there is, Mr. Ambassador. Could you get the *Tennessee* to help us?"

"Are you serious?"

"Yes, sir. That is one fancy boat. Do you think the navy would come through for us?"

There was a slight pause. Then Don heard the ambassador say, "Colonel Dill. I want the duty officer at the Joint Chiefs of Staff on the double!"

"Yes, sir," Don heard Allen say.

"Consider it done," Ambassador Dewey said. "Stand by for a call. If you don't hear in five minutes, call me."

"Yes, sir."

Don handed the mike back to Okawa.

"I like the way you work," Okawa said.

"It's not me, I assure you."

Fred tapped him on the arm. "Thanks for not mentioning my name."

Don grinned in spite of the situation. "I'll leave that to you, Lieutenant. But I don't think you're in much hot water." He paused. "Assuming we get out of this alive."

The boat plunged and tossed as Saeki continued to work his way into the heart of Tokyo Bay. Two minutes later a call came in. Okawa handed the radio mike to Don.

"This is Major Don Stewart."

"Major Stewart. This is Captain Richard Allender, commanding officer of the USS *Tennessee*."

"Good evening, Captain."

"You must travel in interesting circles, Major. The secretary of defense just called me and said I was to contact you ASAP. He said I was to give you all possible assistance—blank check. He said you would explain. What gives?"

Don grabbed a bracket as the boat took a roll. "Hold on to your hat, Captain."

"I'm ready. Shoot."

Don told him all that had happened, condensing it as much as he could. The *Tennessee's* CO didn't interrupt.

"I see," Richard said when Don finished. "What do you want me to do?"

"We need your help in locating the terrorists."

"I figured you didn't want me tied up at the dock. I'm already underway. What are we looking for, and what are your orders?"

Don blinked. He was giving a navy captain orders?

"Wait one," he replied as he turned to Okawa.

"I recommend Fred and I transfer to the *Tennessee* to coordinate their search. Do you have any objections?"

"No. You know what we are looking for, and their crew does not. I will miss you here, but I think you should do it."

"Can your people maintain this radio link with the sub?"

"I will see to it."

Don put the mike to his lips. "Captain, I want to transfer to your boat along with Lieutenant Fred Brown. Can we do that?"

"Affirmative, Major. Does your boat have GPS?"

Don looked at Okawa. "Do we?"

Okawa asked Saeki, then turned to Don. "Yes."

"That's a roger," Don said over the radio.

"Give me your coordinates."

Okawa got Saeki to write them down. Don transmitted them to the sub.

"Stand by," Captain Allender said. "We'll be alongside in a few minutes. *Tennessee* out."

"How are we going to do this?" Fred asked.

"We'll just have to see," Don replied. He had been wondering the same thing himself.

23

Aboard the *Tennessee*

The typhoon hurled the rain against the pilothouse windows so hard Don was surprised they didn't break. The boat rolled and plunged as it fought its way across the storm-tossed bay. It was inky black outside because Captain Saeki had doused all except the navigational lights.

Don picked up the mike when the *Tennessee*'s call came in.

"This is Major Stewart."

"If you've got a spotlight, shine it on your port beam."

Don saw that Okawa was already relaying this to Saeki. The captain flipped a switch. A brilliant light came on, illuminating the slanting downpour. As bright as it was, the beam reached out only a little way before it was swallowed up in the deluge. Saeki turned a handle. The beam rotated around to the left until it was at right angles to their course. There, just within the beam's range, rode a sinister black shape. The tall sail, with "734" painted in white letters, stood out clearly. The sub's decks were awash in the heavy seas.

"We see you," Don reported. He felt his stomach knot up. "How are we going to get aboard?"

"I'm sending a rubber boat for you. Recommend your captain come left to one-two-zero. Our radar shows a large ship dead ahead, range five hundred yards. We pinged it just to be sure."

Okawa relayed this to Saeki. The boat began a cumbersome left turn.

Okawa turned back to Don. "Saeki-san gives his thanks to the sub captain. He says the contact is not in an anchorage, so it must be a ship that has broken free of its mooring. We cannot see anything on our radar. The storm is filling the screen with false echoes."

Don nodded and pressed the mike button. "Thanks for the warning. We're turning now."

"Roger. Now, recommend you slow as much as you can. Tell your captain our boat will be coming up on his port side. We'll be pulling ahead a little to provide some lee shelter for you."

"Roger."

Saeki pulled the throttles back. Soon the boat was wallowing along with bare steerageway. Don traded looks with Fred. It was obvious the young officer was as worried as Don was. If the sub was providing any calming effect on the raging storm, it wasn't apparent.

"Recommend you gents start making your way aft," the radio speaker announced. "Our boat will be alongside by the time you get there."

"We're on our way," Don said. He handed the mike back to Okawa. "I'll call as soon as we're aboard."

"Good luck," Okawa said.

"Thanks." Don turned to Fred. "Are you ready?"

"After you, Major."

Don pulled open the pilothouse door and staggered into the full brunt of the howling wind. A mixture of rain and salt water pelted him as he made his way aft. He had to grab the lifeline repeatedly to keep from being thrown overboard. Saeki's searchlight illuminated the gap between the two vessels. A tiny black shape bobbed like a cork as it sped over and around the raging whitecaps. *We're going to ride in that?* Don wondered.

The inflatable boat came alongside and bounced against the larger boat's side. Three men in black wetsuits were inside, one operating the outboard motor, the other two ready to receive the officers.

"You first!" Don shouted against the howling wind.

Fred nodded, then stepped over the lifeline and stood on the boat's side. He hesitated a moment and jumped. The two sailors caught him as if he weighed nothing. They turned back for their next passenger.

Don stepped over the rail as he had seen Fred do, and turned toward the waiting sailors. He was surprised to see them waving him away and pointing forward. Don looked and for a few moments didn't understand. Then he saw it. A rogue wave rolled past the sub burying its bow. On came the wall of water. Don felt the deck vibration increase as the boat began a ponderous left turn into the wave. The sub began turning as well.

Don's veins seemed filled with ice water. He started climbing back over the lifeline. He got one foot over then the other and started forward. The black mountain of water reached the boat. The bow plunged into it, throwing tons of water over the exposed deck. Don watched helplessly as the flood raced aft. He grabbed a winch and held on. The angry torrent rolled over him, breaking his grip instantly. He bounced once against something hard, and then he was free, rolling around in the raging seas. Everything went black as the angry wave drove him down. He fought his way upward.

His head broke the surface, and he gasped for breath. Not seeing anything, he spun around. He caught a glimpse of the police boat, then it was gone. He couldn't see the rubber boat but knew the low black shape would be hard to see. A wave broke over him causing him to choke. He sputtered and coughed as he fought to stay up. The weight of his clothes and shoes made it hard to swim. He regretted not asking for a life belt before attempting the transfer.

Another wave covered him. This time he heard a faint whining sound. Again he surfaced. He felt something colder than the water when he realized he was tiring. *Did they abandon me?* he wondered.

Don caught a glimpse of something black and glistening. There was a splash, and he felt a powerful arm wrap around him from behind. Don turned his head. A navy swimmer was pulling him back to the rubber boat. They were close now. Fred looked over the side. He and one of the sailors reached over and pulled Don into the boat.

"Thought we had lost you," Fred shouted to be heard above the wind.

"I did too," Don replied.

The swimmer pulled himself up into the boat. The coxswain opened up the outboard. The tiny boat corkscrewed its way through the pounding seas. They rode up one large wave and became airborne. Don held on as they plowed into the following wave. Water poured over the bulbous bow, half-filling the boat.

A short time later Don caught sight of the sub. The huge black shape moved slowly through the water, its deck awash. The coxswain guided the boat up to the hull aft of the sail where other sailors awaited them. One of the swimmers moved close to Don.

"Come with me, sir," he shouted. "I'll help you aboard."

Don crawled forward on his hands and knees through the slopping water. The swimmer grabbed him by the arm and lifted him up.

"Jump!" the swimmer shouted, as he propelled Don forward toward the waiting sailors.

The first sailor grabbed Don and pulled him up on the deck. Two others hustled him to a vertical shaft leading down into the submarine. Don eyed the ladder warily.

One of the sailors leaned close. "No problem, sir! You can do it! Captain says to hustle!"

Don stepped onto the narrow ladder and started down. Below him he could see other crewmen waiting for him. He reached the deck and stepped out of the way. Fred came next, followed by the swimmers.

A chief took the air force officers to some lockers and outfitted them with dry underclothes and wash khaki uniforms. Don and Fred dried off quickly, dressed, and followed their guide to the sub's conn. Captain Richard Allender awaited them. He wore a khaki uniform with silver eagles on his collars and a blue baseball cap on his head.

"Welcome aboard *Tennessee,* gentlemen," he said. He turned to Don. "You must be Major Stewart."

"Yes, sir," Don replied.

"What kind of boat are we looking for?"

"Sort of like the one we were on. Okawa says it's a steel trawler about eighty to one hundred feet long."

"OK. You say you think they're heading for Kawasaki?"

"Yes, and we believe there's a terrorist driving down there to meet them."

"You know what this device looks like?"

"Yes, sir. We found its brother in the Tokyo Tower a little while ago."

"So, what do you want me to do?"

Don took a deep breath. "Locate the boat. Then help us disarm the bomb."

"Captain, incoming message," an enlisted man announced.

Captain Allender grabbed the mike. "USS *Tennessee.* Go ahead."

"Ah, Captain. This is Toshiro Okawa. May I speak to Major Stewart, please?"

The captain handed the mike to Don.

"Major Stewart here."

"We are ready to change course for Kawasaki. Please ask Captain Allender if he can check traffic for us. Our radar is useless."

"Wait one." He turned to Allender but saw the other was already working on it.

Allender turned to his officer of the deck. "Mr. Foster. Do you have the police boat?"

"Yes, Captain. Bearing two-zero-four, range three hundred yards."

"I need a radar report from his position to Kawasaki, and go to active sonar. I want to know everything that's out there."

"Aye, aye, sir." The officer gave the orders.

A few moments later he turned to the captain. "Captain. Radar and sonar indicate clear all the way to the point, except for that contact we plotted earlier. It's moving west slowly so it could be a ship adrift in the storm."

"Does it present a threat to the police boat?"

"No, sir. They should pass to the east of it. Captain, we also got a couple of spooky returns near that drifting contact, but the operator thinks they were caused by the storm. The radar plot is fading fast. We're going to be blind before long."

"Very well." Allender turned to Don. "You heard what he said. Pretty soon it's going to be blind man's bluff."

Don picked up the mike and reported to Okawa.

* * *

Isomura concentrated on his compass and engine rpm gauges. They were traveling completely dark without even navigational lights. This made the boat hard to see, but it also made Isomura nearly blind. All he could see were varying shades of dark shadows. The radar offered no help since its screen was a solid green glow from reflections off the angry waves.

Isomura was using dead reckoning to guide the boat to Kawasaki, depending on a known course and speed. But the boat's motions made even the gyrocompass unreliable, and he knew the winds and waves were causing him to drift. He had allowed for that, but it was only a guess. He didn't know exactly where he was but hoped he was clear of the nearby anchorages.

Isomura caught a glimpse of a red light that quickly winked out. Then he saw it again and knew what it was—a vessel's port navigational light. Icy fear raced down his spine and he spun the wheel to the right and pulled back the throttles. A dark slab of hull materialized out of the murk right in the boat's path. It was a supertanker, and from its position Isomura guessed it had broken free of its mooring.

The boat came around sluggishly. The towering hull came closer and closer. Isomura knew a collision was inevitable; the only question was whether it would sink the boat. He thought about warning Unten but decided he didn't have time. The boat's bow crashed into the tanker. The deck under his feet jumped as the shock rippled through the hull. The bow bounced away, and the boat hit again, this time amidships and harder. The scream of tortured metal carried clearly over the howling winds. The hull shook and vibrated as the two vessels parted.

"What happened?" Unten's frantic voice came from the intercom.

Isomura centered the wheel and advanced the throttles to maintain steerageway. He watched the tanker's hull as it slid past.

"We hit a tanker," he said.

"I am coming up there!"

"No! You must stay where you are. Is there any flooding down there?"

"Are we sinking?"

"Stop it! Go around the engine room. Look for signs of flooding or anything unusual."

"But . . ."

"Do it!"

Isomura checked what he could while he waited. The boat seemed on an even keel, as much he could tell, and the engines were running smoothly. He tried several gentle turns. There was no problem with the steering gear. Maybe they had been lucky.

A few minutes later Unten reported. "No flooding that I can see."

"I think we are all right," Isomura said, hoping to reassure Unten.

"I want to come up there."

Isomura struggled with his anger. "No, Unten-san. I need you in the engine room. If anything happens down there, you are the only one that would know. Our mission depends on you."

"I will stay, then. Where are we?"

Isomura had other things to do but decided appeasing Unten was better than a mutiny. "Nearing Kawasaki. We should reach the dock before long."

The intercom remained silent. Isomura relaxed a little until he remembered he still had to find the dock, without being detected by the police. *That* would not be easy, but it had to be done. Moriya was depending on him.

* * *

Moriya drove over the secondary roads in Kawasaki, looking for the turn that would take him down to the floating dock. His trip had been hard and had required many detours, but now it was almost over. The spare radio was beside him, almost forgotten in all the trouble required to get it.

He turned as he came to the small shipyard. His headlights provided the only illumination as he drove down the blacked-out road. On either side sat boats in varying stages of construction and repair. He heard a metallic twang behind him and heard something fall. He looked in the rearview mirror and thought he saw something lying across the road.

Up ahead, Moriya saw a steel pier and the marine railway used to pull boats out of the water. He slowed to a crawl and watched for the narrow side road. Spotting it, he turned left and drove behind a long building to where the road ended. A long floating dock extended into the secluded inlet, its end hidden by the rain.

Moriya grabbed a flashlight and got out. The wind blew spray into his face and tugged at his raincoat as he walked toward the shore. The dock sections, supported by steel drums, danced up and down on the angry waves. By the time Moriya reached the midpoint, the dock was rising and falling more than five feet. He had trouble staying on his feet.

Finally he reached the end. The boat was not there. He thought about returning to the van, but then he would not see the boat when it arrived. He decided to wait.

* * *

Don heard the familiar voice over the speaker. Captain Allender handed him the mike.

"This is Major Stewart. Go ahead."

"I just received a message from the harbormaster," Okawa said. "A supertanker broke free from its mooring about a half hour ago. The captain reports that an engine room casualty prevents him from getting underway. A few minutes ago the captain radioed again, reporting a collision with a boat. By the time he got to the bridge wing, the boat was almost out of sight. The description fits the one given by our patrol near Shiohama."

"Sounds like the terrorists," Don replied. "You're closer than we are. Can you intercept?"

"I am not hopeful. The boat should be quite close to Kawasaki by now. We will start checking the docks when we get there, but this will take time."

"What do you want us to do?"

"Standby off Kawasaki. If they are going in to pick up their friends, they will be coming out again."

"Will do. *Tennessee* out."

Don handed the mike back to Captain Allender.

24

At Kawasaki

Isomura kept a sharp lookout for the point of land, knowing what would happen if he ran aground. He periodically flipped on the searchlight for a few seconds to check for obstacles, hoping the police would not see it. The boat's rolling motion was worse now, prompting Isomura to order Unten to check it out. The intercom crackled.

"I did what you said," Unten finally reported. "The bilges have nearly a meter of water in them."

Isomura cursed under his breath. There had to be a hole in the hull. He had been afraid of that.

He pressed the intercom button. "Listen carefully. You must start the bilge pump."

"How?"

"Look toward the forward bulkhead near the ladder that goes up on deck. See the box that says 'auxiliary systems'?"

"Yes."

"Open the cover and look in the lower left corner. There is a red button that says 'bilge pump.' Press it. The green light below it should come on. If it does, it is running."

"Let me check."

A few moments later he was back. "It is on. Is there anything else?"

"No. I will check the damage after we dock. Meanwhile, stand by down there."

That was one worry out of the way. The one that remained was how he was going to dock in this storm and whether Moriya would be there when they arrived.

Isomura flipped on the searchlight again. He thought he saw something off to the right. He turned the beam in that direction and saw a dark shadow barely above the waves. It was a point of land, but was it the right one? A few minutes later he was sure. Now all he had to do was make his way through the maze of inlets, piers, and jetties until he found the shipyard's floating dock.

Isomura debated on what to do next. He didn't want the engine room abandoned, but he needed help in docking. He spoke over the intercom, "Unten-san, I need you up here!"

"What about the engine room?"

"Leave it! I cannot dock the boat alone."

Isomura pulled back on the throttles. A few moments later Unten entered the pilothouse. Isomura trained the spotlight straight ahead.

"Take the wheel," he said. "I am going to prepare new lines."

"But . . ."

"Take it!"

Unten did so.

"Now, keep us in this channel, but do not touch anything else! I will be back shortly."

Isomura buttoned his raincoat and stepped out on deck. The wind howled around the superstructure threatening to throw him down. Rain thundered off every surface. The boat's motion was less now, but still quite alarming.

He hurried aft and opened a locker. He reached inside and grabbed two nylon lines to replace the ones they had cut at Shiohama. He attached one to a stern cleat and took the other line forward. After tying that one he returned to the pilothouse.

"Stay up here with me," Isomura said as he took over the wheel and pushed the throttles forward. "When we dock, you must throw the lines to Moriya-san."

"I understand."

Isomura hoped that he did. He played the searchlight about the narrowing spit of land. Then he thought he saw his turn point. He throttled back again and turned the wheel to the right. He drove the boat along with bare steerage way, ready to come about if he was wrong. To his surprise, the landmarks looked right. A little farther on he was sure. He cleared a long building standing on pilings and looked to the left. There was the floating dock.

As he got closer, he saw the dark shape standing on the end. He hoped it was Moriya, but knew it could hardly be anyone else. He saw something else as well. Secluded or not, the dock was moving around—a lot.

"Go up forward and take the line," Isomura ordered. "When we are close enough, throw it. Then take care of the aft line."

Unten left the pilothouse and made his unsteady way out onto the forward deck on the port side. He picked up the coiled rope and waited.

Isomura turned sharply toward the dock knowing the winds were pushing him toward it. He waited until the last moment, then engaged reverse on both engines and pushed the throttles all the way forward. The diesels roared and the deck shook as the propellers dug into the water. Unten threw the line. Moriya caught it and tied them up. Unten raced aft while Moriya followed on the dock.

Isomura brought the throttles back to idle and waited. The stern started swinging into the dock. Isomura turned the wheel full right and ran the port engine up to full reverse. The swing toward the dock slowed. He opened the pilothouse door and looked aft. Unten threw the line, and Moriya made it fast. The boat bumped against rubber fenders on the dock. For a moment Isomura was afraid the impact would break the dock's anchors, but they held.

* * *

It had been a long day, and it was not over yet. When asked by his supervisor, the policeman had, of course, accepted the double shift. With the whole force looking for the terrorists, he couldn't have done otherwise. He shivered as he thought about what would happen if they didn't stop these people.

But the man felt totally useless. He had been close to the waterfront in Shiohama when the dispatcher had ordered him to back up the unit at the bomb factory. But another unit beat him there. Then had come the report of the boat escaping. Checking the location, the policeman figured out *he* would have found the boat, had he continued his earlier patrol. Of course, he didn't know if he could have stopped the terrorists, but he would have tried.

After this had come the firefight with the other patrol. Then the dispatcher had ordered him down to Kawasaki, through nearly impassible streets. This seemed another pointless task.

The man knew from his radio that Okawa wanted all the out-of-the-way docks checked, and he had his list. The first one he hadn't been able to find. Now he was on his way to a small shipyard. That this would be equally futile, he had no doubt.

The policeman slowed when his headlights revealed a light pole across the narrow road. He pulled up to it, stopped and got out. Fortunately the pole was made of aluminum. He picked it up and moved it out of the way. Getting back in his car, he continued through the shipyard until he saw a pier ahead with a marine railway on the right. He drove past a path on the left.

Just before he reached the pier his left front wheel dropped into an unseen hole. The car lurched to a stop, throwing the policeman against his shoulder belt. He put the car in reverse. The engine screamed but nothing happened. The man grabbed his flashlight and got out. He leaned against the raging wind and lowered his head to avoid the driving rain. He staggered around the front of the car and pointed his flashlight down. The bottom of the car rested on the pavement. There was no way he would get out without a tow.

The man turned around slowly, panning the flashlight about. The shipyard was a cluttered, untidy thing, with rotted hulls and large piles of rusting junk amid the boats undergoing overhaul. Thoroughly discouraged, he decided he would continue his search on foot.

He radioed his status to the dispatcher. Rain trickled past his raincoat collar as he closed the car door and started walking toward the pier. He shivered in discomfort. His flashlight picked out many boats, but most were too small, and the larger ones were obviously unmanned. Reaching the end of the pier, he stared back.

* * *

Moriya waited impatiently as he watched Isomura and Unten struggle with the gangplank. Finally they swung it over the side and settled it into place, holding it while Moriya rushed aboard and followed Isomura into the pilothouse while Unten returned to the engine room.

"What happened?" Moriya asked.

"Police spotted us," Isomura said. "I barely had time to get away."

Moriya felt his anger rising. "They are getting close. The police found the factory while I was there. They killed Katsube-san."

"I am sorry."

"He gave his life for our cause."

"Yes," Isomura said with a shallow bow.

Moriya glanced at the bomb, feeling a reassurance at its presence. He looked back at Isomura. "I was beginning to wonder if you would make it. Did you have any trouble?"

"Unfortunately, we did. We collided with a tanker."

"What? How could that happen?"

"It was adrift in the channel—apparently it broke loose from its mooring. I had no warning. The radar is useless in this storm."

"Do you think they reported it?"

"I am sure they did. We hit hard. I think we have a hole somewhere on the port side. Unten-san said we have almost a meter of water in the bilges."

Moriya felt anger surging up inside and struggled to contain it. "Will the boat sink?"

"I think not. I have the bilge pump running. I was going to check the damage after we docked."

Moriya followed him to the rail and looked over as Isomura played the flashlight beam over the battered hull. Then Moriya saw it, a jagged hole several feet above the waterline. He knew it would be submerged much of the time out in the bay.

"Can we go out?" Moriya asked.

"Yes. I think the bilge pump can handle it. Are you ready to leave?"

"As soon as I get the radio."

Moriya started back to the shore.

* * *

The policeman trudged past his car, searching about with his flashlight. He reached the path he had seen earlier and looked down it as far as the light went. It looked wide enough for a vehicle, but just barely. Since he couldn't expect a tow truck any time soon, he decided to investigate.

He leaned into the brunt of the wind as he fought his way along. He walked through deep puddles, soaking his feet. The rest of him was not much drier since his raincoat was almost useless. Waves crashed against an unseen seawall to his right, mingling sea spray with the downpour.

A long building appeared to the left. The policeman searched for a pier but didn't see any. What lay beyond the slanting curtains of rain he had no idea. Up ahead he thought he glimpsed a dark shape at the very limit of his light.

* * *

Moriya reached the shore and hurried toward the van. A flicker of light off to the left caught his eye. It was dim but definitely there. The way it was bobbing around, it had to be someone on foot with a flashlight, and that meant the police. Moriya felt hatred boil up inside. He had not come this far to allow this to stop him.

Deciding he hadn't been seen yet, Moriya dashed to the van, threw open the door, and grabbed the radio. He closed the door and glanced back. The light was a little brighter now. Moriya turned and ran for the boat.

* * *

The policeman thought he saw the dark object widen a little. He blinked his eyes. Now it looked the same as when he had first seen it. He decided his eyes were playing tricks on him but slowed his pace anyway. He felt a sudden chill as his flashlight began to pick out details on the object. It was a small van matching the description filed by the officer ambushed near Shiohama.

He debated what to do. One impulse was to run back to his car and report. But if he did that, the terrorists might get away—assuming they were still nearby, and he had no proof that they were.

He approached the van. After swinging his light all around, he bent down and touched the tailpipe. It was cold. The truck had been there for a while. This trail might be very cold. If so, it would certainly match the rest of his luck that evening.

He crept along the right side of the van. Staying well back, he turned the beam on the driver's window. Not seeing anyone, he came closer and examined as much of the interior as he could. Then he tried the door. It opened easily. The man leaned in and checked the back. The truck was empty.

He closed the door and looked toward the bay. There he saw a floating dock leading out into the inlet. All he could see was the first thirty feet or so. The rest was obscured by the windswept rain.

* * *

Isomura stood there on the dock.

"Here!" Moriya shouted. "Take it to the pilothouse!"

"What is wrong?" Isomura asked, as he took the radio.

Moriya felt his self-control slipping. "Police are on the shore!"

"How many?"

"I am not sure." He *hoped* there was only one. There had only been one officer at the foundry.

"Get on board! We will cast off!"

"No! I must take care of this."

"What if something happens to you?"

"I will not fail!" He paused. *Isomura was right,* Moriya thought. He needed to know what to do if something *did* happen. "I can handle it," he said with a little less heat. "But if something should go wrong, leave without me."

"What about the bomb?"

"Test the new radio. If the link works, we will set the bombs off together. If not, this one by itself. In either case, we must get as close to Harumi Wharf as possible."

"I will remember."

"Good." He looked Isomura in the eye. "I *will* be back."

"Yes." Isomura bowed.

* * *

The policeman took his time approaching the floating dock. He checked to make sure he could reach his shoulder holster through his raincoat but decided not to expose the automatic to the weather unless he had to.

He reached the first section and stepped up on it. The narrow walkway bounced up and down like a wooden serpent as the steel drums rode the waves. The man tested the surface with his leather shoes and found it quite slick. It wouldn't take much to end up in the water. He shuffled along very carefully.

* * *

Moriya, now in his bare feet, stepped to the dock with an agility borne of many years of sumo wrestling. He stood there a moment. In a way, it really was a match. His opponent, he was sure, was even now approaching. That the officer would investigate the dock he had no doubt. Moriya flexed his muscles. He was ready.

He started walking toward the shore with a sure, heavy tread. A few moments later he saw a dull glow ahead. The policeman *was* coming. Moriya had to gauge it right. He stopped and crouched down a little. He smiled as he waited. Just a few more steps.

Moriya charged. The movement of the dock didn't bother him at all. His feet flew over the weather-beaten planks as the flashlight's glow grew brighter. Then he saw the hand that held it, but everything else was lost in the glare. The light bobbed. Moriya knew the man had seen him and was probably reaching for his gun.

Moriya slammed into the officer and encircled him with his massive arms, lifting him up. The flashlight clattered to the dock. Moriya squeezed hard and heard the air explode out of the man's lungs. He smiled as he looked into the terror-stricken eyes. Now to take care of the gun. Moriya encircled the man's right wrist and squeezed. He heard the sound of crushed bones. The gun fell and bounced into the water. The policeman screamed in agony, and his eyes rolled back in his head. He slumped to the dock in a faint. Moriya looked at him in contempt.

Moriya knew it was past time to go. They had to leave now if the mission was to succeed. He looked at the raging waters. The unconscious policeman would drown in that. Moriya lifted him up and threw him as hard as he could. The splash was lost in the tempest. He picked up the flashlight. A hump of plastic floated about twenty feet away, just barely above the water. Moriya smiled. The man would surely die as the wind and waves were carrying him away from the dock. He turned and raced back to the boat.

* * *

The shock of the cold water brought the policeman around. He breathed water and choked. His right wrist burned like someone had driven red-hot needles through it. He looked toward the dock. He saw the glow of a flashlight moving toward the end of the dock and knew it had to be the monster who had attacked him. Then the light winked out.

The man felt something colder than the brackish water. In his brief glimpse of the towering waves, he saw he was being carried away from the dock. Even without his injury, he knew it was impossible to swim back to it. A wave washed over him, and he spluttered after it passed. Using his good arm, he turned around. He couldn't see a thing, but he remembered the pier he had been on earlier. The waves were moving in that direction.

He struggled to keep his head above water but felt his strength draining. He knew he could not last much longer. He listened, and it seemed the sound of surf against the shore was getting louder. But so far there was no sign of the bottom.

The man cried out in agony as he ran into something hard and cold. He wrapped his good arm around it. It seemed to be a steel post. *The pier!* He felt around for a handhold—anything to pull himself out of the water, but there was nothing except the barnacle-encrusted post. He knew he could never climb it.

The next wave tore him away, and he slammed against something hard. The waves broke over his head. He fought his way back to the surface, but he was almost done.

His foot bumped against the bottom. The next wave lifted him, carrying him on. Then he hit again. He stood up, but a wave threw him down. He got back to his feet and staggered toward the sound of breaking water.

Finally he felt something smooth and slick underfoot. He fell hard. He felt with his good hand. It seemed to be concrete and a metal bar. The man remembered the marine railway.

He felt a surge of adrenaline. Although he couldn't see it, he knew his car was near. All he had to do was walk up the railway's inclined ramp and veer a little to the right. He made his way along, feeling in front with his good hand. Finally he reached the car.

The interior lights blinded him as he opened the door. He fell into the seat, exhausted. After catching his breath, he reached for the radio mike.

* * *

Moriya untied the stern line from the dock cleat. Unten pulled it in and threw it down. Water billowed and surged as the boat's stern started moving away from the dock. Moriya moved to the bowline and waited until the boat was almost perpendicular to the dock. Then he loosed that line and jumped. He caught the bow and pulled himself upward with his powerful arms.

The boat backed away into the teeth of the storm.

25

Sailing Toward Armageddon

The *Tennessee* had a moderate roll but nothing like Don had experienced on the police boat. The deck motion was just enough to remind him he was inside a ship—a very large ship. The radio speaker crackled to life, "Okawa to *Tennessee*."

Don took the mike from Captain Allender. "Major Stewart here," he said.

"We have located Moriya," Okawa said over the speaker. "He was at a small shipyard in Kawasaki. The officer who found him got a glimpse of the boat just before Moriya threw him into the water."

"Is the boat underway?"

"Yes. I got a report from the back-up unit. The floating dock is empty." He paused. "What do you think they will do?"

"If they panic, they might set it off now. But I believe Moriya will head for Harumi Wharf since that's where he thinks the *Tennessee* is. If so, he may already be past us since we're off Kawasaki now."

"We are as well. However, Captain Saeki has come about."

Captain Allender looked at Don, who nodded.

"Mr. Foster, bring us about on a course of zero-six-five," the captain ordered.

"New course of zero-six-five, aye, sir," the officer replied. "Coming about." He gave the helmsman the order.

"We're coming about," Don reported to Okawa.

"What do you recommend?" Okawa asked.

"Wait one." He turned to the *Tennessee*'s captain. "Do you have any commandos in your crew?"

"Yes. I have a SEAL detachment on board."

Don picked up the mike again. "This is Major Stewart. Recommend we locate them and send a commando team. Do you concur?"

"Yes. I do not see any other way."

"Do you have the shipyard's GPS coordinates?"

"Yes, one moment please."

When Okawa came back, Captain Allender wrote the location down and called for a chart of Tokyo Bay. Don signed off and watched as the captain leaned over the chart table and started drawing course lines. He looked up when he finished.

"OK, gents," he said. "This is what it looks like." He stabbed a point along the Kawasaki shore. "This is the terrorist's departure point. If they're heading for Harumi Wharf, they'll probably take these courses." He traced a segmented red line. "I'd expect them to stay well clear of the shore until they intersect the channel that leads to the wharf."

"They know the police are after them," Fred observed. "What if they deviate?"

Captain Allender scratched his chin. "It's possible, but they've still got to stay on this general course. See where it narrows up there?" He pointed to some manmade islands south of the wharf.

"Yes."

"They have to be in the channel by then or they stand a good chance of running aground. So however they do it, their base course is going to be around 328 or 329 degrees. If they want to zigzag at first, fine. We can expand our search area, but when they get close to Jonanjima, they'll have to return to the channel."

"How long will it take them to get to the wharf?" Don asked.

"Shortest possible course is thirteen nautical miles. On a calm day, that boat will probably do around ten knots. In this storm, I'd be surprised if they can do eight. At that speed, we're looking at more than an hour and a half. If they zigzag, it will take even longer."

"What do we do now?"

Captain Allender's eyes bored into Don. "Per the secretary's instructions, you're the officer in tactical command, Major. What are your orders?"

Don glanced at Fred. He could tell his young friend didn't care to comment.

"I guess we should commence the search," he told Captain Allender.

"Aye, aye, sir." He called the officer of the deck over and briefed him on the search operation.

"Now, Major," Captain Allender said to Don. "How do you want to go about assaulting the boat?"

Don looked Fred in the eye. "I have to go, since I know what the bomb looks like," he told him. "You want in?"

Fred hesitated for only a moment. "Yes," he said with a nod.

Don turned back to the captain. "The two of us will be going. What do you recommend for the rest of the team?"

"Three SEALs. Two for the assault team, and one as coxswain." He paused. "You gents handy with weapons?"

Don coughed. "Not unless they're hanging on an F-16."

"Lieutenant?"

"No, sir," Fred told the captain.

Captain Allender frowned. "Major, I suggest you and Lieutenant Brown get with Chief Garcia before we launch this operation. He can advise you."

"We'll do that," Don agreed.

* * *

Okawa struggled to keep from falling as the boat rolled steeply to port. He glanced at the captain, but Saeki didn't seem alarmed. Okawa heard water thunder against the pilothouse windows but couldn't see it because they were running without lights. The boat shuddered as the deluge cascaded off.

"Where is the *Tennessee?*" Okawa asked.

Saeki glanced at the GPS readout. "According to their last report, about a thousand meters off our starboard side."

"Where do you think Moriya is?" Sawara asked.

"That is the real question," Okawa said. "Somewhere out in front of us, if our assumptions are correct."

"How will we find them in this weather?"

Okawa stared at the black pilothouse windows. The boat shuddered as the bow plunged into the heavy seas. "I do not know."

* * *

Moriya stood by the bomb. It was completely operational except the red light labeled "link active" remained dark. The radio link with the other bomb was not working. Moriya worried about this but knew there could be any number of reasons, the most worrisome possibility being the discovery of the other bomb. But regardless of the reason, his mission remained the same: set *this* bomb off near the submarine.

The boat rolled so hard to port Moriya had to grab the bomb case to keep from falling. The boat hung there for long moments before slowly recovering. He looked at Isomura, his features in deep shadows since the only light came from the instruments.

Isomura pressed the intercom button. "Unten-san. Check the bilges."

A few minutes later the speaker crackled. "The level is above a meter now."

"Is the bilge pump still running?"

"Yes. Do you want me to check anything else?"

"No."

Moriya felt a twinge of doubt. "Will we sink?" he asked.

"It is possible, if we remain on this course. Every time we roll, water pours through that hole. It is coming in faster than the bilge pump can handle it. If this keeps up, we will sink."

"What can we do?"

"Our present course puts the wind almost on our beam. We need to zigzag to reduce our rolling. It will also make it harder for the police to find us."

"Do it. What about when we get closer to the wharf?"

"The channel is more sheltered there. Let us hope for the best."

* * *

Don, Fred, and Master Chief Garcia sat around a table in the SEAL detachment office. Garcia's brown eyes never left Don's during the entire briefing. The sailor was shorter than Don and had a solid, heavy build that was in no way soft. Don could tell that a sharp mind rested underneath the short, black hair.

Don leaned back in his chair. "That's about it, Chief. Any questions?"

"A few, Major. You and Lieutenant Brown are going on this operation? With all due respect, sir, breaking things and remodeling faces is our line of business, not yours."

"I understand, and I don't want to make your job any harder. But we have special knowledge about the bomb. Our presence is vital to the mission."

"I see. Well, are you two gents qualified on small arms?"

"I qualified with the Colt 45 when I went through survival training."

Garcia grinned. "Oh, so you've dined on rattlesnake and other desert cuisine."

"Roger that. Anything that was too slow to get away."

"Pretty fair training, from what I've heard. 'Course, nothing like what SEALs go through."

"You've got me there, Chief. Don't think I could hack your program."

"It is rather rigorous, Major." Garcia turned to Fred. "What about you, sir?"

"Uh, I got to fire a '45 while I was at the Air Force Academy."

Garcia rolled his eyes upward for a moment. "I see." He looked back at Don. "Major, we need to talk about armaments. I recommend Glock 9mm automatics for you and Lieutenant Brown; seventeen-round clips, with two spares each. Now, do I need to plan for any heavy lifting—are we going to have to blow anything up?"

Don thought for a few moments. "I don't think we'll need any explosives."

"OK. With the major's permission, I *do* recommend we bring along something to help us with locks and such."

"Like what?"

"A Browning Automatic Rifle with armor piercing ammo. Great for blowing doors off the hinges and opening up things."

Don nodded. "Sounds good to me."

Garcia wrote in a small notebook. "And to round things out, me and my sidekick will be packing Uzi submachine guns. Anything else?"

"Don't think so."

"Very good, sir. I'll be planning our mission. When the skipper gives the order, I'll meet you here. I'll help you gents with your SEAL gear and take you topside."

"Right, Chief." Don was definitely *not* looking forward to that.

* * *

Okawa braced himself as the boat plowed into the heavy seas. He glanced at Captain Saeki. If the sailor was concerned, he didn't show it.

"Anything on the radar?" Okawa asked.

"No," Saeki said without even looking. "The storm is blocking out everything on the bay."

Okawa had been afraid of that. It was possible they might sight the terrorists' boat using the searchlight, if they got close enough, but it would also let them know they had been spotted. Okawa could see no way they could perform an active role in the search. He picked up the mike.

"Okawa to *Tennessee*," he said.

After a few moments, "This is Major Stewart. Go ahead."

"We are blind here. Our radar is useless, and I cannot risk using the spotlight. I recommend you take the lead in the search and we will provide backup. I already have ordered the other patrol boats to fall back."

"Just a moment." A few moments later Don came back. "Captain

Allender agrees. We have lookouts up in the submarine's sail with low-light binoculars. Be advised we are preparing to assault the terrorists."

"I understand."

"Captain Allender requests your GPS coordinates."

"Please wait. I will get them."

* * *

The young sailor pulled a sodden rag out of his foul weather jacket and wiped his low-light binoculars, then raised them to his eyes again. Then he saw it—off the port bow—a light green glow of slightly smoother water. It had to be a boat wake.

The man switched on the intercom. "Conn, lookout! Boat wake bearing three-four-zero relative, range less than fifty yards!"

"Conn, aye," the speaker crackled.

The lookout brought his glasses back up. In a few moments he saw the sub's bow begin a ponderous turn to the left, and he felt the light vibration in the deck change.

* * *

Captain Allender turned to Don and Fred. "Well, gents. Looks like this is it." He paused as a stocky chief appeared. "I believe Chief Garcia is ready to fit you out."

"Aye, aye, skipper," Garcia said.

"Thank you, Captain," Don said.

"Good luck," the captain replied.

"Gentlemen, please follow me," Garcia told the officers.

26

Fighting Moriya

Don and Fred were still struggling to pull on their wetsuits when the other members of the assault team arrived. The sailors finished donning their gear before the air force officers were done.

"Shake a leg there, gents," Garcia urged.

"I'm moving as fast as I can," Don said.

"Yes, sir. Let me help you." He grabbed Don's wetsuit and gave a powerful tug, then secured the various zippers and buttons. Another man helped Fred.

Garcia nodded to the two men with him. "Meet the rest of our crew, gents. Chief Jenkins is the fourth man on our assault team." A tall thin man with blue eyes nodded. "He'll carry the BAR—the Browning Automatic Rifle. Good man to be guarding your back. And Lewis over there is our coxswain—none better."

Don shook hands with them.

Garcia handed Don and Fred some rubber-soled deck shoes. He

waited while the officers put them on, then gave them their automatics along with two spare magazines each.

"Careful with those," Garcia said. "They're loaded with a round in the chamber. Safeties are on."

Don took his and hefted it. It was heavy and its black finish spoke of lethal force. He tucked the magazines in a zippered pocket.

"Are we ready?" Garcia asked.

Don took a deep breath. "Lead on, chief."

"Yes, sir. Major, stick with me, and I'll get you aboard that boat." He picked up a nylon bag and slung it over his shoulder. He then turned to Fred. "Lieutenant Brown, Chief Jenkins will do the same for you."

"What next?" Don asked.

"That's up to you, Major. This is your show."

Don swallowed. "Yes, I know, but what do you recommend?"

"Not much we can plan for, sir. This isn't like a normal special ops mission where we train for months. All we know is that there are an unknown number of terrorists on a boat, that we believe carries a nuclear device. This is strictly play it by ear and hope for the best."

"I see. Well, it's not going to get done down here."

"Roger that, sir. If you gents will follow me."

Garcia led the way aft to the open hatch. The deck was wet, and more seawater poured down as an unseen wave broke over the sub. Garcia handed Don and Fred a pair of low-light goggles and showed them where the switch was. Garcia held a submachine gun in his right hand. Jenkins carried one just like it along with the heavy Browning.

Lewis went up first, disappearing into the black hole above them.

"See you topside," Garcia said as he raced up the vertical ladder.

Don went next. He reached the hatch and stuck his head through. A wave broke over the hull and covered him. He spluttered and choked.

Garcia reached down and pulled him up on deck, then did the same for Fred. Jenkins came last and secured the hatch. Don slipped on his low-light goggles and turned them on. The murky blackness changed into sur-real shades of green. Violent waves danced all around them. The slanting downpour limited vision to less than fifty feet.

"This way!" Garcia shouted to make himself heard over the roaring wind.

They held onto a lifeline as they crept farther aft. Lewis was already in the inflatable boat and had the outboard motor running. The tiny craft rose and fell next to the sub's sleek, round hull. Jenkins hurried past, waited for the boat to come back up, and jumped. He landed on his feet and turned to help the others.

Garcia gripped Don by the arm and yelled in his ear. "You first, Major! Wait until I say!"

"Right!"

The boat went down into a deep trough, then started back up like an express elevator.

"Now!" Garcia said.

Don jumped, propelled both by his legs and a generous shove from Garcia. He twisted in midair and lost his balance. The boat and Chief Jenkins rushed up toward him. The sailor caught him under the arms and hauled him upright as if he weighed nothing.

"Great jump, sir!" He said. He guided Don into the back of the boat.

Don watched as Garcia and Jenkins repeated this feat with Fred. The younger officer's leap was better than Don's, but he was plainly in trouble before Jenkins caught him. Garcia jumped in last, landing as agilely as Jenkins had. The sailor up on the sub threw them their line, and Jenkins took it in. Garcia backed away and brought them around to a course roughly parallel to the sub. They quickly pulled ahead and veered a little to the side.

Garcia motioned for Don to come up front, while Jenkins and Fred remained behind.

"See that patch of smoother water up ahead?" he asked.

"Yes," Don replied.

"That's a boat wake. I think we're about to see your terrorists."

* * *

Moriya lurched against the bomb as the boat took another heavy roll. As much as Hong had reassured him of the device's ruggedness, Moriya still couldn't help worrying. Nothing was indestructible. Something had broken the link with the other bomb, and that worried him. If *this* one failed, all his years of effort would be for nothing.

Moriya forced these thoughts out of his mind. He had to concentrate on success, and that meant preparing for what might come. The typhoon was a blessing, in one sense. It made the boat harder to detect, but not impossible. He knew their greatest vulnerability would come when they neared Harumi Wharf. While that was still some time off, Moriya decided it was time to arm themselves.

Isomura held onto the wheel as the boat rolled to port, hung there for long moments, then slowly righted. He pressed the intercom button.

"Unten-san. How much water is in the bilges?"

"A little over a meter, but it is not rising."

"Good. Keep an eye on it."

"I will."

"Tell him to come up here," Moriya told Isomura.

The first mate nodded. "We need you in the pilothouse."

A few minutes later the port door opened admitting a blast of wind and rain. Moriya bent over and opened a locker in the back of the pilot-house. He pulled out a submachine gun, an automatic pistol, and spare magazines for each. He straightened up and handed the weapons to Unten.

"In case we run into trouble," Moriya said.

"Thank you," Unten said. "I am ready." He put the pistol and magazines into his raincoat pockets but held the submachine gun.

In spite of everything, Moriya smiled. "Yes, Unten-san, I believe you are." He turned to the first mate. "Isomura-san as well. Very soon we will achieve our goal. It will be up to those who survive us to restore Japan to the earlier ways. I thank you very much for your service to our cause." He bowed respectfully to both men and received their bows in return.

Unten opened the pilothouse door, went out, and closed it. Moriya turned and faced the black windows. He rested his hands lightly on the bomb's housing.

* * *

Unten ducked his head against the wind-driven spray as he staggered back to the ladder leading down to the engine room. He paused before opening the door and looked aft. He could see very little, only dark shadows. The foaming wake was a little easier to see, especially near the stern. His eyes followed it back to where the curtains of rain hid it.

He stopped and looked again, eyes straining. Something didn't look right. A black shadow was moving slowly up the wake. An icy jolt of adrenaline shot through his veins as he realized what it was. He dashed down into the engine room, grabbed a heavy flashlight and returned to the open deck. He looked aft, straining to see the wake as he felt his way aft. Seeing a winch, he stepped behind it and waited. The black shadow was much closer now.

* * *

Garcia leaned close to Don. "Almost there. I'll go first and help you aboard. Then Lieutenant Brown. Jenkins will come last. Once we're aboard, it's your show."

"OK," Don said. His mind spun into high gear. What *was* he going to do? Where would the terrorists have put the bomb?

The inflatable boat rode right up the wake, closer and closer to the trawler's stern. Garcia got into the bow, placing his hands wide apart on the boat's taut fabric. Then he made a leap Don would not have thought possible. Garcia turned and reached out. Don took his hand, and the chief pulled him onto the trawler's low stern. Don hunkered down next to a skiff lashed to the deck. He turned and looked back. Fred came next. Jenkins tossed the Browning and a bag of ammo to Garcia, who stashed them beside the skiff. Jenkins leaned forward and reached up. Garcia grabbed his hand and pulled, falling backward as his feet slipped on the slick deck.

The night erupted in light and the rattle of machine-gun fire. Jenkins staggered, clutched his chest, and tumbled over backward. He hit the inflatable boat's bow and sprawled inside. Lewis immediately came about and pulled away. Don started to get up, but Garcia grabbed him.

"Jenkins is hit!" Don shouted.

"Stay down!" Garcia yelled over the wind's roar.

Don glanced back. Fred had tucked himself in behind the skiff. A wave swept over the stern. Don grabbed the bottom of the skiff and held his breath as he went under. After the wave rolled past, Don opened his eyes and looked forward. The trawler's cluttered deck stood out in clear, green relief in his low-light goggles, but he saw no sign of their attacker.

"Where is he?" he asked Garcia.

"The shots came from the port side near that winch."

"Suppose he's still there?"

"I'm sure he is. Hold on." Garcia pulled a radio out of the bag slung over his shoulder. "Volunteer, this is Ranger. We're under fire. One man down and being returned to base. Over."

Don inched toward Garcia so he could hear. The chief held the radio so he could.

"Ranger, this is Volunteer. Understood. Expecting a casualty at base. What is your status?"

"Pinned down at the moment."

"Ranger, do you require assistance?"

Garcia looked at Don.

"Absolutely not! If the terrorists see it's hopeless, they'll set the bomb off now."

"They may be getting ready to do it anyway."

Don bit his lip. "True. But at least this way we have a chance."

"Yes, sir." Garcia pressed the transmit button. "Negative, Volunteer. Do not send reserves. Ranger out."

Don saw a dark green bulge appear on the port side of the pilothouse. He tapped Garcia on the shoulder and pointed. The shape remained a moment then disappeared.

"Think he saw us?" Don asked.

"Don't think so," Garcia replied. "Even if he has low-light glasses, we'd be hard to see next to this skiff. Right now, I'm worried about that guy near the winch."

* * *

Moriya shut the pilothouse door.

"What happened?" Isomura asked.

"I think Unten shot at something."

"What?"

"I could not see anything. I suspect the police tried to get someone aboard."

"Perhaps Unten got them. It is quiet now."

Moriya considered it. That was possible, but why hadn't Unten returned? He thought about starting the countdown on the bomb, but decided to wait. There was no indication they were being overrun. *But if Unten was still facing intruders, what he needed was help.*

"Are there lights for the aft deck?" Moriya asked.

Isomura pointed to the switches, and Moriya flipped them on.

* * *

Don's low-light goggles flashed bright green. He snatched them off and winced at the brilliant glare coming from lights high up on the pilot-house. The left-hand light he could see; however the one on the other side was hidden by the skiff.

"Major!" Garcia said.

"Yes?"

"We gotta do something about that guy."

"OK, what?"

A wave crashed over the stern before Garcia could reply. Don spluttered after it passed.

"Can you hit that port side light?" Garcia asked.

"I think so."

"OK. Give me exactly one minute, then plug it."

"Wait . . ."

"Sir, we waste any more time, and we're dead men."

Don couldn't think of anything better. "OK. One minute?"

"Starting now." Garcia tapped him on the leg, snaked around the back of the skiff and disappeared.

Don saw Fred following after the chief. He started to say something but decided to let him use his own judgment. Don looked down at his waterproof watch and marked the position of the second hand. At the thirty-second mark, he pulled back the hammer on his automatic and flipped the safety off. Keeping as close to the skiff as he could, he aimed at the left-hand light and waited.

When the minute expired, Don laid the sights on the center of the glare and pulled the trigger. The gun roared and kicked up. Although Don heard the impact, the light remained on. He fired again. This time the light winked out. Don jumped as he heard a single shot from somewhere to the right. The starboard side light went out. Don slipped on his low-light goggles but couldn't see anyone in his limited field of view. Two more shots rang out, then a groan.

A few moments later he heard a scurrying sound behind him and saw Garcia crawling up, with Fred right behind him. A wave washed over them but quickly receded.

"Got him," Garcia said as the seawater drained away. He turned to Fred. "Thanks for backing me up."

"You're welcome," Fred replied.

"Any more?" Don asked.

"Not on deck," Garcia said.

Don looked forward. He couldn't see any movement but knew that wouldn't last long. Someone would come to investigate; either that or the terrorists would start the countdown.

"It's time to charge the pilothouse," Don said.

"OK," Garcia replied. "How do you want to do it?"

Don thought a moment. "Chief, you and I up the left side. I want you to blow the pilothouse apart. I'll come in after you and take care of the bomb. Fred, go up the right side but stay well back. If anyone comes out that side, blow 'em away—it won't be one of us."

"OK," Fred replied.

"Major, you want the Browning?" Garcia asked.

Don thought about the heavy case on the other bomb. "Yeah, I guess so, but I've never fired one."

"Pay attention, sir."

Garcia pulled the heavy weapon out of its bag, jacked a round into the chamber, and set the safety. "The safety's on," he said, pointing. "Flip it off, and you're ready to go. Be careful! Don't hold the trigger down, or it will go full automatic. Single shots only, or you'll lose control of it for sure. Got it?" He handed it to Don.

"I hope so."

* * *

"What happened?" Isomura asked.

"How should I know!" Moriya snapped. He struggled to regain his composure. With the deck lights out and no more gunfire, he had to assume the worst. How many police were on board, he wondered, and how had they done it? Again he thought about starting the countdown but couldn't bring himself to do it. A few men they could handle. They *had* to get closer to the submarine.

"I need some light on the deck," Moriya said.

"They got all the aft deck lights."

"I *know* that—what else?"

"We have flashlights and flares."

"Where are the flares?"

"In that locker next to the bomb."

Moriya went to it and pulled out several long, red sticks. "Pull this strip?" he asked.

Isomura glanced around. "Yes."

Wind and rain roared through the gap as Moriya opened the starboard door and stepped out into the darkness.

* * *

"Are you ready?" Don asked Fred.

"Ready as I'll ever be."

Don turned to Garcia. "OK, Chief. Let's do it."

Garcia took the lead and started forward. The boat took a hard roll to port. Don grabbed one of the ropes lashing the skiff and held on. The wave swept past as the trawler slowly righted. Don glanced to the right and saw that Fred was keeping abreast.

Don saw him stop. Up forward a large green shadow stood beside the boat's superstructure. The shape moved, and a moment later Don's goggles bloomed into green blindness. Don ripped them off and squinted into the brilliant red glare that was arcing toward them. Off to the right a gun roared.

"Down!" Garcia shouted.

A split second later a rattling chatter erupted up forward, amid yellow flashes. Don heard the slugs tearing into the deck as he fell down near the winch. The sputtering flare lit the deck with a garish red light, while leaving the sides of the pilothouse in deep shadow. Don pushed the heavy rifle aside and pulled out his automatic. He heard groaning.

"Chief? Are you hit?"

"My shoulder."

Don felt panic welling up inside. "Fred—you OK?"

"Yeah. But I'm pinned down."

"Stay there! Can you see the guy?"

"Yeah. Saw him as I fell. He's by the pilothouse, on my side."

The terrorist squeezed off another long burst. Don couldn't see the impacts, but they sounded off to the right.

Garcia looked back, his face red in the reflected light from the flare. "Sir, you better do something or we've all bought it!"

"Like what?" Don snapped.

"Try and flank that guy."

Don reached for the rifle.

"Leave it!" Garcia ordered. "It'll slow you down too much. Take this." He handed Don the compact submachine gun. "It's cocked and ready to go. There's the safety." He pointed.

Don took the weapon and looked forward. The boat took a hard roll to starboard. Don jumped up and ran forward, keeping as low as he could.

* * *

Moriya pulled another flare out of his raincoat and prepared to pull the strip. He stopped when he saw a movement over to the right. He dropped the flare and brought his submachine gun up. Just before he pulled the trigger he recognized the attacker. It was that meddling American. Raw hate boiled up inside Moriya as he clamped down on the trigger. A single round spat from the muzzle before the firing pin struck an empty chamber. The magazine was empty.

Moriya ejected the magazine, grabbed another and inserted it. He chambered a round and hurried back inside the pilothouse.

"What is happening?" Isomura asked.

"There are three of them," Moriya growled. "I think I got one!"

"Should we start the countdown?"

Moriya considered it. Then he thought of Major Stewart. "Not yet. I can handle them." He crossed to the port side, wrenched open the door and stepped out.

* * *

Don saw the huge shape materialize in front of him as he reached the back of the pilothouse. Even in the dim red light, he knew it was Moriya. Don pulled the trigger but nothing happened—he had forgotten the safety. Moriya started bringing his gun up. Don jumped out of the way behind the pilothouse. He tripped over a rope and fell, losing his grip on the gun. It hit the deck, skittered across it and over the side. Behind him a hail of bullets tore down the port side, throwing bright sparks into the downpour.

Don scrambled to his feet on the unsteady deck and faced the direction Moriya would come from. *Lord help me!* He prayed silently.

The boat started a roll to port. Moriya came past the corner, his face ghastly in the flare's light. As he was bringing his gun up, a wave surged over the side, coming up above his knees. He slipped and brought his arms up to regain his balance. Don ducked his head and charged as hard as he could, hitting Moriya full in his immense belly. Don heard a clattering sound as Moriya's powerful arms encircled him in a deadly embrace.

Don couldn't see, but he heard something behind him. He hoped it was Fred. Moriya picked Don up like he weighed nothing and charged. Fred cried out as Don's back plowed into him. Moriya kept shoving until he had Don and Fred pinned against the lifeline. Moriya reached around with a hand the size of a ball glove. Fred cried out in pain. Something hit the deck.

Moriya shifted. His powerful hands wrapped around Don's neck and started squeezing. Moriya's eyes gleamed red in the flare's light, brimming with blind hatred.

Don fought for air, but he couldn't draw a breath. His vision began to grow dim. The deck spun in a dizzy whirl as he felt his consciousness slipping away. Don thought he felt something lurch.

Suddenly the pressure was gone. Don fell onto the hard steel deck and rolled onto his side. His vision cleared. The boat had taken a hard roll to port. Moriya, caught off guard, was trying to keep his balance as he stumbled backward. He hit one of the posts holding up the lifeline and bent it outward. For a moment, Don thought the terrorist was going over the side. But Moriya hung there. Slowly the boat recovered.

Moriya stepped away from the lifeline, his feet steady again. The sumo crouched, obviously preparing to end it. That he could do so easily, Don had no doubt. Moriya came at him with a ferocious speed that left little time for fear. Don braced for the impact.

A gun roared. Moriya sprawled on the deck as if his feet had been cut out from under him. Don eyed the giant cautiously. Then he saw the large hole torn through Moriya's upper chest. Blood poured out, mingling with the downpour. Don looked aft. A dark figure stood there swaying. *It was Garcia!* The man crumpled to the deck.

Don heard a noise behind him and turned to find Fred staggering to his feet, holding his broken wrist.

"Come on!" Don shouted.

He fought his way aft against the wind and rain and knelt down on the deck. He could see Garcia was in agony. "You saved our lives!" he shouted.

"I would have popped him sooner, but I couldn't get a clean shot." He pointed forward with his good arm. "What about the bomb?"

"Don't know." Don eyed the Browning rifle. "We lost our weapons. Is that all we have left?"

"That's it."

Don picked up the rifle. "You stay here," he told Fred.

"I'm going with you!" Fred replied.

"You can't do anything with a broken hand!" But Don could see that Fred wasn't listening. "OK, you take the right side, I'll take the left. Stay back in case I have to use this." Don held up the rifle.

"Don't worry."

"Gents!" Garcia said. "Better do something about that flare."

"Right," Don said. "But I've lost my goggles."

"Me too," Fred added.

"Take mine." Garcia handed them to Don.

Fred started forward. "I'll take care of the flare," he said.

Don followed him forward. Fred picked up the flare and threw it overboard, plunging the deck into inky blackness. Don slipped on the goggles, and reassuring green vision returned.

Don guided Fred forward until they reached the starboard side of the pilothouse.

"The door is about ten feet straight ahead," Don said.

"Right. I can see the glow from the window."

"OK. I'm going to the other side."

* * *

Isomura wasn't sure what to do. He couldn't hear anything outside, but that didn't mean much with the typhoon raging. He had expected Moriya to return quickly, and when he hadn't, Isomura had begun to worry. Keeping the half-flooded boat on course was hard enough, and now he had to decide what to do about the bomb. Finally he realized Moriya's continued absence could mean only one thing.

Isomura glanced back at the weapons locker. He grabbed a submachine gun and returned to the wheel. He pulled the bolt back, let it go and flicked the safety off. Then he turned the bomb's control key to manual and pressed the start button. The large red numerals began their countdown.

* * *

Don crept forward. Light from the instruments streamed through the pilothouse windows, looking like a green searchlight in his goggles. The interior came gradually into view, first the left side instruments, then the wheel and the hands holding it. Don eased closer. There was only one man inside. The boat took a roll. Don stumbled against the door.

The man jerked around, and his hand started coming up. Don saw the gun and jumped to the side. The window exploded outward in a hail of glass. Slugs ripped through the door, blowing the flimsy panels to splinters. Don leveled the Browning rifle, half-expecting the man to come charging out.

A pounding sound came from the other side. Again the machine gun chattered. Don gripped the rifle and raced into the pilothouse, skidding on the debris. The terrorist started turning around, bringing his gun to bear. Don swung his rifle, striking the man's head with the barrel. The terrorist crumpled to the deck like a rag doll, his gun skittering over into a corner.

A head peeked around the corner. Fred got to his feet and came inside.

"Don!" He shouted. "Look!"

The countdown was running. Don's insides turned to ice as he saw the red numerals go from 010 to 009.

"Get back!" he shouted.

Fred hit the deck. Don raised the rifle and said a quick prayer as he aimed at the bomb's panel. He struggled to control the bucking gun as he pulled the trigger repeatedly. Chunks of metal peeled off like banana skins as the armor-piercing slugs ripped the bomb's control panel apart. Don kept firing until the magazine was empty. When the smoke cleared, the firing circuit was shredded junk.

He closed his eyes. "Thank you, Lord," he said.

"Are you all right?" he heard Fred say.

Don opened his eyes and looked at him. "Yes. What about you?"

"Other than my wrist, fine."

Don turned back to the boat's controls. The compass was hard to read, but their course seemed to be around 080—nearly into the wind. He dropped the rifle and took the wheel.

"Find something to tie him up."

Fred disappeared, returning moments later with a length of nylon rope. "You're going to have to do it," he said as he threw it down.

"Right," Don said. "Take the wheel. Keep us on an easterly heading."

"OK." Fred grabbed the wheel.

Don knelt down and tied the terrorist's hands behind his back, then secured his legs.

"That should hold him. I'm going back to help Garcia."

Don made his way aft over the rolling deck. A dark shape lay still against the lashed-down skiff. Don knelt down, afraid of what he would find.

"Chief, how are you doing?"

Garcia's head turned. "I'll survive. Did you get 'em?"

"We did. The bomb's disarmed. Have you still got the radio?"

Garcia pulled it out from under the skiff and gave it to him.

"Volunteer, this is Ranger, over," Don said.

"Ranger, this is Volunteer. Go ahead."

"Weapon disarmed. Send a boat ASAP. We have two wounded, one prisoner, and two dead."

"Roger, Ranger. Stand by."

Don put the radio down and looked at Chief Garcia. "That we will," he said.

27

Reunion

The transfer from the trawler had taken two trips, to provide a crew for the boat and to evacuate Garcia. The second trip had brought Fred and Don back to the sub. The trawler's crew included two marines to guard the surviving terrorist.

Don stood by Garcia's bed in the *Tennessee*'s sickbay. "Thank you, Chief. If it hadn't been for you, none of us would be here."

"It was a team effort, Major. You and the lieutenant found the bomb—and disarmed it."

Don thought about Okawa's men. "Yeah, it really *was* a team effort." Then he felt an inner urging. "It also involved a lot of prayer."

Garcia looked up at him in surprise. "Are you a Christian, Major?"

"Yes, I am. Are you?"

"I guess so. My folks are, and I went to church while I was growing up. And I attend when I visit them."

Don smiled. "I see. Have you ever looked into what it is they believe?"

Garcia's expression grew very serious. "No, I can't say as I have."

"I'd be happy to talk with you about it, if you like."

Garcia didn't reply at once. "Let me think about it," he said finally.

Two hospital corpsmen, a chief and a first class, came up with a gurney. "You'll have to excuse us, Major," the chief said. "Garcia's got a date with the sandman. We gotta patch up his boo-boo."

Don smiled as he stood aside. The corpsmen lifted Garcia to the gurney.

"What about Jenkins?" Garcia asked.

"He's in surgery now," the chief replied. "He was shot in the chest, but it missed his heart and major blood vessels. He was lucky. Only nicked a lung. We'll be transferring both of you to Yokosuka once the weather moderates."

They started to move off.

"Chief," Don called after them. "Any news on Lieutenant Brown?"

The corpsman turned his head. "He'll be out shortly, sir." They disappeared around a corner.

A few minutes later Fred appeared, looking rather pale. His arm was in an immobilizing sling.

"How's the wrist?" Don asked.

"Better now. The doc injected something like Novocain so it doesn't hurt. The X rays show broken bones and torn cartilage. It's going to require surgery. Doc recommended I have it seen at Yokosuka."

Don grinned. "So you won't be spending the night here?"

"No way. All I want to see is the inside of my apartment."

Don felt a tightening in his stomach. "I believe the ambassador will want a word with us first."

Earlier, Don had been a little surprised when Captain Allender had told him they would be docking rather than waiting out the storm. Ambassador Dewey had been quite insistent.

Don and Fred made their way back to the sub's control room. Captain Allender nodded as they came in but was quite busy bringing the sub in. Finally he donned foul weather gear and went up to the bridge.

A few minutes later the ship's speakers announced the sub's docking. Captain Allender came back down and started coming out of his jacket.

"Thank you for your assistance, Captain," Don said, shaking his hand.

Allender still looked grim. Don certainly understood that, but finally having it all over was such a relief, the only thing Don felt was drained.

"Just doing our duty," Captain Allender said. "What we owe both of you is beyond measure. Well done." He turned and ordered raincoats for his guests. "Now, I believe the ambassador said chop-chop."

"Yes, sir, he did."

A few minutes later, Don and Fred were up on deck. The *Tennessee* was again tied up at Harumi Wharf. And on the dock, barely visible through the rain, was a familiar van. Gus got out as they approached and helped them in out of the rain.

The trip to the ambassador's residence was surprisingly short. As they pulled up in front, Don noted that the building still had power. The lights were a welcome sight after a trip through large blacked-out sections of the city.

Don got out and ran to the shelter of the entrance, with Fred right behind him. Ambassador Dewey opened the door. He looked gaunt and bleary-eyed.

"Come in," he said. "Thank goodness you're OK."

Past the ambassador Don saw Doris; Michael, Leah, and Matt waited behind her.

"Don!" she cried out, tears of relief beginning.

She ran to him, burying her head in his shoulder. He took her in his arms, feeling a stinging sensation come to his eyes. He closed his eyes and said a silent prayer, thanking God that it was, finally, all over.

"Oh, Don," Doris gasped. "I didn't know if I'd ever see you again. It was so horrible just waiting, not knowing what was happening."

"It's all right now," he whispered, stroking her hair.

Michael and Leah rushed up. Don put his arms around them also.

"Daddy, I was so worried," Leah said through her tears.

Michael didn't say anything, but Don could see the relief in his eyes. Don glanced over at Matt and motioned for him to come over. He did, with obvious reluctance. Don included him in the hug.

"Uh, glad you took care of that bomb," Matt said. It was awkward, but Don knew he meant it.

"I appreciate what you did, Matt," Don replied. "If it hadn't been for you, none of us would be here."

Matt nodded, keeping his eyes down. Don looked past him and saw Colonel Dill standing beside the ambassador and knew a briefing was expected as soon as possible.

Don whispered in Doris's ear, "Dear, I think Colonel Dill and the ambassador want to talk business."

She looked surprised, but only for a moment. She had been a service wife long enough to understand duty. "Oh, yes. Go ahead." She gathered up Michael, Leah, and Matt and retreated into a drawing room.

Ambassador Dewey stood by the door to his office. "Gentlemen," he said. "Please come in and make yourselves comfortable."

Don pulled his raincoat off and helped Fred with his. They entered the office, and Allen closed the door. The ambassador led the way to his conference table, and they sat down.

"First of all, well done—both of you," Ambassador Dewey said. He paused, and a wry smile came to his lips. "Lieutenant Brown, Colonel

Dill and I were surprised to find out you were on board the *Tennessee*."
He glanced down at some notes. "I believe you're doing research on military bases in Japan. You found some important sources on the sub?"

"Mr. Ambassador, I apologize . . ." Fred began.

"At ease, Lieutenant. Allen tells me you're a resourceful officer—I
think that's obvious. Now, what about that hand?"

"The doc said it's going to require surgery. He recommended the navy
hospital in Yokosuka. I'm going to check into it in the morning."

"What do you think, Colonel?" the ambassador asked.

"It's about the best military hospital in Japan."

"Good," Ambassador Dewey said, then turned to Fred. "I'll call the
base CO and make sure they take care of you. Gus is taking you to your
apartment?"

"I don't know, sir—I guess so."

"Well, tell him what time you want to go tomorrow."

"Thank you, sir."

"Major Stewart, you saved us all from a terrible disaster," the ambassador said. "Our thanks to Michael as well."

Don nodded. "I'm just glad it's over."

"I'm sure we all are. Allen tells me there will be a thorough debrief-
ing on this at a later time." He paused. "But I wanted to have a short
meeting now, to thank you—and to go over a few things." He looked
at Don and Allen. "First of all, my apologies to both of you for pulling
the plug on our deal with Mr. Okawa. Not that it's any excuse, but I
did it because the terrorists threatened to kill Matt. I also ordered Gus
to keep quiet, which caused *him* considerable distress. I'll do my best
to make it right with him—and the police, since it was entirely my
fault."

"But understandable, under the circumstances," Allen said.

The ambassador frowned. "Perhaps, but because of what *could* have happened, it was the wrong decision."

"But you didn't know what the terrorists were up to," Allen said.

"Well, that's something I'll have to live with. But I wanted to assure Don and Fred that I'm going to make things as right as I can, and that includes proper recognition for what they've done."

"Thank you, Mr. Ambassador," Don said for them both.

"No, I thank you." He stood. "Now, I'm sure we're all ready to call it a day."

Don and Fred left together, while Allen lingered behind. Doris and the kids waited near the entrance. A chime rang. Gus opened the front door, and Okawa came in.

"Where's Matt?" Don asked as he approached Doris.

"Off to bed," she said.

"I see. You ready to go?"

"Am I! I can't wait!"

Don looked at Michael and Leah. He could tell they were exhausted, especially Michael.

"Right," Don said. "Gus is dropping Fred off at his apartment. I'll see if he can take us too."

As Don approached, Okawa stepped forward and bowed. Trying to do the right thing, Don attempted the same greeting.

"Stewart-san," Okawa said. "Thank you. I am in your debt." He turned as Fred approached.

They traded bows.

"And Brown-san," Okawa added. "Thank you as well."

"We appreciate all that you did," Don told Okawa. "It was a team effort."

"Yes, it was." Okawa paused. "My office told me where you were. May I drive you and your family back to your hotel?"

"Why, yes, thank you." Don turned to Fred. "Guess I'll see you when you get back from Yokosuka."

"Right." Fred turned to Doris. "Good night." He smiled at Michael. "Hey, dude! You did all right!" He traded an awkward high-five using his left hand. Michael grinned as he returned it.

Don helped Fred on with his raincoat. After Fred and Gus departed, Don and his family got in the patrol car with Okawa. The officer drove them through the wind and rain to the Imperial Hotel. Okawa pulled into the entrance, parked, and turned to Don.

"*Domo Arigatoo,*" he said with a grin, thanking him.

"Uh, how do you say 'you're welcome' in Japanese?" Don asked.

"*Doo-itashimashite.*"

Don tried it, but knew his aim was off a little.

"Close enough," Okawa assured him. "I shall never forget this. We were very lucky."

Don looked at him a moment, then said, "I believe it was more than luck."

"Oh?"

"You know I am a Christian. My family is as well. We prayed about this situation—a lot. Without it, I don't believe we would be here right now."

Okawa looked uncomfortable. "I see."

Don prayed inwardly that he really would. "Perhaps we could discuss it sometime."

Okawa didn't answer at once. "We shall see," he said finally.

Don thanked him for the ride and helped his family out. They hurried inside, grateful that the hotel still had power. He and Doris supervised getting the kids off to bed, which didn't require much effort. Finally they were alone in their room.

Don glanced at the unfinished painting standing by the window. "How are you feeling, Grandma?"

"I'm so glad this is over," she said.

Don saw her eyes were brimming. He held her tightly in his arms. "I thank God for you, dear," he whispered in her ear.

"I thank him for you too." She looked up into his eyes.

He kissed her. "He answered our prayers."

She shivered and rested her head against his chest. "Yes, he did."